The Exiles of Tearlach

By Shannon Tompkins

Copyright © 2021 by By Shannon Tompkins
All rights reserved.
ISBN:

For Maria, who said it could be done.
And for Ozo, who started it all…

Tables of Contents

1~Prologue 1
2~Preliona~ 15
3~Causing Trouble~ 25
4~To the Breezeway 35
5~Coming Together 42
6~A New Deal 51
7~New Blade, Old Hat 57
8~Seeing Double 69
9~Keeping Up Appearances 81
10~A Change of Plans 93
11~A Sticky Send-Off 104
12~The Last Straw 112
13~Secrets 117
14~The First Move 128
15~The Mediocre Mage 133
16~Unexpected Introductions 140
17~Misconceptions 152
18~The Proof You Need 168
19~A Powerful Ally 180
20~Prejudices 190
21~Wisia 208
22~Old Grudges Die Hard 216
23~New Magic 223
24~Friends or Enemies 232
25~Passing the Torch 241
26~The Key to the City 252
27~Unwelcome Guests 268

28~Using the Stairs 276
29~The Thief is to Blame 285
30~Kicked Out and Helped In 289
31~Judgment from the Pool 295
32~Tale of the Twins 309
33~The New Leader 321
34~Unwanted Help~ 335
35~Thieves in the Garden 345
36~Meeting His Match 357
37~The Wizard's Plan 372
38~Alistair Makes his Point 385
39~And Then There Were Five 400
40~A New Watch Chief 420
41~The Other Side of Preliona 427
42~Odin Undone 444
43~The Key~ 460
44~The Blessing 467
45~The Dwarf Lord Makes His Rounds 470
46~Leaving Preliona 484
47~Epilogue 492

1 ~ Prologue

Calen Jase bit his wadded sheet to keep from screaming.

The architect had not been sleeping well ever since construction of the bridge had begun. It was his guilty conscience, he knew.

Calen had no control over how his employer funded the project—how he got his money or how he spent it. Calen did not want to know these things. Calen Jase just wanted to design and build a bridge from barexium—beautiful, solid, safe barexium.

But that was the whole problem. Calen knew that the bridge was not being built from barexium. It was being made of refurbished scrap steel, painted to resemble the rare metal.

And in Calen's dream he stood on the finished product.

Frozen in place by some unseen force, the architect watched in horror as the counterfeit structure he had constructed crumbled beneath the feet of the patrons of his city. Piece by unsafe piece, the bridge collapsed, plunging screaming folk into the depths of the lake.

Soon the destruction would reach him.

Calen wanted to turn and run, but his feet would not obey his command. In slow motion, Calen saw the ground beneath him disappear. Distantly he heard his own high-pitched scream as he crashed into the rocky waters below…

… the architect awoke with a start, sitting straight up in bed.

But he was not falling. He was safely aboard his barge, docked, and none the worse for the wear save being drenched in his own sweat. Calen began to breathe a sigh of relief, rubbed the sleep from his eyes, and began to sink back into his pillows.

His breath caught in his throat when his adjusting eyes fell on two cloaked figures standing, immobile and wraithlike, at the foot of his bed. Calen jumped a mile and clenched his sheets up under his chin. Newly awoken by his nightmare, he was unsure whether the specters were real or imagined.

"Who are you?" he asked, not surprised to hear a quake in his voice.

For a moment neither answered him, and Calen began to wonder if he was still dreaming when one of them finally spoke.

"We are here for the plans to the bridge. Give them to us and we will leave without harming you."

Calen shivered at the sound of the voice. He had never heard its like—he could not place it. Certainly, no one from this city spoke in such an eerie and wholly unnatural way.

"I am afraid I cannot do that," Calen replied, trying to gather his courage. "I do not have them." Calen knew he was a terrible liar, but if these thieves got their hands on those prints, they would not have to kill him. His employer certainly would.

As he feared, they did not believe him. A ring of metal and two gleaming swords were at his throat. Calen gasped. "All right, all right," he panted. "In the drawer next to the bed. Take the damned things."

He considered calling for his guards, but he was too afraid to open his mouth. Besides, if these two intruders had made it this far, his men were probably beyond hearing him.

They were tall, thin creatures, at least as far as he could tell in the dimly lit room. Each of them wore a voluminous, flowing cloak of indeterminate color, the cowl pulled low over his eyes. Calen could see only shadows where faces should have been.

He could see their swords, however. Beautifully crafted of some sort of pure metal Calen could not identify, the shining blades danced in the moonlight from the window, giving them a wavering, liquid look. Calen had never seen anything like it. And the hilts—each one obviously handcrafted, perhaps personally tailored to its owner. They were surely elven. Which practically guaranteed the identity of the intruders. For the life of him, Calen could not see why elves would care about bridge plans.

A grating sound to his right brought his attention back to the rogue leader.

The speaker leaned forward and floated past Calen like a deathly apparition. The other one stayed immobile at the foot of the bed. Calen watched out of the corner of his eye as exceedingly long, thin fingers grasped the drawer handle and slid it open. The plans were right on top. The intruder rolled them up and hid them beneath the volume of his cloak.

But the thief was not done. He now removed a heavy metal box from the desk drawer.

Calen lunged for the box despite himself. "No, not that," he gasped. Sharp sword points at his throat held him back once again. The architect felt the air around him go suddenly quite cold. He wanted to pull his blankets up over his head, but he was too afraid to move.

The cloaked elf stood straight, box in hand. "I am afraid so, Mr. Jase."

He backed away and joined his silent compatriot. "Tell Master Darweshi that *Duak-Thenal* still watches him." Together the strange pair crossed their swords in a sort of salute.

Calen screamed and dove under his covers, certain he was about to die. He shut his eyes tightly, willing the elves to disappear, still hoping they were part of his nightmare. He counted to ten. When the killing stroke he expected failed to fall, Calen Jase opened his eyes a slit.

Gone.

Shocked into action, he leapt from his bed, ran to the window, and leaned out. He saw nothing more than black water lapping lazily against the side of the barge. He trotted to the door and opened it, fully expecting to see four guards in a pool of blood.

Nothing. The hall was empty.

Calen bit his lip in indecision. Should he call the Watch? No, he decided. Not yet.

Calen flew to his desk and rifled through the papers on top of it. There at the bottom of the pile was a blurred but perfectly usable copy of the plans that had just been stolen from him. He caught up the wrinkled papers and kissed them, relief flooding through him.

Then he let out a hiss of frustration as he glared at the empty drawer.

The gold from Malhuria had been in that box -- payment from the southern city for the barexium. The metal had gone south instead of being used for the bridge, giving Calen's employer twice the money he started with. This copy might save his life, but he would still suffer greatly at his employer's hands.

Calen drummed his fingers atop his desk, contemplating his next move.

A glint of metal caught his attention. He reached toward another stack of papers and caught up a small coin, heavily scratched. When Calen held it up to the dim light, he saw a long, jagged X carved into it.

Calen Jase cursed his stinking luck. There was only one group of bandits who left such a calling card. He was now positive of the identity of his night visitors.

Oddly enough, he felt more relief than guilt. At least now his employer would have others to vent his anger on.

— ✴ ✴ ✴ —

Preliona's lake was a narrow one—barely a tenth of a league across and only just deep enough for boats and barges to float on. Any citizen with a decent pair of eyes could see clear across it and wave to a friend on the opposite side.

The human sat on the shore of the eastern side, halfway down the embankment and more than halfway asleep. It had been one long, exhausting day cleaning the streets of Preliona. Home was on the opposite side of the lake and the bedraggled human had ceased to wonder how he was going to get there.

He picked up a stone and tossed it down the embankment, where a thick metal brace rose from the sand. The pebble dinged it and bounced into the flat water of the lake. Newly erected and shining in the moonlight, the vertical beam was one of twelve metal supports that spanned the width of the lake.

The human snorted at the gigantic monoliths towering one hundred feet above the city's only body of water. They had been there for months now, the skeleton of a bridge that had been commissioned by the Council, bought and paid for by the taxpayers. It was being built of barexium, he had heard. But the bridge construction had stalled, and much of the city doubted its completion.

The human, who planned on spending his entire week's salary at a card table in less than a day's time, complained loudly and often about contributing his hard-earned coin to a bridge that would likely take a decade to build. By the time it was finished, he figured, he would be dead anyway.

He chuckled and started to lean back against the sandy incline. It was a warm, breezy night, and he had no desire to walk home. Sleeping here suited him just fine. He settled onto his side and was about to close his eyes when he caught a blur of movement to his right.

Two shadowy figures were sliding down the steep embankment with barely a sound between them. The human would not have noticed them had he not looked in their direction at that exact moment. Their progress down the slippery incline was smooth and agile. Their footsteps were silent, and they moved with confidence and inhuman speed as they stole under the base of the new bridge.

They sniffed about for several moments like scavengers searching for food. Their movements were graceful, sinewy, and fast. Anyone watching would have known immediately that these were no contractors preparing for the morning's work. No builders in Preliona wore long and flowing gray cloaks that swirled the dust at their feet. No builder—or human—could possess the long, delicate fingers now prodding the metal pilings with such dexterity. And certainly, no builder would carry the long thin swords that two sets of hands now grasped and tore from their scabbards.

Both shadows lifted their swords and swung back with a ferocity out of place with the grace and fluidity they had previously shown. As one, they slashed into the metal support of the bridge, leaving a shower of sparks in their wake. Each blade left a deep gash in the metal. The human had a moment to ponder how this was possible, as there was no known metal that could cut into barexium. Then the two figures were moving again. They briefly examined their handiwork, sheathed their swords, and sprinted back up the incline.

The human lay on his back and rubbed his eyes, unsure of what he had seen. Halfway to the top they stopped. At the same time, the human's heart skipped several beats.

The two shadows turned in his direction and the human froze.

They saw him. And they knew he had seen them.

The smaller of the two took a threatening step toward the human, but the larger shadow pulled him back. For several terrifying seconds they stared down at the human. Then, with a swirl of their cloaks, they were gone as silently as they had come.

And the human, feeling as though his heart might burst from his chest at any moment, promptly passed out.

— ❋ ❋ ❋ —

The S'trobenue family had recently suffered the loss of its young matriarch, and much of the large family grieved inside the wealthy townhouse on the southwest side of Preliona. But one lone figure crept into the garden under the shadow of several large trees.

A young man with curly hair and soft brown eyes glanced nervously back at the house he had just slipped out of, and breathed a small sigh of relief when no one followed him out.

Raymond S'trobenue was escaping.

He dropped his meager bag of clothing onto the damp ground and sat on a stone bench to wait. His heart was racing as he clutched the small child in his lap, afraid to let go.

Raymond scanned the expansive, leafy backyard of his late wife's townhouse. He was unsure what he was looking for—hoping that whatever it was would hurry up and arrive.

Contacting a *Duak-Thenal* agent had been incredibly difficult, but he had finally found someone right here in Preliona. The liaison had given him sketchy instructions at best. He said only for Raymond to wait in the shadow of the garden after the child had fallen asleep, and help would come.

Raymond rocked back and forth, hoping for the hundredth time that he had made the right decision. After Edmee had died, his life had been in shambles. Forget for the moment that he had tragically lost the love of his life, but for weeks he had also been the prime suspect in his wife's death.

Edmee's horrible cousins had orchestrated that, he knew. They desperately wanted Edmee's wealth—but his wife had left everything to him. If he was blamed for her death…

Well, with him out of the way, they would get it. Even though his alibi stood and his name had been cleared, the bastards still seemed to have it in for him. Raymond had begun to fear for his own life, and that of his child.

Little Grace slept soundly in his arms. Raymond prayed that she would remain asleep until they reached their destination.

Wherever that was.

Second by waning second, he was losing faith. If his rescuers did not show up soon, he would lose his nerve and go back inside.

A whisper of a breeze caught the hair on the back of his neck, startling him. The night was still. He turned about nervously and then, for no reason, he looked up.

Two darkly cloaked figures dropped from the branches above, landing like cats in front of him.

Raymond leapt to his feet, Grace still in his arms, and stifled a cry of surprise. They had been directly above him and he had never heard them.

The two shadows approached quickly on silent feet. The taller one had a finger to his lips. The smaller one circled the garden, apparently looking for anyone who might have seen them.

"Raymond?"

Raymond's breath caught in his throat as he looked up into the golden face and shining green eyes of an elf.

"Are you Raymond?" the elf asked again.

His voice was like music. So different from anything Raymond had heard before that he could only nod in confirmation. He had once seen a passing dignitary from Lasairian, the light elf city, but this was the closest he had ever been to a real, full-blooded elf. Under the shadow of the cowl, Raymond could make out high cheekbones and blemish-free skin. Wisps of deep red hair peeked out from around long pointed ears.

The tall elf seemed to understand his hesitation. He simply smiled warmly and took his arm. "My name is Kiernan Nightwing," he said. Unerring confidence blazed in his eyes, mixed with a warmth and compassion that comforted Raymond. The elf oozed an attitude of leadership that seemed to both conflict and meld perfectly with his young visage.

And he was young. Raymond knew elves lived hundreds of years, and perhaps this one already had—but to Raymond, who was only twenty-eight, the elf looked to be at least ten years younger than himself.

"This is the Captain." He motioned to his smaller companion. Much smaller, now that Raymond really looked, and extremely slight.

Raymond squinted. *Captain,* the elf had said. Captain of what?

The darkly cloaked figure removed its hood. Raymond gasped as he gazed upon the luminous eyes and small sharp features of a fairy.

Huge blue eyes smiled up at Raymond. He was startled to note the lack of white in the creature's strange orbs. The pupils were abnormally large, and the blue irises took up the rest of the available space. Small pointed ears poked free of the long, jet-black hair pulled back from her pale face.

Not a fairy, for she lacked the delicate wings. Not an elf either.

An imp.

A mischievous cousin to the elves—and surely one of the few fey creatures ever to venture from its home in the Shelkelar forest—a creature Raymond S'Trobenue had never imagined he would see. As far as Raymond knew, there was only one such creature in the Northern Realms—and she was a thief. An incredibly famous one, though at that moment Raymond could not recall her name.

Raymond was about to back away from her, suddenly leery, when, grinning winningly from ear to pointed ear, the imp reached forward with one tiny, pale hand to touch the sleeping child Raymond held.

"Beautiful," she said. Raymond was not surprised to hear the same singsong quality in her voice that he had heard in the elf's. Gazing down at the childlike face of this smiling girl, he suddenly failed to see why he should be the least bit cautious. After all, this creature did not appear to be more than twelve years old.

"Quickly," Kiernan said, leading him to the gate at the far end of the property.

"But the guards…" Raymond protested. "There are several hired men guarding the grounds."

"Taken care of," the imp winked, as if letting him in on some private joke.

Raymond breathed a sigh of relief. For the first time in months, he began to see a ray of hope for the future. Things would be different now. He could feel it.

A sharp cry from the house brought all his fears crashing back upon him.

The three companions turned. Raymond was dismayed to see Edmee's four cousins storming out of the house.

"Raymond!!" Sigmund called out. "What are you doing?!"

"Can you run?" the elf asked, not looking at him but over his shoulder at the four men, who now drew their swords.

Raymond froze with fear as his brutish kinsmen began storming across the garden toward them. "Yes," he replied shakily.

The elf nodded to the gate. "Then do it."

Raymond felt the imp take his arm and pull him toward the gate.

As he ran, he risked a glance over his shoulder. The elf had drawn a long sword with an unusually dark blade and was calmly waiting for the advancing men.

Raymond felt a stab of guilt. Four against one was hardly a fair fight. If Edmee's cousins killed him, it would be Raymond's fault.

Reluctantly, he ran alongside the imp, cradling his daughter and trying not to jostle her too much. They were a few yards from the gate when two of the family's guards suddenly vaulted the fence and charged them.

The imp came to screeching halt. Raymond let out a small cry despite himself. "I thought you said they were taken care of!"

The imp shrugged, apparently unfazed by the sudden change in events. "Missed two."

Raymond gaped at her flippancy.

The imp slid in front of him and drew a foot-and-a-half length of red oak from her back holster. Raymond heard a small click. Suddenly the small piece of wood transformed into an enormous staff, beautifully carved and sporting a wicked spear tip.

Raymond took a step back to give her space to fight, though in truth he did not hold out much hope. The imp stood several inches less than five feet. The two men she faced were at least a foot and a half taller, and twice her weight.

He did not wish to see this creature destroyed before his eyes. "No!" Raymond cried suddenly. "Just leave us!"

To his vast surprise, the imp ignored him and lunged at the closest man, thrusting her staff at his shoulder. Raymond saw a flash of steel a split second before the spear-tip slashed open the man's arm.

Raymond winced and stepped back, clutching Grace to him, as the imp swung her weapon in a wide arc and cracked open the skull of the second attacker. Raymond's jaw dropped in stunned admiration as the imp Captain deftly held off the two guards, moving quicker than Raymond would have deemed possible.

Confident now in the Captain's ability to hold off their attackers, Raymond glanced behind him, where the sound of clashing steel seemed to be lessening somewhat.

Two of Edmee's cousins lay immobile on the damp ground. Raymond could not tell if they were dead or alive. In truth, he was not sure he cared. At that moment, all his attention was focused on the blur of movement that was Kiernan Nightwing.

His hood had fallen back, and his red hair whipped about in the wind like an angry flame. Gone was the sparkling friendliness Raymond had seen moments before. The warm and compassionate young elf had been replaced by a sword-wielding devil with fire-colored hair.

He was confident the two men still fighting would soon join their prone cousins. No one could stand before that darkly gleaming sword and the superbly skilled fighter behind it and live to tell about it.

Raymond watched Vincent and Sigmund S'Trobenue advance. One came in low, the other high, and Kiernan blocked both blows with lightning fast moves. He batted Vincent's sword arm wide and landed his boot into the man's stomach, sending him sprawling back. The elf then spun about in time to block Sigmund's vicious side-cut. Sigmund stepped back, rethinking his strategy, but the elf gave him no time. Kiernan Nightwing stepped in and pierced the man's heart.

Sigmund went down heavily, his mouth wide open in a silent scream of pain.

Raymond covered his mouth and turned away, certain he would see that image clearly for many nights to come.

The imp seemed to be a bit less vicious in her fighting tactics. She wielded her huge staff more on the defensive, choosing to strike at the limbs of her opponents rather than their more vulnerable spots. Though her weapon sported a spear tip, Raymond had seen her make use of it only once.

One guard bled from his left arm, but his sword arm was still free, and he swung his broadsword at the imp with abandon. The man the Captain had hit in the head, however, was fast losing his battle with consciousness. He had lowered his sword and held one hand to his bleeding scalp. The Captain, in full contact with her other opponent, ignored him so she did not see the guard drop his hand from his head and run straight for Raymond.

Panicking, Raymond began to back away, and turned to run. He snagged his foot on a root and fell with a cry, shielding Grace as best he could. He rolled onto his stomach, cradling Grace in one arm and pushing himself to his knees with the other. He looked up at the guard, who now loomed above him. Terror, absolute and all-consuming, swept through him as the injured guard raised his sword above his head.

Suddenly the man's mouth turned into an 'O' of surprise. He fell forward heavily, and Raymond was forced to scramble to one side to avoid being crushed by him. He hit the ground with a sickening thud. Raymond was not surprised to see an elfish dagger protruding from the man's back.

Raymond rose shakily to his feet in time to see the red-haired elf running toward him, his final opponent sprawled on the ground behind him.

"Are you all right?" he asked as he latched onto his arm. He did not wait for Raymond's response, but continued toward the gate.

Raymond nodded, pushing his crooked glasses up his nose with one finger. He swallowed a twinge of fear that grasped at his pounding heart as he ran alongside the elf who had just killed at least one of his wife's relatives.

Raymond glanced up at the tall elf as he ran, terrified he was making an enormous mistake. But the elf smiled down at him with the wrinkle-free face of a teenager, and Raymond felt himself trusting him once again. The vicious fire he had witnessed was no more—in fact, Raymond was unsure it had ever been there at all.

Kiernan propelled him past the fighting imp and through the gate. With his grace and agility, he made Raymond feel old and ungainly.

"But the imp…!" he protested as they passed her.

Kiernan laughed. "I assure you, the Captain is more than capable of defending herself." Even as he said these words, Raymond heard high-pitched and strangely childlike laughter sail over the clash of weapons.

"Finish up please, Captain!" the elf called over his shoulder. He put two fingers to his lips and whistled.

Out of the mist trotted three horses. Kiernan snagged the reins of a pale brown mare and held his arms out to Raymond. "Give her to me," he gently urged, "And climb on."

Raymond hesitated only a second then handed his daughter over to the elf. He climbed onto the horse, and Kiernan passed the sleeping child up to him.

"Wait here," he said, and ran back to the gate.

The fighting had drifted outside the property now. Raymond squirmed when he saw the bleeding guard who still fought the imp. The Captain moved so quickly that Raymond could barely register the movement. Every attack the man began was deftly blocked by the lightning-fast fairy.

"Now, Captain!" Kiernan called, a note of warning in his voice.

"Oh, all right," she acknowledged, sounding disappointed. The blunt end of her staff caught the man at his ankles and knocked him from his feet. He did not get up.

Raymond's rescuers returned at a run and gracefully leapt onto their horses. The elf turned his warm smile on him once more. "Are you all right?" he asked him.

Raymond was far from all right. His wife was dead, her family wanted his money and apparently his life, and now he was running away with two members of the most infamous band of mercenaries in all the realms. Raymond figured it would be a long time before *all right* entered his vocabulary again.

He voiced none of this to the elf and the imp. His life had been saved, and he was profoundly grateful. He nodded his head, unable to speak and shaking slightly as his tension riddled body finally began to relax.

Kiernan nodded and turned his horse away from the townhouse. Raymond followed, with the imp close behind. He risked one final glance back, not at the fallen men, but at the garden his wife had so loved.

2~Preliona~

Althea rubbed her temples and pushed her long white hair from her face. Her head hurt. Her back ached and truthfully, she would have liked nothing better than to get back in bed.

But she could not miss another meeting. Not today.

"Continue, Mr. Darweshi," she said to the bear of a man pacing before the Council.

He gave her a curt nod. "Thank you, Governor," he said, his tone not at all conciliatory.

Althea chose to ignore the boorish young man. Instead she glanced up at the domed ceiling, squinting at the harsh morning light streaming into the Council room.

Nimbus, as it was called, was a magnificent structure, a study in white marble and glass. The enormous pillared edifice sported five domed ceilings, each one built to allow the light of both the sun and the moon to illuminate the rooms beneath them.

The four smaller domed rooms were used for meetings with dignitaries and ambassadors from other cities. They corresponded to the directions of the compass—north, south, east, and west.

The center room, which was the largest and most beautiful, was used solely as the meeting place of the governor and her councilors. On this morning, their daily meeting had ground to a halt due to the sputterings of one Odin Darweshi, a volatile merchant who also happened to be the son of a powerful nobleman.

"My architect was robbed last night by a group of vigilantes calling themselves *Duak-Thenal*." He stopped pacing suddenly and turned his lethal gaze on the Council, who were all seated at an enormous semicircular white oak table. He stabbed one large finger at them through the air and gritted his teeth. "Now, I *know* you have had information concerning these thieves for some time. I demand you do something about them!"

There were grumbles of protest all around the table, but Althea Gaenor had finally had enough. Althea was almost sixty, but she maintained a strength and vigor that compelled everyone in the room to silence when she spoke "All right, Odin, stop fussing and tell us where this unhappy event transpired?"

The foul-tempered merchant flushed the color of his ruby red vest as he turned on the elder woman at the center of the table. "On one of my own barges!" he boomed. "In plain sight of your useless White Watch!"

Althea held up a hand to quiet him. "Your own guards were off for the evening, I assume?"

Odin bristled. "No," he grumbled. "The bastards must be invisible."

Althea nodded. "And did these *bastards* leave any markings behind?"

Odin's black eyes popped in anger. Without a word, he pulled a scratched coin from his pocket and slammed it onto the table.

Several hands reached for the item and it was quickly passed around until it landed in the governor's calloused hand.

She barely glanced at it. "Gregory," she said, calmly handing the coin over to the young scribe at her side. "What do you make of this?"

Gregory Sweep, a dark-haired half-elf, studied the gold piece for a moment. He nodded to Althea and handed it back. "It is indeed the symbol of *Duak-Thenal*," he said.

Odin stormed forward and slammed his hands down on the table to emphasize his point. "Well, who the hell are they? And why are they robbing me blind? They took the plans for the bridge," he continued. "*Your* bridge."

Althea raised one pale eyebrow. "Is that all?"

Odin seemed ready to explode. For a moment he was speechless, his face going so red it threatened to turn purple. "ALL?!!" he thundered.

Althea did not raise her voice, acting as if she were almost bored with the proceedings. "Yes, all. I assume you have back-up plans. Was anything else stolen?"

Odin threw his hands into the air. "Does it matter?! My privacy has been violated; my place of business overrun by elves with swords. This is a serious security breach, whether anything of importance was stolen or not!"

Althea drummed her fingers on the table before her, keeping her cool in the face of Darweshi's tirade, though everyone else at the table squirmed and fretted. Still not answering him, she motioned instead for Gregory to take over.

The half-elf sat up straight. "In elvish, *Duak-Thenal* roughly translates to 'Exiled Warriors.' We have been tracking this group for some time now. Apparently, they are a self-appointed group of vigilantes who have been garnering public notice of late, both negative and positive. We have been unable to confirm any other information concerning their activities."

Odin crossed his arms and glared at the group sullenly. "Well, I suggest you start working a little harder on this, ladies and gentlemen. I seriously doubt many merchants will continue to do business here when they learn of the rampant lawlessness in this fair city."

Althea placed her hands on the table before her and stood quickly, leveling her gaze at the intrepid man. "That is quite enough, Odin," she hissed.

But the merchant went on reaching for the pile of papers he had brought with him, "I hold in my hand a dozen formal complaints! Places *Duak-Thenal* has been sighted, people they have stolen from. I even have one report from a jailer in Yeelan claiming that *Duak-Thenal* orchestrated the escape of a criminal, not two months ago. None of these crimes has been dealt with or investigated—and now they enter this city right under your noses!"

Althea was fuming and seriously considering throwing the man out when Alistair, the Watch Chief, spoke. "Mr. Darweshi," he began. He was an older man, slightly older than Althea, with steel gray hair slicked back over his head and bright blue eyes that flashed with intelligence. "I have in *my* possession the same claims of which you speak. This Council has gone over every one of them and investigated those which we have deemed legitimate."

"Are you saying these people are lying?" Odin sneered.

"No," answered Xanith Creese, another councilor. "Simply that not all of them saw what they thought they saw. And since we have no accurate descriptions to go by, we can hardly issue arrest warrants. Can your architect honestly stand before us and say he saw anything more than two robed figures standing at the foot of his bed?"

Odin frowned, his dark eyes going hard and mean in the expanse of his large square face. "This is your bridge, you know," he repeated flatly. "The one you're paying me to build. All I have to do is pack up and quit. I don't have to finish the damn thing."

"You refer to the bridge that is nearly six months behind schedule?" Althea said, still standing at the head of the table. "I'd almost forgotten about it. If you want our help in this matter, then you had better lose that tone. Especially since you cannot possibly make good on your threats." Althea drew herself up and crossed her arms in front of her. "Or perhaps I should take this issue up with Lord Darweshi himself. I am sure he would be delighted to hear all about the barexium we are paying him for."

Odin paled considerably. "I don't know what you're talking about."

Althea smiled thinly, "Oh, no? Your father's name appears on all the order forms, does it not?"

Odin did not answer, but his flexing fists at his sides belied his efforts to control his mounting anger.

Althea went on. "I wonder how Lord Darweshi would feel, knowing his forged signature appeared on an order for a barexium delivery from Graxton, a city he has long embargoed."

Odin's steely black gaze rested on the governor. The young man was seething with rage. A red dot had appeared on each of his cheeks and his lips formed a thin line across his face. "You wouldn't dare," he breathed.

Althea did not blink. "*I would indeed.*"

The room was completely still, and Althea knew every eye was on her. "Now, as Gregory has said, we have been tracking this little group for some time, but we have been unable to learn their identities or accuse them of any crimes. To date, they have not murdered anyone. What they do steal seems to mysteriously turn up in the hands of the authorities, or some other intermediary." Althea could not be sure, but she thought she saw Odin wince. She suspected he was now wondering where exactly his precious plans had gone. "Now, until I have proof of some real crime, Master Darweshi, I cannot begin to put any serious effort into finding these elusive rogues."

"Are you saying that robbing me is not a serious crime?"

Althea leaned forward. "Not when the missing items have thus far been useless to those of us paying for them." Althea's words dripped sarcasm and she smiled as she saw Odin bite his lip to keep from growling. She had him and they both knew it. Althea Gaenor may have hung up her adventuring hat long ago, but the scathing wit that had made her famous served her well as governor.

The merchant began his fevered pacing again, obviously trying to regain lost ground. "What of the rumors that the imp Captain Tain Elire has been seen with them?" he barked, wheeling back on her.

Althea sighed heavily.

But Xanith laughed. "You speak of a mirage, Darweshi. The rumors concerning the imp thief have tripled these past few years. No one can possibly corroborate them."

"Xanith is right, Odin," Althea agreed. "Whether the imp is involved or not is beside the point. We need evidence, not ghost stories. We appreciate your time, sir, and we will inform you when we have a lead. Make a public show of this, Odin, and I assure you your father and I will be talking sooner than you can blink."

Althea sat down, clearly signaling that the meeting was over. Odin bowed curtly and stormed from the hall, slamming the door behind him. His exit triggered a chorus of grumbles from the other council members.

"All right, all right, ladies and gentlemen, settle down," Althea shouted over the din. She leaned back and smiled. "Let's not let Mr. Darweshi's little tantrum ruin the rest of this lovely morning."

Some of the others chuckled and seemed to calm a bit. The governor had a marvelous talent for soothing the skittish members of the Council.

"You'd best be careful with that one, Your Excellency," began Xanith Creese, sinking back casually into his chair. The elder man was the physical opposite of the governor. While Althea stood straight and tall, Xanith habitually slouched. Where Althea was serious and sarcastic, Xanith was laid-back and calm. She counted on him heavily to balance her out. "Accusing *him* without the proof to back it may not be the wisest thing, either."

Althea scowled at him. "You would have done the same."

"Yes, and you would have cautioned me about it." Other members of the Council laughed along with Xanith and Althea.

"I think it prudent that we continue to discuss this matter today," interjected Quinlan, the Guild Master. He was a thirtyish man of medium build, with raven hair and a caramel complexion. He was exceedingly intelligent and extraordinarily busy. It was a wonder he made it to these meetings at all. "Whether or not we agree with Master Darweshi's current doings, we do have an obligation to the citizens of this city. If there is indeed a renegade band of elven mercenaries making forays into Preliona... well, we must take care of it."

"But quietly," piped Laothist, a middle-aged and rather rotund councilman to Xanith's right. "We cannot afford to have a panic on our hands."

Several others murmured their agreement.

Althea shook her head. "Quinlan, I agree that something must be done, and soon. I hardly need tell you what kind of a fuss Odin will put up unless we at least appear to work on this problem. However, I will not have the Watch running around this city blind. I insist that we do some serious research on this *Duak-Thenal*."

"But, Your Excellency, all efforts to find these rogues have proved fruitless," Laothist stammered. "Their rare appearances in this city have been virtually insubstantial. Anyone who has had contact with them is either fiercely loyal or scared speechless."

"I'll wager they have friends in very high places," said Ranabee Enri, a noblewoman of Preliona high society. "Though I must admit, I have heard nothing of them in the circles I frequent."

"Well, there it is, then," Althea said, crossing her arms. "We all have plenty of *friends in high places,* as Ranabee so delicately put it. I suggest you use them. Find out who has been hiring them and what other types of jobs they have been involved in. Above all, I want to know who they are."

"And I doubt we will get any help from the surrounding elven kingdoms," Xanith ventured.

Althea nodded solemnly. "Agreed. We are on our own. So, I suggest you all get moving."

"What about the imp thief?" asked Iris, a young artisan from the Coral Square District. "If we are to believe Darweshi, then the imp has been spotted with the group. She is considered a criminal, is she not?"

Althea shook her head slowly, "Not exactly. Captain Tain Elire walks a fine line in Preliona. To my knowledge, she has stolen nothing from this city, though there have been reports of her escapades in neighboring towns."

"Escapades?" Laothist asked.

Alistair cleared his throat. "Too many to count. The Captain is a hired thief who rarely keeps what she steals."

"Don't see the point in that line of work," snorted Judith Mercy, owner of the Mercy Inn and Suites, elbowing her neighbor Halberth.

Xanith threw an amused glance in Judith's direction. He slouched even lower in his seat and threw one leg up casually onto the table. "The problem is that as she retrieves items for one party, she obviously angers another. She almost constantly causes a quarrel of some sort wherever she goes. And because many of the items she steals have been stolen before, town officials are usually at a loss as to who to blame."

"Example?" Halberth, the street cleaner, asked. Althea thought he and Judith made an odd pair, as Judith was constantly talking and Halberth rarely said a word.

"Well, is she stealing or simply returning possessions to their rightful owners?" Xanith mused, sitting up. "Put it this way—Villuna wants her dead, while Bellue considers her a hero. It is a controversy we'd do well to avoid."

Most of the Council chuckled.

"But by all means," Althea said, raising her hand for silence, "Find out all you can about the Captain. If she has had dealings here of late, then someone may have hired her. Any information that could lead us to the elves might prove valuable."

"How did the little thief come by the title of Captain, anyway?" muttered Fale Copperhand, a dwarf who ran the weapons school.

Althea frowned slightly at the dwarf's snide tone.

But Gregory Sweep saved the dwarf from a scolding. "I believe Captain Tain Elire led a contingent of light elves in battle against the Crimson Guard. It was the elves who gave her the title," he said.

Fale nodded. "Tall folk wouldn't have followed her any other way."

"Ah yes, wasn't this the battle in which King Kellehar's son was killed?" Xanith asked.

"The same," said Poorez, a haughty jewel merchant. "She stabbed the prince in the back, I understand."

Althea shook her head, not caring for the direction the conversation was going. "That has yet to be proven, Poorez," she snipped. "I hardly think it fair to condemn someone for an untried event."

"As far as the Crimson Guard and their king are concerned, she *has* been tried," Alistair countered, nodding his balding head in deference to Althea. "Whether she attended the trial or not hardly matters to them. Kellehar placed an exorbitant price on her head in Graxton City that has risen every year she has gone uncaptured."

"So I say to you all," Xanith interrupted, opening his arms to the entire Council, "if the Crimson Guard, the most powerful army in Tearlach, cannot get their hands on the elusive imp, then how are *we* to track down her equally stealthy companions?" He leaned back and crossed his arms with finality. "You've a better chance of seeing *Ziyad* himself come down from on high and sit on your midden this Sunday morn."

"Very eloquent, Xanith," Althea said over the laughter of the Council.

The men and women in the great hall calmed quickly, each lost in his or her own thoughts about how to deal with the problem at hand. Althea did not have any qualms about what they faced. She knew what a political nightmare might very well lay before them. Odin Darweshi was certain to make their lives miserable in any way he could. Clearly stirring up a public outcry was his primary plan.

She scanned their faces, memorizing their expressions as expertly as any marksman. She did this not out of suspicion but out of habit. Her Council was strong and trustworthy, but she could not help but think that some of them knew more than they had let on today. And she needed their help and honesty—because, calculating as she was, the governor could not seem to get a handle on this new threat.

Duak-Thenal.

Althea sighed and rose gracefully. She needed a break, a moment away to think. If there was information to be found, then those around her would find it.

And if they did not... well, she had other ways of getting information.

"I suggest we retire for the day," she said. "I would ask that you consider all that has been said here. Discuss it with no one. Use your contacts and gather as much information as you can. We must know what we are up against."

She gathered her gray cloak about her and made to leave. "Above all, use discretion in your dealings. I cannot stress enough how your actions and words may affect those who look to you for guidance. We will meet at the end of the week and discuss our findings. Good day, ladies and gentlemen."

"Good day," said the Council as one.

With the morning light lengthening into afternoon, the First Men and Women of Preliona hurried off to their respective lives… and, Althea hoped, some answers.

3~Causing Trouble~

Gregory Sweep watched the governor exit as he gathered his pile of papers. He could not help but notice that Xanith Creese was the first to his feet. Old as he appeared, one might expect him to be the last to rise, or even topple to the floor without a helping hand.

But Xanith was an enigma. A spry old man, somewhat bizarre, often amusing—and always talking. Now he swept his dark cloak about him and hurried past exiting council members, nearly bumping into Judith Mercy.

"Xanith, darling!" The red-headed woman leaned in and kissed the elder man on both cheeks. "Coming tonight?" she asked.

Xanith waved a hand at her, twirling his fingers in a whimsical gesture. "Judith, really—have I ever missed our game?"

Judith snorted, "Seeing as how you owe everyone in the group money, I don't think you can afford to miss it."

Gregory tried his best to slide past, but Xanith spotted the scribe and reached out to catch the half-elf by the arm. "I'll be there at seven-thirty, Judith. Count on it."

Xanith then brushed past Judith Mercy, pulling Gregory with him.

Gregory groaned, rolling his teal eyes. "Does it not occur to you that I might have business elsewhere, Xanith?"

Xanith clucked at the scholar. "Oh, Gregory, please. It is Monday. What could you possibly have to do on a Monday?"

Gregory gaped at the older man. "Just because *your* business is dark on Mondays does not mean the rest of us don't work!"

Xanith ignored the half-elf and continued to move forward, "Right. Well anyway, I have a thought. These thieves, this *Duak-Thenal*... they have been here before, I am sure of it."

Gregory raised one dark eyebrow. "You have proof?"

"Of course not," Xanith admitted. "But Preliona is the largest city in the Northern Realms next to Graxton—and I know they aren't visiting *that* city. It only makes sense that they would have spent time here." Xanith stopped and pointed, directing Gregory's eyes toward the exiting figure of Poorez Montalbosh, the jeweler. "Or at the very least," Xanith continued, "has made some covert arrangements with the local merchants."

Gregory watched the wealthy merchant hobble out of the main hall. He was a tall man, but you would not know it from the way he walked. He moved about with his shoulders slumped and his head down, as if he were protecting something. His clothing was dark and sleek, even in summer. He favored short vests, long cloaks, and tall hats. He had a fringe of short, dark hair and pale eyes set far back behind tiny spectacles. He looked positively bookish, but he was not studious in the way that Gregory was. He was not a scholar—simply a merchant who was adept at studying people and how best to separate them from their money. Gregory did not care for the man.

Gregory wrinkled his nose. "Poorez. Yes, it would not surprise me in the slightest if that one dealt with thieves."

Xanith followed Gregory's lead. "He practically is one himself. Do you know what he charges for his trinkets?"

Gregory turned and faced Xanith. "Do you think he lied to Althea just now?"

Xanith shook his head. "He doesn't have the guts. But I am betting he has had something to do with the thieves. Maybe he just hasn't made the connection."

"And you think we should be the ones to jog his memory?"

"Yep. Come on."

Xanith dragged Gregory through the swelling crowd now filling Nimbus Hall. Merchants and scholars, artists and business owners, dozens of

Preliona's citizens were arriving for private meetings with the twelve council members.

Fortunately or unfortunately for Gregory, he never had to attend any of these meetings. As Althea's personal assistant, the half-elf was protected from all who might otherwise keep him from doing the governor's bidding.

Everyone except Xanith, that is.

Xanith Creese was incorrigible. As master of the Theatre Guild and its endeavors, much of Xanith's business took place at night. Therefore, Xanith enjoyed a daytime freedom that the rest of the Council could only dream of.

He spent much of his extra time looking for trouble, and for some reason, in this instance he had chosen the much stiffer Gregory Sweep as his ally.

"Poorez will be headed for his shop. He hates opening late," Xanith smiled.

Gregory shrugged. "I can't imagine he'll have too many customers waiting for him. As you said, very few in this town can afford him."

Xanith laughed and clapped Gregory on the shoulders. "True, true, but Poorez doesn't deal much with the masses. His specialty is hard-to-find items. Family heirlooms, lost gemstones. Priceless items, museum quality."

Gregory glanced at Xanith and shook his head. He was amazed at the amount of information Xanith seemed to have at his fingertips. How was it that Gregory himself did not know these things? After all, he was Althea's assistant and in a better position to garner knowledge. And what was Xanith but a silly old performer who worked for nothing more than laughter and applause?

The two pushed open a side door and stepped into the street between Nimbus and the Preliona library. They skirted playing children and rolling carts, skipped over puddles left from last evening's downpour, and finally emerged onto the square.

Nimbus was at their backs, the library to their right. To their left was the Guild House at the base of Dawn Tower, and directly before them lay the main street of the city.

Xanith and Gregory moved toward the tower, but turned right almost immediately after passing the library. This was First Street, or Jeweler's Row, as it was more commonly known.

A small cobblestoned alley dotted with cozy shops beckoned them in. High-priced luxury abodes topped the multicolored awnings of wealthy merchandisers.

Xanith put his hands on his hips. "Who actually lives here?"

Gregory snorted. "You mean your glamorous career does not afford you accommodations such as these?"

Xanith grimaced. "My dear, not even our fearless governor could afford to live here."

Gregory laughed as he scanned the street. About halfway down the lane, a blue and green awning jutted out over the cobblestones. In its doorway stood the stooped jeweler.

Gregory tapped Xanith on the shoulder and pointed at the man.

"Ah, there's the sinner."

Xanith started forward, but Gregory caught a movement to his right that made him hold out his arm to stay the older councilman.

"Hmm?" Xanith said.

Gregory pointed at a spot on the opposite side of the street. Ranabee Enri, a councilor and possibly the wealthiest woman in Preliona, was crossing the street and heading straight for Poorez's shop.

Xanith rolled back on his hip and crossed his arms. "Well, *hel*-lo."

"What is *she* doing here?" Gregory asked.

"She lives here, Gregory."

The half-elf rolled his eyes. "Yes, I know that, but what is she doing *there*? She hates Poorez."

"True. Let us find out."

This time Gregory was unable to make a grab for Xanith when the nimble old man sprang forward, and he was forced to trail in his wake.

— ✳ ✳ ✳ —

Poorez's shop occupied the ground floor of one of the older buildings on the street. For as long as Xanith had known him, Poorez had lived above his shop. He had joined the Council at its inception, though Althea could barely tolerate the man. He ran in higher circles than most. He and Ranabee would have information at their disposal that none of the other council members had access to. And the richest members of society could be counted on to inform one another.

Xanith opened the door of the shop silently enough. He could just make out Ranabee's long black hair and shockingly red dress. He could hear her and Poorez engaged in a heated discussion across the jeweler's counter. He motioned for Gregory to follow him in when a small bell above the door gave them away.

Ranabee stood straight. Poorez glared at them.

Xanith smiled sheepishly, "Afternoon, all. Just out for a stroll, thought I'd drop in."

Ranabee snorted and moved away from the counter, her interest caught by some trinket in the corner. Poorez continued to glare at him in suspicion. "You never come in here, Xanith. What do you want?"

Xanith shrugged and slid gracefully up to the counter, while Gregory hung in the shadows, watching Lady Ranabee out of the corner of his eye. "So quickly you judge me, Poorez," Xanith quipped. "How do you know I am not in the market for some expensive little bauble for my girlfriend?"

"Ha!" Poorez spat, "*Girlfriend*, indeed. Get out, Xanith; I have real business to attend to."

Xanith ignored this insult and picked at his fingernails. "Business that in no way concerns *Duak-Thenal*, I assume?"

Poorez colored considerably and took a step back from his own counter. "I am sure I don't know what you are talking about."

Xanith stood straight and was about to really lay into Poorez when Ranabee floated around a curio cabinet and came to the rescue. "Oh, really, Poorez… you might as well tell them. They'll find out sooner or later."

Xanith grinned at the jeweler and bowed to Ranabee. "Milady, you speak with reason, as always."

Ranabee glared at the performer. Her black, unforgiving eyes, slightly angular, peered from the shadows of her olive skin. "Leave it, Xanith. You will not get high marks from me for snooping around. Look for gossip in dark corners, and eventually you will find it." She pointed a finger at Xanith's face. "But don't think for a moment that I will keep secret your little escapade on the wharf. If you find it necessary to tell Althea anything before I have given you permission to do so, I will tell her everything I know. Then who will she trust more?"

Xanith's eyes widened and he whistled in admiration. "I understand you perfectly, my dear. I won't say a thing. You have Gregory's word on it."

Gregory gritted his teeth, but Ranabee turned to Poorez. "Tell them," she commanded.

"All right, all right," Poorez complained, returning to the counter. "Now, you must know, it didn't occur to me until after the meeting this morning… and I wanted to be sure before I said anything."

"Yes, yes, Poorez, we know you are innocent." Ranabee twirled her hand with impatience. "Get on with it."

Poorez stared at her. "Well, I just want to be sure that everyone understands that I'm not hiding anything from…"

"We know!" Ranabee scowled. Xanith had to cover his mouth to keep from laughing.

"Fine," Poorez pouted. "Here it is. A few months back a customer I had never seen before came in with an unusual piece of jewelry. A large family crest made into a brooch. She wanted to have it appraised."

"To find out how much it was worth?" Gregory interrupted.

"Yes, but that wasn't all. This girl wanted to know how old it was and if I had ever seen its like before."

"Had you?" Xanith asked.

"Yes, of course. Not for some time, but yes. You see, it was a golden eagle crest, made for a specific family. It would have been specially crafted at a cost that rivals anything I sell here."

"And how did this girl come by the piece?" Gregory asked.

"Well, naturally I was suspicious. Such a young girl handling a priceless piece like that -- I mean, it was ancient, many hundreds of years old. But when she did not ask to pawn it, even after I told her its worth, well, my suspicions abated."

Poorez folded his hands, his part of the story finished.

Xanith turned to Ranabee. "Is there more?"

Ranabee turned and leaned her elbows back on the counter, "This morning, during Darweshi's little tirade, I read some of the papers he was waving about. Complaints from people who have been robbed by *Duak-Thenal*. One of them came from a family in Villuna. They said that they hired *Duak-Thenal* to retrieve a family crest for them, and that they failed in the attempt."

Xanith and Gregory exchanged glances. "A golden eagle crest, I assume?" Xanith said.

Ranabee nodded her head.

Xanith laughed. "And you remembered what your good friend Poorez had told you about the strange customer he met a few months back, so you came running over here to tell him."

Ranabee stood up straight. "Don't push it, Xanith."

Xanith held up his hands and laughed.

"Do you remember the name of this family, Poorez?" Gregory asked.

Poorez held up a finger and pulled a large blue ledger from under his counter. "I wrote it down," he said as he opened the big book. He ran one long finger down the page and stopped about halfway down. "Here it is," he announced, and turned the book toward them.

Xanith, Ranabee and Gregory bent over the ledger.

"Seely," Poorez announced. "That is the family name. Seely."

Xanith looked at Ranabee, who was nodding her head.

"Same name as on the papers?" Gregory asked her.

"Yes," Ranabee said. "The Seely family is a large, wealthy gang of looters and thieves from Villuna. They have been around for centuries."

"Gang?" Xanith raised an eyebrow, for Ranabee was not normally given to insults.

Ranabee curled her lip. "Let us just say that they did not come by their wealth honestly."

"Ah." Xanith drummed his fingers on the counter. "So, this Seely clan… crooks, you say… hires another band of crooks to find their long-lost family crest. Make sense to any of you?"

"It does if the eagle crest does not really belong to them," Ranabee said. "That way if the deal went bad—and it looks like this one did—the Seely family has a scapegoat."

"Convenient," Gregory concurred.

Xanith was silent a minute. He was staring at Poorez' ledger again, running his finger back and forth along the name in the book. "If the Seely family hired *Duak-Thenal* to look for their crest, and the crest was never handed over, then why did a family member come into your shop with it, eh, Poorez?"

"I, um… well, I don't really…"

"This girl gave you her first name, too, Poorez?" Xanith pressed.

"Of course, I always insist on first and last names."

Xanith shook his head and pointed to a spot in the ledger to the right of the Seely name. "Look at this."

Poorez donned his spectacles and bent over the book. "Shelly…K… Lar," Poorez read.

"Read it again," Xanith demanded.

Poorez obeyed. "Shelly…K…Lar," he said again. He looked up at Xanith, "I don't under—"

"*Ziyad's blood!*" Gregory swore, sudden understanding lighting his features. Poorez still looked confused.

"Oh, for Kelina's sake, Poorez," Xanith said. "Drop the Y and read it again."

"Shell...ke..lar," Poorez stuttered. "Shelkelar." Then it dawned on him. "Oh, my stars!"

Ranabee slammed her dark hands onto the counter. "Poorez, you fool, you had the Shelkelar Captain Tain Elire in here—and you didn't do a thing about it!"

"I never knew, I swear it! I thought she was a child!" Poorez took off his spectacles and wiped his brow.

Xanith ignored him. "Gregory, get back to Nimbus and double-check those papers. Alistair may want to have a talk with the Seely family in Yeelan."

Gregory disappeared without a word.

Ranabee snorted. "Good luck with that. They will lie through their teeth to protect their interests."

"Maybe, but at least Alistair will be armed with a little more information." He ripped the page from Poorez's ledger and started folding it.

"What are you doing?"

"Putting the evidence in safekeeping," Xanith replied.

"But… but I'll be implicated in this!"

Ranabee rolled her eyes. "Oh, please, Poorez. You aren't guilty of anything more than stupidity."

Poorez looked hurt. "I beg your pardon."

Xanith put a hand on his shoulder in mock sympathy. "Really, Poorez, it could have happened to any one of us. Mistaking the most infamous pointy-eared fairy in Tearlach for a little girl—I mean, I am sure it happens all the time."

Poorez' pale eyes narrowed. He looked positively mutinous. "She was wearing a disguise! And a hat covered her ears."

Ranabee snorted again and slid out the door.

Xanith moved to follow her, but Poorez stopped him with a yelp. "Wait!"

Xanith turned back to him.

"Tell Althea everything if you must, but don't tell Alistair."

"Why not?"

Poorez' shoulders sagged. "Would you want him to know you let the most infamous thief in Tearlach slip through *your* fingers?"

Xanith nodded in sympathy. He suddenly felt for the jeweler. "No," he said. "No, I would not."

4~To the Breezeway

The sun had not yet risen to greet the early morning hours as two shadowy figures approached the Breezeway. They had skirted the north end of Long Lake a few hours before and were now making their way southwest, hoping to reach their destination by mid-morning.

The elf silently watched the rider beside him, amused.

The imp was lounging on her silver horse in her favored position, lying on her back. A wiry little shadow dressed all in black, head resting comfortably on the animal's rump, her feet were crossed and planted on the horse's head.

Kiernan always marveled that the great silver mare did not seem to mind the strange riding habits of its mistress. Algoryn was the horse's name and she was enormous—far too large for the tiny imp, who could not have weighed a hundred pounds. Kiernan supposed it was not much of an inconvenience for the horse.

"I'm starving!" Tain exclaimed suddenly.

Kiernan smiled absently but did not answer, lost in his own thoughts.

"Kiernannnnnnn…" she said, dragging his name out to antagonize him.

"What!" he snapped, whipping about to face her.

She grinned at him, clearly happy to get a reaction of any kind from him, no matter how surly. "How do you think it went?"

Kiernan sighed and looked ahead, not wanting to discuss their most recent job with his partner. He was not finished thinking about it himself.

But Tain went on despite Kiernan's silence. "Because I think it went rather well, all things considered. Raymond and Grace are safe, no serious injuries on our side—basically a task well done."

Kiernan absently wondered how long the self-amused imp would be able to carry on this one-sided conversation. She propped herself up on one elbow and looked at him expectantly. "Well?" she asked, blinking at him with her oversized blue eyes.

Kiernan Nightwing, the leader of *Duak-Thenal,* shook his head in frustration. The elf did not think the rescue had gone well at all. Six men had attacked them, when Kiernan had expected no resistance. His contact was usually so reliable. Four guards were to be at the gate, easily dispatched with sleeping darts. But where had the other two come from? Then there were the cousins, humans whose hearing was poor in comparison to the elf's, who should not have been able to hear a sound from the garden. What should have been a simple mission had very quickly turned into a dangerous situation. The man and child they had come to rescue were at risk of being seriously injured or killed, something Kiernan had never allowed to happen before. The whole affair led Kiernan to one disturbing conclusion: someone other than their contact in Preliona had known they were coming.

None of these issues did he voice to the Captain, knowing she would disagree with him no matter what he said.

"It could have gone better," he finally muttered.

The imp let out a moan of frustration and rolled her eyes. "Ugh! You're doing it again."

Kiernan glared at her. "What are you talking about?"

The imp thief shook her head, her long black braid flipping back and forth over her shoulder. "Picking apart every detail of the assignment until you've convinced yourself that no plan has ever gone worse. Well, I am not listening." And with that she jammed her fingers into her ears and began to sing loudly and hideously off-key.

"I don't know why I bother saying anything to you!" Kiernan shouted over her unearthly vocals.

Apparently, she heard him, for she unplugged her pointed ears and stared at him, "I don't know why you do either," she replied, mimicking his scolding tone perfectly.

Kiernan rolled his eyes. It was hard to be angry with her. Frustrating as she was, and often as Kiernan wished for a more reliable—or at least more mature—partner, he could hardly blame her for her attitude.

Captain Tain Elire was *Duak-Thenal's* master thief, the most infamous one in the Northern Realms—possibly in all of Tearlach.

Some years earlier, before Kiernan had met her, Tain had traveled exclusively with an odious band of cutthroats called the Black Bloods. Every one of those men had been a talented thief, but most of them had been more interested in slaughtering than simply robbing their victims. The fairy's involvement with that group had left her with precious little basis for fair comparison. Everything she had experienced in the twenty years since she had left the Black Bloods was an improvement—so her judgment tended to be a bit clouded and over-optimistic.

Tain would never be able to see last night's rescue as botched in any way.

The imp's stifled snickering brought him back to the present and the freshness of the morning air.

"What are you laughing at?" Kiernan asked.

"I was just remembering the look on Beselmee's face when you walked in the door of his house," she replied, speaking through episodes of snorts and giggles.

Kiernan glared at her, but his stern look only sent the imp into another fit of snorting. "The way his knees buckled when he said, '*My Lord!*' Oh, I thought for sure he was about to kiss your feet!"

Now she was very nearly hysterical. Kiernan had to fight to control his own urge to join her. The Captain had an infectious laugh and could find humor in the grimmest situation.

Kiernan reached into his sack and threw a dried date at her. It bounced off her shoulder and successfully jolted her into at least stifling some of her guffawing. "Not funny, Captain," Kiernan warned.

The imp had suggested another disturbing thought, however—one that was quite sobering. He had been recognized again.

As leader of *Duak-Thenal*, Kiernan rarely made the final contact in a mission like this. There were two reasons for this. First and foremost, the band needed to protect its leader's identity. But there was a second reason.

He was too recognizable to his own kind.

As was evident when he helped Raymond S'Trobenue into his new home in Skelduli.

Beselmee and Rose were elderly light elves who had left the court years before, when Kiernan had been a child. They were a contact for *Duak-Thenal* in Skelduli and had even done some spying for them.

Kiernan's band had never used them for such a large task as last evening's had been. Asking an elf to take in a runaway human for an indeterminate amount of time was a lot to ask of anyone, and Kiernan had thought it best to handle the matter himself.

Beselmee and Rose had met them at the door. Kiernan, thinking only to be polite, removed his hood. Their reaction was immediate.

"Your Highness!" They both exclaimed, dropping into low bows.

Kiernan winced at the formal title, unused to it after several years of living outside his family's walls. He stepped forward quickly and helped both elves to their feet, "Please, it is Kiernan Nightwing now." And gave them a stern look. "Do you understand?"

Things had calmed down a bit after that. Tain had made sure that Raymond and his child were settled and comfortable in their new surroundings. She had even amused the child for a bit. Little Grace had awakened and would not be placated until she had spent some time playing with the wingless fairy.

Kiernan, meanwhile, had tried to give Beselmee and Rose an ample amount of money to care for their wards. They refused it, so Kiernan had passed the money secretly to Raymond, who took it only after swearing he would pay him back.

Before they left, Kiernan had impressed upon the couple the importance of their silence concerning the prince's identity. The two had then said their goodbyes and left without further incident.

The whole affair really should not have bothered him.

Prince Kiernatrialis Aila had been away from Lasairian, the light elven city of his family, on and off for more than twenty years. He had all but forsaken his royal title, so he was almost always startled when he heard his true name pronounced with the awe and respect he had heard last night.

Tain Elire had finally ceased her childlike laughter and was now gazing at him thoughtfully.

Kiernan threw up his arms. "What?!" he shouted in an adolescent tone he could not seem to help.

She did not flinch. "You know, I don't think you realize what kind of effect you have on people, *Your Highness*."

Kiernan scoffed at her flippant use of his title and regarded the imp. She was such a childish little troublemaker most of the time—her large guileless eyes fooled everyone into thinking she was innocent. Despite this, she could be intensely observant and truly adult at times. She knew him better than anyone, and had impressed upon him more than once how mesmerizing he could be, encouraging him to use his unusual elfish look to his own advantage.

Truthfully, Kiernan did not often notice the looks he got from people, the pauses and hesitations in speech and manners that he seemed to cause in the folk he helped. The very idea made him uncomfortable.

Tain was never uncomfortable, Kiernan knew, and she adored attention, whether negative or positive.

Kiernan's mare suddenly shied beneath him, forcing the prince back to the present. The most dangerous part of their journey was nearly upon them.

Kiernan and Tain dismounted cautiously and scanned the landscape before them. The damp, sandy shores of Long Lake had given way to the rocky expanse alongside the larger lake to the west: the Sprawling Edge, a massive sea of rough water that few traveled.

Its stony beach was the last stretch of land to be crossed before the companions reached the back side of The Breezeway.

Tain led the way as both pulled small pouches from their belts. Kiernan emptied the contents into his hand. Pebbles of rock salt spilled into the prince's palm, a gift from the Darkwater clan. It was small protection against the obstacles on the rocky stretch before them, but it was better than nothing.

They walked on in silence, each casting wary glances back and forth, watching for telltale movement in the shadowy rocks. Kiernan was just beginning to think they would make it without incident when Tain came to a frozen halt in front of him.

"Here they come!" Tain shouted.

Kiernan stiffened and followed the imp's line of sight. Directly in front of her was a moving rock. It stood about three feet in height and could be described as nothing more than a living, breathing pile of stones. Coal-like eyes squeezed between slits of rock focused on the travelers with intense hatred. Unstable-looking stacks of slate made up its limbs. Kiernan thought it a feat of physics that these creatures stood at all, much less moved.

They were Spriggans—small, odd-looking creatures that were literally made of the rocks they lived in. No sword, no matter how enchanted, could take down the vicious monsters.

They were a great deterrent to any enemy who might try to attack the Breezeway, and because of that, they had not been done away with. The only time they were encountered was by unsuspecting enemies—or by familiar travelers taking the back shortcut to the Breezeway.

Despite their shaky appearance, the devils could move extremely fast.

The first one charged them ferociously, and Kiernan found himself yelling in sudden fear for his friend. "Tain! Move it!"

Quick as the imp Captain was, the spriggan was nearly upon her before she could throw a handful of crystallized salt at it.

The creature's reaction was great. It threw what could only be its arms in front of its face and screamed. The sound was high-pitched and piercing. Kiernan was forced to cover his ears to keep from screaming himself.

But the keening spriggan did not stop its advance on the imp. Tain was forced to leap out of the way, while the running rock crashed wildly into the leg of Tain's great horse. Algoryn did not shy away. She reared back on her hind legs and brought her forelegs crashing down onto the spriggan's head.

The creature fell apart under the weight of the great horse, but several others sprouted up in its place.

Kiernan heard the two to his right before he saw them. He turned in time to throw a handful of salt at them, stopping them cold. The prince then took a chance with the rocky terrain and leapt onto his horse. He edged the animal forward as fast as it would go, heading toward the imp, who was trying to hold off no less than three small spriggans.

Kiernan's horse raced across the treacherous beach to reach the Captain. The prince tossed the remainder of his salt at their attackers and reached for the imp. "Grab on," he commanded.

Tain did not hesitate, taking the elf's arm and swinging herself onto the back of his horse.

"Go! *Go!*" she yelled putting two fingers to her lips and whistling for Algoryn.

The silver mare was faring better than her mistress had, continuing her strategy of crushing spriggans with her powerful forelegs.

The horse came at Tain's call, but as the group moved quickly away, the spriggans began pelting them with the rocks they lived in.

"Ouch!" Tain yelped from her seat behind the prince. "*Ziyad's blood*, Kiernan, hurry up!"

Kiernan obeyed. "They are getting bolder," he commented.

"Yeah," Tain agreed. She rubbed the back of her head, where a lump was quickly forming. "Let's go the other way next time, okay?"

5~Coming Together

Apart from the Spriggans, the Breezeway was virtually unguarded. The back side was deserted and there was no door, so the companions were forced to lead their horses up the winding stone stairs that led to the front of the compound.

As the two travelers rounded the top of the spiral stairs, the courtyard came into view.

Salmon colored cobblestones covered its entire expanse, and colorful tents lined the circle along the front of the compound. An enormous pink granite fountain carved with ancient dwarven runes sat directly in the center of the yard, spilling enough water over its edge for nearby children to splash in.

The structure of the Breezeway itself was built right into the granite wall. The building was a gigantic, sprawling form of beige and salmon-colored stone, jutting out from the mountain. It looked like a massive inn, a seaside retreat. The front was two stories tall, the upper floor a riot of balconies and parapets, the lower level defined by archways creating a tunneled network of entrances and exits in and out of the many halls of the Breezeway.

Tain and Kiernan led their brave horses across the courtyard, stopping here and there to chat with the many merchants who crowded the circle that morning. As they made their way to the stables at the far end of the courtyard, Kiernan could not help but notice the many merchants who held their cloaks closer and hurriedly guarded their tables as the imp thief passed them by.

Not that their vigilance made much difference. Tain always managed to snag something from one of the booths. He made a mental note to force the Captain to return whatever she had pilfered today. Once the elf and the imp had handed off their mounts to the young stable girl, they turned for the compound itself.

They were stopped by a cheery, musical voice behind them.

"It's about time the two of you showed up."

Kiernan turned and grinned at the sight before him.

Four figures stood together in the shadow of the stable door.

Long, dust-laden cloaks fell about lithe limbs and hid a variety of hand-ready weapons. Pointed ears that caught the smallest whisper of sound peeked through four different shades of hair. Four pairs of eyes shone in the shadows: one the purple of deepest sunset, one gray as mist, one sparkling gold, and one black as the pit of a storm.

This was Kiernan Nightwing's secret group of mercenaries. This was the band of elves whose name was whispered in secrecy and hope, or shouted in anger. This was *Duak-Thenal*.

Kiernan smiled warmly and moved to his comrades. "Good to be back, Nemesio," Kiernan said, clasping hands with a tall brown-skinned elf first.

"Good to have you," the tall elf replied.

Kiernan looked up into the smiling violet eyes and smooth, welcoming features of the tallest member of his group. Nemesio Firebrand was a southern elf from the center of Malhuria, the warmest part of Tearlach. His hair was jet black and he wore it in braids that fit snuggly to his head and ran down the length of his long back. He wore mahogany leathers and wielded an enormous bow. At six and a half feet, he was easily the tallest member of the group, and by far the strongest.

Kiernan turned and hugged the smaller, more slightly built elf next to Nemesio. "Hello, Panas. Miss us?"

The smaller elf pushed Kiernan away. "*Kelina*, but you're filthy, Kiernan! Get off me!"

Panas the Hawk brushed himself off as though Kiernan had dumped mud on him. He was a light elf like the prince, endowed with all the physical features called to mind by the word 'elf.' Flowing golden hair, piercing golden eyes flecked with green, and the cream-colored, blemish free skin of a child.

Panas's clothing was flashier than that of his taller companion. A beautifully embroidered, plum-colored vest covered most of his tunic. His cape was of deep red velvet and hung loosely from his shoulder. Several rings flashed on his thin fingers, and a jewel-encrusted dagger hung from his belt. He carried a score of other weapons useful for any occasion, and was adept at using them all. His current favorite was a slingshot, which he absently spun on his finger.

"Steal anything for me, Captain?" he now asked, taking the imp's hand, and twirling her about.

"As if you have need *or* space for anything new," Tain replied coyly as she allowed herself to dip dramatically into his arms.

Panas screwed up his face. "Then I shall be forced to find myself a new dance partner." He spun her back out.

She caught herself gracefully and rounded on him. "You will be lucky to find someone who can avoid your clumsy feet!"

Laughing at Panas's scowl, she turned to Nemesio, who clapped her on the back and laughed at his blonde companion. "Ignore him, Captain," Nemesio said. "Panas has always been jealous of your dancing prowess."

Tain smiled up at the southern elf. "Wanna dance with me tonight, Nemy?"

Nemesio's purple eyes suddenly went wide as he took a step back from her. "Ummmm, no. Sorry, Captain. If you would like to keep all your toes, you'd better stick with Panas."

Kiernan laughed with Nemesio as he turned to greet the two more silent members of the group.

They were very nearly the same height, smaller than Kiernan and Nemesio, taller than Panas. In many ways they were quite similar, and they worked well together because of that fact. But they were different as well. One was female, the other male. One was tanned and rather wild in appearance; the other was extremely lean and sharp.

Kiernan reached the female first. "Hello, Kiernan," she said quietly. "It is good to see you."

"Hello, Dagmar."

She had long and rather wild brown hair, half of which she managed to pull back from her face. Haunting gray eyes peered out from her sharp features and deeply bronzed skin.

She wore an enormous dark green cape that blended in with natural surroundings. A small crossbow was strapped to her back, and a reed thin sword with a dark golden hue hung from her hip. Her name was Dagmar Coal. She was a wild elf from the mountain woods of Jathaharwel.

Kiernan hugged the wild elf lightly. Of them all, Dagmar Coal would be the least likely to reciprocate a show of affection, and Kiernan was constantly and painfully aware of this.

Tain, of course, had no such qualms and even less subtlety. She crossed her arms in front of her and looked up at Dagmar with disapproval. "Dagmar, you are going to at least let me do something with your hair before tonight, aren't you?"

Dagmar shook her head in a gesture that said she knew she would lose this argument. "Tain…" she began.

Tain fluffed triumphantly. "Panas!" she yelled, cutting off Dagmar's protest.

The flamboyant light elf leapt to her side and bowed dramatically, "My lady?"

Tain grinned mischievously and clapped her tiny hands together, "Ideas, please."

"Well," Panas began, circling the wild elf, and tapping one finger against his chin. He picked at her green cloak, lifting it with two fingers as if loath to touch it. "Green is definitely out this year. Why not try something in rust or burgundy? It would certainly bring out your eyes more, don't you think?"

Dagmar's answer was an elbow in Panas' abdomen. Panas doubled over, sputtering curses, much to the delight of the others. Even Dagmar cracked a smile.

Tain, giving up on her stubborn friend, turned instead and leapt into the arms of the remaining member of *Duak-Thenal*.

Bone-colored limbs caught the airborne imp in a strong embrace. Tain let out a yelp of surprise, "*Kelina!* Talesin!" she said. "Put some gloves on those hands." And she leapt to the ground and glared up at the cold-fingered creature before her.

Though Talesin Darken was by far the most quiet and subtle of his elven companions, he was also the most intimidating. His short hair was so black that at times it appeared almost blue.

Black, pupil-less eyes peered out from beneath long black lashes. Pools of inky obsidian terrifying enough to stop some men in their tracks.

Kiernan approached him without fear, but he did not hold out his hand in greeting. He simply clapped the smaller elf on the back lightly.

"Hello, Talesin."

The dark-haired elf bowed his head slightly. "Kiernan."

Talesin Darken was an ice elf, the rarest creature in the elven world. Ice elves lived far to the north on a huge stretch of frozen land called Serenia. They did not often venture south, as their sensitive skin kept them isolated and their aggressive nature did not lend itself to making allies of their southern brethren.

Talesin dressed entirely in blue and white clothing made for him by Kiernan's people. His long-sleeved blue cloak had been embedded with magic designed to protect his icy skin. He carried a double-bladed sword made of a strange crystallized metal. None but the cold-fingered elf could touch the weapon. Tain had found that out the hard way the first time she had tried to steal it. The fingers of the thief's hand had been numb for almost a week.

Kiernan scanned the group before him and once again remembered how blessed he was to have found them. It was true, after twenty years he knew too little about them. Their names, like his, were fictional.

They were young elves with few ties to either family or friends, who had been willing to leave everything they knew behind. For him, for their cause.

"I'm starving!" Tain announced for the second time that morning. "Let's go in."

Panas took her arm and the two began talking in hushed, excited tones as the rest of *Duak-Thenal* shook their heads and followed their friends inside.

— ✹ ✹ ✹ —

If the outside of the Breezeway seemed like a bustle of activity, the inside was a veritable bazaar of animation.

Hundreds of people of every race moved about in a blur of energy, rushing in and out of hallways in a kind of agitated bliss that was exhausting to watch. So much activity went on in these halls, concerning so many types of people, that Venk Darkwater and his clan had kept expanding the compound to accommodate the increasing influx of visitors.

The Breezeway was split into four quarters, each specifically tailored to the diverse living conditions of the races that sought hospitality here.

The companions entered Oak Hall, which Kiernan considered the most beautiful of the four, first. Dozens of full-grown oaks towered overhead, their branches and foliage intertwining so that a great green blanket became the ceiling of the hall. Rope bridges dangled above, linking tree to tree in a mesmerizing network of web-like roads and alcoves beneath the mountains.

Six round tables stood under the shadow of the trees. On each tabletop was inlaid a detailed map of all the surrounding lands with whom the Breezeway traded.

All six tables were currently surrounded by groups of people who were shouting and pointing. It seemed as if each table competed with the other five for some unknown treasure. This was a common sight in Oak Hall during the day, for most of the caravan business of the Breezeway was conducted here.

The companions converged on the table nearest them, their boots scraping softly on the cobblestone floor. Surrounding this table was a crowd of bellowing dwarves, who were so busy shouting and cursing that a herd of goblins could not have caught their attention.

Tain suddenly held her arms out wide, stopping the elves' advance, and grinned mischievously.

Kiernan recognized the wicked glint in his friend's eye. He followed the imp's gaze to the first table, where one exceptionally large dwarf had his back turned to them. Kiernan guessed the imp's intention and lunged forward to grab her arm.

Too late.

The Captain was already running straight for the unsuspecting dwarf. An instant before she reached her quarry, Tain Elire let out a whoop of warning and, placing her tiny hands on the dwarf's shoulders, she vaulted up and over his head.

The startled dwarf stumbled backwards and landed on his backside, sputtering curses as the nimble imp landed in a graceful crouch at the center of the table.

The other dwarves were stunned into silence only for a moment, their wrinkled faces frozen in mid-curse. Then they all began shouting at the rude interruption, waving their arms and hollering at the imp.

Tain completely ignored them. "Hiya, Venk!" she shouted, much to the amusement of the five elves, who were now laughing heartily. The sight of the imp playing leapfrog with the dwarf leader was highly amusing to the tall folk.

"Dammit, Tain!" Venk Darkwater clambered to his feet and brushed himself off. "If I told ya once, I told ya a thousand times!"

Venk then turned and glared over his shoulder at *Duak-Thenal.* "You... shut up!" he hollered. Of course, this only made the elves laugh harder. Panas was on his knees and the others were holding onto each other for support. Kiernan put his head in his hand to avoid the dwarf's murderous look.

Venk Darkwater, the powerhouse behind the Breezeway and the coordinator of *Duak-Thenal's* missions, was taller than every other dwarf at the table. Tain herself stood only an inch or two above him. Black curly hair, just brushing his shoulders, framed his rounded, ruddy face. His black beard, unlike the others', was clipped and neatly trimmed. A single gold ring hung from his ear.

Venk Darkwater turned his furious glare on his tormentor, who was now sitting cross-legged in the center of his map, still ignoring the vicious scolding of the other dwarves. The dwarf raised one finger and stormed back to the table, looking as though he intended to do serious damage to the imp thief.

It may have been her smile that stopped him. Or perhaps it was her eyes. Those enormous blue eyes that looked at him so adoringly.

Kiernan watched the dwarf's anger melt. He settled for simply shaking his finger at her.

Tain Elire's smile widened, if that was possible, and she stood and stepped lightly to the edge of the table, meaning to jump off. Venk stopped her with a hand and motioned for her to bend down to his level.

She did, and before she could back away, Venk had grabbed her pointed ear in two stubby fingers. "Hey!" she protested, but Venk held on, and pulled her off the map with one flick of his hand.

Tain went stumbling and tripped over Panas, who was still kneeling on the floor. Both landed in a heap. This time the dwarves joined in with the elves' raucous laughter.

"Now stay offa my table!" Venk concluded with a harrumph, turning back to the map.

The hubbub of negotiation, which Tain had interrupted, started up again before Kiernan could get a word in with Venk.

He stepped forward, but the large dwarf stopped him with his voice. "What're you long-legs standing around fer?" he yelled over the din. "Go feed those thin stomachs a yours. And take the mini-thief with you."

Panas laughed out loud, and Tain kicked him in the shin. Kiernan shrugged and motioned his friends from the hall, knowing this was not the time to press the busy dwarf.

Venk stuck an arm out as Talesin passed, catching the elf at the waist, and stopping him. "Got somethin' fer me, boyo?" he asked, not looking up at the elf.

A rolled-up piece of parchment appeared in the elf's hands and Venk took it. "Any trouble?" he asked quietly.

"Is there ever?" Talesin asked, a hint of sarcasm crossing his chiseled features.

"Good boy," Venk commented, patting Talesin on the arm. "Go eat."

Talesin nodded and moved past Kiernan.

"Meet me in the Grove at ten o'clock, ya hear?" Venk called after them.

The tired and hungry crew waved their assent and continued to the Darkwater Arms.

6~A New Deal

Odin Darweshi stalked through the warehouse, enjoying the way his heeled boots echoed off its stone halls. The floors were flagstone and the walls were built of cedar, thick and impervious to the damp air by the pier.

At this late hour, the warehouse was nearly empty. Most of the laborers had gone home. Only a few clerks flitted from place to place, taking notes and signing invoices. Odin ignored them all and continued to the upper level. Darweshi absolutely loved roaming the halls of the enormous building he would one day inherit. And it gave him great pleasure to carry out his illegal endeavors right under his father's nose.

At the far end of the warehouse Odin took a right turn and walked down a lengthy hall. This area was restricted to all his father's employees. There was only one door, and only Odin had the key.

He reached out to insert the key in the lock, but before Odin could grasp the cold handle the door flew from his extended palm and flung wide of its own accord.

The merchant was startled but not really surprised. He did not fear magic. In fact, right now, he embraced it. The Mage who backed him enjoyed exercising his skills almost as much as Odin enjoyed making him wait.

"I suppose I deserved that," Odin stated flatly, addressing the seemingly unoccupied room.

"You deserve far worse, actually," came the cryptic response. The door slammed shut behind him before Odin could touch it.

Odin let his eyes adjust to the semi-darkness of the spacious room. There was not much to it, really. A few small pieces of plain furniture clung to the corners. The sky was darkened by clouds, so the moon did not shine through the two small windows above. A couple of low-lit lanterns, one on the table and another on the floor, threw dim yellow light about the room and cast shadows across a large, hulking mass of metal in the far right corner.

This Odin ignored in favor of the room's only occupant – a mage dressed entirely in dark red. Odin had only just now spotted the man seated in a wooden chair, his cowl pulled low over his eyes.

This was who he had come to see, the man who made all his corrupt dreams possible. Stealing barexium from Graxton caravans, selling it to Malhuria, and building a bridge out of scrap metal without the city's knowledge required the touch of a wizard. Odin had found exactly what he was looking for in this mysterious mage.

"Sit down, Darweshi," the mage said, gesturing to another chair. "We have much to discuss."

Of course we do, Odin thought. He was afraid this relationship was starting to wear thin. Odin was used to working alone, being in control. He butted heads with the Red Mage more often than not recently.

He crossed his silken-clad arms across his chest and smiled wryly at his guest. "Do you own me now, LaRante? Because I seem to remember something about this being an equal partnership." Odin pointed a finger at the seated mage. "That being the case, I hardly think you have the right to command me to do anything."

Instead of an apology, Odin was greeted with a throaty chuckle. The merchant repressed the urge to tear the Mage's throat out.

He had never seen LaRante's face. But Odin guessed the man to be in his late sixties by the way the mage moved and spoke—slowly and raspily, and in that order.

Odin had never seen LaRante's eyes. He was unsure he ever wanted to.

"Be careful, young Lord," the Mage said through his sporadic laughter. "You are forgetting to whom you speak."

"As are you, I'm afraid," Odin responded, neither moved nor cowed by the man's threat. "A word from me brings my father's guard."

"And a gesture from me would burn your foolish tongue from your blabbering mouth." The Mage's voice changed drastically as he leaned forward in his seat. Gone was the lounging conversationalist, replaced by a sharp and powerful old man with a venomous ire to match Darweshi's. Odin was surprised to find himself swallowing hard.

The rusty Red Mage sat back, calm once again, and gestured again to the chair. "You forget why we have come together, Lord Darweshi," the Mage said calmly. "I am the solution to your problems."

Odin narrowed his eyes. "You've certainly done a smashing job thus far," he spat, finally taking the proffered seat. "In one day alone, I am robbed, and my bridge is vandalized. Please, oh great LaRante, give me your solution!" Darweshi made himself comfortable, leaning back in the chair and resting his arms behind his head. "I await the plethora of ideas that will surely waft from your wizened tongue."

"Have you spoken to the S'Trobenue brothers lately?"

Odin sneered when LaRante did not take the bait, disappointed. But he gritted his teeth at the very mention of Edmee S'Trobenue's cousins. "Those idiot cousins of Edmee's were supposed to be watching Raymond!"

LaRante folded his thin hands across his abdomen. "Yes, I know. And now he is gone."

Odin stood, furious at the mage's relative calm. "*Duak-Thenal* slashes the supports of my bridge. They steal the plans and the barexium money, and then they spirit away the one person who could finger me for Edmee S'Trobenue's death. Whoever those bastards are, they have certainly been busy destroying my life."

"True. But take heart, dear Odin, this time *Duak-Thenal* has slipped up." He leaned forward. The scant light in the room lit up a well-trimmed gray beard. "I know two of their number."

Odin froze. "Tell me."

LaRante did not hesitate. "The Shelkelar Captain Tain Elire is one of them."

Odin's eyes widened with pleasure, "I *knew* it!" he hissed. "I knew she ran with them. Now that pompous Alistair will have to listen to me. Who is the other?"

LaRante shook his head. "The Captain is enough of a revelation for now. I suggest you use her identity to your advantage. The other… well, that will be my little secret."

Odin was more suspicious than grateful. He sat down slowly. "How did you come by this information, LaRante?"

The Mage paused, petting his gray whiskers as he made Odin wait.

Odin tried to stay very still and not allow LaRante to see the angry twitch of his fingers against his thigh.

"I was there when they helped Raymond escape."

It took several seconds for Odin to register what the mage had said. When his words finally sank in, he leapt to his feet, tipping the chair backwards. "Why didn't you stop them?!! Damn!! Our problems could have been solved by now, you old fool! Or are you no match for an imp thief and a handful of elves?"

LaRante raised one index finger. Red sparks streaked from it. They darted toward Odin's head, stopped just short of his eyes, and exploded in his face. The merchant shrieked and stumbled backward. He moved to draw his sword but discovered it had suddenly turned crimson. Odin howled and dropped the weapon, his hand seared by the burning metal.

LaRante had barely moved and his snide expression never changed. "You are the fool, Darweshi." The Mage's voice did not even rise. "How do you think it would have looked for me to hand over two members of *Duak-Thenal* to the Watch? Even if I could have overwhelmed both of them—and it would do well for you to remember we are dealing with incredibly dangerous warriors who have some magic of their own—what good would it do to have only two of them behind bars? There would never be enough evidence to convict them of anything, and there would be too many questions about my involvement. I cannot be a known participant in your plans, Odin. The Council is on your trail as it is. You are doing enough damage to your reputation without my help."

Odin was so angry he was finding it difficult to breathe. He snagged the chair and righted it with a crash. Then he sat down hard and faced the mage. "You could have killed them," he pouted.

"I would have had to kill Raymond, too. Again, too suspicious."

Odin scowled. "Yes, and now he's out there somewhere, waiting to point a finger at me."

LaRante shifted in his seat slightly. "Raymond will never come back here, Odin. He doesn't know anything. I assure you he wants nothing more than to be away from this city. Forget him. *Duak-Thenal* did you a favor."

Odin wasn't convinced. "I'd rather he was dead. Edmee's cousins would have taken care of that for me sooner or later."

"And they would have botched it somehow. Believe me, you are better off this way. As for *Duak-Thenal*, they will dig their own grave soon enough."

Odin leaned his head against the back of his chair and sighed. "We don't even know how many they are."

"Does it matter?" LaRante asked. "We need to turn things around. I have set plans in motion to make the authorities in this city stand up and take notice. We will prove to them that *Duak-Thenal* is indeed a dangerous group of outlaws."

"How?"

"There is another shipment on its way from Graxton now, is there not?"

Odin nodded slowly.

LaRante leaned forward and placed a large leather bag and a gold coin into Odin's hand. "Send this to the caravan. Have your men leave them behind."

Odin stared at the coin for a long moment and then looked up at the mage with surprise. "How did you get this?"

The mage smiled and gestured at the coin. "This is your future."

He had to admit the Mage's plan was a good one. He could already imagine the outrage of the Council when he reported the carnage visited upon one of his caravans. And the praise he would receive when he identified the perpetrators of the crime.

"There is of course one more thing."

Odin threw up his arms in exasperation. "Of course there is."

"Traveling with the caravan is a young magic user," the Mage said. "In his possession is a powerful magical artifact. It's yours, provided you make sure the boy does not make it to Preliona."

Odin grinned. "That's the kind of payment I am happy to make."

LaRante laughed. "I had a feeling that would please you. Now, what is the Council doing today?"

"Nothing, as usual. Althea won't let Alistair make a move before she knows the color of the criminal's eyes."

"Did you tell them about the supports?" LaRante asked.

"No. I figured Alistair would want to take a look, and I didn't want to risk it."

LaRante nodded. "Good. Keep complaining to Alistair. Put on a good show."

Odin leaned forward and rested his hands on his knees. "What about the Governor? She threatened to go to my father. As much as he dislikes her, he hates me more. He will believe anything she says if it doesn't favor me."

LaRante smirked. "Leave Althea to me. Soon there will be no need to worry about Preliona's warrior governor."

Odin raised one black eyebrow. "And pray tell, why not?"

"Let's just say Lady Althea is about to be taken out of the picture."

Odin Darweshi smiled and sighed, finally satisfied with his benefactor. "Oh," he said, resting his hands behind his head. "That is the best news I have heard in weeks."

7~New Blade, Old Hat

The Weapons School of Preliona was a long, squat structure behind the library. It stretched the length of two street blocks and housed more than five hundred students, many of whom would eventually be recruited for the Watch. Althea herself often saw to this job, assisted by Alistair, the Watch Chief.

On the afternoon of Odin Darweshi's Nimbus tirade, Althea found herself in the school's Hall of Smiths, testing Fale Copperhand's latest invention.

"Is the balance right fer ya, Governor?"

Althea stood in the center of a wide room facing a young opponent who was so covered in protective padding that one could not identify the brave soul.

The governor had removed her voluminous outer cloak, giving her arms free reign with the new sword. Two-handed, she held the beautifully crafted weapon by its pearl-inlaid silver hilt. The blade was an interesting length, somewhere between a short sword and a long sword.

The two opponents circled one another, one masked and covered by full dwarven body armor, the other quite unprotected, wearing nothing more than her everyday garments.

The governor twirled the blade quickly, first to her right side then to her left, as her masked opponent did his best to dodge and block. She brought the blade down in a vicious sideways arc that rent the air before her with a keen whistle.

Her opponent leapt backwards, narrowly avoiding the shining new blade. He brought up his own weapon, blocking the governor's expert attacks with some difficulty until his back came up against the far wall. The governor's new blade pressed into his padded breast.

Althea smiled and stepped back from her young opponent. "It's perfect," she announced.

Fale folded his arms in satisfaction. The padded opponent removed his faceplate, shaking loose a head of unruly blond hair as he bowed to the governor.

Althea patted the boy on the shoulder as the rest of the students in the room breathed a collective sigh of relief.

"And the weight?" Fale asked, making his way toward the governor.

Althea took a moment to toss the weapon from hand to hand before settling it comfortably in her left, spinning it once and then whipping it about to place the silver blade directly under the dwarf's chin.

The move met with applause and a bit of laughter from the dozens of students and smithies who crowded the room, eager to get a look at the master swordswoman testing a new weapon.

"Save it," Althea said to her admirers as she lowered the sword. "Ramsey here wasn't even trying—were you, my dear?"

The blue-eyed student smiled and looked at his feet. "You would have bested me no matter how hard I tried, Your Excellency," he said.

Althea shook her head and laughed at the boy's modesty. "You are a brave soul, Ramsey, but a terrible liar."

The other students laughed and applauded again as Ramsey bowed and moved toward his crowd of friends.

Althea beckoned the dwarf to her as the young men and women left for their classes. Quinlan, the young Guild Master and councilman, who until now had been hiding in a corner, followed Fale. He moved quietly, stealing furtive glances at the retreating students.

"What's the matter, Quinlan?" the governor asked. "Too many vibrant young souls in one room for you?"

"I hated school," he grumbled.

"Come now, Quinlan, you were young once. Still are in my book. Is it not refreshing to be surrounded by youth once in awhile?"

The Guild Master grimaced. "Quite honestly, Your Excellency, no."

Althea waved him away and turned to the dwarf. "I must admit, Fale, I did not think it could be done, but the weapon is flawless. You have achieved what I have been seeking for years." Althea lifted the silver weapon in her hand. "It is light and yet not too delicate. It has power and reach, and yet it will not scrape the ground when sheathed."

Fale crossed his mighty arms nodded with pride. "A blade with the thrust of a short sword, the weight and timbre of a rapier, and the sheer might of a broad sword."

Althea sliced the air once more with the shining blade, admiring the way in seemed to sing as it cut downward. "Make a hundred more. Two dozen for the Watch and the rest to Quinlan."

The Guild Master perked up. "Thank you, Governor," he said.

"Oh, don't thank me too soon. You'll pay me back when you sell them all."

Quinlan made a small bow of his head as he whipped out his ledger and began to write furiously.

Althea sheathed the new weapon, and then drew it again. "So, what have you got for me, gentlemen? News, I hope?"

Quinlan glanced at Fale and put his ledger away. He cleared his throat. "I am afraid we have found very little."

Althea frowned and went back to practicing with her sword, "How little?" she asked.

"There has been a surge of merchant caravan attacks of late, but it is difficult to say who is responsible for them..."

Fale grunted and uncrossed his arms. "Aw, come off it, Quin! Ya know damned well there aren't many but an organized group o' vigilantes could pull off the attacks we been hearin' about."

Quinlan shook his head, apparently unwilling to elaborate.

Althea dropped her sword tip and turned to face the Guild Master. "Quinlan," she began, "Withholding information from me, no matter how implausible, will not win you favor."

The young man smiled uncertainly and shifted on his feet.

"How many attacks have there been?" the governor pressed.

Quinlan continued to look at the floor. "A dozen in the last year."

Althea raised both of her high eyebrows and glanced at Fale. The dwarf shrugged and leaned against the nearest table. "And your losses?"

Quinlan shrugged. "Not so much to myself as those for whom I have organized. I have shelled out some money for damages, but I am afraid I cannot repair my reputation." Quinlan looked up at her and Althea was surprised to see a rare flash of anger cross his face. "I cannot afford the kind of protection these caravans suddenly seem to need. If this keeps up, I will lose money in the long run—for no one will trust me to get their goods from one place to another."

Althea regarded Quinlan's dark eyes and nodded solemnly. "I wish you had told me this sooner, Quinlan."

"I did not wish to bother you." Quinlan ran a hand through his long black hair and turned away with a heavy sigh.

Fale stood straight. "And sure, now the boy sees he was wrong in not comin' to ya."

"I am not a boy, Fale," Quinlan growled from the opposite side of the table.

Althea held up a hand to silence the younger man, but Fale plowed on. "He was wrong not comin' to ya in the first place," Fale repeated, "'cause our problems appear to be linked."

Althea sheathed her new sword and sat down slowly.

"Surprisin' number a deaths have accompanied the attacks," Fale explained.

Althea watched with interest as the Guild Master paced on the opposite side of the room. He rolled his eyes in frustration but made no move to silence the dwarf.

Althea leaned into him, understanding where the conversation was going. "And you think the elves are involved."

"It's possible," Quinlan said, shuffling around the table. "But I must admit we have little evidence to go on."

Althea looked to Fale, who seemed more willing to dole out details. "We have only been able to investigate four a these attacks. In one of 'em, two people were killed—both men of questionable character." Fale came around the table and sat next to the governor. "Most of the other merchants had run off, but one shaken-up survivor gave us a sketchy description. Four extremely tall cloaked figures attacked the caravan, killed the two drivin' the wagon and then ransacked the contents."

"Only the one wagon?" Althea asked.

Quinlan nodded.

"And what makes you think the elves were involved?"

"The manner in which the two men were dispatched," Fale explained, "Single stroke straight ta the heart. Wounds were so small I could barely find the entry. Not many I know could deliver a killin' strike with such grace. Exceptin' yerself, of course."

Althea grunted. "Well, I am a bit rusty, Fale, so I guess you can rule me out as a suspect."

The dwarf chuckled. "Regardless, someone wanted whatever was inside that wagon and was willin' ta kill ta get it."

"Unless the thieves had no intention of killing," Quinlan said.

Fale grunted. "Course they did! Ya don't go cutting people up like that unless you intend to, my friend."

Althea looked from dwarf to man and back again, Fale with his gruff exterior and fiery orange eyes and Quinlan with his somber brown orbs and serious, somehow placid demeanor.

Oil and vinegar.

Yet these two got along better than any other two council members.

"Should I even ask who the wagon belonged to?"

"Odin Darweshi," Quinlan shot back.

Althea closed her eyes with a sigh. "What was stolen?"

Fale got up and started to polish one of the many swords littering the table before him. "Near as we can tell, money, some documents maybe. Nothing more."

Quinlan continued to stand and shift back and forth on his restless feet. "The second caravan yielded no deaths but literally dozens of thefts. Everything from money to jewelry, documents to clothing. No descriptions this time. In fact, no one knew the items in question were missing until they stopped."

"And how many of *those* wagons belonged to Darweshi.?"

Fale nodded to Quinlan, who swallowed. "All of them."

Althea raised an eyebrow, "Really? And no one died."

"Not a one," Fale said. "But before I could speak ta anyone involved, Darweshi gathered his employees and hustled 'em away."

"So, we have no idea who saw what."

"No," Quinlan admitted.

Althea nodded, "And the other two caravans?"

Quinlan did not answer.

The dwarf continued to polish his swords. "The other two caravans had no survivors."

Althea raised her head and looked from Quinlan, who dropped his eyes under her heavy gaze, to Fale, who did not look up at her at all. She could feel her temper rising and she clenched her fists, trying to keep it in. "How long were you planning to keep this from me?" she finally hissed.

Fale shrugged, calmly shaking off the governor's ire as though he dealt with this all the time. "Didn't seem all that important at the time."

Althea stood and slammed her hands onto the table, sending several smaller daggers bouncing across the surface. She leaned in toward the dwarf, forcing him to stop his work and acknowledge her. "Since when do *you* decide whose death is important and whose is not, Fale Copperhand?"

The dwarf placed the sword calmly on the table and turned to face her, his copper eyes unflinching. "Merchants die on the road all the time, Yer Excellency. Now, I know that might seem unlikely to some other governor who's spent their life inside a buildin', but you know better. You spent half yer life out there."

"Yes," she spat at him, furious at the scolding. "Spent most of my time protecting them! And I expect to be told about the deaths of merchants on the road to my city!"

Fale crossed his arms. "With all due respect, Yer Excellency, you don't need to know. Yer own Watch Chief has had this information fer months now, and he hasn't seen fit to tell ya the details. If you want ta take yer ire out on someone, it really oughtta be him."

Althea blinked and took a step back. She forgot again. She was governor, not the Watch Chief, and certainly no longer an adventuring warrior responsible for only herself and a few companions. She was one of thousands who worked for this city and she needed to trust in those people to do their jobs. And Fale was right: she did not need to know everything.

Quinlan cleared his throat, "The truth is," he began, "We did not see the significance of this information until today. If we had, or if Alistair had, we would have said something by now."

Althea sat down. She put her head in her hands and rubbed her temples. "I hate to ask…"

"In the last two caravans, none of those wagons belonged to Darweshi." Quinlan said at once.

Althea dropped her head back and let out a long stream of air. "What else?"

Fale shrugged, "Rumors. And sketchy ones at best."

Althea was silent for several seconds. Fale went back to polishing. Quinlan moved closer to the dwarf, alternately elbowing Fale and glancing at the governor with a wary eye.

Althea ignored them both. *Why would Duak-Thenal kill everyone in one attack and no one in another?* She thought. *Why the inconsistencies? Unless…*

Althea suddenly launched herself from her seat and began to pace the floor, startling Quinlan. "In the first attack, only two men died, correct?"

"Yes," Fale concurred.

"And what was stolen?"

Quinlan flipped through his notes, "Money, some papers, a couple of small chests. No one could tell us what was in those, of course."

Althea did not care. "Did anyone else on that caravan work for Darweshi?"

"No."

"And the second? No deaths, only robberies?"

"Correct."

"Did any of those items belong to Darweshi?"

Fale and Quinlan exchanged glances. "Several, in fact," Fale answered.

Althea spun about to face Quinlan. "So, it is safe to say that those two caravans were targets."

Quinlan opened his mouth and then shut it again without saying anything. He turned to Fale for help, but the dwarf continued to polish metal, leaving Quinlan to answer the governor's accusation. "Well… I suppose you could draw that conclusion, but…"

"But what?" Althea crossed her arms and stared at the Guild Master.

Quinlan held out his arms to her, clearly unsure if he should press the issue. But Althea beckoned him to continue. "Well… why wasn't anyone killed in the second attack?"

"Perhaps no one put up a fight," Althea mused turning a critical eye on Fale, "And the last two, where everyone was killed. Did you get a look at the victims?"

"Yes," Fale answered tightly.

Althea glared at him, her gray eyes smoking. "It seems you know the answer to the question I am about to ask, Fale. Why don't you save me the trouble?"

The dwarf grunted and threw down the dagger he was working on. "Fine! Yer victims were slaughtered, all right? Run through by brigands who wouldn't know a fair fight if it stabbed 'em in the eye! Barely a clean kill among 'em. Looked like whatever group done 'em in was in a big sloppy hurry."

Althea crossed her arms and smiled in triumph. "I see."

"See what?" Quinlan asked, plainly confused.

Althea sauntered by him. "Ask Fale," she said.

"Fale?" Quinlan began.

But the dwarf brushed the merchant away. "Ahh, leave off."

"No! What does it all mean?"

Althea perched herself near the perturbed dwarf and shook her long white hair from her face. "It means the elves couldn't possibly have been responsible for the deaths in the last two attacks."

Quinlan shook his head and turned to the dwarf. "But you said…"

"Never mind what I said, dammit," Fale growled. "The governor is right."

Quinlan turned to her for an explanation.

"The chances of elves killing that way are slim to none."

Quinlan sat down and let that revelation sink in. Althea felt for him. Ten minutes ago, he had been a worried Guild Master, concerned only for the wellbeing of his customers and the security of his business. Now he had become an unwilling investigator into a series of crimes they were far from solving.

One thing seemed certain, however: Odin Darweshi was right. The elves were involved, and they were not just thieves, they were killers.

"Has anyone talked to Darweshi about this?" Althea asked.

Quinlan looked up. "He came to me about two months ago. He said he would be hiring his own guards for his caravans from now on."

Fale snorted. "Hence the reason we have seen nothing of late. Odin's guards take care of themselves."

Althea nodded. "And they clean up any messes they make."

"So even if they are being robbed, we are not hearing about it," Quinlan concluded.

The governor stood. "When is the next shipment of barexium due in?"

Quinlan checked his notes. "It left Graxton yesterday. It should be here at the end of the week."

"Watch it. See if you can keep track of the contents."

"I will try."

Fale harrumphed and began to lead the way out of the finishing room. "We'll have to do more than try, Governor."

Althea and Quinlan followed, the latter grabbing the governor's cloak and handing it to her. "And what would you suggest?" she asked.

"I'd put my own men on every one of Darweshi's caravans. Then we'd see what's what."

"And risk their lives, Fale?" Quinlan protested. "*Duak-Thenal* kills as often as they don't."

"If they are indeed doing the killing," Althea suggested.

Fale stopped and turned to her. "In at least one instance they did. Who knows how many others there are? And maybe yer elves did kill all those others. Maybe they botched it to cover themselves."

"And maybe they weren't there at all," Althea countered.

Fale took a deep breath. "Point is, with Darweshi holdin' all the cards, we'll never know."

"So, you would send in the Watch?"

"Watch?" Fale blustered. "Who said anything about the Watch? No, no, yer Excellency, I'm talkin about a spy."

Althea smiled, feeling a bit of her reckless youth come back to her. "Quinlan," she said. "Have we got someone up North who can get on that caravan out of Graxton?"

The Guild Master nodded, not much liking the way things were going. "Yes, we have someone. I'd have to move pretty fast to get in contact with him, fill him in on what we want him to do."

"No need," Fale said. "We've already got someone on the inside." He elbowed Quinlan in the side. "Old merchant friend o' ours. He talks too much, but he listens even better. He'll be able to tell us what's been goin' on if someone attacks."

Quinlan was stunned. But Althea was beaming. "Brilliant, Fale," she said. "I shall expect his report as soon as he arrives."

And with a swirl of white she was gone.

— ✺ ✺ ✺ —

Quinlan turned back to Fale, incredulous. "Did I miss something? Are we actually sending someone to spy on the biggest merchant in Preliona?"

"Yep."

"Isn't that illegal?"

"Not when the governor of Preliona approves it."

"No, I'm pretty sure it's still illegal."

But Fale only laughed and began walking back to his workroom.

"You knew it would go this way, didn't you?" Quinlan accused, suddenly seeing the old dwarf in a new light. "You knew she would agree with you."

Fale smiled but did not answer. But the golden gleam in his eye was enough for Quinlan. He plopped himself down onto the nearest bench and shook his head. "I feel so used."

Fale smacked his friend on the back, making the man stumble forward out of his seat. "Ah, get over yourself, Quin. You did everything right."

"According to *your* rules, maybe. But I certainly wasn't expecting to put the life of one of our own in danger."

"I hate to break it to you, Quin, but those men are in danger every day, and maybe they know it better than you do." Fale looked wistfully at the place where the governor had stood a moment before. "And that one knows it better than anyone."

Quinlan sighed. "I still think it's risky."

"Ayuh. It is. But if she's willin' ta take that chance, then I'll go along with it."

Quinlan shook his head. "*Ziyad's blood!* You two are just alike."

"That's right, boy," Fale said. "And one day she'll realize that I'm the one she's meant to be with fer the rest of her days!" The dwarf cackled hysterically at his own joke and went back to work, wiping tears from his golden eyes.

Quinlan rolled his eyes and left without saying goodbye. It was going to be a long week.

8 ~ Seeing Double

A raucous group of musicians, a dance floor filled with people of every type, empty plates scattered across every table, and a drink in every hand: The Darkwater Arms was a place of high spirits this evening.

In the Breezeway's largest dining hall, the house band had whipped the crowd into a dancing frenzy. Those who stood or sat on the side clapped along with fervor. Tables had been shoved aside to make room for more dancers. Those who could not find room on the floor stood on the second level outside the doors to their rooms, extending the revelry so that the entire hall was alive with movement. A mass of pulsing limbs dangled over the balcony, complementing the sea of bobbing heads that flooded the dance floor below.

Kiernan Nightwing shook his head in amazement as he gazed up at the dancers who now hung from the rafters. A young man was swinging from one of the five wrought iron chandeliers, hooting and hollering, threatening to come crashing down on the heads of the patrons below. Kiernan would be vastly surprised if the entire population of the Breezeway were not present here this eve.

"Look at them, Kiernan," Dagmar said with a small, light laugh. The wild elf sat across from the prince; her chair tilted back so that she leaned precariously against the wall. Talesin sat next to her, as absorbed in the surrounding entertainment as the prince was.

Dagmar pointed into the crowd, drawing their attention to their two companions dancing at the edge of the floor. Captain Tain Elire and Nemesio

Firebrand, an oddly matched couple, to say the least, were holding hands and attempting to dance. Tain and Panas had made it a point to learn all the most popular dances of every race. Of course, the two argued regularly about who knew the correct steps to each dance. After one particularly loud set-to that ended in Tain's announcement that Panas had all the grace of a teenage troll, the light elf had stalked off. Tain was now attempting to teach Nemesio.

It was not going well. When Tain tapped her tiny foot forward, Nemesio promptly tripped over it.

The tall warrior fell flat on his face while the imp howled in pain and hopped about on one foot, much to the amusement of Kiernan and the others. The prince clapped loudly and Dagmar and Talesin fell forward onto the table, clutching at each other to contain their laughter.

"Ha ha," Tain sneered, limping over to their table. "I don't see any of *you* braving the dance floor."

"Believe me, dear Captain, you alone can represent our company out there," Talesin said, wiping tears of laughter from his black eyes.

"Look at poor Nemesio!" Dagmar stood and pulled out a chair for the bruised elf.

"Oh, he's fine," the imp scoffed, leaning her elbows onto the table, and plopping her tiny chin into her hands. "At least the Malhurian is willing to come out of the shadows occasionally. He proves that *some* elves, at least, have rhythm."

The comment was met with more laughter from the elves as they hurled several bits of leftover dinner at the sarcastic imp.

Tain hurled them back with better aim, managing to make contact with the heads and shoulders of each of them. Then she sighed dramatically. "Well, I'm off to find another dancing partner, seeing as Nemesio suffers from two left feet."

The southern elf took a swing at the Captain, but the nimble imp was already halfway across the floor and well out of reach. Nemesio dropped his head back and blew a stream of air from his mouth. "I wish that I had half of that one's energy," he said. "I expect she'll still be climbing buildings and swiping jewels long after we've retired."

"Perhaps whatever drives the Captain is infectious," Talesin commented.

"I doubt it," Nemesio returned, removing his boot. "We've been together almost twenty years now. She has not rubbed off on me -- if anything she wears me out more. I would tell her to grow up, but…"

"She is younger than the rest of us," Talesin said, in an effort to defend the imp's actions.

"Not that much," Nemesio replied, rubbing his feet. "I turn two hundred and one in a few months."

"Ouch, no wonder you are limping about like an old man." Kiernan teased.

Nemesio threw his napkin at the prince. "Another twenty years and you will hit the double century mark, Kiernan. And it will fly for you, my friend—mark me."

Kiernan grinned. "Maybe, but you will still be the oldest, Nemy."

"That's the truth of it," Nemesio leaned back in his chair and put his sore foot up on the table. "You think the imp will be as tired as I am when she has lived two centuries?"

Dagmar shook her head. "I don't think it matters. The lifespan of an imp is much the same as an elf's. The difference is that we, while slower than humans, will physically attain adulthood. Tain will continue to resemble a pre-teenager for the rest of her life."

"So I suppose there is no chance of her catching up to us mentally," Nemesio said with a grin.

Kiernan patted Nemesio on the back. "I suspect the Captain hides more knowledge behind that mischievous grin than we will ever know, Nemy. The imp can no more curb her childlike outbursts than a dwarf could curb his surliness."

"Perhaps that is why you chose her," Talesin commented quietly. "Perhaps her immense will is what will sustain us all in what lies ahead."

The three others stared at their friend, but he did not look back at them. He stared off into some dark recess of the room as if contemplating the meaning of his own words.

It was true that the imp Captain was a driving force of *Duak-Thenal*. Many of their missions could not have been accomplished without her. On the other hand, the imp's boundless supply of energy had, on more than one occasion, nearly cost them their lives. Kiernan was unsure how that same unbridled and often dangerous enthusiasm could be the tie that bound them on their future missions.

The prince had no more time to think on Talesin's words, however, for the host of the enormous party had caught his eye. Venk Darkwater stood at the entrance to the hall, his powerful arms crossed over his chest. He motioned for the group to follow him and turned about, not waiting for a response.

Kiernan glanced at the great clock on the wall and cursed himself when he saw that it was half past ten. "Let's go," he said, rising with the others. "The Darkwater powerhouse requested an audience, and we're late."

"Lovely," Nemesio said, shoving his boot back onto his sore foot. "A hazing by the mutant dwarf is all I need to finish my night."

"Where is Panas?" Dagmar asked.

Talesin pointed over his shoulder. "The bar."

Kiernan grinned. "Venk has a new bartender."

The four laughed and moved to the hall entrance, picking up the flirtatious Panas and the light-footed imp on their way.

It had been an enjoyable evening, the prince thought, marred only by the lost chance for a dance with Dagmar. He risked a glance at the wild elf as they left the hall. Kiernan felt his heart skip a beat when she returned his look. Swirling mists of gray stared at him. Those were eyes that the prince of the light elves always found difficult to see into.

They were friends, of that he had no doubt. Kiernan knew that the wild elf was implicitly loyal and embraced his cause as much as the others.

But he knew little of her life before she joined his band, and he wished to better understand her unusual gifts and her reasons for lending them to his cause.

Kiernan sighed and looked ahead. The dwarf was out of sight. The six companions had to run to catch up with him.

They rounded the corners of several stone hallways, their boots echoing off the walls until they felt the stone beneath their feet disappear and instead grind on the gravel and dirt of an open road.

A tangled forest to their right and fields to their left expanded for what seemed like miles. Except the Breezeway had no forest; the only thing you could see for miles was the great ocean called the Sprawling Edge.

And they were not outside.

Now it appeared to be night, even though the star-filled sky above was no more than a granite ceiling. Come morning the sun would rise here just as it did outside along with whatever the weather happened to be doing.

Welkin Grove, third of the four halls of the Breezeway, was an illusion, and a very convincing one. Kiernan could smell the pine needles that had fallen from nearby trees, and could hear the quiet hum of nighttime insects. He wanted to close his eyes and drink in the night air, but he could not.

The sorceress who had created Welkin Grove did not visit often. But when she did, it was important to be punctual.

The members of *Duak-Thenal* made a loud and untimely entrance. They skidded to a halt when their eyes fell on the pale ethereal form of the image floating in the center of the Grove.

Tain scowled. Panas swore under his breath. The others narrowed their eyes, suspicious of the sorceress's presence.

Kiernan simply folded his arms and gazed at the elf who he considered to be the most powerful mage in the realms, and the source of many of his recent headaches: his sister, Princess Kalliroestria Aila.

There could be no doubt that the two were twins. Their height, their features, even their stances were nearly identical. But while Kiernan's features were smooth and gentle, even angelic, his sister's were hard and chiseled, ofttimes frightening.

Green eyes the color of seafoam swept over the group, giving all a cursory nod. Her gaze slowed when it passed over Talesin. Then it continued until it finally came to rest on Venk and Kiernan.

"Greetings, Venkarius." Her voice was like crystal, so sharp it seemed it would shatter. "Thank you for seeing me on such short notice."

Venk bowed his head, wincing slightly at the use of his full name. "Of course, Yer Highness, the Breezeway is always open to you."

The sorceress nodded and turned to her brother. "Hello, dear brother," she said, a hint of sarcasm in her crystalline voice. The other members of *Duak-Thenal* shifted uncomfortably behind their leader.

"Hello, Kal," Kiernan replied, purposely shortening her name. "Sorry we're late."

Kalliroestria narrowed her eyes, thinly veiled anger sweeping her angular features. "You are lucky I have a link to this place, Kiernan. I would not have been able to hold the spell for this long under normal circumstances."

Usually Kalli would have to perform a complicated spell to transport her astral self anywhere. But in Welkin Grove the sorceress could simply utter a password and her form appeared on the road of her own magical artwork. It was her creation, her private portal and there was no limit to the time she could spend here, in astral form.

Kiernan smiled, unwilling to let his sister's condescension bother him. "My apologies, Kalli," he repeated, putting his hand to his chest, and bowing slightly.

It was not a mocking gesture, but Tain snickered behind him all the same. The sorceress sent a scathing look in her direction. Tain straightened quickly and backed away to stand near Nemesio and Dagmar.

Kiernan watched his sister's sea-green gaze go hard and flat when she looked at the imp. In fact, there was little compassion or warmth in the paler eyes of his sister. Her features were sharp and angular, almost boyish. Her face was too square, her cheekbones too high, her figure too straight. There was beauty there, but it was marred slightly by the extreme seriousness and fiery anger that she constantly exuded. "I take it your last trek into Preliona proved fruitful, since I see you are all still alive."

Her voice did not hold a note of concern.

"Not disappointed, are you, Kal?" Panas quipped lightly.

The princess raised an astral eyebrow. "I'll get right to the point," she said. "I have an assignment for you. You leave tomorrow."

The announcement was met with something less than enthusiasm. The band groaned loudly.

"All right, all right," Venk raised his voice. "Let's hear her out."

Kalli nodded her thanks to the dwarf, "I do not need to remind you of the recent rash of highway robberies in Hunter Heights, as you were a part of them."

"Not all of them," Tain piped up.

The princess glared at the imp, "Of course not all," she sneered at Tain, "But it may surprise you to know that many of the robberies have been committed by Odin's own people."

"Wh..,whaat?" Nemesio stammered.

Kiernan narrowed his eyes. "How do you come by that information, Kal?"

The sorceress smiled. "I have as many secret sources as *Duak-Thenal* has, Kiernan -- and I do not choose to reveal them to you."

Kiernan tensed, bit his lip to keep several scathing words behind his teeth.

Panas saved him, "Sounds like we didn't need to steal the bridge plans after all. Darweshi is sabotaging himself."

"But why?" Dagmar asked. "Why would he rob himself?"

"We don't know exactly," Venk replied. "We had hoped the bridge plans you stole would reveal something, or at least halt the building process until we could find out. The money you and Talesin brought back was from Malhuria. It looks as though Odin is selling the barexium south."

"Then what is the bridge being built from?" Kiernan asked.

"Not barexium," Nemesio spoke up. "Panas and I took a little trip to the bridge while we were in Preliona." He drew his two-toned sword, gold on one side and silver on the other and held it lengthwise for all to see. "I slashed the supports with this blade. If the metal were truly barexium, my sword would have sustained some damage. As you can see, there is not a nick on it."

"The same cannot be said of the bridge," remarked Panas.

Venk nodded with a grunt. "Could be enough to convince the governor."

"The bridge and the robberies hardly concern me," the sorceress said with a wave of one pale hand. "It is the help that Odin is undoubtedly receiving that has caught my attention. There is a mage involved. One who has a stolen magical artifact in his possession. I suspect he is in league with Odin."

Nemesio uncrossed one arm and held up a finger. "You suspect, or you know?" he challenged.

The princess glared at the southern elf. "Does it matter?" she hissed.

"Only in our approach to the situation, Your Highness," Talesin replied, holding open his hands. "We'd hate to accuse anyone when we are unsure that he's done something."

Kiernan noticed his sister's eyes soften when she turned to the ice elf. "My sources speak for themselves," she replied.

"What exactly is this artifact?" Venk asked.

"A key," Kalli replied. "It is made of silver, with a large blue sapphire set at the end. It can open any door and it has teleportation powers, as well. The mage who stole it is a student of Lorcan De Cresler. My former mentor reported the key stolen, and his student missing, three days ago. The boy has since signed a charter and is traveling to Preliona with a caravan from Graxton."

Kiernan shook his head in amazement at his sister's seemingly endless stream of information.

"A coincidence, perhaps, Your Highness," Dagmar suggested. "Why would one of Lorcan's pupils betray him?"

She shrugged, causing her billowing blue robes to flutter about her, sweep the floor and float about her feet as if some unfelt breeze fanned the material. "The young mage ranks only in the middle of his class. His chances of attaining an apprenticeship are minimal. What better way to improve his chances in life than signing on with Preliona's resident crime lord?"

Kiernan shook his head. His sister's hatred for humans always surprised the prince. "You speak as though a life of crime were the only avenue open to a mediocre human mage. Not all humans turn to evil when their chosen paths take a different course."

Princess Kalliroestria leveled her gaze and glared at her brother over the tip of her nose. The sorceress's red hair, a shade lighter than her brother's and the color of the early morning light, suddenly blew about her face and fanned behind her, refusing to settle. "You wish to refuel our oldest argument at this time, dear brother?" she challenged. "Believe me, if I had the time, I would indulge you. As it stands, that key gets closer to Odin's hands by the minute. I want it in mine by week's end." Kalli concluded her tirade and folded her arms across her chest. Her long hair returned to its original state as she waited for the group to acknowledge her command.

"Why doesn't the mage simply teleport himself to Darweshi and hand the key to him?" Tain asked from behind the relative safety of Nemesio's back.

Kalli sighed heavily at the inconvenience of having to speak to the imp. "My guess is he is charged with traveling with the caravan, overseeing whatever evil will soon befall them."

"I don't like it, Kal," Kiernan interrupted. "Too many loose ends. If Lorcan suspected his student, why didn't he expose him before now?"

For the first time the sorceress' confidence wavered. Kiernan saw a slight spasm of uncertainty crossed her striking features. She recovered quickly, though, and any doubts she may have had were wiped from her face. "Lorcan has not made the connection—I have. It would break his heart to know a student had betrayed him."

Kiernan stepped forward. "So, you are ordering us to attack one of his own without his council?"

Kalli's eyes flashed dangerously. "Attack is a harsh word, brother."

"What would you call it, then?" Kiernan asked, refusing to back down from his powerful sister.

"I'd call it an assignment. Retrieving things is what you do best, isn't it, Kiernan?" Kalli threw back at him. "One of the most powerful mages in Tearlach requests your help and you refuse him?"

"No," Kiernan sighed heavily. "I simply question his motives and your information."

Princess Kalliroestria's green eyes narrowed. "Let me put it this way, then," she hissed. "If that key is not in my hands in four days' time, I will be having a talk with Alistair the Watch Chief of Prelona. And if he has not figured out who kidnapped Raymond S'Trobenue and where they have taken him and his child, I will be sure to drop him a few clues."

"Kalli, you wouldn't…!" Panas blurted out.

"I would indeed."

"Yer Highness…" Venk cautioned.

But the princess did not tear her eyes from her brother's, a tiny hint of a smile touching the corners of her mouth.

Kiernan was furious. He could feel a cloud of anger filling his chest, pushing at his throat, and threatening to choke him. She had him and she knew it. He clenched his teeth and held his breath. He barely moved as he spoke. "Raymond S'Trobenue's safety depends on the secrecy of his whereabouts."

The sorceress did not flinch. "And the secret of your identities depends on whether or not I get that key. *You decide.*"

For several long seconds, the siblings stared each other down, neither willing to break eye contact. Two sets of intense elven eyes, emerald and seafoam, each boring into the other, and neither giving way.

"Get the key, Kiernan," Kalli said finally, smashing the moment. "Bring it to me. Do it any way you can." Without a word of goodbye, the sorceress faded from sight, leaving the companions on the darkened road of Welkin Grove.

Kiernan stepped into the space where his sister's image had been seconds before, and paced about. "Damn her," he hissed, clenching his fists.

"Well, that's that, I guess," Panas began lightly. "The all-powerful has spoken." The sarcasm in his voice was not missed.

Venk scratched at his black beard and sighed deeply. "I think it's safe ta say that at least part of what the princess has said is the truth. I realize Kalli is sometimes given to scrambling her facts a bit, but she would never lie outright."

"So, we go after the young mage?" Nemesio asked.

"Yes," the prince replied tightly. His head was reeling with all the things he wanted to say to his sister, and he could not seem to unclench his jaw. "But with utmost caution. Either Kalli is deliberately hiding something, or she doesn't have all the information."

"And she is threatening to expose us," Panas reminded them.

Kiernan felt his face flush with anger, and he paced away slowly.

"I think she is bluffing," Talesin offered.

Kiernan saw Venk nod. "Perhaps, but let's not take a chance, eh?"

"Well, even if this escapade turns out to be nothing, at least we can see that the barexium shipment reaches Preliona." Dagmar offered.

"If we have time," Nemesio said. "Four days is barely enough time to get to Kalli's school barring any missteps—let alone a side trip to Preliona."

Venk crossed his arms over his chest. "Harrumph! Don't know why that Council gave Darweshi the rights ta that bridge in the first place. Told the governor a hundred times the Darkwater clan'd do it for her. And for a mite less too! Serves 'em right if they never get that metal."

Tain bounced over to the dwarf and slipped her arm in his. "Now, you don't mean that, do you Venk?" she purred. "Perhaps that old governor was simply blinded senseless by your charm."

The others laughed as Venk disengaged himself from the imp's grasp and stomped out of the Grove. "Ya'd best get some sleep!" he hollered over his shoulder. "You leave at first light."

"Does anyone have a sleeping preference?" Panas asked.

"Oak Hall!" Tain Elire announced, pushing past the others. "Race you there, Dagmar."

Dagmar shook her head in mock disbelief. "Guess my choice has been made. Anyone care to join me?"

"No thanks," Nemesio said. "Last time I shared a tree limb with the Captain I ended up face first in the dirt. No, a bed in the Arms is calling to me, my friends. You coming, Panas?"

"I am indeed," the light elf replied, clapping his southern friend on the shoulder. "You don't mind if we stop by the bar first, do you? I should like to finish the conversation I was having."

Nemesio rolled his violet eyes. "One drink. That's it."

Panas grinned. "Good night, all," he said, disappearing around the corner.

Kiernan watched the others disappear, knowing they were fleeing in the face of his brooding. But Dagmar waited for him at the door, silently, not looking at him, only waiting calmly.

Kiernan sighed and caught up to her, then turned back suddenly. "Talesin?"

Talesin Darken hung back from his companions a bit, scuffing one black booted foot in the gravel of the open road. "Actually, I was thinking of staying here for the night."

Kiernan looked back to the place on the road where his sister had stood, and suddenly he was not quite so angry. He smiled at his friend. "Goodnight, Talesin," he said, and turned to follow Dagmar to Oak Hall.

9~Keeping Up Appearances

Alistair was sweating.

After days of rain, the miserable spring weather had broken and decided to give Preliona a steamy taste of summer. The waves of heat and humidity came suddenly and without mercy. It was the kind of heat that did not so much burn as it pressed on the population beneath. It fell upon the earth in thick layers, a yellow haze that made it difficult to see, let alone walk, without dripping.

And for each degree the temperature rose, the Watch Chief's fragile temper slid up another notch. It was a dangerous circumstance made worse by the tiresome presence of Laothist Benrist.

"Well, as it turns out, Alistair," Laothist drawled, "This blasted *Du-ak-Thenal* has been gallivanting all about us for quite some time now. I've been speaking to my liaisons in Bristlemoore and Bellue, and it appears the elves have been hired by several citizens in both towns."

Until this point Alistair had been barely tolerating his fellow councilman. It was well past noon the day after the council meeting. Laothist Benrist clung to Alistair, who was actively trying to shake him loose, all but ignoring the barrage of words at the man's disposal.

But now he suddenly stopped and put out his hand to halt his walking companion.

Laothist braked ungracefully beside the Watch Chief. "What?"

Alistair shook a handkerchief from the inside of his coat and wiped his sweaty brow. "Appears," Alistair repeated. "You said 'appears.' Does it *appear* that the elves have been hired, or have they *actually* been hired?"

Laothist blinked. "Ah… well, my contacts in Bristlemoore assure me…"

"Your contacts!" Alistair laughed and rolled his eyes, but Laothist stumbled on.

"… that *Duak-Thenal* has been spotted there on several occasions."

"Doing what?" Alistair asked, closing his eyes.

Laothist pursed his lips. "Well, I'm sure I don't know, but I assume…"

"Assumptions don't help me, Laothist!" Alistair turned to go.

Laothist loped along behind him. "Well, Althea did not insist on specifics."

Alistair stopped and turned back on the round man. "No, but she did ask for credible sources."

Laothist sputtered. "I will not stand here and be insulted!"

Alistair threw his hands in the air. "Then don't!"

Laothist did not move. He pouted. "Don't you want to hear about Bellue?"

"NO!" Alistair roared. And he spun and stalked away.

"But—but it has to do with the Captain!"

Alistair stopped. More than anything he wanted to move on, but his curiosity got the better of him and his feet simply would not obey. He blew a thin stream of air through his tight lips and slowly turned. "Well," he said, his hands open. "What have you got?"

Laothist licked his lips and took a tentative step forward. "She's been there recently. In Bellue. My sources inform me that the imp makes a visit there at least once a month."

"So? She is a hero there, Laothist. I wouldn't be surprised if she has dinner with the Mayor once a week." The Watch Chief crossed his arms. "You'll have to do better than that."

Laothist drew himself up, suddenly defiant. "I spoke to one of the mayor's assistants myself. He says the Captain is never alone." The councilman leaned in conspiratorially. "He says she is always accompanied by a tall companion."

"Description?"

"Sorry?"

"A description! Or is *'tall'* the only thing that comes to mind?"

Laothist opened his mouth to speak but Alistair cut him off.

"And does the mayor's assistant have any credible information about actual jobs *Duak-Thenal* has been hired for?"

Laothist shifted guiltily and looked at his feet. "Well…"

Alistair nodded. "That's what I thought." He turned his back on the merchant for the final time and walked away.

"I'll get back to you when I speak to the mayor's man again," Laothist called.

Alistair waved a hand over his shoulder as he stormed away. "Don't bother," he grumbled.

The Watch Chief growled and raked both hands through his thinning white hair, as if to shake Laothist out. How on earth did he always wind up with the one man he truly had no patience for? It was beyond him. Laothist Benrist was the type of person who had no idea how annoying he was.

Between Laothist and Odin Darweshi, the week was shaping up to be a long exercise in frustration. *And* heat.

And it was only early afternoon! He had yet to meet with the Watch and he wanted to interview the architect Calen Jase within the hour. Alistair picked up his pace, slamming his steel-toed boots against the street, and headed for Opal Tower.

There were four Watch Towers in the city—The Dawn, The Moon, The Odessa, and The Opal. Dawn was on the east side of the city. It marked the main entrance to Preliona and was by far the largest tower. It housed quarters for the overnight guard and served as the post for everyone entering and exiting the city. Dawn Tower also housed the Guild House on its main floor.

The western lookout was the Moon Tower. It stood at the far end of the city and was the least populated. The north tower, Odessa, was situated in the heart of Preliona's business district. Theatres, museums, many restaurants and inns, and a school campus were under its guard. It was an area already well covered by Xanith, Ranabee, Halberth and Judith. This fact alone made it the busiest, loudest, and most crowded building in Preliona.

Opal was the south tower, so named for the lake it overlooked. Docks surrounded it, the rickety domiciles of Artist District denizens abutted it, and the scaffolding of a half-constructed bridge faced it. Opal was a giant structure – large enough for a carriage to pass through. Eventually, if all went well—and Alistair was not at all confident that it would—the bridge would pass right through the old Opal Tower, finally connecting the city's south side workplaces with north side homes.

But for now, it was still a guard tower that sat close enough to the barges of Odin Darweshi's architects that Alistair could demand the presence of the one man who had most recently seen *Duak-Thenal* and lived to tell the tale.

At mid-afternoon, Opal's front hall was empty, save for one soldier working the intake desk.

The bookish older woman perched behind the table was dwarfed by its height. Even standing, she stood barely a head above the monstrous wooden lectern she leaned upon.

"Hot enough for ya, Chief?"

Alistair raised an eyebrow at Lieutenant Helga Bellen and grunted. He removed his cloak and hung it on the hook behind the desk.

Unfazed by the lack of response from her superior, Helga pushed her tiny glasses further up her even tinier nose and rattled off the log for the first half of the day. It was short, as was to be expected, but something caught Alistair's attention.

"Hold it, Helga. Did you miss someone?"

"Sorry?"

Alistair walked around behind the desk and pointed at a spot about halfway down the log. "Where are Sylvan and Donegal? They should have checked in early this morning. Where are they?"

Helga ran a crooked finger along the lines of log entries twice. Then she leaned back and crossed her arms. "Huh. Well, I'm sure I don't know, sir," she said, perplexed. When she looked up at Alistair's face, however, she moved far more quickly than her squat form belied, sliding from behind the table and heading for the door. "But I guess I'll be going to find out."

"Yes," said Alistair, rubbing his head. "You do that." He sat on her wooden stool and started to lower his aching head onto his arms.

But Helga poked her head back inside the door. "Ooh, almost forgot. The architect—Calen Jase? He's waiting for you in the corner room."

Alistair growled.

"Right then," said Helga. "I'll be getting along."

Alistair waved her away. Then he pushed himself to his feet, a stab of pain shooting through his shins, and shuffled along down the front hall.

The interior got darker the further he went in and the gray walls were pleasantly cool. He turned right at the end of the hall, followed the circular curve of the tower for a few paces and then came up against a corner where a curve and a straight wall met. The door before him was open a crack, revealing a small interrogation room furnished only with a long wooden table, two rickety chairs and an unlit lamp. A tiny window let in a stream of light and the hot sticky air.

Alistair peered in at the room's occupant, who was pacing and biting his nails nervously. He was of average height, shorter than Alistair but a bit wider. His salt-and-pepper hair was combed and slicked neatly back onto his head. His gray and green robes were clean and pressed, but Alistair could see sweaty patches across the man's back and under his arms. His brown watery eyes darted about the room quickly and his shoulders were bunched up around his ears. He nearly jumped out of his shoes when Alistair came in.

Alistair pretended not to notice. "Please, Mr. Jase, have a seat."

Calen Jase, hand to his chest, took a deep breath. "I, ah, I don't have much time, Alistair. I hope this won't take too long."

Alistair smiled thinly. "It shouldn't. I just have a few quick questions."

The architect settled himself into his chair, carefully avoiding the Watch Chief's eyes. "Of course, of course," he demurred. "Anything I can do to help."

"Mmm-hmmm," Alistair mused as he took the other chair. Something in the architect's demeanor bothered the Watch Chief. He shuffled his papers and picked up a quill and readied himself to write. "What time would you say you were attacked the other night?"

"Oh, I wasn't attacked."

Alistair looked up sharply.

Calen Jase flushed under Alistair's inquisitive gaze. "I mean to say, I was not hurt… that is." He cleared his throat and wrung his calloused hands. "Those two rogues stole property that belongs to Mr. Darweshi."

Alistair stared at the architect. "Yes, I know." He flipped a page. "Bridge plans. However, will you finish?"

Jase did not miss the sarcasm in the Watch Chief's voice. "Well, fortunately we have copies."

Alistair nodded and looked back to his paperwork. "Did they take anything else?"

Calen sat back in his chair. "Oh, no," he said, suddenly relaxing.

Alistair raised an eyebrow. "Nothing?"

"Nothing," Calen confirmed.

Alistair put his pen down. "Mr. Jase, forgive me, but I find that very hard to believe."

Jase blinked. "You do?"

"Those two thieves got past two dozen guards without a sound, made it through three locked doors, and left without disturbing the water you floated on and all they took were bridge plans?"

"Copies," Calen corrected.

Alistair again raised an eyebrow. Calen shifted nervously in his chair. "I can't explain it, Alistair," he said. "I was too terrified to speak."

"Do you think these are the same thieves who have attacked Darweshi interests before?" Alistair asked.

"Possibly."

"What do you think they were really after?"

"How should I know?" Calen blustered. "I don't pretend to know the inner workings of the minds of thieves."

"No, of course not, Mr. Jase. But you do know the inner workings of Odin Darweshi's endeavors. Think about it, why would two expert thieves take nothing more than copies of plans for a bridge?"

"Perhaps they stole more from other barges?" Calen suggested.

Alistair shook his head. "They did not break into other barges, Mr. Jase. Just yours. Is anything missing, Mr. Jase? Anything you want to add."

Calen Jase swallowed and stared out the window of the tower. It gave a perfect view of the scaffolding. Alistair watched the man's eyes go fuzzy and unfocused. "Dreams are a funny thing, Alistair. They make you see things differently than when you are awake. They can inspire you or they can scare you into absolute silence, lock away your fears so that they only come out at night."

He wiped one hand across his forehead and focused on the Watch Chief, his eyes clear again. "The thieves took the bridge plans," He said decisively. "That is all I know."

Alistair nodded. "I understand you, Mr. Jase. That will be all for today."

The architect practically ran from the building and did not look back.

Alistair stacked his papers and followed him out. He sighed. The city's chief architect was a coward. Not that Alistair blamed him. When your main employer was a lying ogre like Odin Darweshi, some dodgy answers were called for.

Alistair missed Edmee. Edmee S'Trobenue would never have lied to him. Of course, Edmee would never have let Odin push her around, either.

And Alistair seriously doubted that anyone could have stolen *her* plans without a fight.

But Edmee was dead, and life went on, sadly, without her.

Alistair stopped at the front desk. Helga was back. "Well?"

"Well what, sir?"

"Sylvan! Donegal! Where are they?"

"Relax, Chief! I was only havin' fun with ya. Turns out those two were off duty last night. No one has seen them since. I sent Milland downtown to check their homes."

Alistair nodded. "Send for me when you find them."

He stepped into the late afternoon sun and immediately missed the coolness of the stone tower. He could have removed the outer layer of his uniform, but Alistair was too old and too professional to loosen anything more than his top button. He started down the hill, turning his head slightly to shield his eyes from the afternoon glare.

It was then that he saw her. If he had kept his eyes straight ahead, he might have missed her altogether.

Iris was wandering around the outside of the tower, picking through the weeds at its base. Her long blonde hair hung in tangles about her face. As he watched, she absently tucked it behind her ear a few times. Finally, she gave up, pulled a strip of fabric from her apron pocket, and pulled it hastily into a ragged ponytail.

Alistair cocked his head and looked around. No easel, no brushes. As far as he could see, the frizzled artist had not come up to the tower to paint the view. He knew she lived not far from the docks, so it was not a total surprise to find her here.

Alistair cleared his throat and hailed the girl. "Miss Iris!"

The girl started so badly that she jumped out of one brown sandal. She whirled about and looked in three directions before her green eyes fell on Alistair.

Alistair held out his hands. "Easy," he said.

Iris put one dirty hand to her throat and breathed deeply. "You scared me, sir." But she smiled at him.

Alistair nodded. "My apologies. Can I help you with anything?"

Iris wiped her grubby hands on her apron and grinned sheepishly. "I was looking for you, sir, but I got distracted by the cornflowers over there."

Alistair looked over the girl's pointy shoulder to the hodgepodge of weeds hovering near the tower wall.

Iris leaned into him and whispered conspiratorially. "Do you think I might pick a few of them?"

Alistair laughed out loud. "Those weeds belong to no one. You may pick as many as you like."

Iris smiled and brushed away the smudge on her cheek, simultaneously leaving another on her upturned nose. She was not a terribly pretty girl, but she had a natural, raw charm, which under the dirt and grime was infectious and attractive. Despite her air of dreaminess, Alistair liked her.

"Now, what can I do for you?" he asked.

"Oh, I had a visit from some friends from Yeelan today. I got to talking about *Duak-Thenal* and one of them mentioned that she'd seen 'em recently."

Alistair froze. "When?" he hissed.

"About two months ago, it was. They returned a picture to one of the museums there."

"Returned?"

Iris smiled and nodded. "Yes, they were hired by the curator, apparently."

Alistair had to work awfully hard to stay calm. He did not want to appear too eager and scare the girl into silence. "When you say hired, you mean they were paid?"

"Well, that's just it, they weren't. Not in the traditional sense anyway."

Alistair twirled his hand, motioning for the girl to continue before she lost track of the subject at hand.

"They were looking for something—an artifact, or family heirloom or the like. Anyway, the museum curator provided them with an idea of the whereabouts of the piece, and two days later the elves showed up with the missing painting."

Alistair scratched his chin and started to walk away from her, down the hill.

Iris took a step, starting to follow, but just as quickly Alistair changed direction and came pounding back up the hill toward the girl.

Iris squealed and leapt backward to avoid being trampled.

"How many?" he asked.

"Sorry?"

"How many elves brought the painting back to Yeelan?"

"Oh. Three. My friends said three."

Alistair nodded. "Yes, that would be about right," he mumbled. "No sign of the imp, I suppose?"

Iris shook her head. "No. Just three elves."

Alistair nodded again.

Iris stepped forward, suddenly remembering something. "But didn't you say sir, that the imp thief wasn't allowed in Yeelan?"

"That was Villuna," Alistair corrected, shaking his head. "But I wouldn't be surprised if she were banned from Yeelan as well. Did your friends say anything else?"

"Only that they knew the elves had been there before." Iris smiled. "They were full of stories, but honestly, sir, I am not sure I believe them."

Alistair leaned in close to the girl. "Why don't you let me decide, eh?"

Iris stared past him. Alistair recognized that the girl's limited concentration was almost at its end. He motioned her to go ahead and followed as she dropped to her knees in the dirt and grass.

"Well," she began, "My friend … mentioned one instance where a family lost a child."

Alistair raised an eyebrow. "Kidnapped?"

"That is what they thought. The family hired *Duak-Thenal* to get him back."

"In exchange for another artifact?"

Iris shrugged and yanked a puffy white weed from the dirt. "Probably. Something went wrong, though, because they didn't bring the child back. My friend says the elves were arrested but they escaped, and they paid the family with jewels and art to keep them quiet."

Alistair snorted. "I find that hard to believe."

"Either way, it seems they do favor artists." Iris smiled at this thought.

Alistair cocked his head at her words, sensing something in her voice he had not heard before. He slowly knelt beside her. "Have you seen them, Iris?"

Iris laughed nervously and yanked at another cornflower.

Alistair laid a hand on the girl's arm, stopping her frantic pulling. She did not look up at him. "Iris, if you have any information, anything at all, you have an obligation to tell me."

Iris licked her lips and shrugged her shoulders. "Well, it's not as though I actually *saw* anything sir."

"Iris…" Alistair pressed.

Iris sighed and stood up. "Remember the fire at the harbor two years ago?"

Alistair nodded. "Yes, of course. You and several other artists lost your studios, as I recall?"

"Our houses, actually, and everything we owned. I spent two nights on the streets and two more in the city poorhouse."

Alistair cast his eyes down. He had not known that. Of course, he had not known Iris then, either. She had not been on the council yet. But she was elected shortly after. Alistair was sure of it. The fire was in the spring and Iris was on the council by that fall. By then, the entire artist district had been rebuilt. Alistair remembered it happening extremely fast. He hadn't really given it much thought at the time. After all, he had little cause to go to that section of town. It was not particularly crime-ridden, and he was not exactly a patron of the arts.

Now his suspicions were aroused, however. How had an entire block of buildings been erected in such a short span of time, and with whose money?

"Who helped you?" he asked.

Iris shuffled her feet dragging one toe through the grass, "Well, Xanith was going to let us move into one of the older theatres over on Peacock. The small abandoned one? We were having a meeting there late one night when in walked one of Laothist's couriers. He handed us a large bag and left."

"What was inside?"

"Gold. A lot of it. And right on the top of the pile was a dwarven coin with a great big X carved into the center."

Alistair was silent for a full moment. "No note? No explanation of where the money came from or what it was to be used for?"

Iris shook her head, looking guilty.

"And when your entire life was rebuilt in less than three months, no one ever questioned where you'd gotten the money?" he asked a little too harshly.

The girl's blonde head snapped up. "Do you think anyone really cared? Did you?" Iris swallowed and stepped back suddenly, remembering who she was talking to. "Sorry, sir. I didn't…"

Alistair held up a hand. "No, I deserved that. Have they ever been back? Anyone. Anyone asking you to repay them in any way?"

"No, sir. As far as I know, no one in Coral Square or the surrounding area has ever heard from them again."

Alistair nodded. He had expected no less, really. If mysterious gift givers were one and the same as kidnappers and thieves, then he was going to have a much harder getting cooperation from witnesses then he had expected.

Sensing her time was up, Iris folded up her apron and started to go.

"And if you did…?" he asked suddenly. Iris stopped and turned slowly back to the Watch Chief. "If a tall, hooded elf suddenly showed up on your doorstep and asked you for a favor…what would you say?"

Iris suddenly looked much older and wiser than her nineteen years. "I'd say yes," she said without hesitation or fear of repercussion. "I'd say yes in a heartbeat."

10~A Change of Plans

It was late and the sun was setting fast in Preliona. Althea was planning to go to dinner with Judith Mercy, but Xanith had sidetracked her with a story of Poorez and a certain famous thief. And so dinner had been skipped. With a small stack of reports provided by Alistair tucked under her arm, the governor headed for the library to find Gregory Sweep.

The heels of her gray boots rang on the stone floor as she sailed across the courtyard. The walkway to the library was open; pillars studded the walk every sixteen feet or so. A dozen stairs on either side also bordered the passage.

There were few places to hide, so when the girl in the apron slipped around the base of a pillar to her right, Althea came to a dead stop and threw up her arms in frustration.

"*Ziyad's Blood!* Is anyone working here today except me?" Althea hollered to the empty corridor. Immediately three grey garbed Watch soldiers appeared. They spotted the girl and, surprised as they seemed by her appearance, quickly made their way to the newcomer.

But Althea held up her hand and waved them away, "Too late, too late," She grumbled. She was unconcerned for her own safety, for she had already seen who had chosen to visit her, uninvited and unannounced.

"Muriel, what are you doing here?"

Muriel, a bartender who worked for council member Judith Mercy, froze at the advance of the Watch, her green eyes darting back and forth. But having recognized the girl as well, the three guards went away, grumbling.

Althea frowned at Muriel and with two fingers beckoned the thin blonde girl over.

She was Judith's youngest employee and her fastest. Muriel practically ran the remaining twenty feet, covering the distance between them and skidding to an ungraceful halt at the governor's feet. "Your Excellency," the girl gasped. She opened her mouth to go on but began coughing instead.

Impatient, Althea whacked the girl on her back a few times. Muriel leaned over her knees and gasped for air. "Calm down, girl," Althea said. "Whatever it is will wait until you can find the breath to say it."

Muriel shook her head. "Miss Mercy only gimme fifteen minutes and you can bet she'll dock me but good if I don't get back ta my tables in half that time."

Althea rolled her eyes. Trust Judith Mercy to make a wager out of getting a message to the governor. The owner of the Mercy Inn ran several different semi-legal operations out of her establishment. The governor had turned a blind eye because Judith was an invaluable source of information. Plus, she sat on the Council. Althea had no interest in bailing government representatives out of jail.

"What is the message, Muriel?" Althea asked.

Muriel caught her breath, "Right then. Miss Mercy told me ta tell ya ta keep yer eyes open fer Edmee S'Trobenue's cousins."

Althea raised an eyebrow, "Really. I wasn't aware Edmee had any cousins."

"Oh, she does. An' they were in the bar all mornin', stinkin' drunks. Didn't cause no trouble or nothin', which is odd 'cause usually they're a bit o' a handful. Anyway, they musta been up real late last night, 'cause they looked even worse than usual."

"They come in on a regular basis, I take it?" Althea asked.

Muriel nodded. "Yes'm. Me an' Miss Mercy didn't catch much o' their conversation. Truth ta tell, there wasn't much ta hear, but Miss Mercy wanted me ta tell ya that one of 'em was missin'. Don't know what that means, but the old bag… sorry… I mean Miss Mercy… thought you should know. Said it might be important."

Althea did not see how, but she filed away the information all the same. "All right, Muriel, thank you for the information. Please tell your employer our usual deal will suffice."

Muriel made a clumsy bow and slipped away.

Althea continued more slowly than before, lost in thoughts of a dead friend.

Edmee S'Trobenue was an architect and the original designer of the current bane of her existence, the Opal Bridge. At least she had been until she was killed several months ago.

She remembered Alistair breaking the news to her. Robbed of her money, jewelry, and set of plans, Edmee had been stabbed a dozen times by a knife with a distinctly serrated edge. To date, Alistair had not been able to find the blade to match those wounds.

Edmee had been a council member and the group had taken her death hard. She was young, argumentative, ambitious and a damned pain in the ass. Althea had adored her.

The governor had not been aware of any cousins, and could not see why Judith would think it necessary to inform her about them now.

Four hours later she had completely forgotten about her hurried conversation with Muriel.

"Most of these reports have little detail and none are backed up by more than one witness!"

Gregory and the governor spent the better part of their evening meticulously going through Alistair's pile of complaints against *Duak-Thenal*. Most of them turned out to be little more than useless bits of fake sightings and unsubstantiated claims against the elves. The exception was Gregory's report on Poorez's chance meeting with the Captain, Tain Elire.

"There is never an accurate account of *Duak-Thenal*'s number. Most witnesses are unsure how many elves they saw. If they are sure, then there are never more than two or three!" Althea threw the reports across the table and sank into one of the leather chairs.

Gregory Sweep reached for them, unperturbed by his mistress' impatience. The half-elf's brown hair fell over his bright blue-green eyes in long curls that never seemed to tangle. His delicate fingers deftly gathered all the scattered papers about him, expertly shuffling them into a single small pile. "An interesting side note," he said. "Though many eyewitnesses claim to have spotted Captain Tain Elire traveling with *Duak-Thenal*, not even one of these reports mentions her."

Althea's brow furrowed as she leaned forward. "That *is* strange."

Gregory held up one finger. "Not when you consider the Captain's track record. The imp has absolutely never been caught. For twenty years that we know of, she has been marauding in the Northern Realms. And as we know, even the Crimson Guard has been hard pressed to get anywhere near her."

"Point taken," Althea said. "I have always figured that only about half the stories I have heard about her are true."

"Look at this," Gregory picked up a piece of parchment from the pile. "Here is the prison break last month in Yeelan that Darweshi was so keen to tell us about." He started reading quickly, "Five elves of varying race broke into Yeelan prison late last night. Six Yeelan guards were injured in the battle. It is not known if the elves sustained any injuries. It is noted here that the group carried with them one Clope Rainell, a bard from neighboring Bellue. The man appeared to be unconscious. It is not known whether this was a jailbreak or a kidnapping. A gold coin marked with an 'X' was found in the bard's cell. There is no accurate description of the bandits, but it is the opinion of government officials that this was the work of the vigilante group who call themselves *Duak-Thenal*. There has been no further sign of the group or the man they took with them."

Althea sighed and took the report from her assistant's hand, "Well, I hate to say it, but Darweshi may be right on this one. I would say that this is the first real piece of evidence we have. I wonder at the number, however," She mused. "Five and no mention of the imp thief."

"Well, there wouldn't be would there?" Gregory said. "She is already wanted in Villuna. It would probably be too dangerous for her to make an appearance in Yeelan."

"It is really too dangerous for her to make an appearance anywhere, but that does not seem to stop her." Althea stood to stretch.

That was when the screaming started.

Gregory jumped up and Althea grasped the pommel of her sword. She rushed forward and whipped open the door.

Xanith Creese stood in the doorway, looking slightly bemused at the governor's battle-ready stance. "Excuse me, Governor," he said, pressing his palms against the doorframe. And though he had clearly run down the hall to reach her, Althea did not see the man labor for breath.

Althea released her sword pommel, "I suppose you have come to tell me that something of great importance requires my attention outside?"

Xanith crossed his arms. "Ah, I always knew you were the psychic one among us." He opened an arm to the hall and motioned for her to follow. "Now I do hate to drag you from your intellectual pursuits, but I believe our dear Alistair is at the end of his rope. We will either have a jail full of brigands this night or several dead men on your back step."

Althea was already moving. "Read on, dear Gregory. With any luck I will be back before tomorrow."

She needn't have left the directive, she knew. Gregory had barely lifted his head at Xanith's appearance.

Althea sailed past Xanith in three long strides, not stopping to wait for the council member. Her colleague seemed used to this and automatically matched her long-legged stride, handing her cloak to her on the way.

"It is getting cooler out, Your Excellency," he said.

Althea swung the gray wool about her and continued to steam down the halls. "What time is it?" she asked, glancing out the arched windows on her right. The sun was much lower than she expected it to be and the sky was quickly turning red.

"About seven, I think."

Seven o'clock. How little she had accomplished today, she thought. "And how long has this 'situation' of yours been going on?"

"About twenty minutes. And it is hardly my situation, I was simply passing by when I saw the need for your presence and came to claim you."

Althea snorted. "Is your faith in the Watch Chief so poor, Xanith? I am sure he can handle whatever it is." But as the shouting grew louder, Althea began to doubt her own statement.

"I have the utmost confidence in Alistair. But something reeks outside this evening, and I do believe it is the scent of Odin Darweshi."

Althea shot him a troubled glance. "Are you saying our most decorated soldier needs protection? From Odin?"

Xanith turned to her, the crooked smile gone suddenly. "Yes," he said without breaking stride. "Yes, that is exactly what I am saying."

Althea stared straight. Shelving that last statement in the back of her head, she placed both hands on the double doors in front of her and pushed her way out to the courtyard.

The sheer number of people that had gathered at the side door of Nimbus surprised her. A few dozen citizens had gathered on the street and several more were milling about the columns watching the commotion.

The disturbance consisted of four men, only three of whom were among the living.

A blanket-covered mass that could only have been a body lay at an awkward angle halfway up the stairs. The three living men stood on the stairs at varying levels around their fallen comrade. All three were yelling unintelligibly at Alistair and his guards, who stood impassive and unmoving above them.

All but the Watch Chief himself had drawn their swords. Althea could see it would only be seconds before the three newcomers drew their own.

"What's going on?!" she thundered.

The shouting match came to an abrupt halt. It was several seconds before anyone moved, startled as they were by the sudden appearance of the mistress of Nimbus.

Alistair finally broke the silence. "Good evening, Your Excellency. Sorry to have disturbed you." The Watch Chief did not relinquish his position, but spoke to her over his shoulder.

Althea moved purposefully to stand at Alistair's side. Xanith followed her but kept himself back and slightly in her shadow. "And who might these fine gentlemen be?" she asked.

Alistair kept his pale blue eyes trained on the men before him. "These are the cousins of Edmee S'Trobenue. They have…"

"I don't need you to introduce me!" one of the men shouted. He had lank blond hair and mossy green eyes. He took several steps up the stairs toward the governor, ignoring the swords suddenly raised around him.

Althea could see the man had been drinking, but he held himself rather well despite this. "Edmee don't enter into this," he spat. "Edmee is dead, and we, her cousins, have our own names. The governor ought to know who we are without remembering Edmee first."

Althea raised an eyebrow. These men could not possibly be related to Edmee. Not only did they look nothing like their dead cousin, their manners were like to lower-class dockhands. Not at all like the cultured architect Althea had come to know. "Very well," Althea began cautiously. "Introduce yourselves."

The man smiled, though his lips never parted. "My name is Vincent S'Trobenue. These are my brothers Maddox and Marek. "This," he said, reaching forward and snatching the blanket from the inert form on the stairs, "Was my brother Sigmund. I demand justice be paid to the one that slew him!"

Without a word, Althea moved past Vincent S'Trobenue, not affording him even a glance, and down the stairs to examine the body. She felt the air around her intensify, the Watch clearly uncomfortable with her decision to put herself between them and the three men. She saw Alistair hold out a finger to keep his patrol in place and Xanith move forward, slipping neatly next to Alistair on the top stair.

She ignored them all, feeling supremely confident in her ability to deal with three drunken men. She bent down to get a better look at the dead man. He had been expertly dispatched. A clean sword thrust under the ribs and apparently straight through the heart. He had died quickly, that was certain. And whoever had held the sword knew exactly what he was doing. *Elves,* she thought.

"This man has been dead for a day at least. Why did you wait so long to report this?"

Vincent's brow furrowed. "Well, we been grievin', haven't we, Gov'nor?"

Althea stood and faced Vincent. He stood two or three steps above her and seemed extremely disappointed that the sight of his dead brother had not shocked the governor at all. All four men looked very much the same. In fact, Althea knew already that she would never be able to remember which man was which. Already their names had begun to blur in her mind. Althea wasn't sure if this were a sign of age or simply the fact that these men were so undifferentiated and unmemorable. Even in death Sigmund resembled his brothers… one could not help but forget them. "Why don't you tell me what happened?" Althea said.

Vincent took a step toward her. "I already told *him*!" he hollered, pointing to Alistair. "Let him fill you in."

Althea turned her back on the man and began to mount the stairs. "If the Watch Chief can simply fill me in, Master S'Trobenue, then what is all this yelling about?"

"I just wanted to be sure that you heard directly who done this, seein' as how you've been looking for them elves."

Althea looked up and caught Xanith's eye. This, then, was why he had been in such a hurry to find her. She tore her eyes from Xanith's and turned back on Vincent slowly. "And what elves would those be?" she asked coyly.

Vincent's reddened eyes narrowed dangerously. He should not have known about the investigation and he knew he had slipped up by saying something.

"The thieves!" Maddox chimed in—or was it Marek? "The same ones that broke into Lord Darweshi's barge."

Odin again. There then was the connection. Althea's gray eyes flickered about, looking for the scoundrel in the crowd, but if he was there, he had hidden himself well.

The governor nodded to the three remaining cousins and began to turn away. "Give your report to the Watch Chief, gentlemen. Though if that is all the information you possess, I am afraid there is little we can do for you."

All three men immediately surged forward, but Alistair's troops were quick to hold them back.

Althea, only a few feet from them, turned and yelled over their mounting tirade. "If you have information pertaining to *Duak-Thenal*, gentlemen, then I suggest you give it! If you do not, then go away and bury your fallen brother. You are wasting my time and he is staining my steps."

Shock crossed the uniform faces of the three men. But Vincent finally gathered his wits and spoke. "A red-haired elf entered our home last night. He killed Sigmund and took Edmee's husband and child with him."

The news of Raymond S'Trobenue surprised her, though she did not show it. And one elf was hardly a posse of thieves. Also, that put them in Odin's barge and Raymond's garden on the same night. Althea was reluctant to believe that her famous White Watch had slipped so far into inefficiency.

"Is that all?" she asked them.

"What more do you need?!" Vincent howled, trying desperately to push past the guard, "Murder? Kidnapping? You should be tearing this city apart by now, looking for 'em!"

Althea moved directly in front of Vincent S'Trobenue. Her height made her level with him and she stared into his eyes with a conviction that made the man blanch. "First of all, I hardly need *you* to tell me how to do my job.

And second, anyone who would do what you have claimed would not be hanging about the city waiting to be caught. No, the elf you seek is long gone. We will carry out an investigation to verify your claims."

Althea was speaking loudly enough for the people gathered at the columns to hear her. She wanted to assure them that she was in control and that they were safe. "I am sorry for your loss, gentlemen. We will do our best to see that your home is protected from further attack." Now she lowered her voice so that only the three men before her could hear. "In the meantime, you may give a full report to Alistair. Take your brother and go home. And stop taking advice from Odin Darweshi."

Ignoring any further commentary from the cousins, Althea turned and made her way back inside, Xanith Creese hot on her heels. "Well," he began. "That was interesting. I'd say you have lost a vote or two for Humanitarian of the Year."

"Xanith, don't start with me. You know as well as I do that those boys were hiding something. They were just as guilty as the one who killed their brother. It only remains to be seen what they are guilty of. Besides, how do we even know they are telling the truth about what happened? Red-haired elf, indeed. Whoever heard of such a thing?"

"We can't possibly know whether or not they are lying. Though I seriously doubt they have the brains between them to make up such a story."

"Odin Darweshi could have made it up, though."

Xanith snorted. "True. But do you really believe that in that state they could have gotten anyone else's story right?"

Althea shook her head in resignation. "No," she said. "No, I don't. Which means we now have real reason to go after *Duak-Thenal*. I will be forced to send out scouts to the surrounding towns. Perhaps send a dignitary to Lasairian." Althea pounded her fist against the stone wall as she passed. "Damn!" she hissed. "This is exactly what Darweshi wants, and we are no further ahead in our own investigation than we were this morning!"

The governor was practically flying through the halls now—even Xanith was hard pressed to keep up. They had already rounded the corner to the connecting walkway and headed back toward the library where Xanith had first found Althea.

"Althea, if you wish, I will go to Lasairian myself. Tonight, if need be. If there is such a thing as a red-haired elf or even a *Duak-Thenal*, then I am sure Gilleece would say so."

Althea stopped. She turned to the councilor and sighed. "Xanith, I need you here. But…"

"But you have no one else you can trust to go to the elf king." The elder man smiled mischievously. "And of course, you have always loved me best, and I am the smartest man in all of Preliona, and so on and so forth."

Althea took Xanith's crinkled hand and looked into his light brown eyes. "You know, you *are* all of those things and so much more. I am sorry for this, but I must ask you to go. Perhaps the king of the light elves can shed some light on our situation."

Xanith rolled his eyes. "Don't count on it. King Gilleece can be very evasive when he wants to be. He has a bit of a flair for the dramatic, if you ask me."

Althea smirked. "Precisely why you two get on so well." Now she frowned. "You will have to leave tonight."

Xanith flashed his slightly crooked grin and patted her hand. "I have already packed."

11~A Sticky Send-Off

Venk Darkwater had been up and moving since sunrise. Preparing for *Duak-Thenal's* journey without the help, or hindrance, of the actual group was something he rather enjoyed doing. Somehow, feeding and brushing horses, packing saddlebags with food and water skins, and ordering stable hands around relaxed the dwarf almost to the same degree as gazing at a chest full of rubies.

Besides, the six warriors had been on the road for two days and before that for three weeks without a break. He supposed they deserved a few extra hours of sleep in the one place they could call home.

Venk had been planning on a lengthy break for his exhausted crew after a year full of hazardous assignments. Talesin had injured a few prison guards when the group rescued a bard from a Yeelan town jail. Dagmar had been laid up for a week after the group had been sent by a family of mages in Windy Cove to retrieve a pet falcon and the bird turned out to have been cursed. Talesin and Panas had been accused of kidnapping a boy, and Nemesio had nearly lost an ear in a confrontation over a stolen cache of books outside of Bristlemoore.

And Tain…well, with Tain there would always be gray hairs for Venk. The amount of bounty hunters trolling for reward money had lessened somewhat in recent years, but they were always there, even if the rest of them had grown complacent. Just last month Tain walked into a trap in Villuna, set up by Sifron Seely's nephew, a bounty hunter for the Crimson Guard. Tain had barely escaped. She was not allowed anywhere without at least one elf's escort now. It was simply too dangerous.

Yes, the last year had been less than favorable for the group, and Venk feared that the current assignment was stumbling headlong into disaster. After last night's unexpectedly heated meeting with Princess Kalliroestria, Venk's mind had been whirling with possible approaches. With so little information provided by the evasive sorceress, the dwarf was unsure how to direct *Duak-Thenal's* first move. Should they catch up to the caravan and attempt a direct attack? That would mean taking the risk that the mage in question might be a lot more powerful than they suspected. Or should they ride directly to Preliona, the city they had left in secret two nights before, and enlist the help of the governor and the city's council, perhaps?

Venk took a breath of the crisp sea air and scanned the early morning grounds of his home.

It was deceptively warm for early spring. The stable hands and merchants were already shedding the layers they had donned, shivering, only hours before. The sun had crested the horizon and was beating mercilessly on the morning workers below, glinting off the pink granite and forcing more than one person to shield their eyes with a hand.

Velorinne Darkwater, a cousin of Venk's, had just turned on the fountain. The first spray of water splashed several children who scampered nearby. Venk chuckled as the children, ignoring their wet clothing, practically fell over each other to get a taste of the first sticky buns of the day.

Venk Darkwater smiled as he finished saddling Tain's horse. As he turned around and leaned against the huge silver animal, he caught the barest hint of movement coming from the shadowy stable to his right. A flash of white skin and a swoosh of dark blue cloth was all the dwarf's keen eyes caught of Talesin Darken before he slipped into the stables.

If one was up, the others were bound to follow. He sighed and moved toward the stables. Before he could cross the threshold, he was cut off by two bickering elves.

Nemesio Firebrand and Panas the Hawk rounded the corner of the foremost stall, arguing loudly and blocking Talesin from Venk's sight.

"What are you grumbling about, Nemy?" Panas was asking, with a wave of his hand.

Nemesio stopped walking and put his hands on his hips, glaring at the light-haired elf. "Well, Panas, maybe it has something to do with someone kicking me out of my room at three o'clock in the morning."

Panas reached the stable door and spun about to face his friend, golden eyes flashing with merriment. Venk suddenly wished to be out of earshot of whatever the elf was going to say.

Panas took a tentative step toward the larger elf. "I am sorry about that, dear Nemesio, but…. your bed was bigger."

Venk smacked himself in the head with the palm of his hand. Nemesio closed his eyes. "Not the bartender..."

Panas leaned gracefully against the door jam and batted his golden eyelashes at the dark elf. "I told you he liked me."

"Panas!" Venk bellowed, taking a threatening step toward the gold-haired elf.

Panas held his hands up and began to back away. "Now, Venk…"

"I told you to get some sleep, Hawk, not stay up all night doing I-don't-want-to-know-what with my bartender!"

Panas grinned and slid past the angry dwarf. "Sorry, Venk," he said. "No sleep for me, but I assure you I feel remarkably refreshed." And with that, the light elf skipped into the sunlight before Venk could get hold of him.

The dwarf gave a low whistle and turned to the fuming Nemesio.

He stood stiff and straight, his fists clenched at his sides. "I'm going to kill him on this trip, Venk, I swear."

If he didn't know any better, Venk might have taken the dark elf seriously, but those violet tinged eyes were smiling.

He shook his head and looked down at the dwarf. "We really don't need him, right?"

Venk snorted. "Why don't you go check on Tanadia? She threw a shoe and old Vade's workin' on her now."

Nemesio nodded and disappeared into the darkness of the stables.

Like a father sending his children off to school, Venk Darkwater counted heads as he strapped packs filled with food to each of their horses, checked saddlebags and supplies. So far, he counted three. He was turning towards the Breezeway entrance when Kiernan and Dagmar emerged, talking quietly with their heads close together. When they spotted Venk, they broke off their conversation, and without a word headed off in opposite directions.

Venk raised an eyebrow as he watched Dagmar stroll off toward the stables and Kiernan make his way toward him. "Got somethin' ta tell me, boyo?" he asked.

Kiernan cocked his head. "What?"

Venk smiled. "'What,' yerself," he said. "You and Miss Dagmar...."

A glare from Kiernan kept Venk from finishing his sentence. He held up his hands defensively. "All right, all right, I was just makin' an observation, Yer Highness—don't get yer ears all bent, now."

Kiernan smirked. "Any news on the caravan?"

"It left Graxton yesterday afternoon," Venk said. "You should be able to catch up to it tomorrow at Hunter Heights. Find out what else is on that caravan, and have Dagmar send word."

Kiernan nodded and turned to check his horse's saddle, closing the conversation without another word.

Venk was not bothered by the prince's curtness. He had every right to be concerned, and Venk was glad the elf felt that way. It was at his most pessimistic and overtaxed that the young leader of *Duak-Thenal* performed his best.

Venk scanned the sunny courtyard. "All right, you lot, let's go now!"

Panas, who was already seated atop his white mare Spiro, covered his ears. "Venk, do you mind not shouting quite so loudly?"

Venk Darkwater rounded on the light elf. "If you had gotten a good night's sleep like I told ya to, yer ears wouldn't be so sensitive, Hawk!" Venk shouted.

Panas nearly fell off his horse as Venk turned back toward the courtyard, muttering under his breath. He caught sight of Talesin, Dagmar and Nemesio coming out of the stables. Suddenly he remembered that he had intended to speak with the ice elf. He was about to make a second attempt with Talesin, but he did a quick head count instead and found himself missing one member of the team.

"Where's the imp!?" he roared.

The elves did not answer, but threw a glance across the stone walkway toward the gathering morning merchants.

Until that point Venk had not noticed the somewhat unwieldy crowd of underage patrons assembled near the breakfast booth. Winnie and Jack's was always the first stand open. They catered to early morning travelers with their assortment of sweet pastries and hot drinks. Their stand was by far the largest and therefore the most difficult to attend to. Under normal circumstances this did not pose a problem—patrons were patient and willing to wait for their favorite breakfast treat. No one would dare steal from the two best bakers in the Breezeway.

Well… almost no one.

Before the thunderous pounding of tiny feet, before the shouts of laughter, even before the unmistakable high-pitched peal that could belong to only one creature, Venk guessed what was happening.

Captain Tain Elire was moving across the grounds at a dead run, followed by no less than a dozen children, human and dwarven alike. In one hand high above her head the Captain carried a tray of bakery treats, and her flock of followers was screaming for them. Venk could scarcely believe the imp was able to keep the assorted goodies from flying off the tray, given the speed at which she was running. "First one to touch me gets the whole tray!" she shouted over the din of shrieking children.

Venk glanced toward the vendors, already knowing what he would see. Sure enough, Winnie and Jack were standing outside of their stand with their fists raised, shouting curses at the imp and her fan club.

Venk groaned aloud and clenched his eyes shut, wondering how much it would cost him to calm the husband and wife team this time.

Talesin, Dagmar and Nemesio had caught up to the water trough by then and were marking the imp's progress around the fountain.

"Winnie and Jack's again?" Dagmar asked.

"Mm-hmm," Panas and Kiernan affirmed together.

"More kids than usual today," Nemesio said. "Faster, too."

"Shut it, the lot of ya," Venk growled, sending the group into a wave of giggles. The dwarf turned back to the festivities led by Tain Elire, the bane of his existence. If the imp didn't manage to drive him off a cliff in the next year, he'd be shocked.

Rounding the bend like a horse in the final stretch of a race, the imp thief led her band of panting followers to the base of the fountain. Tain leapt onto the ledge of the pink granite monolith. Several of the braver kids came bounding after her. But the Captain was not content with this height -- her escape plan aimed higher yet. To everyone's surprise, the spry imp managed to scale the statue itself, slipping only once and not dropping a single bun. She balanced precariously, one foot resting on the extended arm of the stone dwarf, the other mashed into its bulbous nose.

Once they were over their initial surprise at their friend's unending resourcefulness, the elves doubled over with laughter.

"Oh my, that's a new one, I think," Panas tittered. "She's never made it all the way up to the head before."

Venk glared at the light elf. "And she won't again!" He rounded on the others. "And a fat lot of help the rest a ya are! TAIN!"

Tain's head shot up and she nearly lost her balance. The children screamed as she barreled her arm to keep from falling. Then she righted herself and received a round of applause from the surrounding children.

"Yes, sir!" she called to Venk, giving him a strange sort of salute with her free hand.

"In case ya haven't noticed, the rest of yer comrades stand ready ta leave."

Tain grinned at the dwarf's attempt at sarcasm, seeming almost impressed. "I am ready, Your Royal Surliness." She even managed a small bow.

Venk folded his arms and growled from deep in his throat. Tain could see he was done with conversation. Her eyes widened slightly, and she swallowed a comment that would surely have sent the dwarf into a raging fit.

"How do you plan on getting down, Captain?" Nemesio called, standing beside the dwarf.

"Ummm, haven't thought of that yet, actually." She looked down and saw that the children had surrounded the fountain. It looked as though she would have to throw the sweets down to escape. "Don't suppose you'd like to lend a hand, eh, Nemesio?"

Nemesio crossed his arms and chuckled, clearly enjoying the Captain's plight. "Sorry, Captain, I had my toes stepped on one too many times last night." He turned and walked back to his horse. "I am afraid you are on your own."

Tain scowled. "As usual."

Venk stepped forward again, "Tain Elire, ya have five seconds ta get down offa there, or I swear I'll...."

"All right, all right!" Tain said. The children groaned their disappointment, but the Captain thief still had a glint in her eye. Bringing both feet together and grasping the tray in two hands she bent her knees…

And jumped into the fountain.

The ensuing splash created by her booted feet sprayed the screeching children on all sides of her. Those that turned to cover their eyes created a path for the imp to dart through. Over the furious shouts of Venk, Tain scrambled out of the fountain and ran straight for the dwarf.

"TAIN!" he roared and reached one huge arm out for her.

The imp didn't stop. She ducked under the dwarf's arm as she passed by him and placed the tray of treats in his outstretched hand. The imp kept going, and the children, who were soaking wet and hot on the Captain's heels, crashed into the dwarf, bowling him over in their attempt to get at the tray.

The Captain did not wait for the howl of anger that followed. She leapt onto Algoryn's back and trotted off. "Bye, Venk," she called. "Watch out for the turnovers, they're still hot."

Panas and Nemesio, who were laughing so hard that tears jetted from their eyes, quickly followed Tain. No one wanted to be around when the dwarf regained his feet. Talesin too took off after the Captain, the corners of his mouth turned up slightly.

This left Kiernan and Dagmar to peel the dozen or so children off the irate dwarf on the ground. Exchanging worried looks, the two elves began pulling wet and sticky forms from the pile.

Most got up on their own, half of them running after the departing Captain and waving goodbye, the other half licking their fingers, already searching for a new game to play. When they finally uncovered him, Venk Darkwater lay flat on his back, arms crossed as though he waited in his coffin. He seemed oddly calm.

Kiernan and Dagmar looked at each other quizzically and reached down to haul the dwarf to his feet. He had crumbs in his beard and frosting plastered to his forehead, neither of which he seemed to notice.

Instead, he uncrossed his arms and latched onto the elbows of the elves beside him, pulling on them so hard that the elves were forced to come down to his level, "I want you to leave her at Kalli's school," Venk growled in their ears. "Let the princess babysit 'er awhile. With any luck, the sorceress'll kill 'er and save me the trouble."

12~The Last Straw

Althea was almost asleep at her desk. She slouched sideways onto the cushiony arm of her white chair and let her head droop into one hand. It was nearly morning and she had not been to bed. She was vaguely aware that she was drifting in and out of a fitful dream and was trying to get up enough energy to move and fall into bed when Alistair walked into her office.

He did not barge in, exactly, but neither was his entrance quiet. He rapped his bony knuckles on the half-open door once and stepped inside.

Althea's lidded eyes shot open and she sat up with a start.

Alistair held up a hand. "Sorry to disturb," he apologized.

"It's quite all right," Althea said, rubbing at her face. "Clearly I needed someone to wake me up."

Alistair smiled wanly. He too looked exhausted and he had every right to be. The old Watch Chief had traveled to Yeelan, Villuna and Bellue the night before. Althea was awaiting his report.

But the Watch Chief did not start the conversation with his findings in those towns. Instead he dropped a pair of leather binders on the governor's desk, pulled out a chair, and plopped himself into it. "Sylvan and Donegal are dead."

Althea leaned forward. "Who?"

"Two of my officers, missing these past few days. They were killed the other night while moonlighting as house guards for the S'Trobenue family."

Althea very slowly sat back in her chair. "Killed by whom?"

"Good question. Their bodies were mysteriously returned to their families, who buried them the next day."

"Do the families know what happened?"

Alistair sighed and rolled his eyes. "They were told that the men died in a drunken brawl in a bar on the other side of town."

Althea knew Alistair did not believe that story. "And what really happened?"

"I interviewed the other house guards," Alistair said, folding his hands over his chest. "There were six of them that night. Four of them were drugged and did not come to until the next morning, when they were promptly fired by Vincent S'Trobenue. But at least two of them swear they saw Sylvan and Donegal on the grounds that night."

Althea pursed her lips. "So, either they left early…"

"…Or they met with foul play," Alistair finished.

"Like Siegfried S'Trobenue."

"You mean Sigmund," Alistair corrected.

"Whatever." Althea leaned forward and wearily dropped her chin into one hand. "And what do the S'Trobenue boys have to say for themselves, if anything?"

Alistair shrugged. "They claim they don't remember seeing any guards that night—just one red-headed elf."

Althea studied the Watch Chief. "You think this one elf killed two guards and Sigmund S'Trobenue?"

"According to the families, one was stabbed in the back. The other sustained a pretty major head wound."

Althea grimaced. "Consistent with a barroom brawl."

"True."

"But you are not convinced."

"Not remotely."

Althea tapped her fingers on the white marble desktop and casually flipped through the files of the dead men. Middle aged, middle income;

one married, the other single; moderate recommendation letters from their superiors; both known to go out drinking nearly every night. These were just the sort of men who worked during their off hours. Men who needed a bit of extra change to support their extra-curricular activities. And it seemed that Sunday night they had gotten much more than they bargained for.

Althea's eyes burned with fatigue. She was having a hard time making much sense of the whole situation—something a decent night's sleep would substantially help, surely. She decided to change the subject. "How was your fishing expedition? Find anything new?"

"No," Alistair stated flatly. "The mayor of Bellue, Benjamin Oolab, was very tight-lipped."

"Humph," Althea snorted. "Well, I can't say I am surprised. Ben is not about to give us anything on Tain Elire if he thinks we are going to charge her with something."

Alistair ran a hand through his thinning hair. "He wouldn't even acknowledge the existence of *Duak-Thenal*. Ben isn't going to help us unless we force him to."

"And that I am not going to do," Althea admitted.

Alistair nodded in agreement. "Villuna was a different story altogether. I met with Sifron Seely, the head of the family with Poorez's golden eagle crest. He had numerous unkind words for *Duak-Thenal*."

Althea smirked. "I'll bet."

"Sifron confirmed the story. He had hired *Duak-Thenal* to retrieve a family crest for them. The man claims he and his house guards were attacked by no less than ten elves, who killed several citizens of Villuna on their way out of town."

Althea rolled her eyes.

"Sifron also claims he himself nearly captured the imp Captain."

"Ha!" Althea laughed. "Sifron Seely is a liar. I've known that old windbag for years."

"I know. I got out of there before he could lodge any more complaints. But I did manage to sneak in a conversation with one of the Seely house guards on the way out. She claimed the odds were a bit different that night. One elf for every two guards, and there were ten guards. According to her, the Seely house guards ran the elves out of town. And the only people killed were three of *Seely's* men."

"And somewhere in between those two stories lies the truth," Althea concluded. "What about Yeelan?"

Alistair shifted in his chair and dropped an elbow onto Althea's desk. "Yeelan…. Yeelan was interesting. Iris's story about the kidnapped boy checks out. There is indeed a family in Yeelan missing a son."

Althea sat up. "Really?"

"Yes, but there is one problem. The son in question is eighteen years old."

Althea sank back into her chair and sighed. "There was no kidnapping, was there?"

"No. The boy left home. But his family refused to believe it. Since *Duak-Thenal* was hired to find the boy, when they came back empty-handed the family blamed the elves for the boy's disappearance."

"It is possible they had a hand in it."

"Oh, it certainly is," Alistair replied, "though I am not sure what *Duak-Thenal* would get out of keeping the young man. And as with almost everything we have discovered thus far about this group, nothing is black and white. I found several young artists on the streets of Yeelan who were willing to swear that *Duak-Thenal* consists of dozens of members whose sole purpose in life is to help the poor denizens of artistic communities all over Tearlach."

Althea dropped her head into her hands. "Infuriating," she growled. Althea suddenly felt incredibly old. When she was young, life was easy. Bad was bad and good was good. "So, what do we have? Thieves who dine with politicians, who spend their money to build homes for the poor? Bounty hunters who refuse to do their jobs. Kidnappers who take someone away from a home he fears. Are they murderers? I just don't think so."

"If they killed Sigmund S'Trobenue and my two men, they are," Alistair said with finality.

Althea stared at him. The Watch Chief's pale blue eyes were unforgiving, and his jaw was set and firm. He was right, of course. *Duak-Thenal* could rob from the rich and give to the poor all they wanted, but if they had indeed killed these three men, then one or all of them were killers—and therefore subject to the charges carried by such a crime. Preliona was responsible for investigating those three deaths—and somehow, some way, that job would be done and done well. This was the last straw.

Alistair leaned forward. "Governor?"

The governor shook her head slowly and smiled. "I was just thinking Alistair, there is one person in town we haven't spoken with yet."

Alistair nodded, knowingly.

"Cornelius."

13~Secrets

It was only a couple of hours before morning when Althea moved silently across the square, skirting the lighted walk of The Dawn and successfully avoiding the eye of the guards. The governor hated being so secretive, but it would not do for the city's Watch to know of her destination this night.

She passed the library and turned left, following a small, unmarked path to its end. There she stopped and took in her surroundings. She had not gone far, only a matter of yards, when the scenery changed drastically. From where she stood, she could still see the white lights of Nimbus Hall.

But now she looked down the mouth of an alley. The gray and coral cobblestones common to the streets of Preliona had not been laid down here. In its place, dull black gravel swirled in the wind and blew up dust at her passing. Small, darkly canopied shops replaced the shiny gray marble of the façades in the square.

The buildings here looked like they had been shoved together, all with windows difficult to see into. The doors were so small that an average-sized person would need to duck to enter.

This was Dirt Alley, a haven for the city's seamier vendors with their string of questionable establishments. Keepers of pawn shops and dealers in magical artifacts resided here. Mercenaries and bodyguards unapproved by the White Watch could be hired down the way. Mysterious mystics, palm readers and their ilk wandered in and out of the shops, selling their services to any with a question in their hearts and money to spend.

The most upstanding citizens of Preliona had announced their public intention to be rid of Dirt Alley and its occupants. But in private, Althea knew, it was these very people who visited the lane most often, probably keeping it afloat. There was mystery here, and danger. Even the most conservative of denizens eventually found a reason to sneak in and out of the shadows provided by the deep awnings and dark enclosures of Dirt Alley.

For the governor's part, she appreciated the Alley for its unusual array of vendors and the silence and secrecy she was able to enjoy here.

But there was another reason Althea had allowed the Alley to stay, which had little to do with the secret comings and goings of nobility.

The truth was that the dark emporium established a healthy fear, an excellent deterrent for those brave souls foolish enough to stumble upon the Master here. Though most did not know it, Preliona's most feared and whispered-about sorcerer had conjured this thin path, and the daunting tower at its end.

Althea pulled up her hood and lightly ducked in and out of the shadows, making her way toward the pencil-like structure.

It was made entirely of pale, porous stone. More gray than white, the lightweight rock was eerily smooth and shone like mist in the moonlight. The tower was not a smooth cylinder, but jagged here and there, with spikes jutting off to form small turrets with no apparent doors or windows.

A wrought iron gate hemmed in the dark grounds of the tower. Althea Gaenor touched a familiar brick to the right of the gate, then stretched out her hand. Instead of pushing open the gate, her hand sailed right through it.

Althea shook her head, always amazed that the magical illusion seemed so real, and made her way to the foot of the tower, careful to step only on the white stones of the pathway. She did not hurry, exactly, but neither did she dawdle. The governor had seen things in her life that would have made grown men faint. Still, even she could not help but shudder at the shadow cast by the wizard's tower. It was not the darkness that bothered her, but the knowledge that no matter from which angle the moon shone, the elongated shadow never moved. She could not shake the feeling that it was alive.

The door ahead of her was already partly open, waiting for her. Althea slipped through the small opening and let it swing shut behind her.

A warmly lit study, a circular room with a glowing fire, greeted her. Shelves of books lined it and rose to the ceiling. The colors were dark and warm, the floor covered entirely by throw rugs and furs.

Standing behind a worn leather chair was a large, wide elderly man with ancient black eyes that were used to drinking in everything around them. He stood only a few inches above the tall governor, but nearly doubled her in width. He dressed in loose and flowing black leggings that cinched tightly at the waist. A huge trail of ochre cloth was loosely wrapped about his shoulders and torso, like a winter scarf gone out of control. Much of his chest and arms were bare, showing several fading tattoos etched into his brown skin.

"Well, well," Althea began, shrugging out of her hood and cloak. "Isn't this a surprise!"

"Per your specifications. Satisfied?"

"Perfectly," she replied, hugging the large man before her.

Cornelius' study usually rested four floors above this one. This was one of the wizard's favorite tricks—a spell that enabled him to change the floor plan of his tower at will. With a word, he could switch his bedchamber with his kitchen, and back again. Althea seriously doubted the man had climbed a stair in years.

Tonight, the mage had magically moved his favorite meeting place to ground level to accommodate a guest who had made it clear she would not be hiking up dozens of winding stairs this evening.

"You look wonderful, as always, 'Thea," Cornelius said with a grin.

"Save it, Neil," Althea returned. "I don't care to be flattered by someone who is a year older than me and doesn't even have a hint of gray in his hair."

Cornelius laughed loudly and absently ran a hand over his bald brown head. "Why do you think I shaved it off, my dear?" The wizard motioned to a plush chair before the fire.

"Not all of us have that luxury, my friend," Althea replied, plopping herself into the proffered seat.

Cornelius sat opposite her in his favorite purple chair. The color provided an eerie background for the stark black and yellow outfit the mage was wearing. He did not wear the colored robes common to mages of Tearlach. At a young age, mages begin to exhibit their own aura, a color that marks all future spells cast by them. Traditionally, mages choose to wear robes that match their aura.

For Cornelius, this color would have been white. But the older Malhurian wizard did not favor wearing such an easily dirtied color.

He was in impeccable shape, much like Althea; he looked nowhere near his age.

Althea raised an eyebrow. "Neil, when are you going to get rid of that awful chair?"

Cornelius put a hand to his massive chest and feigned shock. "But I love this chair."

Althea ran her eyes over the patches on the well-worn armchair. "It shows," she replied dryly. But she smiled over the bridge of her nose at her friend.

Cornelius handed her a glass and raised his own to her. "Cynical to the very end, 'Thea," he said. "I suspect you'll outlast us all." He swallowed and then became suddenly thoughtful, his black eyes drifting somewhat. "There are only three of us left, you know."

"Yes, I heard about Cassian," she said absently.

Cassian was once part of a group of adventurers. Now, more than twenty years after *Glory* had disbanded, two of its surviving members sat gazing at each other, remembering times long past.

Neil's words were still ringing in her ears. Althea did not much like the prospect of outliving everyone she had ever known and loved. But after the deaths of four members of their old group, that possibility sounded more and more plausible.

Cornelius nodded over his glass and quickly changed the subject. "So, had a little tiff with the enigmatic and always well-dressed Darweshi scion, did we?"

Althea nodded grimly. "Been *scrying* on me again?" she asked.

"Nothing so complicated, I'm afraid." He pointed at her. "It's written all over your face. You always get that scrunched-up look over your eyebrows when you've been dealing with that worm."

Althea rolled her gray eyes and set her drink on the table before her. "He's up to something, I know it. So far all I have succeeded in doing is embarrassing him in front of the Council. Something I am sure I'll regret. He's winning this spitting match, and I hate the thought of losing."

Althea dropped her head in her hands, agitated and frustrated.

"You aren't giving up, are you?"

Althea's head snapped up immediately, marking the concern on Cornelius' face. "What! No. Of course not." She sat back. "Actually, it's because of Odin that I'm here. Neil, what do you know of *Duak-Thenal*?"

The wizard was silent for a long moment. He leaned back in his chair and took a slow sip of his drink before answering. "Well," he began, "The name is certainly elven, and I am fairly certain there was an ancient band of vigilantes that once went by that name..."

Althea waved her hand at him. "I know all that. What do you know about the current namesakes?"

Cornelius put down his glass and rested his chin on one fist. He gazed at her with the eyes of someone who had known her longer than anyone alive. "'Thea, what's going on?"

Althea knew she would get nothing else out of him without an explanation. "Two elves claiming the name of *Duak-Thenal* robbed Odin Darweshi's architect and stole the plans for the bridge. According to Darweshi, these same rogues are responsible for the last two caravan attacks, which resulted in the loss of more barexium."

Cornelius lifted his chin and opened his hand. "Maybe this *Duak-Thenal* is a solution to your problems with Odin."

Althea laughed mirthlessly. "I doubt it. Though this group is certainly making Odin suffer, they have shed no light on my problems with him. If anything, they are complicating the issue. Much as I love seeing Odin sweat, I cannot ignore the fact that unidentified, skilled and possibly dangerous thieves are prowling my city."

"*Your* city?" Cornelius's brown eyes twinkled. "Really, Althea, seeing as how I built the most attractive part of it, I think it should be referred to as 'our city'."

Althea wanted to play along, but her heart was not in it.

Cornelius must have recognized this, for he immediately became serious again. "I guess I could speak to Gilleece for you. Take a trip to Lasairian, perhaps."

She shook her head. "Xanith has already gone." She looked up at him. "Do you think it will help?"

Cornelius poured himself another glass and shrugged. "Well, I can tell you that the king of the light elves is not going to recognize any Exiled Warriors, even if he knows them. Xanith can call in as many favors as he likes, it will not make a bit of difference. The elves protect their own."

Althea, her head resting on one hand and her eyes closed against a mounting headache, suddenly stared at her friend. It took her several moments to catch his mistake, but when she did, she froze. "I never referred to them as Exiled Warriors, Neil."

The wizard's face went blank, completely masking any surprise that might have been there. He leaned back and away from Althea's narrowed eyes, "The translation," he replied, smoothly covering his mistake. "I was referring to the translation."

Realization dawned on her as she slowly sat up and gripped the arms of her chair. "*You know them, don't you?*"

Cornelius did not answer.

Althea leapt to her feet, nimble as ever, and furious, to boot. She began feverishly pacing the room, her white hair trailing wildly behind her. "Damn!

How could I have been so blind? I have been racing around looking for answers everywhere and here they were all along, right under my nose! No wonder the rogues are able to get in and out of this city without alerting a single guard!"

Cornelius twiddled his thumbs and tried to look innocent. "Maybe your guards aren't as well trained as you think," he offered lightly.

Althea's eyes widened and she stalked over to him and placed her weathered hands on the arms of his chair, "*I* trained them, Cornelius!"

Cornelius had not given up his casual posture during her rant. He remained infuriatingly calm, collected in a way Althea had not felt in days herself. "Are you finished?" he asked.

"*Hardly,*" she hissed. "You knew—you helped them."

"What if I did?"

Althea threw up her arms in frustration. "I'd expect you to tell me!"

Cornelius opened his hands in defeat, finally appearing conciliatory. "I couldn't do that, 'Thea."

"Well, why the abyss not?!" she asked, throwing herself into her chair. "You do not trust me, after all these years?"

Cornelius winced, his black eyes blinking with guilt. "You, I trust. But as governor, you would be duty-bound to inform the rest of the Council. How many secret missions could there be, once Judith or Poorez got wind of that information?"

Althea could not argue with that. "This is a problem, Neil," she said, running a hand through her white hair. "I can't have who-knows-how-many renegade elves…."

"Five, actually," Cornelius interrupted.

Althea stared at him. "Would that be including, or in addition to, one imp thief?"

"The latter," the wizard replied.

"And how many other excursions into the city have you sponsored, old friend?"

Cornelius hung his head. "More than you would like to know, but all implicitly necessary. This is more complicated than a bunch of thieves, 'Thea."

Althea gritted her teeth. "Neil, tell me who they are."

Cornelius Pav, *Duak-Thenal's* contact in Preliona, sighed heavily and rose to his feet, "Only for you." He pulled a small leather-bound book from one of his many shelves and handed it to her. "*Duak-Thenal* actually means 'Exiled *Nobles*'."

"They're *nobles?!*" She took the book from him and cursed under her breath. "So even if I have them arrested…"

"It is possible their respective families would save them from any legal action you might take," Cornelius finished.

"Then Gilleece knows about this?" Althea asked, already knowing the answer.

Cornelius nodded. "Most likely, though he would deny it. I can't speak for the other elven kingdoms, though."

Althea shifted in her seat. "You mean to tell me there are elves from Jathaharwel?"

Cornelius nodded. "And Malhuria and Serenia."

Althea was incredulous. "Impossible."

"I'm afraid not."

Althea shook her head and turned back to the book in her hand. "What is their purpose?"

Cornelius leaned over Althea's shoulder and flipped through the book. He stopped on a page with a detailed map representing the four estranged elven kingdoms.

"Several hundred years ago," Cornelius began, "The four kingdoms lived in relative peace with one another. Each one had a Champion, a noble warrior who represented his kingdom in battle. When it became apparent that an influx of other races would soon disrupt the harmony of the Northern Realms, the kingdoms went their separate ways, each retiring to a more secluded corner of Tearlach."

He pointed to the bottom of the page, "The southern elves replanted themselves in the huge desert city of Malhuria." Cornelius slid his long finger up the page and stopped at a spot to the right of where Preliona was marked in black ink, "The light elves remained here, building Lasairian." Althea's eyes followed the trail north, where the mapmaker had sketched out a triangular mountain range. "The wild elves pulled themselves deeper into the highland woods of Jathaharwel in the Boaz Mountains, rarely making an appearance again. And the ice elves…" Now the wizard's finger moved sharply north. "Reclusive and somewhat hostile from the start, they moved even further north into the ice and snow of Serenia."

Cornelius turned the page. Here was a map of a dense forest, with the picture of a fairy on one side and a horrible goblin on the other.

Althea nodded. "The Goblin Wars."

"Yes. The Champions rallied their homelands to fight a monstrous battle. Together the four elven kingdoms beat back the goblin and fairy hordes."

"Then what happened? I should know this…"

"Everyone dispersed. The elves went back to their own lands. The separation left the four Champions without a home. They became the Exiled Warriors, vigilantes really, traipsing around the country in a desperate attempt to hold their kingdoms together. Of course, it didn't work, and the legendary *Duak-Thenal* faded away."

Althea was silent a moment, still flipping through the book while Cornelius shifted nervously behind her.

"So, what you're saying," Althea began, closing the book, "is that our little group of nobles is trying to reincarnate their ancient idols in an attempt to unite their estranged kingdoms?"

"Sort of," Cornelius replied, taking the book from her and replacing it on the shelf. "At least, that was the original intention. But since the group formed, they have spent more of their time aiding unfortunate members of society than furthering their own cause."

Althea found herself getting impatient again. "And this has *what* to do with Odin's missing bridge plans?"

"Apparently someone's gotten wind of Odin's illegal activities and has hired the group to hinder him."

"Something you had nothing to do with, I'm sure."

Cornelius smiled thinly. "I am not their only contact, 'Thea."

Althea eyed him as he made his way back to his chair. "You realize this puts me in a very awkward position."

Cornelius spread his arms out wide, "Precisely why I did not wish to tell you, my dear."

Althea shook a finger at him. "I have to give Darweshi *some*thing. As it is, he has been screaming from the rooftops for days now. We cannot ignore him forever."

"Mm-hmmm. And you have another problem as well. Raymond S'Trobenue left town."

Althea raised her eyebrows. "Yes, I've heard. What do you know?"

Cornelius clasped his hands together and put two fingers under his chin. "He came to me a couple of weeks ago, terrified that his dead wife's cousins were bent on killing him. I hired *Duak-Thenal* to get him and his daughter out of here."

"Yes, well, unfortunately one of the cousins was killed in the fray, along with two moonlighting guards from the Watch."

Cornelius winced. "Is there any proof it was the elves?"

Althea frowned, remembering the precision with which Sigmund S'Trobenue was dispatched. "They were seen. Proof enough in some people's eyes."

Althea waited for a response from the wizard, but he continued to stare at her, forcing her to make the next move. Her visage softened suddenly as she saw something in his face she had missed before. A slight downturn at the corners of his eyes, perhaps.

"They are your friends, aren't they?"

Cornelius hesitated, and then nodded grimly.

Althea stood. "Keep them out of town, Neil. I will do my best to divert attention from them. I can only send the Watch after them if they enter the city. But if they do, mark me: they will be arrested and charged with murder."

Cornelius placed his hands on his thighs and stood. "I understand."

Althea sailed past him and made for the door. As she reached for the handle she stopped and turned back. "*Why* didn't you tell me?" she asked again.

"Up until this point, *Duak-Thenal* has thrived on fear and secrecy. I believe they can survive without it. Their leader does not."

Althea did not even bother asking her friend who that leader might be. "And so, you go on protecting them?"

"Their true goal may be unattainable. *Ziyad* knows they have a lot of ground to cover. But this group has a penchant for protecting the innocent of all races, and that's something I am a bit of a sucker for."

"Reliving your youth through them, Neil?"

Cornelius smiled sheepishly.

Althea shook her head and smiled up at her old friend. "Times have changed, Neil. Is there really room for marauding adventurers anymore?"

The wizard took the governor's hand. "I sincerely hope so."

Althea patted his hand. "We'll see," she said. "But from now on, I expect you to keep me better informed, Neil."

Cornelius opened the door. "Now, what would a great sorcerer be without his secrets?" He leaned forward and kissed her cheek lightly.

"Just keep them out of here, Neil. I will do the rest." She patted his face and, in a swirl of white, she was gone.

— ✴ ✴ ✴ —

Cornelius Pav closed the door behind her and leaned against it heavily. With a whisper of arcane words, he transferred his study back to the fourth floor. The main floor of the tower was now just an empty white room with cold stone walls. An enormous scrying pool was the only object in the room. It was to this pool that the sorcerer walked with resigned steps. "Well, my friends," he said aloud, placing his hands on its edge. "Things are about to get complicated."

14~ The First Move

It took Althea Gaenor a moment longer than it should have to realize that she was being followed. She was still running over the strange conversation she had just finished with Cornelius, so she was not as attuned to her surroundings as she would normally have been. By the time she realized she had company, it was far too late to turn back to the tower.

Her first thought was not of the identity of her pursuer, but the fact that she had not brought along a better weapon than the two daggers she always carried. As she did not think her current choice of shoes would allow her to make the short dash out of Dirt Alley without spilling herself face first onto the stones, Althea kept her pace casual, as though she suspected nothing.

Halfway between Cornelius's gate and the mouth of the alleyway, her pursuers made their move.

Before the first dark form detached itself from the shadows, Althea had unsheathed the dagger hidden at her hip. A flick of her wrist and the closest assailant fell, clutching his throat and gurgling.

Althea turned, grabbing the second dagger from her ankle, and faced her remaining attackers.

There were two, dressed in black from head to foot. They bore no markings that she could see, which meant that whoever had hired them did not wish to be found out. "Only three of you?" she asked, twirling her dagger casually between her long fingers. "What a pity."

The two remaining men answered by drawing their weapons, the long, curving swords common to many mercenaries in the Northern Realms.

Althea's eyes flashed dangerously. "Well, come on, then," she challenged. "It's been awhile. I can probably use the exercise."

They did not hesitate. Both men came in together, circling their weapons to the outside and cutting across their bodies, crossing their swords at the last second. They aimed to cut her down, finish her immediately. But the veteran warrior had no intention of making things that easy.

It took only seconds to size up her opponents and determine the best course of action. The most obvious move would have been to back up and reset for a better defense, something the two men clearly thought she would do. Had she a longer weapon she could have blocked them, but her remaining dagger would not do for that defense.

Instead, the spry elder woman stepped to the side, catching one assailant's sword arm on his follow through. With her left hand she dug her nails into his wrist and with her right she slashed her dagger across the man's face, splaying his cheek wide open.

The man hissed in pain. The cut was deep and stunning. He yanked on his sword arm, pulling loose of Althea's grasp, and stumbled away, letting his partner fill the gap.

The second man came in like a blur, swinging with fierce abandon. But Althea did not give any ground. She aimed to prolong the fight long enough for the noise to bring on the Watch. She would be damned if she would call out for help.

Blow after blow she deftly blocked, desperately trying to stave off a long sword with what might as well have been a kitchen knife. The battle would end soon if she did not get her hands on a better weapon.

Suddenly the man slashed crossways. Althea deflected the blow, but not before the blade nicked her shoulder. She ignored the searing pain, determined to act before the man could follow through. She stepped in and plunged her knife into the shoulder of his sword arm. Muscles tore and her attacker's weapon clattered to the ground. The black-clad assailant dove for it, reaching with his uninjured left arm and leaving his front exposed.

Althea raised her arm and caught the assassin's cheek with her fist. He stumbled to the street and she stalked after him, giving him no chance to recover. "I want you to know that twenty years ago it would have been my boot that connected with your face, and this fight would be over now."

Althea snatched up the fallen sword. Her attacker came up swinging, but Althea ducked under his good arm and plunged his own sword into his ribcage. Warm blood spilled onto her hand, but she could not tell if it was her opponent's or her own. She could feel a steady stream of blood trickling down her injured arm and noticed her vision getting fuzzy around the edges.

She felt the presence of the second attacker behind her a second before she felt the sting of his blade sliced open her shoulder. She spun about, letting the other man slide to the ground behind her. She glanced at the growing crimson stain on her sleeve and knew that a similar one was spreading across her back. "Now, was that fair, young man?" she hissed through gritted teeth.

Althea raised her arm, but before she could strike, she felt a slight breeze and heard a whisper of arcane words. The air was suddenly sucked out of the alley. Althea murmured a small prayer of thanks to Cornelius, who must have finally decided to join the fight.

She was wholly surprised, then, when she felt a wave a heat roll over her. She was thrown viciously forward, a brutal burning pain ripping up her back.

Althea hit the ground hard, dropping her weapon and slamming her palms into the stones to catch herself. She felt skin rip as the heels of her hands skidded along the gravel. She steeled herself for the impact and had every intention of leaping back to her feet. But her legs would not obey her command.

And then an all-consuming pain stabbed into her like a thousand bees, stinging her repeatedly. She tried to push herself up, but waves of nausea kept her from raising her head. Her arms quaked when she put pressure on them. Blood, flowing freely and burning with every passing second, coursed down the governor's back. She could feel it soaking her clothes and seeping into the pavement beneath her.

Out of the corner of her eye she caught a glimpse of steel. She was shaking uncontrollably but she managed to close her fingers over her dropped weapon when she heard the soft tread of slipper-clad feet.

She froze. No longer sure who she was dealing with, and nearly blind from the pain in her back, Althea listened as the floating feet came toward her.

A red slipper stepped onto her hand.

"No need for that anymore, Governor."

The voice above her was not at all what she expected. Through a haze of pain Althea made out a cultured, mature affect to the speech. Male, but certainly not one of the brawny mercenaries she had just fought.

Steeling herself against the fire in her back, and desperately trying to hang onto consciousness, Althea Gaenor looked up at her true attacker.

A hooded man stood above her. In her current state, that was all the governor could tell about him.

"I must say, I am impressed, my dear," he began. "I did not think you had a killing strike left in you, let alone two. I am glad to see that years of playing governess to the overprivileged population of this city has not erased the fighter I once knew."

Althea heard something eerily familiar in the smooth and silky voice that now rained down upon her. Her head throbbed, however, and she could not focus enough to recognize him. "Who are you?"

The robed man did not give up his casual pose as Althea struggled with the memory that lingered just at the edge of her mind. "Someone who has the utmost respect for you, and deeply regrets what he is about to do." He nodded to the one remaining assassin.

— ✳ ✳ ✳ —

It took only one blow for the injured governor to lose consciousness. The mercenary raised his arm again, vengeance flashing in his eyes.

But the robed man stopped him with his voice. "Wait," he said, kneeling and placing a small gold coin near her body. "Do not kill her. I do not need a martyr. Not yet."

He stood and moved away into the shadows, his henchman dragging the two dead bodies behind him. "*Duak-Thenal* will have much to answer for."

15~The Mediocre Mage

Devon Bane had taken in enough fresh air to last him a lifetime. His head hurt, his face was red from the bite of the wind, and his boots were soaked straight through to his feet. At that moment, the young mage wanted nothing more than to be in his warm compartment, reading his spell book and sipping hot tea.

Of course, he had tried that strategy during the first leg of the journey. Not quite an hour out of Graxton, the rocking motion of his wagon had forced him into the open air, grasping the edges of the door, breathing heavily, and praying he would not be violently ill.

So, for the second day running, Devon had ridden out front with several of the merchants, even making an acquaintance or two. He was especially fond of Jonah, a portly middle-aged man with many stories, some historical, many not. "Hey, hey, you guys remember the time I sold my cow, right?"

Groans from the other merchants. Jonah ignored them and latched onto Devon's elbow. "No, really—listen to this." The merchant then launched into a lengthy and mostly fabricated story that Devon only half remembered. Subjected to this type of entertainment for the better part of an afternoon, the mage put his mind on hold until the caravan came to a halt for the evening.

The merchants numbered an even two dozen. They were a hodgepodge group of mostly middle-aged, rather unkempt men and woman used to long days and nights on the open road. They dragged with them five passenger wagons, including the one Devon had to himself, and one long wagon with only a brown tarp covering whatever it carried.

Jonah and the others made him feel welcome. They did not question his reasons for joining them, which was a nice change of pace. As a student, Devon had been questioned all the time. It was oddly liberating to be in the company of adults who treated him as a fellow traveler and not as some ignorant child on an errand.

The clearing they had chosen for the night was small, and many of the wagons had to be left just outside of it. Devon's was one of them.

After a filling dinner, which the merchants ate separately from the hired swords, Devon said his goodnights and made for his wagon. On his way he had to pass the dozen or so men and women that made up the group sent to guard the caravan, and he gave them a wide berth.

Devon had never been part of a caravan before, but the young mage had seen enough guards and soldiers in the last few years to know that this group was different. The soldiers at his school were clean-cut, uniformed men and women, well spoken and well trained, who all carried the same set of weapons.

The guardians of this caravan, by contrast, had no uniting features. Some were slovenly and dirty, some clean and well put together. Some sported tucked-in tunics, others were so disheveled that they more resembled overworked kitchen grunts than battle-seasoned warriors.

They talked in pairs and groups or stayed to themselves altogether. What bothered the mage, however, was the wide array of weapons he saw displayed. Scimitars, dirks, bow-staffs, short-swords, long swords, and a slew of daggers, which were being used for everything except defense. Picking teeth seemed to be the most popular pastime. Axes, clubs—with or without spikes—it was an arsenal belonging to a ragtag group of roughnecks.

Devon sighed as he neared their camp. He had no right to judge them, really. Even at sixteen, he was painfully aware that his privileged upbringing had kept him extremely sheltered. He realized that many other young men his age were already earning a living in ways that closely resembled the lives of the people with whom he was traveling.

"Young mage! A word, if you please."

The voice was cultured and friendly. Still, Devon started at the sound. He turned and froze as one small, reed-thin man approached him.

Devon's initial reaction was to back away. Even though the man was small, he carried a curved sword, a wicked serrated dirk, and who knew how many hidden weapons. Cursing himself for what he perceived as cowardice, Devon took a breath and reminded himself that he had his own weapons at his disposal. He readied a defense spell and turned to face the hired sword.

The warrior reached the mage and extended his hand. "Jinin Aurek," he said.

Devon took the offered hand, but cautiously, taking in the newcomer's appearance. The man's hair was black, but Devon could clearly see it had been dyed. Badly. Hints of yellow shone from the part in the center of his head, and streaks of the same color peeked out at his temple.

With that odd exception, the man seemed otherwise well put together. He was dressed entirely in black, tunic tucked in and belted, laces done up on his leather boots.

"I wanted to introduce myself," Jinin Aurek said. "You are the mage from Lorcan DeCresler's school, correct?"

"I am." Devon could see no reason for not answering the man. "My name is Devon Bane."

Jinin smiled. "My pleasure, Master Bane. Lovely evening, isn't it?"

Devon nodded, becoming slightly more comfortable in the company of the black-clad man. "It is." He was not tall—around Devon's height, which was just over five and a half feet. Devon was a terrible judge of age, but he knew that the warrior was at least old enough to be his father. Still, there was a hint of youthful mischief in his features.

"Did you enjoy riding out front today?" he asked.

Devon stared at the man, wondering how he knew what the mage had been doing that day. Then again, it was his job to oversee the goings-on of the caravan. "I did, actually," Devon replied. "More than I thought I would."

"Good, good," Jinin nodded. He removed his gloves and tucked them under one arm. "Better to be breathing nature's air than smelling nothing but your own bad breath and bodily stench while tossed about the back of a wagon."

"With no windows," Devon added.

"And smaller than a Preliona prison cell!"

Devon burst out laughing. He had been comparing his tiny wagon to a jail just the day before. That Jinin Aurek gave words to the mage's thoughts was both amusing and relieving to him.

Jinin Aurek laughed as well and clapped him on the back like a new found friend. Devon found he did not mind the familiarity.

Their laughter trailed off and Devon stood straight again while Jinin stared off into the distance. "Listen, if you would like to do the same tomorrow, I will make provisions to guard your wagon for you."

"I don't plan on straying far from my compartment, but…"

"Still, one should be prepared." Jinin began to rub his calloused hands together as if to restore circulation to them. "I have had reports of bandits in the area we will be traveling through tomorrow. I am sure you are most capable of defending yourself and your package, but I would not feel comfortable unless a few of my people were nearby."

Devon studied the eyes of the hired sword. They were pale blue and flat. But the mage could detect no avarice there. Not that he was the best judge of character anyway. Lorcan was always telling him he was too trusting. He would not let his mentor down on this important mission though; he was determined to use caution. "Are you expecting trouble, sir?"

The hired sword bowed his head slightly. "Please, it is Jinin—and the answer is no, not exactly. I am simply trying to do my job to the best of my ability, and that means being prepared for any eventuality." He smiled. "It would help if you would allow me to do that."

Devon hung his head a moment. He was being paranoid, he knew. There was no reason at all that Jinin and his crew should not be guarding his wagon, when it was their job to do so.

"Of course," Devon replied. "I did not mean to question your judgment, Jinin. I would welcome any assistance you offer."

Jinin nodded. "No apology necessary, Devon Bane." He waved his hand grandly and Devon was again struck by the oddness of the man's colored hair. It seemed drastically out of place with the well-mannered and intelligent man before him. "Good night, then," Jinin said, nodding to the mage and backing away.

Devon slept well that night. The next morning, he left his wagon and climbed aboard the front of Jonah's carriage, intending to spend the day riding with him.

As he had promised, Jinin kept a watchful eye on Devon's wagon. The black-clad man rode up next to Devon and Jonah every half hour or so to give them a report. "Good morning," Jinin said early in the day. "Looks like another lovely day."

Devon was about to agree when Jonah grunted at his side. "Looks like rain to me."

Jinin narrowed his eyes but kept a grin on his face. "Really, Jonah, the sky couldn't be clearer."

Jonah, much to Devon's surprise, favored Jinin Aurek with a disgusted look. "My knees are throbbing. It's going to rain." He turned back to the road before him and left Devon to continue the conversation with the swordsman.

Jinin shrugged and smiled as if the merchant's words did not bother him. "Your wagon is well guarded, Devon," Jinin assured him. "Let me know if you need anything at all."

"I'll do that. Thank you."

Jinin fell back to converse with his fellows. Devon turned to Jonah, intending to question him about his behavior. But as he opened his mouth to scold the merchant for his rudeness, Jonah beat him to the punch and began to tell another story. "Did I ever tell you about the time I sold a bolt of Malhurian cloth to the wizard of Preliona?"

Devon had to laugh about that. The little he knew about Cornelius Pav led him to believe that the wizard was not one to truck with caravan merchants, or haggle over the price of cloth. The story was amusing, however, and Devon forgot about Jonah's odd behavior as he settled back to listen.

Hours later, Jonah's prediction about the weather came true. Black clouds rolled in, shutting out the afternoon warmth completely and forcing most extra riders into their wagons.

"Best get inside mage," Jonah said. "Don't think this'll get better any time soon."

Devon was inclined to agree. He leapt off the wagon bench as gracefully as his wet robes would allow and ran through the mud to the back of the line nodding to Jinin on the way. He tripped once and was forced to put one hand in the mud to keep from going down on his face. He wrenched himself to his feet and clambered into his wagon, now filthy and soaked to the bone.

He stripped off his wet robes and flung them toward the far corner of his cubicle. Teeth chattering, he hastily pulled a fresh tunic over his head and wrapped a heavier robe about his shuddering, lanky frame. *Ziyad's Blood*, but it's cold," he muttered, and snatched up several rumpled blankets from his makeshift bed. Throwing himself down on the pallet, he curled himself into a ball and closed his eyes against the cold.

Devon heard the knocking at his wagon door as part of his dream. It was his mother pounding on the ceiling of their kitchen with a broom handle. The kitchen ceiling was his bedroom floor, and his mother was notorious for finding new and inventive ways to wake him. *Well, at least it had not been a bucket of cold water,* he thought.

The banging was louder now, more insistent. Devon cracked one eye open, desperately trying to hang onto the image of his mother.

As soon as he saw the bland wooden door to his wagon he sat up. "What is it?" he yelled.

"Master Devon, Jinin Aurek has asked that you remain inside your cabin."

Devon stood up, blankets falling about him in a wrinkled heap. "What's going on?" he asked. "Why have we stopped?" For the mage had only just now realized his cabin no longer rocked in that seasick sort of way.

"It's nothing," the disembodied voice outside explained. "The rain has flooded parts of the road and one of the wagons is stuck. Jinin is asking everyone to stay inside until we are on our way again."

Devon was silent for a moment. It had stopped raining. Devon could tell it was dusk by the meager light coming through his cracked wagon door.

"Master Bane?"

"Yes—umm, where are we?"

"Hunter Heights. Now, if you do not mind, I'll be getting back to the others."

Devon heard the man walk away and risked a peek out his door. Steam from the warm ground rose from the mud, obscuring much of the caravan from the mage's eyes. In the distance, several lumbering figures worked in the shadows, pushing against one very stuck wagon. Several times the carriage lurched forward a few feet, only to be mired once more down the path. Horses whinnied, men shouted and slid in the mud. Devon could see enough to know that they would be here awhile.

He closed the door and slumped back onto his mound of blankets. He rested his head against the wall, grabbed his spell book and began flipping through it. He had just settled on a spell to study when the sound of horses' hooves and clashing swords caught his ears.

Devon Bane surged to his feet, startled by the change in the voices of the fighters outside. Shouts and curses carried clearly into the relative safety of his quarters.

They were under attack—as Jinin had warned they might be. Devon Bane, never having used his powers in a real fight before, dove for his spell book and frantically began flipping through the pages.

16~Unexpected Introductions

Kiernan swung his dark sword in a wide arc, catching the man in front of him in the chest and following through in time to block a thrust from the women behind him. He and Nemesio had come in from opposite sides and were currently fighting two opponents apiece, hand to hand. The good news was that the merchants had apparently climbed inside their wagons, leaving only the dozen armed mercenaries for *Duak-Thenal* to deal with. Kiernan could only account for ten of those now – but he assumed Tain and Panas would take care of the other two.

Things were not going exactly as the prince had expected, however. The first thing Kiernan had noticed when he engaged the hired swords was the way they looked. From a distance, the group had resembled any other ragtag bunch of mercenaries, cheaply hired to guard a merchant train. The fighters before him were no such animal, though.

The second they caught sight of Kiernan and Nemesio, the four fighters surrounding the mired carriage snapped into fighting formation, giving substance to his fear that these men and women not only knew how to fight as a group, but had been expecting to do so on this particular journey.

Not that they did not have the decency to act surprised. As Kiernan and Nemesio came in from the sides, Talesin and Dagmar appeared on the road before the other six. The appearance of the four vastly different looking elves, especially the extremely frightening ice elf, was enough to startle even the most steadfast among them. But Kiernan saw that the advantage they had hoped to gain was lost. They rushed forward before *Duak-Thenal* could take any of them down. Kiernan found himself instantly batting away two sword tips from aggressive fighters intent on keeping the prince from the wagons… and his friends.

— ✳ ✳ ✳ —

Panas's job was to cover the Captain. But from his high perch, Panas could see that his companions were in trouble. Ten to four was hardly fair odds. Not that they had never faced worse, but Panas had noted the same readiness in the mercenaries that Kiernan had. These fighters had been hired as a group, and were clearly here for more than a standard job. They were guarding something important. It looked as though they were unusually well prepared—and now all four elves were on the defensive, battling skilled opponents instead of off-guard hired swords.

Panas winced and tore his gaze away from his friends, turning his attention to the task at hand.

Tain was focused on the covered wagon below her, judging the distance and measuring the perfect place to land. Panas was unsure the imp even heard the sounds of clashing swords as she dropped onto the canvas wagon top.

The light elf scrambled to lower branches to mark her progress. The imp had landed silently, but Panas kept a lookout for any sign of the mage. He swung his legs over a nearby branch and hung his knees over it. Then, drawing his slingshot, he lowered himself headfirst so that he dangled upside down several feet above the front door of the mage's wagon.

Panas fully expected the door to open, regardless of the Captain's silent feet. He was startled then when he heard Tain call out and saw two men clamber up onto the wagon, racing toward her.

Panas twisted his torso painfully and let the band of his weapon loose. The tiny metal ball caught one mercenary between the eyes and knocked him clear off the wagon top.

The second man was quicker. He was on top of the imp before the elf could reload his weapon.

Panas fished in his pockets for more ammunition and cursed under his breath. He wanted to call out to Tain, but he feared giving away his position. The spry thief had already dodged her attacker twice and was currently leaping over the rips in the canvas made by the mercenary's sword. The wagon top was in tatters as the swordsman hacked his way toward the imp. Tain, having the better balance of the two, simply stood atop the metal hoops and let her opponent destroy the ground on which he stood.

Breathing heavily, the mercenary made one last attempt at moving to the imp. Panas' metal ball hit him in the back of the head, toppling him head over heels onto the damp ground below.

— ✳ ✳ ✳ —

Kiernan glanced over his shoulder to see how Nemesio was faring. He need not have worried. The huge dark elf was wielding both his weapons with abandon, alternately swinging his sword and firing his bow. He had managed to knock down one of his own attackers and pick off two of Dagmar's at nearly the same time. Clearly, he aimed to finish off this last man so he could go to the aid of his outnumbered friends.

Kiernan was going nowhere soon. The woman he fought was a true warrior. It was going to take longer than he would have liked to best her. Nemesio saw this too as he finished off his own opponent. He caught Kiernan's eye and nodded toward the front of the line, where Talesin and Dagmar still fought.

Kiernan nodded back and turned his focus fully to the fighter before him. The light elf thrust ahead, knocking the woman's sword arm aside and overbalancing her so that she was forced to fall back. Kiernan pressed the advantage. He stalked the fighter, slashing his sword down and across in a blur of movement.

But the woman managed to block him and come back with several offensive slashes and thrusts. "I know who you are," she spat.

Kiernan was slightly surprised, but he did not give any ground. "If you know me, then you know what I will do to you."

She lunged forward. The prince blocked with a downward sweep and thrust his heel forward, catching the woman on one hip. She fell back but recovered in time to parry the prince's next thrust.

Kiernan dove forward, barely giving the woman time to catch her breath. "Tell me who *you* are, and I might let you live."

The fighter grinned, revealing a row of artificially sharpened teeth. "My name will mean nothing to you," she snarled and lifted her sword high, leaving her midsection exposed for a split second.

It was long enough. Kiernan Nightwing lunged forward, plunging his sword through her ribcage and into her heart. She collapsed, taking the prince's sword with her as she sank to the ground.

Grimacing, Kiernan yanked his sword from his opponent's body and sprinted off in search of the rest of his crew.

— ✻ ✻ ✻ —

Dagmar was angry. She was bleeding from several small nicks and cuts on her arms and Talesin did not have a scratch. Dagmar looked enviously at Talesin's double bladed sword and suddenly wished for a weapon with more of a reach than her smaller thinner blade. Still, the ice elf had not made any more progress in this fight than she had. Out of the six who had attacked them, four still stood -- and Nemesio was responsible for downing the other two.

Dagmar spun into the nearest fighter, grabbing his sword arm, and thrusting back with her foot. She heard a sickening crack and the ensuing scream of pain as the man went down with a crushed kneecap. She ducked under the swinging sword of her other attacker and dove aside to avoid the foot that was aimed at her head. She felt the man's heel connect with her shoulder. Wincing, Dagmar rolled with the blow and came up in a crouch, ready for the next attack.

Instead, however, Dagmar found herself watching the human's bobbing head running away from her and mounting his horse. Talesin's two opponents were also retreating. Even the human with the crushed kneecap was attempting to get to his horse. He did not get far. Nemesio chose that moment to hurl one of his arrows into the fray. The missile nailed the already injured human dead to the ground.

The rest of the attackers galloped off, leaving three stunned members of *Duak-Thenal* staring after them.

Nemesio sprinted up to his friends. "Where are they going?"

Dagmar shrugged. "Don't know—they just took off."

"Were they losing?" the southern elf asked.

Dagmar held out her cut and bleeding arms. "Not exactly," she replied grimly.

Nemesio whipped a handkerchief out of his pocket and held it to the wild elf's skin.

"Listen," Talesin said. He was standing between two mired wagons, his black eyes narrowing in concentration. "Where are the merchants?" he asked.

Nemesio and Dagmar glanced at each other, then at the silent wagons around them. Lifting her sword again, the wild elf walked to the nearest wagon. There was no sound coming from inside the wagon. Even if the merchants had chosen to hide inside, her sensitive ears would have picked up their breathing.

Dagmar knew what she would find even before she stepped onto the stair of the wagon. Still, she was unprepared for the gruesome sight that greeted her when she pulled back the canvas flap.

Three humans, a man and two women lay in a heap on the wooden floor. A dark brown pool spread in a wide circle from their lifeless bodies and the same color stained the walls. The wild elf did not need to look any closer to see that their throats had been slashed.

The wild elf's heart sank, but she forced herself to stand her ground. She bent and touched a finger to the nearest pool of blood. The humans had not been dead long, for warmth still lingered in their blood.

From her crouch, Dagmar Coal peered into the faces and open eyes of the lifeless bodies. She did not know them, but that thought did not make her any less angry at the senseless carnage before her.

Talesin suddenly appeared at her side, looking even more grim than usual. He said nothing, but Dagmar could feel her companion tense at the gory sight. He immediately turned to guard their backs. "Check the other wagons." she ordered.

Talesin nodded. "I doubt the sights will change," he said, and disappeared.

Dagmar jumped to the ground and took a long breath.

Nemesio stared at her. "Dead?" he asked.

Dagmar nodded. "Let's find Kiernan."

— ✺ ✺ ✺ —

Devon Bane spent the fight silently preparing as many defensive spells as he could when he heard something land on the canvas above him. It was so light that it could have been a squirrel, but Devon reached into his pouch and grabbed a handful of sand, readying the first spell that came to mind. Another considerably louder thump overhead rocked the entire wagon. He looked up in time to see a sword tip slash through the roof. Devon dove to floor and looked up as several more rips reduced his wagon top to tatters. He did not know what was going on up there, but he figured he was not in the safest place now. The mage scrambled to his feet and opened the door.

Instinct told him that this was not the best course of action, either. A high-pitched sound in his ear and a slight breeze to his right forced him to dive aside, stumbling into the doorframe. He was stunned to see a small ball bearing had buried itself in the wooden frame of the wagon.

Shaking at the near miss, the young mage dragged himself to his feet. A whisper of words and small jets of orange lightning flew from his fingers, smashing the tree branches above him and setting the leaves on fire. Devon heard a cry of fear or pain and saw a shadowy form slip several feet and land on branches more level with the mage's eye.

Devon was about to raise his hands to strike again when he noticed that the sound of battle above him had died away. There was a slight breeze and a high-pitched voice shouted above him. "Hey!"

Devon whirled about; his hands raised in defense.

A blur of movement and two black booted feet came swinging down, catching him in the chest and throwing him backward out of the wagon. The mage landed hard on his back, cracking his head on the dirt, and getting the wind knocked out of him in the process.

It took a moment for the world to come back into focus and Devon was startled to see the tip of a spear hovering dangerously close to his nose. "One sound out of you, young man, and I will personally mar that perfect complexion of yours."

The voice that spoke to him was like music. It was high-pitched, childlike, and most decidedly feminine. It was a voice that had no business speaking in any type of commanding manner whatsoever.

Devon narrowed his eyes and looked past the long staff, up at the face that belonged to the voice.

Huge luminous blue eyes stared down at him with a mixture of anger and amusement. A small, sharp-featured, and extremely pale face was attached to a petite, lithe body dressed completely in black. Pointed ears should have marked her as an elf, but Devon remembered enough childhood lore to know exactly what stood over him.

"*Kelina*—a fairy," he breathed.

The creature cocked her head and frowned at him slightly. "Imp, actually. Fairies have wings, silly boy. But I forgive you. It is a common misconception." Then, remembering her first words, she placed one hand on her hip. "What did I just tell you?" she scolded, her gigantic eyes narrowing in some childish mockery of anger. If he had not been staring down the end of a spear-tip, Devon might have found the irritated imp amusing.

A sound of rustling leaves to his left kept the fairy from following through on her threat. "Tain!" shouted a pain-filled and concerned voice.

"Over here!" Devon's captor called out.

A second later, the owner of the disembodied voice emerged from the brush. Devon's jaw dropped as a light elf stumbled toward them. His golden hair was singed slightly, and his clothes were smoking. This must have been his attacker from the trees. It appeared his spell had not totally missed its mark. Now, however, Devon almost wished that it had. The elf was furious. Devon did not speak elvish, but he knew a curse when he heard one.

"*Kelina*, Panas, what happened to you?" The imp's attention was on the elf now. Shocked as he was, Devon used the moment to attempt to rise.

But though he had barely moved, the fairy heard him. Both hands were immediately back on her staff, pressing its tip closer to his throat. "Be a good boy and don't move, eh, mage? Can't have you burning everything out of the trees now, can we?"

Surprisingly, the little imp stepped back. Devon assumed she was letting him up after all until he felt long thin fingers grab the back of his collar and haul him to his feet. Before he could even try to break away, he was roughly spun around to face the golden-haired elf. "Look at my hair," he practically shrieked. "And my new vest," the elf pointed to his smoking red vest. "I'll have you know I expect you to replace this, mage."

"Maybe he can magic you up a new one, Panas," the imp quipped from beside him.

Panas frowned and released him. Devon stumbled back a step, realizing for the first time that he had been dangling above the ground in the tall elf's grasp.

Both strange creatures stood a few feet away from him now, each gazing at him with wholly different expressions. The elf was still brushing the soot off his clothing, and the imp gazed at him as if he were some interesting bug ready to have its legs pulled off. "I don't suppose you'd condescend to tell me what you want."

The elf and the imp traded bemused looks and laughed. "Why don't you have a seat, mage," the blonde elf told him, barely raising his eyes from his charred outfit.

"I'll do no such thing until one of you tells me what's going on!" Devon announced. He was getting braver by the moment and was preparing another spell.

The imp was shaking her head and chuckling. "Tell me, mage, why are you humans so impatient? Is it because your life span is so short? That must be it. You've got to get everything in as quickly as possible before your time runs out, huh?"

Devon was about to tell the sarcastic imp that anyone in his position, human or not, would be intolerant by now, when more voices came from behind him.

Startled by the sound, the mage whirled about and let loose the spell he had recalled. Dimly he heard the imp call out a warning to the newcomers, but Devon had already raised his hands. An orange gooey mass streamed from his fingertips, slamming into the first figure to emerge from the trees. With a yelp of surprise, the newcomer was propelled backward, arms flailing. He landed with a dull thud against the trunk of a tree and stuck there.

Devon had raised his hands, ready to dole out more justice to the next attacker, when he got a look at the creature he had dispatched.

The orange goo covered the chest and arms of his victim, but Devon had a clear view of his face. Deep brown skin covered smooth features and high pointed ears. A set of extremely angry violet eyes glared at him. The mage was so startled at the sight of his victim that he dropped his hands.

The two creatures behind him, however, had both drawn their weapons and now had them trained on him. "Do that again, mage, and you'll find your tongue on the ground," Panas said from his side.

The imp meanwhile let out a high-pitched peal of laughter. "Oh, *please* do it again," she begged, dancing in place and pointing at her gummed-up comrade. "That was brilliant."

Devon gaped at her, unsure if he was being mocked or praised.

Devon was just wondering where Jinin and the other hired swords had gone—for he no longer heard clashing metal or angry shouts and curses—when three more elves emerged from the trees.

By now they had all removed their hoods, giving Devon a clearer view of his current situation. Two of the three remaining elves approached him, their swords drawn. One had flaming red hair and striking green eyes. The other, a tall brown-haired female, was clearly a wild elf. She was the plainest of the group but her gray eyes held a strange frenetic quality.

Most curious of all, and that which froze Devon in his place, was the presence of the ice elf. Though he stood some distance away, trying to pry his dark companion loose from the tree, Devon found himself shivering in his presence.

The red-haired elf stood before him, his jewel-like eyes boring through the mage, scanning his features as if searching for some hidden message. "Did you ask him?"

Behind Devon the blonde-haired light elf answered, "No, we thought we'd wait for you."

"Ask me what?" Devon said impatiently. "I don't know who you are, but…"

His tirade was cut short as a gleaming sword of dark gray steel came up and caught him at the throat. "First things first," the elf said. "Your name."

Devon started to object, but the elf's sword suddenly pressed deeper into the skin at his neck. His name seemed to burst from his mouth of its own accord. "Devon Bane," he gasped.

The elf nodded in satisfaction. "My name is Kiernan Nightwing," he returned. "Panas and Tain you have met. To your right is Dagmar. Over there is Talesin and the fellow you have so successfully stuck to that tree is Nemesio."

Devon glanced at the writhing form of the southern elf, silently congratulating himself on how well his spell had worked.

"Can you turn him loose?" Kiernan Nightwing asked.

Devon considered lying—but only for a moment. What good would it do? Out of the six, he had only managed to take down one of them. He certainly could not defend himself against the other five.

"Yes," he said with a sigh of resignation.

"Good. Do it," the light elf commanded, and stepped back to give him room.

Devon thought the elf showed a lot of trust for someone he had just met. Devon could easily have cast any number of spells that have might rendered at least some of his captors unconscious.

He did not, however. He tried to tell himself it was because he was outnumbered. That he would be dead before he had uttered one arcane word. That was not it, though. As he reached into his pocket and pulled out a handful of rust-colored powder, he silently cursed himself for being the coward he knew he was.

Sighing, he blew into his hand and whispered the words that would release the elf from his gooey prison. The southern elf fell to the ground, sputtering curses. The ice elf helped him to his feet, and for one terrifying moment Devon thought they were about to approach him. He was enormously relieved when they stayed where they were.

"That's better," Kiernan Nightwing said. Devon did not think he sounded any happier than he had been before. The flame-haired elf showed little emotion. "Now…"

"Who are you, and what have you done with the merchants and guards?" Devon shouted suddenly, finding sudden reserves of courage.

Kiernan Nightwing raised one red eyebrow remarkably high. It was the kind of look a patient father might give a wailing child. Only it did not quite work here, because the elf did not appear to be much older than Devon himself. In fact, now that Devon truly took in the faces of all the elves and the imp, the whole crew seemed extremely young.

Devon knew that was impossible. Elves aged about one year for every ten or so that they lived. He was not so sure about imps and fairies, but elves he had learned enough about in school. Devon was quickly doing the math in his head. Judging by the smooth, wrinkle-free faces that now surrounded him, he figured these elves to be no more than one hundred and fifty to two hundred years of age.

Which meant they were teenagers, like him. Teenagers with swords and the skill to use them—but teenagers, nonetheless.

"Your *soldiers* have run off, I'm afraid," the elf announced. "As for the merchants, we found them dead in their wagons."

This news hit the young mage hard. His vision suddenly went fuzzy around the edges and he desperately wanted to stagger back several feet. But the presence of an elf and an imp kept him from doing that.

Each put out a firm hand to steady him, but the mage shook them off. *Poor Jonah.* "You killed them!" he accused, and watched Kiernan Nightwing shake his head.

"No, we didn't."

"Murderers," Devon hissed.

The elf's emerald eyes flared. "I don't have time to argue this point with you, mage, and I don't much care what you think either way." The elf was moving closer as he spoke. His voice was forceful and commanding, but his tone was light and airy. Beautiful, at striking odds with his demeanor.

Devon found himself backing up until he felt the wooden wall of the wagon at his back.

The fiery elf put his angular face close to Devon's, "All I want is the key."

17~Misconceptions

Devon's eyes went wide, "No," he whispered defiantly.

Kiernan Nightwing backed away from the mage a step and scanned his blue eyes, taking stock. "It doesn't really matter whether you tell us where it is." Now he grinned. "We will find it anyway."

Devon stuck out his chin in one final attempt at defiance. "All my possessions are warded, and I won't release them." Then, as an afterthought, "You'll have to kill me first." He really had not meant that, but he thought it sounded good.

The elf smiled. "Bold words," he remarked, and then turned over his shoulder. "Captain," he called, "it's all yours."

"Captain..." Devon began looking around for whoever the elf had spoken to.

The little imp beside him flashed him a cocky grin and bowed slightly. "Captain Tain Elire at your service," she announced. "You sure you don't want to tell me where that key is, boyo?"

Devon shook his head weakly. He knew her name. But he ransacked his memory for some clue as to what exactly the fairy was captain of. "Suit yourself," she said with a shrug, and bounded up the steps of the wagon.

"Wait!" He lunged after the imp. "Didn't you hear me?" he gasped. "It's warded!" Devon saw the irony of warning his enemies of the potential dangers they faced inside his wagon, but he had no wish to see the tiny thief fried by one of his magical protections.

The imp stopped on the top stair of the wagon, "Heard you the first time, little mage," she replied nonchalantly. Then she put her hands on her hips and looked at the surrounding elves. "I don't think the boy knows who I am."

The elves laughed at that. "No, Tain, I don't believe he does," Kiernan said.

Devon tried to get past the elves who were blocking his path. "You're a fairy, not a mage, and if you go in there and start touching things you'll be burnt to a cinder!"

But the elves only laughed harder, and the imp Captain shook her head in condescension. "Have some faith in me, please," she said, placing a hand to her chest in a gesture that showed she was deeply offended. "My dear young man, do they teach you nothing of history in that silly school you go to?"

Panas the Hawk rolled his golden eyes. "Really, Captain, you cannot expect everyone to tremble at the sound of your name."

Clearly offended, Tain Elire glared at him, spun on her heel, and stormed into the wagon.

Devon clenched his eyes shut and waited for the inevitable explosion.

When he heard nothing but the laughter of the elves, he dared to open one eye just a sliver. The wagon remained unscathed. Devon caught a glimpse of a shadowy form milling about inside. "How…"

"The Captain is a thief, mage," Kiernan Nightwing said from beside him. "She has broken through stronger magic than yours in the past. No offense."

Devon was not so much offended as he was embarrassed that his wards had been so easily defeated. He frowned at the light elf and turned away, scanning the rest of the group.

The southern elf, Nemesio, had recovered completely from Devon's spell and was currently examining some superficial wounds on the wild elf's arms. He kept throwing annoyed looks in Devon's direction and the mage quickly dropped his eyes. Panas the Hawk was sitting on a tree stump shaking bits of leaves out of his singed golden locks, and the ice elf had disappeared altogether. Kiernan Nightwing was the only one paying any attention to him now.

He stood a few feet away, arms crossed, leaning casually against a nearby tree. He had fixed Devon with an unnerving stare, and the mage found himself squirming beneath it. "Shouldn't you be guarding the perimeter or something?" Devon snarled, unable to help himself.

"Being done," the elf assured him.

"By one man?"

"Elf," Kiernan corrected, "and yes."

Devon gritted his teeth in frustration and paced back and forth. "So, what are you, some kind of freedom fighters?"

The elf gave him an amused look. "What makes you say that?" he asked, not shifting from his casual position.

Devon threw up his hands. "Oh, I don't know—the planned attack, the murdered merchants, stealing my things—take your pick." Devon pulled himself up to his full height of five foot eight, rather short next to the over-six-foot elf, and made a vain attempt at looking threatening. "Are you trying to make some sort of political statement or something? Because I think you could have done it without killing innocent bystanders."

"I told you we did not kill anybody," the elf said with finality. "The merchants were dead when we got here." Not a shred of emotion crossed the elf's face as he said these words. His sharp features remained cold and unchanged. At that moment Devon thought him quite capable of murder.

Devon swallowed, "Who did it, then?"

The elven leader shrugged and walked toward him. "Your runaway mercenaries, perhaps?"

"Why would they do that?" Devon asked, his courage melting away the closer the elf got.

Kiernan Nightwing sauntered past him, leaning in toward Devon's ear as he did so. "Why would they run?" he whispered.

This last comment jolted, and he was left with a rather unpleasant notion: Jonah had been right. The cowardly hired swords had run. Jinin and his gang had abandoned them. Devon had been a fool to trust the wiry mercenary—and now it was too late. Jonah and the others were dead, and the mage felt a weighty responsibility for their fates.

"Tain!" the elf called into the wagon. "A little faster, please."

"Do not rush an artist, oh fearless leader!" came the sarcastic reply.

Kiernan turned back to the mage and shrugged almost apologetically. Devon glared back at the elf and crossed his arms. The mage was not sure he could win a staring contest, but he was certainly in the mood to try.

But then the imp thief sauntered out of the back of Devon's wagon. In her tiny white hands, she carried the box that Devon had spent the last week protecting.

Without even realizing what he was doing, the mage lunged for the wooden case, thinking to snag it from her before the imp could pry it open.

She was too quick for him. She whooshed her prize away and dangled it just out of his reach. Meanwhile, Panas and Kiernan had hooked their long hands around his arms and pulled him away from the thief.

"Take it easy, Devon Bane," Kiernan said.

"I guess it's safe to say that our quarry lies in this box, as our little friend seems so intent on getting his hands on it," Panas commented lightly.

The imp grinned. "Yes, and besides, I've checked everywhere else." The Captain whipped out a tiny white pick and aimed it at the lock on the box.

"Wait!" Devon shouted, struggling madly. "It's…"

"Warded?" the imp finished for him. She shook her head and laughed, and Devon simply shut his mouth with an audible snap.

He watched in awe as the fairy's fleet fingers moved too quickly to see. The blur of movement was itself almost magical. Tain Elire bypassed his ward spell and popped the lid of the box before Devon could utter another cry of protest.

She did not say anything right away, only stared into the wooden case.

"Well, what is it?" Panas asked, impatient.

Tain looked up at them and turned the box around to show them the contents.

And Devon felt the strength go out of his knees.

"I hate to break this to you, ladies and gentlemen," Tain began. "But someone beat me to it."

The box was empty.

"No," Devon whispered as the elves released his arms and let him slip to the ground. He buried his face in his hands and rocked back and forth on his knees. "No, no, no, Lorcan will kill me for sure."

For a moment no one moved or spoke. Then the mage felt someone take his arm and gently but firmly lift him to his feet. Panas steered him over to the nearby tree stump and allowed Devon to collapse onto it. "Well now, what do you expect?" he asked soothingly. "Stealing a magical artifact from a powerful wizard? And your own teacher, no less. Then losing it—I must say you make a pretty poor thief, my friend."

Devon had only been half listening to the light elf, but these last words caught his ears. "Thief?" he asked, his head snapping up. "Me?"

The others nodded solemnly.

"I'm no thief!" Devon protested.

The four elves started to gather around him in a tight circle that made the mage want to crawl away. Four sets of otherworldly eyes looked down at him with suspicion. With growing alarm, Devon began to realize that it was he who was suspect, not them. "It's obvious that filthy band of hired swords stole the key," he stammered, scrambling for some shred of defense.

"Yes, we gathered that," Kiernan replied. "Seems that key has been stolen a lot lately."

Devon scowled. "I told you I didn't steal it. Why would I take something from my own teacher?"

"Why indeed?" the southern elf quipped.

Devon stared at them all. "You have to believe me. I have no reason to steal such an object."

The elven leader chuckled. "Oh, I can think of a few."

Devon bristled at that. "What does an elven mercenary know of a magical artifact?"

Kiernan Nightwing shrugged. "Very little, I admit, but I imagine the benefits of having one are much like any object of power. It has more to do with what it can get you than what it can actually do." The red-haired elf stepped closer to the mage. Try as he might, Devon could do nothing but shrink under that emerald glare. "I'm betting that key could get you just about everything you want. Money, magic, perhaps the death of a merchant or two."

Devon felt his jaw drop. "Are you actually suggesting I killed those people?"

The elf backed away a step, considering. "No," he said with finality, "I'm not."

Devon closed his mouth, realizing suddenly that the elf had just made a point. If Jinin had stolen the key, and it was certainly looking that way, then he was probably responsible for the death of those poor men and women in the other wagons.

"Kiernan, what are you saying?" the elf called Dagmar asked.

The green-eyed elf sighed in frustration. "I am saying that my sister was not as well informed as I had hoped."

"You don't think *he* stole it?" Nemesio pointed at Devon, a note of surprise in his voice.

Kiernan Nightwing shook his head. "No, I don't." He locked eyes with Devon Bane. The green eyes sparkled, not in anger but in challenge. And Devon suddenly understood something: Neither of them was guilty. They were going to have to help each other.

As if he had read his mind, the red-haired elf asked Devon, "What do you say, mage? Want to join us in finding your key?"

Devon bit his lip. What did he have to lose, really? He had to get that key back and he certainly couldn't do it on his own. The mage nodded his assent.

"Good," the light elf said, brightening. "Now why don't you tell us why you had that artifact and where you were taking it?"

Devon suddenly felt bolder. "What do I get in return for the information you want?" he said, realizing he finally had a chip to bargain with.

Panas leaned into him threateningly. "How about your life?"

Devon shrank away from the light elf. "Look, I want that key back, and if you're going after the man who stole it, then I'm coming with you."

The southern elf laughed out loud at that, clearly questioning Devon's commitment. "I'll find Talesin," he said as he walked away.

"You don't understand," Devon pleaded, suddenly concerned they would leave him behind. "Lorcan DeCresler entrusted that artifact to me. I was to bring it to Cornelius Pav in Preliona."

Kiernan held up one long hand. "Does Cornelius know you are on your way?" he asked.

Devon nodded eagerly. "Yes! Lorcan told me it was imperative that Preliona's mage receive it immediately."

Devon instantly beheld a knowing glance between Kiernan, Panas and Dagmar. He got the distinct impression he was missing something.

"I still do not understand why Lorcan didn't just magic himself to Preliona and give the key to Cornelius in person," Tain interrupted, bouncing up alongside Devon.

Devon shook his head. "We are in the middle of spring semester. Lorcan cannot possibly take time away from his classes now. This was the only way."

"But then why did Kalli say…" Panas began, but Kiernan cut him off with a glare.

Devon caught that exchange as well, and narrowed his eyes.

But then Kiernan turned back to him. "Devon, who were the merchants who rode with you?"

"A group of locals from Preliona. They were on their way back from Graxton when they picked me up."

The elf's eyes widened slightly. "And the hired swords? Any idea what they were guarding?"

Devon hung his head, despairing again. "Obviously not me." He slammed his fist down on the palm of his other hand. "Damn that Jinin and his filthy thieving band!"

"Jinin?"

Devon and the elves turned to the imp. "Yes, Jinin Aurek," Devon confirmed. "You know him?"

For the first time since he'd seen her, the imp looked serious. The mage began to wonder if her childlike antics had been his imagination.

"Yes," she replied solemnly. "I know him."

"What kind of hired sword is he, Tain?" the female elf asked.

Tain Elire laughed, but the sound was forced. "He's not." she replied. "He's a thief, and a very good one."

"Could he have gotten past that ward spell?" Kiernan asked.

"Yes, and leave everything looking as though it had never been touched." She turned to Devon. "You would have gotten all the way to Preliona without ever missing it, mage."

Devon rubbed one hand absently through his unruly hair. "I have to get it back," he whispered. It wouldn't just be embarrassing to return to Lorcan after such a failure, Devon thought, it would be a devastating mark against him. Lorcan wasn't exactly a forgiving teacher, and though he liked Devon Bane, this misstep would indelibly scar their relationship now and forever.

"I have to get it back," he said again.

No one answered him, and Devon thought he was about to be abandoned when he saw Kiernan Nightwing's gray booted feet shift slightly. "We will help you get the key, Devon Bane."

Devon looked up quickly, meaning to thank the elf. But the words stopped on his lips when Devon saw how deadly serious the elf's smooth features were. Devon licked his lips. "You still haven't told me who *you* are."

Kiernan Nightwing smiled devilishly. "We are called *Duak-Thenal*. Perhaps you've heard of us?"

Devon had, but he could think of nothing better to do than nod weakly. He had suspected as much, but knowing it for a fact seemed to knock the rest of the fight out of him.

The imp clapped him on the back, making him stumble forward. "Come now, mage, it's not all that bad. You might have some fun traveling the countryside with a band of outlaws. Perhaps you could write our memoirs." The imp seemed to find this idea particularly amusing. She slapped her knees and rocked back and forth with laughter.

Devon scowled and turned to his wagon.

"Kiernan, over here!"

Devon started at the shout and turned in time to see *Duak-Thenal* running to the back of the caravan. Devon followed, his curiosity getting the better of him. He tripped on his orange robes and nearly laid himself out on the hard ground, but he hiked up the voluminous material and jogged to catch up with the others.

Afraid of seeing dead merchant bodies, Devon slowed down as he rounded the corner of the final wagon. He had steeled himself for the inevitable gory sight, determined not to blanch in front of these new and strange creatures.

But the ice elf had not called them all to see more dead bodies. Devon found himself breathing a sigh of relief when he laid eyes on the uncovered wagon at the rear of the caravan.

It was the only one with no roof. Its contents had been covered by a great tarp, which was currently folded back, revealing gleaming metal bars that ran the length of the wagon. Piled on top of each other, the silvery metal struts made for bulky cargo, to say the least. It was immensely heavy. Devon could see that the metal-rimmed wagon wheels had begun to buckle under its weight.

Duak-Thenal had surrounded the wagon and Kiernan Nightwing was running one long finger along the front of a huge piece of metal, "Barexium?"

He addressed Talesin Darken, who had perched himself on top of the pile and was squatting down to answer his leader. "It is. I can only assume this is the latest shipment to fail to make it to Preliona."

"Does that mean Jinin Aurek and his crew are responsible for all the robberies?" the southern elf asked.

"Perhaps," Kiernan mused. "But it looks as if the artifact was more valuable to them this time."

Dagmar turned to him and opened her hand. "Maybe they intended to abandon the wagon all along."

Panas' jaw dropped open so far that the others, including Devon, rushed to see what it was the wild elf was holding. Devon wasn't exactly included in the circle, but it did not prevent him from standing on his toes and catching a glimpse of what looked like a heavily scratched gold coin.

"That's not one of ours," Tain was saying.

"Yes, but unfortunately that wouldn't have mattered had it been found by authorities from Preliona," Dagmar said.

There was a silence that Devon took for perplexity. He opened his mouth before he thought not to. "You believe someone is trying to frame you?"

The entire group turned to him as one, each cocking one colorful eyebrow at the human. "It would appear that way, mage," Kiernan said finally.

"The question is," Dagmar reasoned, "Why this ragtag group of hired swords? What could they possibly gain?"

"I doubt it is Jinin and his band who so cleverly orchestrated our incrimination," Nemesio Firebrand said.

"What?" Panas asked, perplexed.

"He means that Jinin left this little token behind, but someone bigger and better told him to do it," the imp translated.

The light elf looked at the imp, then back at Nemesio, and shook his hands in the air. "Why couldn't you just say that?"

Kiernan stepped in between them in what Devon saw as an attempt to curb an argument. "Tain," he said. "What do you think?"

The imp had taken a seat near Talesin and, sitting cross-legged, was currently tossing the false coin up into the air and catching it in her tiny hand. "I think Jinin was here, but Nemesio is right: he was taking orders from someone else."

There was a silence after she spoke. Devon sensed an unspoken thought in the air that they would not voice in his presence.

The ice elf suddenly reached across and snatched the coin out of the air, eliciting a cry of protest from the imp. He ignored her and shook the coin at his leader. "A single coin is not so easily spotted."

Kiernan nodded in understanding. "Fan out," he commanded. "Scour the rest of the wagons and take care not to disturb the deceased. Dagmar, send a message to Venk and be sure to tell him where he can find the barexium."

Before Devon could say anything, the company was on the move. Devon might have offered to help but something was bothering him.

He lunged forward suddenly and grabbed Kiernan's arm. "Wait."

The flame-haired elf turned, eyeing Devon's hand with a cold glare.

Devon swallowed and immediately let go. He backed off a step but bravely pressed forward with his request. "We cannot leave the merchants as they are."

Kiernan nodded, his green eyes softening. "I understand your distress. Believe me, we would like to take the time to give them a proper burial, but unfortunately…"

Devon cut him off. "Unfortunately, you are too concerned with saving your collective behinds right now to be bothered, right?"

Even Devon was stunned by the force of his own words.

But the elven leader remained unnervingly calm. He raised his chin slightly and took a deep breath. "If that is the way you choose to see it, mage, then I will not bother to convince you otherwise. I will say, however, that the fact that *you* remain alive will seem just as suspicious to the Prelionan authorities as any marked coins that are found." He took a step forward and Devon desperately wanted to step back. "Think on that," the elf hissed. "And after you have done so, make yourself useful and help us look."

The elf spun on his heel and walked away.

Devon was furious. There was no way he could be implicated in any of this. Though he badly wanted to get his hands on Lorcan's key, he was quite willing to delay the trip in order to bring peace to the souls of the deceased.

"You would leave them here to rot?" he called after the retreating elf.

Kiernan did not turn as he spoke. "If you wish to join them, I am sure that can be arranged."

Devon clamped his mouth shut. He had no idea how serious the elf was. After all, the group really had no need of him. They were more than capable of finding Jinin on their own.

No, it was he who needed them.

Unable to bring himself to help with the search, the mage retreated into his cabin and gathered his things. He emerged once again to find the tiny imp thief outside his door. In her hands were two silver daggers, one with a jet-black handle, the other with a blue diamond set in the blade. As Devon watched, the Captain bent down and unsheathed two other less remarkable daggers from their scabbards at her ankles. She examined them for a moment, then shrugged and tossed them aside. She quickly holstered the two new daggers and stood. She paced around for a moment and then nodded in satisfaction.

Devon did not need to guess where the imp thief had gotten the daggers. There were dead bodies all around them. He was hoping she had at least taken the two new weapons from Jinin's dead men, and not the innocent merchants. But he would never know for sure.

The Captain smiled brightly and waggled her fingers at him.

Devon swallowed hard and waved weakly back as she sprang away.

As she bounced past his wagon, Devon noticed the wild elf standing just beyond the line of wagons.

Dagmar Coal was tall and thin like the others. Her clothes were green and brown and blended with her surroundings. She was plain for an elf.

Her hair was brown and wildly curly. She did not have the dark allure of the southern elf or the sparkle and verve of the light elves. She certainly could not match the sheer coldness and sharpness of the ice elf. But Dagmar Coal had a serene air about her that Devon liked instantly. She was calm and quiet, and unlike her companions, Devon was not afraid of her.

The wild elf stood about thirty feet from him, arms hanging by her sides and gray eyes turned up toward the sky. She did not move, hardly breathed. Just when Devon wondered if she might be a bit touched, an amazing thing happened.

A falcon, a red one, dove from the sky straight for the elf. Devon heard the screech before he saw the bird. It startled him so that he stood and came down off the step shielding his eyes and peering into the sky.

The bird was moving at an alarming rate, "Hey!" Devon said, suddenly concerned the bird would attack the elf. "Hey! Watch out!"

But Dagmar held out a palm toward him.

A second before the bird would have crashed into her, Dagmar stepped back and held out her arm. Devon sucked in his breath as the red falcon reared and brought its feet forward. Shooting its wings outward, the graceful bird crested to a halt, landing on the elf's outstretched arm, where it began to coo and nuzzle its head near Dagmar's cheek.

Stunned, Devon cautiously moved forward. "How… how did you do that?"

Dagmar Coal turned her misty eyes on him and smiled as she petted the head of the falcon. "You might say I speak another language." She put her lips close to the bird's head. If she said anything to the animal, Devon did not hear. Then she threw her arms into the air and the bird was off.

Dagmar brushed her hands on her deep brown leathers and moved past him with a polite nod. Devon turned around and watched her go, stunned by this somewhat magical display.

Kiernan stood a few feet away "Are you ready, mage?" Kiernan asked.

Devon didn't answer, but slung his pack over his shoulder and moved toward the group.

"Good," Kiernan said, as if Devon's lack of response did not bother him. "You ride with Tain. Her horse is the largest and can easily carry two."

Devon was about to question why the smallest member of the group was in possession of the biggest horse when he came nose to nose with the animal. Two huge red orbs blinked at him. The mage let out a yelp of surprise and staggered backward.

Tain's horse was enormous. It completely dwarfed its mistress. Easily twenty hands high, it lacked the girth that seemed necessary to an animal so tall. It was as thin and sinewy as an elf. Its mane was—and here Devon had to rub his eyes—silver. Its coat was gray, with a metallic sheen that gave it an unusual shimmering quality.

And then there were the eyes. Devon hadn't been wrong. They *were* red.

He looked up at the imp, who seemed minuscule atop the gray monster. The proportions were all wrong. And yet it seemed appropriate that this creature from the land of fairies should have such an ethereal horse.

"Her name is Algoryn," the Captain announced.

Devon only stared at her.

"It means Joy," she explained.

Joy? Devon thought. In his opinion, the animal looked anything but joyful. It looked more like a demon's steed.

"Your horse has red eyes." It was the only thing he could think of to say.

"Wonderful observational skills, mage, simply wonderful," Panas said, trotting over on a white stallion. "Shall we expect an overabundance of perceptive wit on this journey, or are we out of clarifying declarations for the day?"

Devon decided he had had enough of the sarcastic light elf. "You know, fire-tip spells come in several sizes. The one I used on you was an extra-small. I'd be more than happy to demonstrate some of the larger ones for you."

"Oooooh…" Panas teased, waving his fingertips at the mage.

Devon ignored him and reached for Tain's outstretched hand.

"Leave him alone, Panas," she said. "If you hadn't been so busy falling out of that tree, he never would have hit you in the first place."

"I'll have you know I was in the process of saving your head, little one," Panas snapped at her.

"Well apparently you were doing it loudly," the imp shot back, hauling Devon onto the back of her horse with surprising ease.

Panas puffed out his chest. "It is not my fault those tree branches were wet and slimy."

The other members of *Duak-Thenal* laughed at the light elf.

"So, it's to Preliona, then?" Devon asked, trying to settle in on the back of the Captain's horse.

Dagmar rode up beside them, "Actually, no. Your friends headed toward the Pearl Song Trail. I assume they are making another stop."

"But their destination will eventually be Preliona. We should head there anyway. Cut them off?" Devon offered.

"We will catch them before Preliona," she replied with confidence.

Devon had to press the issue. "But would it not make more sense to head straight to the city where…"

Dagmar cut him off with a smile. "No," she said and urged her horse forward, ignoring any reply Devon might wish to give.

Devon was confused. "But…"

Nemesio leaned into the mage. "Events are unfolding in Preliona which we believe involve key people in the city. We do not wish to be dragged into that."

Devon narrowed his eyes. "Because you are outlaws, aren't you?"

"That's not true," Tain chimed in. "The Council knows about *Duak-Thenal*, but not who they are."

"They?" Devon asked.

"Most of our names have yet to be discovered by the Watch Chief. But he has issued warrants for the Captain," Nemesio said.

"He has not!" Tain protested. She looked over her shoulder at Devon. "I didn't steal anything from Preliona."

Panas leaned over to Devon. "She stole something from Yeelan."

"Several things, actually," Nemesio announced.

"*And…*" the imp sneered, "The Watch Chief got wind of it and has been snooping around ever since. No warrants, though."

"Yet," Nemesio added.

"The point is," Tain said, glaring at the southern elf, "Even though I'm the only one whose name is on paper in the city…"

"It's still a risk for all of us to enter right now," Nemesio finished.

"Why?" Devon asked.

"Because we were just there," Panas answered.

"Doing what?" Devon asked, genuinely curious.

Nemesio shook his head, "So many questions, mage."

"And too personal. After all, we just met," Tain added.

Nemesio rode ahead then and Tain offered nothing more, so Devon Bane was left to his own thoughts. Should they really be taking up time running after Jinin when they could just as easily cut him off and possibly elicit help from the Council at Preliona? And was the wild elf correct in assuming that Jinin would take the Pearl Song Trail? And if so, shouldn't they avoid that path altogether? And what had the elves done in Preliona? How many secrets were they keeping?

Devon felt a sudden chill and glanced to his side. Talesin Darken rode nearby on his black horse.

The ice elf was close. Too close, Devon thought. He could feel the frigid air emanating from the elf.

Suddenly the ice elf turned. Depthless pools of black stared at him. Devon froze. He could not look away, though he desperately wanted to. Talesin Darken's irises took up so much space in his eyes that only a sliver of white could be seen around them. His face was still and completely unreadable. The mage was more than glad when the strange elf finally turned his gaze away.

Devon offered up tiny prayer to *Ziyad* for a short, easy journey.

18~The Proof You Need

Mid-afternoon and Nimbus was living up to its name. The Council room was bathed in brilliant yellows and oranges as the sun passed overhead. The prism-like crystals in the room shot slivers of blues and purples into any shadowy crevice that natural light could not reach.

Under normal circumstances the sight would have been comforting. However, today was turning out to be anything but normal.

Gregory, half-elven scholar and aide to Governor Gaenor, had not been asleep since the night before last. Often up until the early morning hours, Gregory had been one of the first to discover that the governor had been attacked. He had been consulting with healers, council members and one large, angry wizard ever since.

Gregory covered his teal eyes with one hand and sank further into his chair. Twenty minutes after one o'clock, and the meeting had yet to start. It was amazing how disorganized things got when Althea was not around.

The governor's assistant glanced over at Cornelius. The wizard had taken a seat off to the right of the table. Other than drumming his fingers on the arm of his chair, he gave no sign that he was just as worried and tired as the half-elf.

Cornelius must have felt Gregory's gaze, for he suddenly looked in his direction. Though startled, Gregory managed to hold the man's rather intimidating stare. Cornelius blinked once and then rolled his eyes and nodded in the direction of the yammering councilors. Gregory snorted and nodded in return, sharing a private moment with the wizard.

"Ladies and gentlemen, would you please take your seats!"

Gregory jerked upright and smoothed his wrinkled robes as best he could. Not that it mattered. Everyone in the room was in the same rumpled shape he was.

He glanced over to the center of the room, where Laothist Benrist was attempting to get some attention. "Umm… excuse me, folks, if you could all take your seats. Yes, that's right, sit down now—thank you, thank you."

Gregory shook his head and muttered to himself as he glanced around the room. Most of the remaining council members were indeed moving to their seats, but certainly not with the air of urgency they should have had. No one wanted to listen to an overfed, underworked, hand-wringing merchant who couldn't bring a meeting to order any faster than he could run a marathon.

Gregory watched with growing unease as the salesman began waving his hands about. He stood on his toes and hopped up and down in an attempt at getting the Council's attention.

Suddenly Alistair was standing beside the merchant. He placed a heavy hand on Laothist's shoulder, keeping the man from making another undignified leap into the air. "Ladies and gentlemen!" Alistair boomed. The voice of military authority cut through the babble of the men and women in the room.

Gregory sighed at the silence.

Laothist practically beamed up at Alistair. "Sit down, all of you," Alistair growled. Without a word, the sleep-deprived occupants of Nimbus' main hall trudged to their seats. Alistair continued speaking, obviously in no mood to wait for scraping chairs and creaking knees. "Odin Darweshi is due to walk through that door in less than half an hour, so if you don't mind, I would like to discuss our next move before we all drop dead of exhaustion." Alistair threw himself into his chair and wiped his forehead with a handkerchief. "I don't suppose any of you would object to having some sort of plan formulated before the hotheaded son of a whore, pardon my language, starts frothing at the mouth again?"

Gregory snorted with laughter despite himself. But the rest of the Council seemed to have gone collectively pale at the Watch Chief's choice of words. Not a mouth remained closed in the semi-circle of faces. You had to give the old man credit—he sure knew how to get attention.

"Laothist," Alistair said with a small gesture to the merchant. "You may begin. Again."

Laothist clasped his hands together and gave Alistair an appreciative salute. Alistair rolled his eyes. Laothist seemed not to notice, turning instead to his captive audience and placing his stubby fingers on the table. He breathed deeply, as if he were about to give a lengthy oration. "As you know, Governor Althea was attacked last night by an unknown assailant. I defer now to Alistair to give you the details."

Laothist sat down and smiled at the Watch Chief, apparently pleased with his job so far. He seemed completely unaware of how close to death he was, as Alistair now eyed him with something close to a blistering rage.

The Watch Chief shook his head and pulled himself to his feet with an audible groan, moving to take Laothist's place at the center of the table. "Althea Gaenor was found in Dirt Alley behind the library at precisely three forty hours this morning by Cornelius Pav. She was brought directly to Nimbus. Healers have been with her ever since. I can tell you that she is alive, but I have little information beyond that. She was hit from behind by what Cornelius believes to have been a form of fireball spell. She has yet to regain consciousness. Until she does, if she does, we have no way of knowing exactly what happened."

Iris raised her hand, but Alistair held up one bony finger and she quickly dropped her arm back into her lap.

"After examining Dirt Alley, my people found evidence of a fight. Several pools of blood, not all of which could have been Althea's, were found there. I am fairly certain Althea was fighting off at least two assailants other than the mage who felled her." He scanned the room, looking at each of them over the bridge of his hawk nose. "I have already ruled out Cornelius as a suspect, so get that thought out of your heads right now."

Gregory shook his head in disgust as several people quite suddenly lowered their eyes, trying to find an interesting spot on the table to focus on.

"I absolutely guarantee that Odin Darweshi will blame *Duak-Thenal* for this attack, and in truth I have not ruled out this possibility. However, I caution you to be careful what you choose to do in these next few hours. Our leader is severely injured, and I have requested that Xanith Creese, our second in command, remain in Lasairian until further notice. Laothist," Alistair sneered, "Is *technically* in charge."

Gregory wondered how in the name of *Ziyad* this was possible. Laothist was a nice man with a good heart, but he had no head for leadership. His assistants ran his businesses for him. And yet by some strange fluke he remained the third from the top in the chain of command within the Council.

"I have asked Cornelius to stay here and observe today, though I have no doubt he would be here with or without my invitation." Alistair sat down, apparently out of bluster, for his voice took on a tired, listless quality. "So, we are down to ten. The two oldest and wisest among us have been taken unexpectedly out of the picture, and we are left to make decisions for a city they practically built. Again, I urge you to be careful of what you say and do now, for while I am a member of this Council and abide by its rules, I have a responsibility first and foremost to protect the walls of Preliona." Alistair clenched a fist and hammered it onto the table. "I *will not* allow an overprivileged son of a merchant dictate how I do my job." The Watch Chief settled again and pointed to the chamber door behind them. "For the sake of that lady in there, I hope you will do the same."

Gregory watched with newfound respect as Alistair scanned the table, eyeing each council member with conviction.

Laothist stood and waddled around the front of the table again, clearing his throat as he went. "Any questions?" Several hands went up at once. It took Laothist a moment to choose whom he would call on first. "Ummm… yes, Ranabee."

"We heard a rumor that a gold coin with an *X* scratched into it was found near the governor's body. Is that not the calling card of *Duak-Thenal*?"

Not surprisingly, Laothist wrung his hands and looked to Alistair for support.

The Watch Chief shrugged his shoulders and threw his hands into the air.

Laothist's brow furrowed. Gregory could tell he was unsure if Alistair meant him to answer the noblewomen's question or not. "Umm…well…hmmm…"

"Excuse me."

Every head in the room swiveled in the direction of the new voice. Cornelius Pav moved toward Laothist without waiting for an invitation. The sorcerer practically glided across the floor, his black, sleeveless cloak dragging on the marble behind him.

"If I may, sir," he began, "I believe I can be of some assistance regarding Lady Ranabee's question."

Gregory saw that Laothist was having some difficulty controlling the workings of his jaw. He was, along with most everyone else in the room, clearly terrified of the wizard. He couldn't have spoken if he wanted to.

Cornelius seemed to realize this, and simply smiled and nodded. "Thank you, sir," he said and gestured for Laothist to take his seat. Whether the merchant did so of his own accord or Cornelius' gesture was a motion of magic that helped Laothist along, Gregory did not know. Either way, he was thankful that the merchant had been silenced for the second time that afternoon.

Cornelius Pav stared directly at Ranabee Enri, who seemed to have shrunk into her chair a bit. "In answer to your question, milady, you are quite correct. I found the gold coin to which you refer."

Murmurs and grumbles of mistrust slipped through the group. Fale and Quinlan seemed particularly annoyed. The two had their heads together at one end of the table.

But if Cornelius noticed the two, he did not let on. "I do not believe that one scratched coin is much proof, especially since the governor had just such a coin on her yesterday."

Gregory only half listened as the rest of the council members went back to their grumbling. He had his hand in one of his many pockets holding tight to the very coin Cornelius was referring to. Althea had left it with him the night before. The half elf didn't know what Cornelius was playing at, but for the moment he was inclined to keep quiet.

"But Cornelius, surely you can't ask us to sit back and do nothing," Poorez said. "The people will demand that we act!"

"And you must resist the urge," the wizard replied.

"What would you have us do, exactly?" The jeweler stammered. "Tell the city folk that everything is all right?"

Cornelius remained calm in the face of Poorez's objections. "Do you have another suggestion?"

"Yes, dammit! Hunt the bastards down and see them punished!" Fale exclaimed.

Cornelius turned to the dwarf. "I would remind you of Governor Gaenor's own words: Do not act without the proof you need."

His speech was met with silence. Even snobbish Poorez had nothing to say. Gregory glanced about at his comrade's faces.

"The truth is, ladies and gentlemen," Cornelius went on, "Not a shred of evidence has come to light to connect *Duak-Thenal* with the type of unwarranted assault that occurred last night."

"What about the attack at the S'Trobenue house?"

Every member of the Council started at the sound of the voice. Together they turned to meet the man whose arrival they had been dreading all morning.

He was dressed in a deep purple today. His short cape fairly flew out behind him as he entered the room. Odin's large frame was powerful and intimidating. Gregory knew that without Althea and Xanith to hold him in check, the merchant could walk all over the Council this day.

With the merchant was a small entourage of heavily armed men. Gregory wondered just exactly how they had made it past the Watch.

Cornelius faced the merchant lord and crossed his massive arms before him. "You have proof of some wrongdoing, Lord Darweshi, or do you simply bring friends to tell us what you want us to hear?"

Gregory sat up tensely as Darweshi's jaw clenched. "Sigmund S'Trobenue was killed, and we have three witnesses who say it was at the hand of a red-haired elf."

"Edmee S'Trobenue's cousins have spent most of their evenings rip-roaring drunk for as long as I can remember, Odin," said Cornelius with a wave of his hand. "What is your point?"

One of the large men at Odin's side took a threatening step toward the wizard, but Darweshi held out a hand to stop the advance.

That must be one of the cousins, Gregory thought. The man had listless blond hair, as did the two young men behind him. They were as nondescript as they were dangerous. Gregory was quite impressed by the hold Odin seemed to have over the S'Trobenue clan. Odin now said, "My point, dear councilors, is—what if the elf was responsible for the death of Edmee as well?"

Alistair snorted in response and shook his head. "You are reaching, Odin," he said.

But Darweshi pressed the issue, his dark eyes flaring. "You will ignore this information, then? Fine. I am sure the public that you profess to protect will have something to say about that."

Alistair was on his feet faster than Gregory had ever seen the older man move. He was across the room in four quick steps. A foot or so from the merchant he stopped. "Do you dare threaten me, Darweshi?"

Odin held out his hands in a gesture of complacency. His large square face was all innocence now. "I would simply make sure that the rest of the city was as well informed as you seem to be, sir."

Alistair was seething, Gregory could see from his diagonal view, but he was holding his anger in check admirably. "I have been over Edmee S'Trobenue's case and I consider it closed. No evidence of the involvement of elves has ever come to light."

"No evidence has come to light, period," Odin challenged. "We all know what a thorough job you always do, Alistair, but if you have found nothing at all. Doesn't that make it possible that *Duak-Thenal* might conceivably be suspect?"

There was a moment when Gregory sincerely hoped the Watch Chief would punch the merchant, but Alistair turned away, pursing his lips and clenching his jaw.

"Lord Darweshi!" Judith Mercy called out. "If your accusations are true—if *Duak-Thenal* is responsible for Edmee S'Trobenue's death—then what were they doing at her home the other night? Finishing off the rest of the family?"

Odin smiled. "Why not ask her husband?"

Gregory sat up straighter in his chair as a murmur went around the table. "Explain that comment, please," Quinlan said.

The merchant folded his arms across his chest and raised both his eyebrows. "I am simply suggesting that you speak to her husband—if you can find him," Odin said.

Gregory could no longer keep quiet. "Lord Darweshi, I hope you are not honestly suggesting Raymond S'Trobenue had anything to do with the attack on the family home—his home, I might add."

Odin barely afforded Gregory a glance. Instead, he turned to Cornelius and a knowing smile passed his lips. "I have said no such thing, scholar. Because the truth is, Raymond is gone."

"What do you mean? Where has he gone?" Poorez asked.

The chatter around the table rose again but Gregory had just noticed Alistair whispering to Cornelius, who did not seem at all surprised by Odin's revelation.

"Raymond *is* gone." Alistair announced. "But how do *you* know that?" he asked, taking a step toward Odin. "This matter was brought to Althea's attention days ago, but you were not there. Why the sudden interest?"

Odin remained calm in the face of Alistair's mounting suspicions. "These honorable men here informed me." He motioned to the S'Trobenue cousins. "As to my interest, well… I only wish to see to the wellbeing of my dead architect's family. I adored Edmee and would hate to find out that some foul play had befallen her family." Odin puffed out his bottom lip. "I have come to help Alistair," he pouted.

Alistair turned from him with a snort.

"Give us information if you have it, Darweshi," Judith said flatly. "Or else go away and let us solve our problems in peace."

Odin bowed slightly to Judith, though the look in his eyes carried not one ounce of respect for the woman. "The last time Raymond was seen, he was in the garden of his house and dangerously close to a red-haired elf." Gregory saw one of the cousins lean close to Odin and whisper something into his ear. Odin shifted his gaze and looked directly at Alistair. "Oh yes, and I almost forgot. The imp was there as well."

Alistair's eyes widened. "What!" he growled.

That's it, thought Gregory, *we've lost him*.

Odin smirked. "Thought that might get your attention."

Alistair stared at the cousins and moved slowly in their direction. "Why didn't you tell me this before?"

"We didn't make the connection," one of the men offered. "We were unsure if it was indeed the Captain thief."

Alistair eyed them. "And now you are?"

The man shrugged. Alistair sighed and turned to the Council. "It appears I will have to reopen the case."

Odin rushed forward. "Then of course you admit that there is a possible connection between Raymond's disappearance and the attack on Althea!"

Alistair rounded on Odin. "I'll admit nothing of the sort! I am yet unaware of any evidence that would condemn either *Duak-Thenal*, whose members we have yet to find a description of, or Captain Tain Elire."

Odin scowled, his dark eyes going dangerously black. "You know that the Captain runs with the group. As far as I'm concerned, that alone guarantees the red-haired elf is part of the group!"

"Can you even prove to me that the imp they saw was indeed the infamous Captain?" Alistair pointed out.

Odin laughed. "You know of another black-clad imp that shows up in the gardens of unsuspecting humans?"

Several council members chuckled at that, and Gregory knew that Alistair had lost the battle. He glanced over at Cornelius, who had remained strangely quiet during the proceedings, chin in hand and brow creased. Gregory couldn't be sure, but he thought the wizard looked worried.

"You must admit there is more than a coincidence here, Alistair," Poorez said quietly.

"And of course, there is the matter of the coin," Odin pressed, one hand resting lightly under his squared chin. He hit on the original doubt of the Council as if he were hammering a nail in a coffin.

Alistair had gotten very stiff off to one side. He was nodding his head at Odin, as if to say, *you win. I cannot fight you on this one.*

The thin old man turned to the Council. "Vote, then. I have had my say, and *he* has certainly had his. It is in your hands."

Alistair threw himself into his chair as Laothist stood and cleared his throat. "Right, then. Those in favor of treating this… *Duak-Thenal* as a dangerous threat to Preliona, of treating them and the Captain Tain Elire as suspects in the death of Edmee S'Trobenue, the disappearance of her husband, and the attack on Governor Althea Gaenor…"

"And of the attack on my architect," Odin interrupted.

Laothist raised an eyebrow and looked to Alistair who nodded. "Right," he said, "And of taking the highest actions against them?" Laothist turned back to the Council, "All in favor?"

Eight ayes echoed through the marble hall.

"All opposed?" Alistair and Gregory voiced their nays almost under their breaths.

"Motion passed." Laothist sat down with a relieved sigh.

Alistair placed his gnarled hands on the arms of his chair. "Consider the case of Edmee S'Trobenue reopened, Darweshi," he said. "I will assume that Raymond is missing for now. Until further evidence comes to light, I am unwilling to tack kidnapping onto the list of crimes the imp Captain is accused of—though I cannot account for the company she keeps." He turned now to address the Council. "I will also consider what impact these events have on the current situation involving Governor Gaenor, though I would warn you all, nothing that has been said here today proves anything. I will expect these conversations to remain in this room, people. I look to you to keep these proceedings confidential."

Odin scowled. "But the public should know…"

"*The public will know when I see fit to tell them!*"

As frustrated as Gregory knew the Watch Chief was, he couldn't help but grin when Odin took a startled step back.

But the outburst was over as quickly as it had begun, and Alistair was all business again. "Rest assured, friends, security will be stepped up to its highest level and I will be discussing those plans with you all at further length." He stood with a sigh and placed his hands on the table. "Now if there is nothing further, I move to dismiss this meeting."

Gregory was about to second the motion when a small voice at the table's center spoke up. "Umm… excuse me, Alistair?"

Laothist had his hand up. Alistair swung his gray-haired head in his direction. "What."

Laothist took a deep breath. "It's my job to dismiss the meeting."

Alistair's eyes widened and Gregory was almost sure that Laothist would be the next to incur the Watch Chief's wrath.

But instead, Alistair spun on his heel and stormed out of the room without a nod of acknowledgement to anyone.

Cornelius watched him go and wondered if he should follow. If anyone deserved to know what was really going on, it was Alistair. He did not move, however. Odin had pushed all the right buttons today and Alistair needed time to recover his crumpled ego.

The wizard left the Council room, intent on going back to Althea's quarters. For the first time in as long as he could remember, he was uncertain of what steps to take next. He risked exposing himself by involving the Watch Chief, but Cornelius figured he could deal with that. It was this cloak and dagger game he was tired of. He was too damned old—and now his best friend had nearly died because of it. For he had no doubt now that whoever had attacked Althea had done so for some reason connected to the elves.

Cornelius could clear *Duak-Thenal's* name right now. But before he did that, he wanted to talk to Kiernan Nightwing. He could not defend *Duak-Thenal* without uncovering their identities. He had already done that with Althea, and minutes later she had been attacked. He would not risk that again.

No, the best he could do was to try to hamper Alistair's efforts. Steer him in the wrong direction, if that was possible. The Watch Chief had certainly been willing to drop the *Duak-Thenal* angle. Right up until Odin mentioned the Captain, that is. She was not exactly public enemy number one in Preliona, but she was infamous enough for Alistair to want to catch her.

Cornelius saw no easy way out of this. Every trained eye in Preliona would be watching for *Duak-Thenal* now, and they would all recognize the Captain when they saw her.

And Cornelius had no way of warning them.

19~A Powerful Ally

According to Dagmar, they were only a couple of hours behind the fleeing group of thieves. If they continued to move at their current pace, they should catch up to Jinin and his mercenaries by nightfall.

The wild elf was currently scouting ahead without her horse, most likely clambering through the trees overhead. So far, the ride through the Pearl Song Trail had been uneventful; there was no reason it should not have been. Most of the long stretch of dry, dusty land served as an ancient burial ground to a tribal group of humans who used to wander this section of the Northern Realms.

Kiernan knew the route well, having traveled it with his crew many times, so he was wholly surprised then when his scout appeared on the trail before them, running at top speed, frantically motioning them off the road.

Talesin moved first. "Off the road, move!" he hissed at them, and spurred his black horse over to one side.

Kiernan and Nemesio followed as the prince motioned for Tain, Panas and Devon to take to the opposite side of the trail. The clamor the human made grated on the prince's nerves. He could only hope that whatever had followed Dagmar down the path did not have the keen hearing the elves did.

Kiernan slid off his horse and crouched down next to Talesin. He could clearly make out the shapes of the others across from him. Panas and Tain had placed Devon between them, and both had drawn their weapons. To his credit, the mage was trying to be as silent as his neighbors.

Nemesio had silently drawn his bow and was aiming it at the now deserted road. Dagmar had vacated to a safer place, apparently, as Kiernan no longer saw her. He badly wished she would give them some sign that she was safe, but Kiernan knew she would not chance it. All they could do now was wait.

And they did not have to wait for long.

A strong gust of wind suddenly swept through the trail, picking up dirt and dry leaves as it went, forcing the company to shield their eyes. The sounds of the world were sucked from the space, making the area a tunnel through which only one noise was heard: a high-pitched keening that tore along the forest floor, a vanguard to the frightening sight that followed.

A cluster of translucent creatures flew toward them at top speed. They traveled as a group, their corporeal forms overlapping so that the prince could not get an accurate count of their number. He could see them well enough to recognize torn and tattered remnants of the clothing they once wore.

Someone had disturbed the burial ground and its spirits.

They moved so quickly that at first Kiernan was hopeful the ghosts would pass them by entirely.

The spectres came up short, however, directly in front of their hiding place—as if they sensed the presence of living beings. Kiernan was mildly surprised by the sound of his own breath catching in his throat. They were greenish in hue and nearly skeletal in shape and form. He could see no way past them.

The keening noise lessened somewhat as the spectres split up. They loped about, slipping back and forth through the air, blurred fragments of their former selves, searching the area for those who had disturbed them.

Then without warning, the spirits shot into the air and disappeared among the leaves of the trees. The prince turned to Talesin, who shrugged his shoulders. Nemesio let out a sigh of relief. "That was strange," he said.

"Indeed," Talesin agreed.

Kiernan looked up again and saw nothing. He was about to give the signal to come out when Panas let out a yell of surprise and came tumbling out of his hiding place.

Kiernan and Talesin stood as Panas rolled into the road, came up to his knees, and turned in time to duck under one diving, screaming ghost. The light elf flattened his body onto the dirt as Talesin and Kiernan lunged forward, swords drawn. Both elves felt the whoosh of air near their ears that signaled the release of Nemesio's arrows.

But the flying weapons sailed harmlessly through the attacking ghosts.

Panas was attempting to gain his feet when another ghost dive-bombed him, forcing him to the ground again. Panas cursed loudly as a spray of dirt clouded around him. Kiernan and Talesin reached him just as Dagmar dropped from the trees above. She grabbed Panas by the collar, hauled him to his feet and shoved him out of the way.

The wild elf dove in the opposite direction, leaving Kiernan to face another swooping specter. He heaved his sword into both hands and stood ready to lash out, though he knew it would do little good. After all, what did a ghost have to fear from a blade, even a black one?

But the apparition aimed to surprise, for it came up short a few feet from the prince. Kiernan was startled but did not give up his stance. The creature hung in midair, misshapen and gaunt, its ghostly clothing hanging in tatters and its eyes swiveling about. The prince was slightly disturbed to see the ghost studying him as if looking for a weak spot in its opponent.

If it found one Kiernan never knew, for the ghost lunged at him. The prince ducked and spun about, slashing his sword clear through the thing. He should have come up behind the specter, but he had not. He spun around again and came face to face with his opponent, its leering visage so close he could feel the cold radiating off it. The prince took a step back and prepared to dodge again.

This time he swore the ghost grinned at him before diving at him.

The prince held his ground. Holding his sword in both hands he swung across his body, slicing into the ghost.

The specter never even slowed. Before Kiernan could move, the creature passed right through him.

There was a panicked moment when his vision went gray and Kiernan had a clear look at the world through the eyes of a ghost. Everything before him took on a drab and colorless quality that immediately saddened him to the point of utmost despair.

Then the ghost was gone. Kiernan felt as if he had been frozen. He was cold and stiff and the wind had been knocked out of him. He felt himself gasp once, and then he could not seem to get a breath in or out. He clutched at his chest and his sword clattered to the ground. Dimly he heard Talesin call to him… and then he was falling.

Kiernan Nightwing hit the dirt with such force that his forehead nearly met the ground. He managed to lift his head enough to see Talesin standing over him, but the rest of his body seemed unwilling to obey his commands.

Talesin had his back to the prince and was holding off several other specters. To Kiernan's surprise, the ice elf seemed to be succeeding. His massive double-bladed sword connected with the diving ghosts, glowing an eerie blue each time it made contact. He hit one ghost after another, sending them screaming away. They kept coming back, but it was obvious Talesin was hurting them.

"Your sword…" The rest was lost in a fit of coughing, but Talesin seemed to comprehend.

"Dagmar!" he called out, motioning for the wild elf to come closer.

Kiernan looked up to see Dagmar and Panas dragging a stumbling Nemesio between them. "One of them flew right through him," Panas announced as he and Dagmar let the southern elf slip to the ground. Nemesio landed next to the prince, also gasping for air and shivering uncontrollably.

Kiernan looked up at Dagmar. "Tain?" he coughed.

"Over there," Panas yelled, and pointed over their shoulders.

Everyone except Talesin turned to see Tain Elire fiercely swinging her staff at several specters. Like Talesin, she seemed to be having some luck. The ghosts were hanging back. Each time one moved to attack, the Captain's staff would emanate a bluish arc of light that held the specters at bay. Kiernan had never seen her staff act that way before. He knew the weapon was unbreakable, but he had never thought of it as magical.

The orange clad mage stood near the Captain. Kiernan had completely forgotten about the boy. He could dimly see him now behind the bright orange flashes of light shooting from his fingertips that created fiery explosions.

"Well, well. The little boy can defend himself, after all," Panas snorted.

"Get them over here," Kiernan gasped, his voice cracking.

Talesin was yelling for the imp. In a moment they both were running toward the group, followed by the rest of the ghosts.

"Everybody down!" the imp yelled. She leapt clear across the huddled group of elves, and landed like a cat, positioning herself directly opposite Talesin. Without a break in stride she was swinging her staff once again, desperately keeping the damned souls away from her friends.

Kiernan reached for his fallen sword and tried to grasp it. But he could not quite wrap his fingers around the pommel. Frustrated, he tried to gain his knees, but Dagmar reached out and gently pulled him back to the ground.

"There is nothing you can do," she said simply.

Kiernan was about to argue when a bright flash of orange forced him to shield his eyes. When his vision cleared Kiernan saw Devon Bane standing over him.

The mage's back was to him, but Kiernan still caught a glimpse of dexterous fingers circling the air. Arcane words slipped from his lips, bringing about another flash of light, much larger than the last. Devon's spell disintegrated one of their attackers.

Kiernan's mouth fell open. "Can you do that again?" he asked.

Devon glanced over his shoulder, and then turned back to the task before him. He smiled. "Actually, I planned on it." And another burst of orange lit the air. Another ghost gone.

Kiernan nodded in admiration, "How about getting rid of them all at once?" He suggested.

Devon didn't even turn. "Too dangerous," he said.

"For who? You?"

"All of us," Devon growled over his shoulder.

Kiernan crawled closer to the mage. "But it can be done?"

"Yes, but it is an extremely complicated spell. I could over-calculate and kill us all. We'd end up floating around like them. It's too dangerous," he said again.

Kiernan grabbed the mage's robe and pulled.

Devon cried out in surprise as he was forced to crouch down in front of the prince. "What is dangerous," Kiernan said through gritted teeth, "Is eliminating them one at a time. Talesin and Tain can only hold them off for so long before they tire and one of them gets through."

"The explosion could fry us all!" Devon protested. "I'm telling you it's a bad idea."

Kiernan tried to remain calm. "And I'm telling you - we're not going to get out of here if you don't." He cocked his head. "Or can't you?"

"I didn't say that," Devon hissed, trying to pull away from the elf. But Kiernan held on.

He looked around at the only two members of his group who were able to fight. The imp and the ice elf were taxed to their limit holding off the remaining attackers. The ghosts did not dive as a group but took turns menacing Tain and Talesin endlessly. It was not possible for them to hold their end of this fight much longer. "I am afraid we have little choice left to us, mage." Kiernan said. "You will have to attempt something."

The mage locked eyes with the elf and frowned. "Fine," he spat, and stood up.

Tain, who had overheard the conversation, turned to Panas. "Pick me up," she demanded.

Panas wasted no time with smart comebacks. He whisked the tiny imp into the air. Resting precariously on the light elf's shoulders, the Captain began to twirl her staff over head like a baton. The five-foot-long piece of wood glowed an eerie blue and kept the specters far enough away so that even Talesin was able to lower his weapon.

The wide berth gave the mage the room he needed to recite the complicated spell.

"Don't worry mage. If you fry us, we won't hold it against you."

Kiernan saw that Devon was ignoring Panas and was now completely immersed in the casting of his spell. Only three sounds broke through the silent trail – the high-pitched screaming of the ghosts, the whirring of Tain's twirling staff, and the whisper of arcane words coming from the young mage next to him.

And then the sky exploded.

The prince did not so much dive to the ground as he was pushed by an enormous wall of hot air. He crashed into Panas' legs accidentally taking the light elf down with him. He heard Tain howl and caught a glimpse of the imp flying. Then he was forced to cover his head or have his eyes burned from their sockets by the immense orange light surrounding them.

The screaming of the ghosts reached an unbearable pitch and then there was a great popping noise. It was the only way the prince could describe the sound he heard. A zap in the sky—and then silence.

Kiernan slowly lifted his head.

Panas was sprawled on the ground next to him and was just beginning to raise himself. He nodded to the prince, signaling that he was all right, and stood shakily.

Kiernan got to his knees and turned around. Talesin stood nearby, brushing off his blue cloak and moving toward his leader. He held out a hand to Kiernan, who took it and allowed himself to be pulled to his feet. The two elves looked about for their friends. Panas had helped Nemesio up and both were digging Dagmar out from under a fallen branch.

"Is she all right?" Kiernan called out, taking a step forward.

"She's fine," Panas yelled back, nearly laughing aloud at the string of curses emanating from the wild elf's lips. "Where is Tain?"

"Up here!"

Talesin and Kiernan looked up. The imp was perched on the limb of a nearby tree. Unfortunately, the tree was a tall one and its trunk too thin and slippery to scale down. She was stuck. Talesin chuckled. "Need a hand, Captain?"

"I'll thank you not to laugh," she said, jumping down into Talesin's waiting arms.

"Kiernan, where is Devon?" the imp asked once she was safely on the ground.

The prince's heart skipped. He turned and scanned the area around them for signs of the mage who had saved them.

Dusk had caught up to them and it was difficult to see. Kiernan focused his keen eyes into the gloom, narrowing his search for the human. The horses had scattered but the prince could hear snorting and stomping hooves not far off. Through the misty air he could just make out a brownish lump at the base of a tree.

Kiernan's breath caught. "*Kelina!*"

The prince ran and slid to his knees near the mass of rusty robes, praying that he would not find a burned human beneath.

With a surprisingly steady hand he pulled back the robes.

Devon Bane lay unconscious on the ground. A small trickle of blood ran down the side of his head.

"Is he dead?" Talesin asked.

Kiernan reached for the mage's throat, intending to feel for a pulse. As soon as his fingers touched the human's skin, the mage awoke with a start.

"What happened?" he mumbled, thrashing about.

Kiernan took the mage by the shoulders. "Calm down, Devon," he said. "You are hurt."

Devon's eyes fell on the prince and his eyebrows rose in surprise. "You're still alive."

Kiernan laughed. "And so are you. We all made it, thanks to you."

"They are gone?" the mage asked.

Kiernan nodded. "They are. How do you feel?"

Devon put a hand to his bruised head. "I feel like I hit a tree."

Kiernan looked up at Talesin, who was staring down at the mage with as much respect as he had ever seen the ice elf muster for anyone. "Stay here," Kiernan commanded, and he stood up. "Tain, take Panas with you and round up the horses. Nemy, how do you feel?"

"Still a little stiff, but I'll live."

Kiernan nodded. "Can you look at our magical friend here? He got into a bit of a mess with that tree."

Nemesio knelt next to the human as Kiernan motioned for Dagmar and Talesin to follow him.

The three huddled out of earshot of the mage. "What are you thinking?" Dagmar asked.

Kiernan looked at Devon then back at the two elves. "I'm thinking I'm glad he's on our side."

"More powerful than you expected, isn't he?" Talesin said.

"Yes. And more powerful than probably he or his teacher realizes."

"Should we be leery of him?" Talesin asked.

Kiernan shook his head after thinking a moment. "No."

Talesin and Dagmar were silent a moment, waiting for the prince to continue.

When he did not Dagmar asked, "What do we do with him?"

"Nothing," the prince responded. "If the mage wanted to be rid of us, he could certainly have done it before now—he's more than powerful enough. He could easily have let us be defeated by those banshees back there, but he risked his own life instead. No, I think the mage is not only innocent of Kalli's accusations, but is caught in the middle of a situation we have yet to comprehend."

Dagmar sighed. "I will be happy when this is over. I suggest we move as soon as we are able and find a suitable place to stop off the trail. We will never catch up to Jinin this night."

"Agreed," Kiernan said.

They dispersed. Kiernan and his exhausted crew mounted their skittish horses and prepared to travel at least far enough to put the graveyard behind them.

Kiernan watched as Nemesio boosted Devon onto the back of Tain's horse. He wondered how it was that his sister could have been so wrong about this. He intended to ask her as soon as they reached her school. A talk with the elven sorceress was long overdue.

20~Prejudices

It took them the better part of two hours to find a suitable place to camp. The troop could have stopped just on the other side of Pearl Song Trail, but none of them was eager to sleep with the thin road still in sight, ghosts still fresh on their minds.

Devon was so tired that he would have been perfectly happy to bed down at the base of the tree he had hit, but the elves would not allow it. They were slave drivers, he decided, certainly not the cowards he had accused them of being, for he had seen them fight and that sight had left a lasting impression on the mage's mind.

With the rocking motion of a gigantic horse underneath him, Devon had fallen asleep against Tain's back. The little thief had tried her best to keep from waking him, but the fairy's bony shoulders did not make for much of a pillow, and the mage did not sleep long.

Slightly shaken but no worse for the wear, *Duak-Thenal* stopped for the night in a small shelter about one hundred yards off the road. An enormous maple, whose lowest branches came down to a level twice the height of Nemesio, served as their protection from the light drizzle the evening offered.

Panas, suddenly friendly, helped Devon with his things and set him up under the tree, giving him a wink when he was finished. Devon didn't know why he was surprised. The light elf seemed subject to a mood swing every hour or so—Devon had begun to expect them.

Devon scowled at the elf and watched as the others set up a perimeter for the night. Dagmar immediately disappeared, grabbing her crossbow from her back, and slipping into the woods. Nemesio and Panas unloaded the horses and hid the animals from sight. Tain seemed to be collecting stones, presumably for a fire pit, and Kiernan covered their tracks with branches and leaves.

Talesin took the first watch. On his way he passed near the mage. Devon didn't want to look at the ice elf, but he couldn't help himself. He was like a ghost himself. He floated across the dirt and grass in almost total silence, wearing long layers of cool dark blues that hid the double-bladed, magical sword he had wielded so fiercely earlier that evening. He kept his hood up as he passed, but Devon still caught a glimpse of black depthless eyes peering out at him. Talesin may have been smaller than the others, but he was certainly no less intimidating.

Devon was afraid of him. He had to keep himself from cringing as the elf passed—so he was genuinely surprised when Talesin nodded to him as he went by. Caught off guard, the mage attempted a smile, but what he produced was more of a grimace than anything. If the ice elf noticed or cared, he did not show it and Devon sighed with relief when he had passed.

By the time the rest of the elves had finished setting up camp, the rain had stopped. Tain came skipping over, dropped several stones onto the ground and plopped down beside him. She crossed her legs and grinned at him. "How're ya feelin'?" she asked.

"Much better," he lied. Truthfully, the sound of Tain's armful of stones hitting the hard ground had brought Devon's headache crashing back. He didn't tell the imp this.

He had something else to talk about. "May I ask you something?" he said.

The imp's wide blue eyes blinked slowly at him. "You may."

For a moment he hesitated. The imp's eyes were so guileless and seemingly full of innocence that staring at them made him feel like he might lose himself in the depths of their blueness. The fairy's entire face was an exercise in contradiction. Eyes too big for her face to hold, a mischievous smile that practically erased the innocent youthfulness of her features. He had no idea how old this creature was, but she had outlived him multiple times—of that he was certain. She gazed at him now with a knowing look that made Devon squirm.

"Go on, Devon Bane," she said quietly. "Ask me your question."

He cleared his throat. "It's about Talesin," he began. "Aren't ice elves supposed to be vicious, cold-blooded killers?"

The imp did not even blink. "Aren't human mages supposed to be greedy, power-hungry tyrants?"

Devon was taken aback. "Of course not!" he objected.

He waited for the fairy to respond but she only gave him a smiling look of reproach.

Devon closed his eyes and shook his head. "I'm sorry," he said. "That was a thoughtless thing to say."

"It was," she acknowledged. "But I accept your apology." Tain opened her pack and spread out her blanket. "Talesin can be a bit scary at times, I admit, but you must realize what type of life he has led."

"You mean where he grew up? What was it like?" Devon pressed, curiosity getting the better of him.

Tain stopped arranging her things and cocked her head. "I don't really know."

Devon opened his hands. "But you just said…" He sighed and put his hands back in his lap. "Then how do you know his environment is responsible for his actions?"

"I don't," she replied in all seriousness. "No one does. I was referring to Talesin's life when he first left Serenia."

Devon's brow furrowed. "Oh? Which was what?"

Tain folded her hands in her tiny lap and leaned forward. Her eyes were dark and sad. "Talesin spent time in a prison called Che'ne, far north of here."

Devon's eyes widened. "For what?"

Tain shrugged. "He has never said. But the place was run entirely by human mages."

Devon got the picture. "They tortured him?"

The imp nodded solemnly.

"That would explain a lot," Devon muttered.

He wanted to ask more when Panas and Nemesio joined them. Both elves dropped their packs and began setting themselves up for the night. Panas sat unnervingly close to Devon and the mage afforded him a sideways glance.

The light elf hardly seemed to notice. He sidled even closer to the mage and Devon inched away.

"So, Devon," Panas began. "Are you married?"

"What? No!" Devon exclaimed. "I am not even out of school."

"Geez, Panas, he's a bit young, don't you think?" Tain asked.

Panas rolled his eyes. "Well, how do I know how old a human is?" he protested. "He looks older than you, Captain."

"And that would make him over one hundred." Nemesio said.

Question answered, Devon thought.

"My point is, Devon, do you have a girl or something at school?"

"Well there was this one girl, but..." Devon suddenly noticed that Tain and Nemesio were snickering and that Panas was gazing at him with more than passing interest. "What!?" the mage said, throwing his arms in the air.

Tain was laughing harder now. "Devon... Panas doesn't..."

"Hush, Tain," Panas hissed. "Devon and I are discussing the status of him and his lady friend. Now, Devon, how serious are you and this little girl sorceress?"

Devon narrowed his eyes and studied the light elf. He seemed genuinely curious, but Devon found something suspicious about the elf's look. "Things didn't work out," Devon hedged. "Why do you want to know?"

Tain could hold it in no longer. "He's not interested, Panas!" she said, through snorts of laughter.

"Tain!" Panas shouted. "I was not flirting—I was simply curious!"

"You were too, Panas," she went on. "You're always flirting."

Devon glanced from the imp to the light elf and back again and suddenly his eyes went wide. "Ohhhhh," Devon whispered, realization suddenly dawning on him.

He turned and looked at Panas, who wiggled the tips of his fingers at the mage.

"I... ah... I..." Devon sputtered.

"It's all right, mage," Panas said, laying a hand on his shoulder. "I'm not interested in you." He sighed, his golden eyes glazing over. "But I do so love hearing about the love lives of others."

Devon found himself laughing with the others. He could not help but be charmed by Panas the Hawk.

"So, what were we whispering about, little ones?" Panas quipped.

Tain threw him an apple from her bag and then handed one to Devon and Nemesio. "The mage was curious about Talesin's limitless hospitality."

Panas snorted and Nemesio smacked him in the back of the head. "Let me guess," the southern elf said. "The mage wants to know why we let a heathen ice elf into our ranks?"

Devon began to protest. "I didn't mean..."

But Nemesio held up a hand. "Of course you didn't, but curiosity has a way of turning your words around, doesn't it? Whatever you were thinking in your head did not come out of your mouth the way you had planned, did it?"

Devon frowned in embarrassment, thinking of his stuttering reaction to Panas the Hawk moments before. "I guess not."

Nemesio smiled warmly. He possessed the kind of control Devon expected to see in a much older man. Wisdom, kindness and understanding oozed from him. Nemesio had the features of a young elf, dark, but sharp and angular, with violet eyes that, kind as they were, flashed with intelligence and scrutiny. "Do not be too hard on yourself, mage; we all did the same thing at one time or another."

"You mean *Duak-Thenal* was not always a happy-go-lucky group of adventurers?" Devon asked, a note of sarcasm edging into his voice.

The three paused and looked at each other. Then they all laughed. "You don't miss much, do you, mage?" Nemesio concluded.

Devon shrugged. "Simple deduction. There are six of you from five quite different cultures. You could not all have started out as friends."

"Well, no swords were drawn on our first meeting, but few friendly words were exchanged either," Nemesio conceded.

Devon shifted slightly, trying to get more comfortable. "So how did you manage? You can't tell me that overnight you forgot your differences and became the fighting force you are today."

Panas looked at Nemesio. "Cynical little pint, isn't he?"

But Nemesio ignored him and continued to eye Devon with his strange purple orbs. "Let me ask *you* a question," he said calmly. "Imagine you are walking down a well-traveled road. Moving toward you from the opposite direction is a large troll. What do you do? Ready a spell? Draw your weapon? At the very least, would you hide or even run back the way you came?"

Devon opened his mouth, but Nemesio did not give him time to answer. "Of course you would," he said, "Because all trolls are evil, right?" The southern elf dropped his voice slightly and leaned in toward the mage. "But what if this troll was simply looking for directions?"

Devon slowly nodded in understanding. "Your point is taken," he said. "Not all ice elves are vicious and cruel, just as all human mages do not torture helpless prisoners."

Nemesio turned sharply to Tain. "You told him that?"

Tain shrugged. "He asked."

Nemesio frowned, but Devon went on. "Explain to me, then, why it is that while you few choose to live together, the rest of your kind remain secluded in their own faraway kingdoms."

Panas smiled and nodded in growing admiration. "Can't put anything past you, eh?"

"Perhaps we should let Kiernan continue this conversation," Nemesio said.

Devon looked up and watched as Kiernan Nightwing and Dagmar Coal approached. The red-haired elf moved sharply, constantly glancing about his surroundings as if he expected an attack at any moment. His long brown cloak hung over his arm and his pale blue tunic only made him look younger than Devon already suspected he was. The mage scanned the light elf's tanned features and suddenly decided he did not wish to press any further into the lives of this company. It was not that their leader looked angry, but Kiernan Nightwing's brow did seem to be in a permanent furrow.

This is a creature who could worry even on the sunniest of days.

Dagmar Coal, on the other hand, seemed completely at ease in her surroundings. The ethereal wild elf moved with the grace of a wolf next to the quick sharp movements of her companion. She did not remove her green cloak, but instead let it float about her, puckered by her slightest movement. If she anticipated danger, she did not show it. She looked straight ahead, casually brushing her unruly brown hair from her face.

Fire shone in Kiernan's green eyes, but a smooth gray mist clouded Dagmar's. They could not have been more different.

"What conversation would that be?" Kiernan asked as he and Dagmar put down their packs and took a seat.

"Why, the history of bigotry among our races!" Panas answered grandly, leaning back on the grass.

Nemesio kicked him. "Not exactly. The mage was simply curious about our long-suffering cause."

Kiernan settled himself between Dagmar and Tain and studied the mage. "So, you have come to the conclusion that we are not the murderous bandits you thought we were?"

"Not yet," Devon replied, becoming slightly defensive.

Kiernan Nightwing was not fazed. "Well, I see no reason not to tell you the truth. As much as we can, anyway," he said pointedly, looking at the others. "You've more than earned it. Very well, the history of *Duak-Thenal*."

Tain and Panas pounded on their thighs with their fists: a drum-roll introduction.

Dagmar laughed. Nemesio rolled his eyes. "Go on, Kiernan."

Kiernan stretched his legs out in front of him and leaned back on his hands. "Well Devon, how's your knowledge of history?"

Devon shrugged. "How far back are we going?"

"About a thousand years."

Devon grimaced. "Rusty at best," he admitted. "Not many humans around the Northern Realms at that time."

Kiernan nodded. "Correct." He sat up and dug around in his pack. He pulled out a small, battered map and spread it out on the ground before them. "All right, a little geography lesson for starters, then." He turned the map toward Devon and pointed to a large wooded area on the left. "This is the Shelkelar as it stands today." He moved his finger upwards. "Here is Graxton, the Gray Ash Mountains, and way out here…" He moved his finger left and off the map, "are the Ledges, and then the ancient Dwarven lands. Familiar?"

Devon nodded that he was following.

Kiernan went on, "A thousand years ago everything I just pointed to, with the exception of the dwarves' land, was a part of the Shelkelar."

Devon looked up sharply. Then he dropped his head back to the map and let out a low whistle. "It was huge."

"Yes," Kiernan agreed, "Vast and out of control, its inhabitants outnumbering the rest of the Northern Realms. Goblins had taken to terrorizing the locals, so Lasairian moved itself back to the fork in the Inid River."

"Where it is today," Devon interjected.

"Yes. Leaving an enormous stretch of empty land between." Kiernan sat back, leaving the map for the moment. "The goblins and their king wreaked havoc daily. The Goblin King wished to rule everything he could get his hands on, and at the time the fairy queen was on his side. Together the entire force of the Shelkelar was large enough to wipe out Lasairian."

Devon had to interrupt. "Captain, you are from the Shelkelar?"

Tain eyed him, her expression sly and dangerous. "This was before my time."

"Yes, but do you not serve the current king and queen?" Devon pressed.

Tain recoiled dramatically. "They do not rule together, and I swear allegiance to neither."

Devon shook his head in confusion. "But…"

Nemesio placed a hand on his shoulder. "At the time of the war, the king and queen were more likely to agree with one another."

Panas held up a hand. "Unlike the current holder of the title, the past queen was just as power-hungry and unmerciful as her counterpart. In an unusual and rare union, they joined forces and for the first…"

"… and last…" Tain interrupted.

"… time in history, fairy and goblin fought side by side," Panas finished.

"So, there are two separate monarchs of the Shelkelar," Devon offered.

"There are *hundreds* of monarchs in the Shelkelar," Nemesio confirmed. "Those that are recognized by others and those who have appointed themselves."

"I don't understand," Devon said to the imp.

"I don't expect you to," Tain retorted.

"Rules do not exist there the way you understand them, Devon," Dagmar explained.

"What…"

"Shhh, mage. Just listen," Panas scolded.

Kiernan went on, clearly eager to avoid an argument. "The more unpleasant members of the Shelkelar had become quite a menace, and Lasairian was hard pressed to continue to hold them off. Members of the court thought it likely that they would have to elicit outside help. One elf, a nobleman, volunteered to go. He traveled to the three other kingdoms in search of any who might be sympathetic to his cause. He found only one elf in each kingdom who would listen to him."

Here Kiernan paused and looked to each of his companions. They all nodded in agreement and Kiernan turned back to Devon, his green eyes sparkling. Devon sat up, realizing the elf was about to reveal something important.

"Their names were Nightwing, Coal, Firebrand and Darken."

There was silence as Kiernan's words sunk in for Devon. "Your names," he breathed finally.

Kiernan nodded.

Devon held open his hands, waiting for the elf to go on, but he did not. Devon scanned the faces of his company and saw that they all wore the same expression. They wanted him to know the truth. "Then either you are all distant relatives of the original band or you are all using aliases?"

"The latter," Panas said.

"You have taken on the names of long-dead heroes?!" Devon exclaimed.

"Correct."

Devon was reeling. "But there are five of you," he said, "Not including the Captain."

Kiernan held up a hand. "I will come to that."

Devon was intrigued and motioned for him to go on.

"The four elves found they worked well together, despite their differences. Each member began convincing his kingdom of the benefits of coming to Lasairian's aid. They succeeded, and the group led their races against a horde of goblins and fairies…"

"… and Kelina knows what else," Panas sneered.

"Shut up, Panas!" Tain yelled.

"Basically, everyone with wings, claws or green skin qualified…"

The imp pelted Panas with her apple core.

"So, what happened?" Devon asked, inserting himself between the quarreling imp and elf.

Kiernan did not seem at all bothered by the bickering. His smooth features betrayed little emotion. "Thousands died, but when the dust cleared, the elves had won, and the goblins and fairies and their monarchs retreated into their forest."

"And the elves?" Devon asked.

Kiernan stared straight at him with those sharp green eyes. "They went home."

Devon's mouth dropped. "What!?" he exclaimed. "After all that?"

Kiernan's thin lips turned into a wry smile. He was enjoying this, Devon saw. "Though their champions got on well enough, the rest of their kingdoms could not stomach each other." Kiernan sat back again and let that sink in for Devon.

"So, what about *Duak-Thenal*?" Devon asked.

"With the exception of Lasairian, the other members were exiled from their countries. Shut out."

"But they were heroes!" Devon objected.

Kiernan held up a hand. "The members of *Duak-Thenal* wanted to stay behind. They felt they had found their calling; that they were part of something new, a coming together of cultures, the like of which had never been seen before. They had witnessed firsthand what could be accomplished by combining strengths instead of coveting them -- and they wished to do more. Not on as grand a scale as the war, perhaps. But protecting the freedom of the light elves, at least, was something they seemed well fit to do."

Kiernan sighed. "It was seen as an insult when they did not return home to their respective kingdoms. As humans began entering the realms and the heroes began aiding them too… well, they became an embarrassment. Ignoring what their brethren thought, the four elves continued their escapades, at times treated as heroes and at others referred to as outlaws, until they faded into history."

The elf stopped.

There was a long pause during which Devon glanced at them each in turn, grappling with something. "Why five elves?" he asked suddenly. "Why are there five of you when there were only four of them?"

Kiernan nodded. "Ah yes, I forgot. Well, mage, you know now that the previous group was made up of nobles, therefore you must conclude that we are as well. Unlike the ancient group, we cannot advertise that fact. Nemesio, Dagmar and Talesin's kingdoms are far away, but mine is not."

Devon nodded in understanding. "Panas serves as a decoy."

"Much as I hate to admit it, I rather need it at times."

"But he looks nothing like you," Devon said.

"You don't think so, mage?" Panas objected. "Look at my eyes," he said, pulling on the skin below his eye.

"They are gold," Devon announced.

"No, no, no, don't you see the flecks of green?"

Devon squinted, "Barely. And how do you account for the hair?"

Panas flung his golden locks away from his narrow face. "In the right light, usually the moonlight, my hair is as red as Kiernan's."

"Perhaps it is not a prefect match," Nemesio interrupted, "but it has been enough to sow some confusion among our enemies."

Devon was pleased with the information he had received, but it worried him a bit. "Why do you tell me this?" he asked. "It seems these are *Duak-Thenal's* best-kept secrets. Or will you simply kill me on this journey?"

Kiernan met his gaze. "We have no intention of harming you."

"In fact," Panas continued, "You should count yourself lucky that you ran into us first. There are others who would not have been so... ummm... lenient."

Devon ignored Panas and studied the red-haired elf before him for a long time. It seemed to the mage that the elf was daring him to speak his mind, challenging him to voice an opinion. For it was now obvious to the mage what the story had been meant to reveal.

Against his better judgment, Devon spoke. "And so, you think you will revive the memory of *Duak-Thenal* by becoming them. Bring together your estranged kingdoms by reminding them of the good deeds of a few who lived a millennium ago."

Kiernan nodded. "That was the plan."

Devon blinked. "I think you're insane."

The others laughed. "No, really," Devon protested. He climbed to his knees, trying to gain some leverage. "This strategy failed for your ancient heroes. What makes you think it will work now, especially when the other elves have had a thousand years to strengthen their convictions?"

"Times change," Kiernan said. "Whoever would have thought humans would move so far north, or that the dwarves would cross the mountains? These things were thought to be impossibilities by great scholars of the time, and yet they came to pass."

Devon wasn't convinced. "It is also true that history can and must repeat itself."

"You predict another war, mage?" Nemesio asked.

"No," Devon said, backing down a bit. "But if a war of that magnitude failed to bring unity to the four kingdoms, then what will? The six of you? Old grudges die hard. Can you honestly tell me that any of you has been a guest in the other's land? Lasairian, maybe. I'll wager even the Captain's been allowed there. But the others?" He looked around at them.

"We've been to Malhuria," Panas protested weakly.

But no one else said a word. Their silence made his argument for him. None of them had traveled to or even been allowed inside Jathaharwel or Serenia. Devon was betting it was the same with the Shelkelar.

Devon was suddenly uncomfortable. He shifted slightly, unable to meet their eyes. "I simply wonder if you are being realistic."

The entire group now focused on Kiernan, who folded his hands across his chest and regarded the human mage. "I think your viewpoint is very near the mark, if a bit pessimistic."

"I consider myself a realist," Devon replied cautiously. The volatile elf was agreeing with him far too much. Devon began to distrust his motives again. "Please," he said changing the subject, "Continue the story."

"There is no more to tell," Kiernan said.

Devon cocked his head. "Well...what about the Shelkelar?"

"It was cut back drastically," Kiernan went on. "And the king and queen and their entire horde barricaded themselves in the deepest part of it. Which is why you see extraordinarily little of the likes of the Captain, here, today."

Devon was thinking of the war twenty years ago with Graxton. The fairies had certainly come out in force again for that battle, and Devon knew that the Captain had been there. "Where do imps fit in?" Devon asked cautiously, for the Captain seemed no longer interested in the conversation.

Tain danced away and smiled mischievously. "Somewhere in between."

"Between what?" Devon asked trying to follow.

But Tain was flitting about, untying bedrolls, and flinging them around the ground, making no attempt to unroll them or find out whose was whose.

"They are not part of any faction, per se." Nemesio took over. "Most of them could be loyal to a different ruler on any given new moon. It is a constant game, a competition between the king and queen."

Devon appreciated Nemesio's lesson, but he wanted to hear it from the fairy. "But *you* serve the queen, don't you?"

Tain turned and grinned. "For now."

Devon scowled, knowing that she was deliberately sidestepping him. "Then what are you doing here among elven nobles? Hmm? How is it that you have a place in an ancient band of heroes?"

His question was met with silence. He glanced around and found that none would meet his eye. Kiernan shook his head. "That is a story for another time, I'm afraid."

Confused, he turned back to the imp, who had stopped her busy movements and now stood very still.

Devon froze, certain he had touched a nerve. "I'm sorry, Captain, I meant no offense."

He thought she might have frowned at him but then she began to walk away, "None taken, mage." But she did not look back at him. "I'll relieve Talesin," she called over her shoulder.

Devon moved to follow her, but Dagmar stood in his path. "Do not bother, mage."

Devon regarded the wild elf curiously. For someone who had spoken hardly a word all evening, she certainly chose a strange time to object.

Devon turned to Kiernan, who was also standing. In truth, he had a rather good idea as to why the Captain remained outside her forest. His curiosity now got the better of him. "Is it true she killed the prince of Graxton?" he blurted out.

Kiernan flinched and then his eyes flickered to the remaining members of his party. The three elves took the hint and moved away out of earshot. "Why? Not thinking of that reward money, are you?"

Devon laughed. "No! Of course not. It's just that I cannot believe a mysterious, even child-like creature such as the Captain could be capable of stabbing a man in the back."

Kiernan features darkened as he stared off in the direction the Captain had taken, "How do you know that was even the case?"

"Well, I read a small account of the Graxton war in school…"

"And automatically you assume she is guilty," the elf snapped.

Devon fidgeted slightly. "Well, it was a *historical* account…"

Kiernan drew himself up, his face flushing in anger. "Of whose history, do you think?"

Devon opened his hands, trying to understand. "I don't remember exactly, but it was a well-documented event."

Kiernan took a threatening step forward and the mage was forced to back up. "Documented by whom? Scholars from Graxton! Men who were so disposed to steal land from the fairies that they never expected their hero to be defeated by one?" The elf pushed his face closer to Devon's. "What about *her* side?" he hissed. "Do you think that was documented? Not a chance. You know why? Because there were no witnesses! None. Everything you have read was fabricated by angry people who were not even there. *Listen*," Kiernan said. He lowered his voice and grabbed Devon's arm, pulling him back toward the tree. "We have all had to defend ourselves or our homes at some point or another. The Captain is no exception."

"You are saying she was defending herself and the Shelkelar against Prince Tavares?" Devon asked, somewhat relieved at the prospect.

Kiernan straightened. "I am saying people will believe what they want to believe. Honestly, no one knows the truth. Not even me. It is a subject you would do well to avoid, Devon Bane. It is one that has caused a great deal of pain and aggravation for us all. Tain is a fugitive because of it."

"She is a fugitive because she is a thief," Devon countered before he could stop himself.

Kiernan shook his head. "That is her nature, as yours is magic. And she never keeps the things she steals."

Devon raised an eyebrow. "The daggers?" he asked, referring to the parade of constantly changing weapons at the imp's ankles.

"Weapons of the dead are of no use to them in this world."

Devon had a lost a step in this debate and now he was scrambling to keep his footing. It seemed everything he said only made things worse. "I mean no disrespect. I like the Captain, which is why I am trying to understand the death of a hero at her hands."

Kiernan remained stony and pointed a finger in Devon's face. "Tavares caused his own death, and he was no hero."

The light elf whipped past him without another word. Devon Bane was left alone to ponder revelations of a history he thought he had known, disappointed that the conversation had ended on such a sour note. He spent the rest of the night poring over his books, trying to find some mention of the Captain thief as the fun-loving imp he now knew.

— ✳ ✳ ✳ —

Kiernan had made a wide circle around the perimeter of the camp to locate the Captain. Admittedly he had not searched very hard. If the Captain did not wish to be found, she would not be—there was really no use in breaking a sweat over a search. He did not think the mage had upset Tain too badly, and after all, he hadn't meant to. Still, Kiernan would have felt better had he been able to speak to her before she had taken off.

Twenty minutes or so after he had started out, the prince found himself on the opposite side of the road with a slightly skewed view of their camp. Kiernan knew that his crew lay on the grass. The only thing he could see was the tip of Dagmar's head, and that only because the wild elf was still sitting up. She had chosen their position well. An enemy casing the camp from this angle would have been unable to get a true count of their number.

Dagmar stood. Even though she should not have been able to know his position, she began to make her way over to him.

Kiernan remained where he was, not really surprised that the wild elf had spotted him. All the elves and the imp had impeccable vision, but Dagmar's seemed most fit for peering into shadows and spying things that had chosen to blend in with the foliage. Her pace was even and firm and yet she slipped across the dirt road without a sound. She did not speak a greeting but simply leaned against the same tree, barely inches from the prince.

There was a long silence that Kiernan hesitated to break. The night was beautiful. Mist rolled across the road and over the treetops, the moon was out in full, squeezing through the clouds and sparkling off the raindrops and puddles... and he had a quiet moment alone with Dagmar.

"Did you find her?" she asked.

Kiernan shook his head, still unwilling to speak.

"Worried?" she asked.

"Not really," Kiernan replied, finding his voice. To his ears it sounded a bit raspy, he hoped she did not notice. "I'm just glad she was out of earshot for the mage's last few ignorant statements."

Dagmar paused a moment. "You were a little hard on him," she said quietly.

Kiernan turned his head to her. "You take his side?"

Dagmar shrugged. "There is no side to take. His comments were not meant to hurt the Captain or the rest of us. He is only curious. You cannot fault him for asking such questions."

Kiernan nodded. "You think I was too defensive."

"I think you are overprotective of someone who hardly needs it."

Kiernan pushed himself away from the tree. "Oh, she needs it," he said. "Whether she likes it or not."

"She has never been caught," Dagmar offered.

Kiernan snorted. "More thanks to us."

"Do not give yourself too much credit, Kiernan," Dagmar scolded. "She is hard to catch. Besides, it has been twenty years. They will have given up by now."

Kiernan winced, but he did not let Dagmar see it. He had been with the Captain when the Crimson Guard attacked the Shelkelar. He had seen what they could do. "No," he said, "they will never give up." He growled under his breath and turned to face her. "Graxton has enough power to condemn someone for an incident no one was witness to and then manage to convince the world it is true."

Dagmar Coal smiled in the face of Kiernan's anger and stepped toward him. Kiernan held his breath.

"Not everyone believes the tales. And those who do—well, you seem more than adept at changing their minds."

Kiernan laughed. In a quick show of affection, he reached out and clasped the wild elf's' hand. Her long, thin fingers, darker than his own, squeezed his and then let go. She moved past him as smoothly as water and disappeared into the forest. The moment was so fleeting it should have meant nothing, but to Kiernan that light touch was enough to calm his nerves for a whole night.

21~Wisia

It took them another whole day to reach Wisia.

Nothing was said on the journey, and Devon could not help but think he was the cause. They had allowed the mage to voice his opinions last night. The air around him was now filled with the thickness of thought.

Devon was suffocating in it.

It was not that they blamed him, for Devon knew with strange certainty that they did not. Even the Captain, whom Devon was sure he had offended, treated him with the same amity she had at their first meeting. They were quiet now because they were questioning themselves much the same way he had questioned them the night before.

Devon wished he had never said a word. He had placed a small bump in their self-righteous road. Devon did not think they would begin to doubt their cause because of his probing, but it was clear they were distracted. Devon did not want to meet Jinin Aurek with a distracted group of outlaws.

His nerves were raw when, near sunset, the group finally made the outskirts of the small town of Wisia.

"Split up," Kiernan said. "Find out where Jinin and his crew are. Meet back here in one hour."

"Kiernan, we don't have much time." Nemesio looked meaningfully at Kiernan.

Kiernan held up a hand. "I know. One hour, no more."

The elves split so quickly that Devon could scarcely be sure who went with whom. He was left alone with Kiernan Nightwing and the light elf led him quietly through the gates.

They skated swiftly over the plain gray streets of Wisia, barely disturbing the dust — of which there was little, Devon noted. He knew Wisia was the most industrious of Preliona's four surrounding towns, that it was filled with people who worked constantly and had little use for magic or art, books or music. They had only one form of entertainment, one refuge, one place to relax at the end of their taxing days: The Washbin.

The Washbin Pub was already filling at this early hour. Through large bay windows patrons could be seen drinking, laughing, and relaxing at tables and booths inside. From the street the bar could not be seen, but it was reputedly enormous.

Kiernan stopped and slid his lanky frame under the awning of a tiny shop across from the Washbin. He pulled Devon under with him and together they leaned against the brick wall and waited.

Devon watched patrons of the Washbin enter in groups of two and three. He let the silence between him and the elf last a quarter of an hour before he could stand it no more.

"Time for what?" he asked suddenly.

Kiernan Nightwing slowly swung his green gaze towards the mage. "What's that?"

Devon swallowed under the elf's heavy look. "Umm, well, Nemesio said you didn't have much time. Time for what?"

The light elf stared at the mage for only a second before he turned away and faced the street again. "To get the key, of course. Cornelius is expecting you, isn't he?"

His response came too quickly. Devon was suddenly suspicious again. He bit his lip and turned back to the road. He was missing something, he was sure of it. For all the openness and trust *Duak-Thenal* had shown him last night, he really did not know them at all. He had no idea what their true intentions were.

He spent the next three quarters of an hour counting the cracks in the sidewalk and worrying about what would happen next.

At almost exactly the hour mark, Tain and the elves returned. "He is in the Wisia Arms," The imp announced.

"Can't be sure which room," Talesin added.

"He'll have taken the largest suite."

Tain turned her head sharply and started at Devon. "Why do you say that?"

Devon shrugged. "I don't know. Just a feeling I get about him, I guess."

Tain's eyes widened. "Well, you are right," she said. "That is exactly what Jinin would do."

Devon wanted to say more, but Talesin moved forward. "The larger rooms are above the pub," he said.

"Four suites are occupied; all by the same party," Nemesio said. "There are windows around the back."

"Go," Kiernan commanded, and Talesin and Dagmar disappeared into the shadows.

Tain reached up and touched Devon's shoulder. "I need to know how the key works, Devon," she said.

"Why?"

She cocked her head as if she were surprised he did not know the answer to his own question. "Because I intend to take it from him, and I do not wish to be burnt to a cinder in the process."

Devon closed his eyes and tried not to laugh at the irony of her words. "It has no wards. You should be able to handle it as long as Jinin doesn't use it."

"And how would he do that?" Tain pressed.

It was amazing to Devon how serious the imp could become. One moment her voice was high-pitched and childish, the next it dropped drastically. It was at these times Devon noticed that the imp betrayed her age. The tone that infused her voice now was that of one who had lived long and seen much. To the teenage Devon, it was downright frightening.

Devon swallowed. "It works in two ways. First, it can unlock any door."

Tain twirled a hand and nodded as if she already understood this part. "And its teleporting abilities?"

"It's quite simple, really. He would hold the key in front of him and with a clear thought about where he wanted to go, he would push down on the sapphire. Then he would disappear."

Tain sighed. "I suspect he has already used it," she said.

"Then it will be all the harder to take it from him," Devon said.

"Why is that?" Kiernan asked.

Devon turned to the elf. "Well, imagine how it would feel to be able to open any door, to teleport yourself anywhere, anytime. How would you feel?"

Panas nodded grimly. "Like a god."

The three remaining elves stared at each other in silence a moment. Then, as one, they turned to the imp thief.

"Can you handle him?" Kiernan asked.

Tain grinned. "Oh, I don't think Jinin will give me too much trouble. He likes me."

Kiernan took a threatening step forward. "I don't care if he's head over heels in love with you, Tain. You get that key and you get out!"

"All right, all right," Tain said, holding up her hands. "Why don't you go have a drink and let me do my job, okay?"

With a growl Kiernan grabbed Devon by the collar and steered him toward the Washbin while Tain, Nemesio and Panas trotted off in the opposite direction. Devon had no idea how the imp and elves intended to get upstairs but he had no more time to think about them as he was being pushed through the door.

"Wait, we're going in?" Devon said, trying to dig his heels into the ground and stop the hasty elf.

Kiernan grabbed the mage's arm and dragged him forward.

The bar was at the center of the room and was the only well-lit portion of the place. Above the bartender hung a square of oak low enough for him to reach the many drinking glasses that dangled from it. All around the outside of this square, small, round lanterns, strategically placed and shining brightly, lit up the bar and shot enough light into the rest of the room so that no other light was needed. As far as Devon could tell, the top part of the bar was suspended by huge black cables that also supported each corner of the oaken square. These in turn extended up toward the ceiling, coming together at a center point.

It looked sturdy enough, but Devon wondered how much it would take for the whole contraption to start swinging if he pushed hard enough.

Kiernan steered Devon toward a stool and motioned for him to sit. The bar of the Washbin was fashioned of blonde oak, so well cared for that it shone. Devon could see his reflection in the surface. Kiernan, his gray hood pulled up to cover his features, ordered them drinks.

Devon spun about on his stool and took in the rest of the room. Nearest to him was a cluster of small round-topped tables surrounded by groups of people. At the far end of the room large rectangular tables took up most of the floor space. It was difficult to tell with all the people there, but Devon thought he counted fifteen tables. As that was still not enough space to accommodate the throngs of people. Booths clung to the walls back to back all around the outside of the room.

"Ya gonna drink that, lad?"

Devon started at the voice and spun around to face the scrawny bartender.

The man was old—close to seventy. But the mage could see he was strong and spry for his age. Devon glanced at the man's fingers, which were currently wiping the inside of a glass. They were slightly gnarled, but if they gave the bartender any pain, he did not show it. His piercing blue eyes gazed at Devon with a measure of intelligence the mage had never seen outside of school.

"Hey, kid," the bartender was saying. "You in there?"

Devon shook his head. "Sorry, sir," he said. "What was the question?"

The bartender smiled wryly. "Right. So are ya gonna drink that or not?"

Devon looked down at the glass before him. It was a goblet and it was filled with a dark liquid that seemed to have a bluish tint to it, "Ummm, yeah."

With much trepidation he lifted the goblet to his lips. The drink went down quickly and instead of the throat-closing reaction he had expected, Devon was pleasantly surprised by its taste. As sweet as berries, with an aftertaste that lingered. Devon could not stop licking his lips.

"Do you like it?" Kiernan asked beside him.

"It's wonderful. What is it?"

"Berlys," the elf replied. "It's a rather common elfish drink and one of the less intoxicating ones. I thought you might like it."

Devon set his glass onto the bar top and nodded to the bartender for more. And Devon found himself easily downing a second glass.

Kiernan grabbed his arm. "I said it was weak, Devon, not spirit-free. I wanted to tell you to sip it, but I guess it is too late. How about some water?"

Devon watched sadly as the bartender slid the glass away. He could already feel his legs go to liquid. "Shouldn't we be waiting outside? Preparing the horses for a quick escape?"

Kiernan smiled. "We don't intend to run."

Devon was stunned. "But...but what if Jinin's crew engages us?"

"They most likely will."

Devon leaned in to the elf. "What do you plan to do, kill them?" he whispered.

Kiernan sipped his drink, "If I have to."

Devon blinked. "You're not serious."

Kiernan rolled his green eyes. "Never would I harm anybody unnecessarily. I am an elf, Devon—I do have morals."

Devon smirked, his brown eyes squinting in anger. "Unlike me, of course, who is human and therefore has none."

Kiernan frowned at him. "You know what I mean. Believe me, I would like nothing more than to leave here quietly and unnoticed. If we can slip out once we have the key…"

"If Tain gets it."

Kiernan lowered his gaze. "*When* she gets it, we will first try to leave without a fight. When that does not work, and it won't…"

"Why not?"

Kiernan Nightwing opened his hands in a gesture of helplessness seemingly uncharacteristic for him and sighed, "Mage, our thief is in the lead right now."

The elf stared at Devon, as though this statement should explain it all. But Devon did not understand. "So?"

Kiernan rolled his eyes and turned back to his drink. "So…I have learned to be…flexible where she is concerned."

Devon narrowed his eyes in concern. "What does that mean?"

Kiernan folded his hands on the bar and stared at Devon. "It means, Devon, that with Tain, nothing ever goes quite according to plan."

Devon opened his mouth, but Kiernan turned back to the bar. "Sabon," Kiernan called to the bartender.

Devon watched with interest as the bartender sauntered back over to them.

"Are any members of the upstairs party down here?" Kiernan asked.

Sabon picked up Kiernan's glass and turned away, speaking over his shoulder to the elf. "Two tables behind you and to the right."

Devon immediately started to turn but Kiernan grasped his arm. "Do *not*," he hissed. "Sabon has told us all we need to know."

"But how many are there?"

Kiernan shrugged, "Two tables, four chairs at each, I assume."

Devon squirmed, "Then we are badly outnumbered."

"Better down here than upstairs. There were twelve in all, correct?"

Devon's brow furrowed. "I think so. But twelve with or without Jinin I cannot remember."

Kiernan tapped his fingers on the bar. "Three we left behind. Eight are down here. That leaves Jinin alone upstairs. Good."

Devon threw a look over his shoulder that was too quick to get an accurate head count. "Good, huh? You sure about that?"

"The less distraction Tain has, the better her chances of getting the key without a fight. I am hoping she will be able to talk him into giving it over."

Devon thought back to the conversations he had had with Jinin Aurek. He did not think the enigmatic thief would simply hand anything over—no matter who was asking.

22~Old Grudges Die Hard

Jinin Aurek entered his suite of rooms above The Washbin casually, with much less caution than he would normally afford himself.

He was gloating, and allowed himself the luxury of using his loyal crew to guard his back. He hardly thought the elves could be following him now, delayed as they were by the un-dead. It would be some time before *Du-ak-Thenal* escaped that haunted trail. Awakening the Pearl Song Trail ghosts had been a brilliant ploy. Jinin reveled in the knowledge that perhaps not all the elves would escape.

Payment for the deaths of three of his crew.

Jinin grasped the large silver key in his pocket and grimaced. The key had sidetracked him, he knew. The thief had made use of the magical item more than once in the past twenty-four hours, and its power was seriously beginning to grow on him. He could enter any room he wanted in this little town—steal any item he wished without disturbing a lock. He had acquired from the hamlet of Wisia more than he could carry—and still he wanted more. He no longer cared what he was stealing. He simply reveled in the fact that he could do it with such ease.

He closed the door behind him and peered into the gloom.

"Why don't you turn on the light?"

The voice startled Jinin more than he would ever admit. No one should have been able to make it into his suite of rooms undetected.

He also recognized the voice. It belonged to the one creature in Tearlach who could cause Jinin a problem at this point in the game.

Cursing under his breath, Jinin Aurek lit the lamp nearest him.

Captain Tain Elire was seated comfortably in his enormous red velvet chair, one tiny knee pulled up casually her arm flopping over her drawn leg. Leaning back in his chair, her pointed chin resting in her hand, the imp looked as though she had been there for hours. "Hello, Jinin," she grinned at him.

Jinin scowled at her and quickly glanced around the room. "How did you get in?"

Tain ignored him. "You seem to be doing well for yourself, Jinin. New curtains, new clothes, and this…" She ran her hands across the arms of the chair. "This is very nice."

"Thank you," Jinin replied blandly, not much caring for the air of familiarity the imp was taking with him. There was a time when Jinin would have admitted to knowing the imp, even working with her. But that was many years and hundreds of jobs ago. "What are you doing here?" he barked.

Tain's storm blue eyes sparkled. "You have something I want."

Jinin sighed and turned his back on her. He made his way to a desk near the door and began removing his cloak, all the while keeping his eyes open for any company the Captain may have brought along. "Cryptic Tain," he replied. "Can't ever give a straight answer, can you? Why do you always have to be so damned evasive?" He saw her grin over his shoulder as he tossed his new coat over the back of a chair.

"I want the key, Jinin," she said calmly.

Jinin hesitated, breath catching, but only for a moment. "What key?" he asked.

"*Now* who's being evasive?" the Captain asked, swinging both legs over one arm of the chair.

Jinin turned to face the imp thief and leaned back against the desk. Knowing he would not succeed in lying to her, he simply smiled. "I don't know what you're talking about."

He was about to go on, to stall the Captain if he could, but he saw that the imp now held a small pouch at the end of a string. She dangled it between two tiny pale fingers, and she was swinging it back and forth casually like some sideshow hypnotist.

The motion may not have worked on Jinin, but the sight of the pouch, which obviously held a good amount of money, interested him, nonetheless.

"I can pay you," she said and tossed the pouch in his direction.

Jinin caught it in one hand noting its weight. "How much?" he asked, curiosity piqued.

"One thousand," Tain replied, not missing a beat.

Jinin looked at the pouch, seriously considering it. Then he reached into his pocket again and wrapped his fingers around the cold metal of the key. It was his now. Odin had said so.

Jinin licked his lips, indecision staying his hand.

He could kill her and take the money and the key. Ending the imp thief's life was something that held mounting appeal to Jinin the more he thought about it.

There was a problem with that, though—something that had been nagging at him since he discovered her in his room. Tain Elire supposedly ran with *Duak-Thenal*. He had not seen her among the elves in the attack on the caravan, but that did not mean she had not been there. If she was here now, how many other members of *Duak-Thenal* had tracked his group here? Perhaps it would be better to stall until he knew just how many enemies he had lurking in the shadows.

"You know, Captain," he began, placing the pouch on his desk and taking a step toward the thief, "I am particularly good at what I do. I work very hard, but I see little profit."

The imp snorted. "And I suppose that jeweled dagger you're carrying and those Malhurian leather boots would not be considered profits."

Jinin smiled wryly. "Perhaps I am looking for more esteem than a good pair of boots can offer me."

"Perhaps," Tain said cocking her head. "If you worked for someone other than Odin Darweshi you would have the celebrity you seek."

The Captain's sharp words gave Jinin pause. She knew about his involvement with Odin. Perhaps he would have to kill her after all.

But still he hesitated. It had been years since he had last seen the imp, and he wanted a moment to brag. "Look around you, Tain," he said, spreading his arms wide. "How else would I have access to things such as these?"

Tain Elire leaned forward. "You didn't work for this, Jinin," she accused. "You stole these things with the use of a magical artifact that a thief has no business possessing."

Jinin rolled his eyes. "Pretentious Tain. You use more than your fingers to pick locks with."

She smiled, egging him on. "But I don't cheat," she said. "I don't use magic."

Jinin curled his lip. He opened his mouth to berate her, but the Captain cut him off.

"What do you intend to do with all this?" she asked, swinging her arms about. "You can't be staying here long. Do you plan to make the hamlet of Wisia your new base of operations? Or will you steal a whole new set of furniture at your next stop?"

Her sarcastic tone was not lost on Jinin. He crossed his arms in front of him and glared down at her. "You know, Captain, not all of us have that unconventional need to give away the things we steal. You seem to forget that though our jobs are the same, the end results are vastly different."

Captain Tain Elire smirked at him down the length of her tiny nose. "Giving and returning are two entirely different things," she replied in her own defense. "And *return* is what I intend to do with that key."

"To whom?" Jinin asked, assessing just how quick he would have to be to draw his dagger before she could reach one of hers.

"To its rightful owner."

"A sorcerer."

"Yes," the imp affirmed. "You don't need it. You are a fine thief."

Jinin raised one blond eyebrow. "Flattery, Captain? That is exactly the type of pleasantry that got you kicked out of the *Black Bloods*."

Captain Tain Elire's blue eyes widened ever so slightly and her angular jaw clenched. "I was never kicked out. I left."

Jinin smiled in triumph and took another step toward her. "Oh, please. You forget, I knew you before the title of Captain made you fearless and famous. I knew you when you were nothing but a petty little pickpocket."

The imp did not defend herself, so the wiry thief continued with a dismissive wave of his hand. "Either way, your leaving was just as well. Your sympathy for our victims would have gotten you killed sooner or later."

He had hit a nerve, Jinin knew, for the mischievous light in the imp's eyes had gone out like the flame of a candle. In truth, he did not know how Tain had escaped the *Black Bloods,* and he did not care.

"What about you, Jinin?" she asked him suddenly. "Did you leave willingly, or were you forced out?"

Jinin's face darkened. "You know what happened, Tain. *You* were there."

"Yes, I was. And I was not sorry to see you go."

"You replaced me!" Jinin growled. "You were like a new toy to the others. I was shoved aside."

Tain sat up. "You could have fought for yourself, Jinin," she countered. "Tried to stay top thief. But you gave up. Just like you are doing now—letting magic do your work for you. How long will it be before you do not remember how to pick a lock?"

Jinin shook his head, stunned by the unending gall the imp seemed to possess. "You speak as though I have used the key for years, not mere hours."

"You deny that its power eats at you? Doesn't the magic control your wants and needs?"

Jinin stood straight and threatening. "I am controlled by nothing," he insisted. When she did not press the issue, he chuckled softly. "I don't have years and years of life left like you, Tain. I need this…"

"It's retirement you want?" she asked, cutting him off. "Take the money then. Use it to move to some peaceful town and settle down. There is more than enough there."

Jinin was stony again, years of pent up anger at the imp threatening to bubble over. He touched the handle of his short sword. If the Captain saw the move, she did not show it. "I am not giving it to you," he growled.

Tain set her jaw. "I wasn't giving you a choice."

Jinin was across the room in a second, drawing his sword and pointing it at the imp's chest. "I'll kill you first."

Jinin had only just finished his threat when the air in the room suddenly shifted and he felt the bite of two sword tips, one at his neck the other at his back.

"I don't think so, Jinin," Tain replied calmly.

Jinin's eyes went wide with anger and shock as he distinctly heard arrows being fitted to notches nearby. It seemed quite impossible for him not to have noticed anyone other than the Captain in the room with him. If the intruders had swung through the window since he had threatened her, they had moved with unbelievable speed and stealth.

Jinin swallowed hard and his breath came in short audible gasps. He was so angry he was tempted to make a move on the imp, consequences be damned. At that moment, all he wanted to do was plunge his sword into Tain Elire's chest and watch her stormy blue eyes close for good.

But the decision was taken quickly out of his hands as one of his attackers snatched his weapon away.

Tain stood, smiling that evil little smile, and reached for Jinin's pocket. Instinctively, the blonde thief made to smack her arm away. He was immediately grabbed by the two sword wielders behind him. He struggled with them and as he did, he caught a glimpse of pointed ears and sparkling eyes.

He froze.

It was true, then. Tain Elire did travel with *Duak-Thenal*. And it seemed she had quite a measure of control over them. This discovery opened a wealth of possibilities to Jinin. The identity of *Duak-Thenal's* leader was information much sought after in the city of Preliona.

The wheels in Jinin's head were turning, but he was suddenly light-headed and dizzy. A light scent of jasmine and woodland leaves assaulted him. The smell was intoxicating, and it sent off alarm bells in his head.

He was being drugged! He lunged for the Captain, only to collapse to his knees. "You're dead, Tain," he hissed. "Do you hear me, imp? I'll kill you!"

But his voice was barely audible to his own ears. He saw the imp kneel beside him and expertly remove the key from his pocket. He cursed and reached out to grab at the imp's black boots, but she danced lightly away from him.

But even as the floor rose to meet him, his body, hardened over the years against the effect of poisons, fought against the imp's drug. Jinin did not panic. He was sure he would have his chance at her before she could set foot out of the Washbin.

23~New Magic

Devon was scanning the bar again when he spotted Talesin standing in the middle of the room. Devon had not seen him come through the door or down the stairs. The eerie ice elf had just appeared there as if he had been there all along.

So intent was the mage on Talesin's appearance that he did not hear Tain creep up behind him and drop something into his drink.

Devon spun about as the imp slipped between him and Kiernan and frantically began to fish the key out of his glass. "Captain!" he scolded. "Do you have any idea how much this thing is worth?"

"Oh really, Devon," Tain said brushing him off and leaning against the bar, "If a key like that cannot survive a dunk in a Wisia beer, then believe me, it has no business being magical."

Talesin and Kiernan laughed loudly, but Devon continued to scowl at the imp as he caught the silver key from the bottom of his glass with a spoon.

"How did it go?" Kiernan was asking Tain.

"He has been using it," she said, leaning across the bar and suddenly becoming serious. "He did not give it up easily."

"He did not give it up at all," Talesin muttered from Kiernan's left.

Kiernan eyed the Captain, who was glaring at Talesin. "Any trouble?" he asked.

Devon watched the imp's face shift from anger to something resembling worry. It was gone in a moment, quickly replaced by the confident mien Devon had become used to seeing.

"Of course not," she said. "I told you, Jinin likes me."

At that moment, a piercing shout of anger cut through the din of the crowd. Devon and his newfound friends turned sharply toward the voice. Stumbling down the stairs and fumbling for his sword was one very drugged Jinin Aurek. "Carys! Jory!" he shouted at the tables full of his crew. All eight of them jumped to their feet at the sight of their incapacitated leader. "The imp at the bar. Bring her to me!"

Mouth open in surprise, Devon turned to the Captain, who was smiling sheepishly at Kiernan.

"Tain…" Kiernan eyes were wide with anger. "You said…"

"Impeccable judge of character as always, Captain," Talesin said, interrupting Kiernan's scolding and vaulting over the bar.

Tain shrugged, "I probably shouldn't have drugged him."

"I'm going to kill you, Tain!" Jinin was roaring over the scraping chairs behind them.

Tain looked up at Kiernan's furious face and laughed nervously. "I'm sure he'll get over it." Then she leapt onto the bar and readied herself for the inevitable attack.

Jinin made it to the bottom of the stairs and leaned against the wall, head in his hands. The man looked intensely drunk. It was obvious that whatever the imp had given him was potent indeed. Still, Jinin's will power must have been great, for the Captain was clearly surprised that the thief had appeared at all.

Kiernan Nightwing swore under his breath, drawing his sword as several screams rang out and many of the patrons of the Washbin made for the doors. But so crowded was the establishment that over half the men and women were stuck in the center of a violent rumble.

Talesin had already engaged with several of the hired swords. Dagmar and Panas were right on his heels.

Two members of Jinin's group had managed to break away from the swinging weapons of *Duak-Thenal* and were headed toward the bar. Devon reached into one of his many pockets and began to prepare a spell, but Kiernan suddenly grabbed his arm and pulled him away. "No, Devon," he said. "Do not waste your spells here." Kiernan pushed the mage behind the bar, "Get down!"

Devon objected. After all, it was because of him they were here. But Kiernan was insistent. "You are supposed to be dead, remember?"

Devon threw off the elf's arm. "Don't you think Jinin got a good look at me standing right next to the Captain?"

Devon began to push past Kiernan, but the elf shoved him back and held him in place. "I am counting on his focus being totally on the Captain. In the state he is in, let us hope she is all he saw." And with that he disappeared, leaving Devon to cower behind the deserted bar.

The bartender had disappeared, he noticed, and after about five seconds of hiding Devon risked a peek over the edge of the bar. He nearly got his head taken off by a flying bottle. The offending green glass shattered next to his ear, forcing him to dive aside or be splayed by the shards.

The brief glance had afforded him enough of a look at the fight to know that it now raged fully. Many patrons had managed to clamber out of the pub, but the bulk of folks at the center of the room remained dangerously close to the fray. Fortunately, most of these people were too drunk to care much about the swords slicing the air very near their heads. This at least made things easier for the elves, who were valiantly trying to protect citizens while defeating mercenaries. One man had gone so far as to pick up a few verses of a lewd drinking song and was waving his glass about in tribute to anyone who scored a hit.

Devon looked up. Tain Elire had begun on the bar, successfully masking Devon's hiding place. But after only a few moments she grew bored with that spot and went in search of higher ground.

As the imp looked up at the chandelier-like creation over her head, the man she had been fighting made a dive for her feet. Devon nearly shouted out a warning, but it was unnecessary. The Captain made a graceful leap straight into the air and snagged the hanging piece above the bar with one hand. Before the man had a chance to grab her Tain had swung her tiny feet upward, catching the wood between them.

Her opponent immediately leapt onto the bar and slashed at the imp's dangling form with his sword. But Tain scrambled out of the way. Vaulting herself up and over the beam, she planted her feet firmly above the mercenary. The square swayed but Tain balanced herself easily. She then began dancing across the beams, teasing the mercenary below and laughing wildly all the way.

"Cut the cable, Carys!"

Devon again peeked over the bar and saw that Jinin had now made it to a nearby table, slumped over its top. His black-blond hair hung wildly about his face. He was awake enough to shout out orders but no use at all in the fight. He must have dropped his short sword somewhere along the way to the table, for Devon could not see it.

"Good idea, Carys," mocked Tain, "I hope this doesn't come crashing down on your big head." The imp laughed and began jumping up and down on the oak square, causing it to swing threateningly.

Jinin made a clumsy attempt to raise himself onto his arms. They promptly collapsed beneath him and dumped him onto his face. The thin thief struggled to lift his chin and ground his teeth. "Get her down, Carys! I don't care how you do it!"

But Carys could not reach the cables with his sword. And he was apparently not brave enough or stupid enough to attempt to climb up after the imp. Devon figured the Captain was safe for the moment. As Jinin's man pondered how best to reach the fleet-footed fairy, Devon turned his attention to the lower portions of the room.

Panas had taken to the stairs. The light elf was busy ushering people out of the door when two mercenaries charged him. Devon nearly applauded when the nimble light elf kicked the first man in the stomach and used his opponent's doubled over form as a springboard to launch himself at his second foe. The second man swung his sword wide and missed badly. Panas easily blocked the blundering move and grabbed onto the man's arm. The surprised mercenary found himself being hurled into the stair banister.

The first man recovered, and the light elf was currently battling him up and down the stairs with dancer-like grace.

Dagmar had skirted the room, remaining far outside the bulk of the fighting. That was not to say that members of Jinin's troupe had gone unscathed by the wild elf. From his low vantage point Devon could see the slumped-over form of a female clearly not of Wisia dangling over a table. After standing protectively over several drunk or frightened patrons, Dagmar had decided to take her part of the fight outside. Devon had not seen her since.

Talesin had disappeared, as well. In fact, Devon could not recall seeing him leave. The mage silently wondered how it was that these six could ever defeat their foes when they seemed so intent on splitting their forces.

The clash of steel against steel snapped his attention back to the center of the room, where Kiernan and Nemesio battled against no less than four foes. Kiernan stood on a table and Nemesio slashed at his opponents from the floor. Both elves were a blur of movement, each deftly holding off two of Jinin's group apiece.

The Malhurian elf's fighting skills belied his physical appearance. He was larger and more muscular than most elves, but Nemesio moved with the same sinewy grace as his companions. At the same time, the force with which he dispatched his enemies was frightening, to say the least. As skilled as Jinin's crew obviously was, they could not seem to get near the southern elf. Nemesio, smiling, seemed to be thoroughly enjoying himself.

And Kiernan Nightwing was on fire, his black sword stabbing and blocking so quickly Devon could scarcely follow the flow. All he could see was the arc of a silver blur left in the wake of his blade. It seemed a miracle that either of his opponents still stood.

Devon itched to make a move. He watched for a pattern in the swordplay, an opening that would allow him the second he needed to blast someone with a spell. But there was none. If the elves did not soon end the fight with their sword tips, their opponents would surely die of exhaustion.

Someone had to give soon. The Captain's little balancing act above his head would only distract for so long before Carys really did heed his master's command and bring the whole contraption crashing down, regardless of the danger to himself. If Kiernan was stalling for something, the time was up. It was time to go.

A sliver of movement toward the front of the tavern caught the mage's attention. Dagmar had left the front door ajar after ushering people out and moonlight spilled through the doorway, enough to light up a figure Devon had not noticed before. A small young woman was stealing her way across the floor, gracefully avoiding all swinging swords that disturbed the air. She was dressed in dark, loose-fitting clothes much the same as the rest of Jinin's group.

The girl was headed for the center of the room, her focus clearly on those that fought there, her movements as silent and undetectable as the elves'. When she pulled a dagger from the sheath at her wrist Devon knew he would have to act, for the elves would never see her.

Nemesio and Kiernan now fought back to back on the floor. The new player in the game remained on the blind side of both elven warriors. Even as Devon fished in his pockets, he knew it would be too late for a spell.

The girl raised her hand to strike and Devon did the only thing he could think of.

"To your left, Nemesio!" Devon heard himself scream.

He must have shouted louder than he had intended, for the dark-skinned elf jerked violently as if the warning call had pained him somehow.

He did not hesitate, however, and his sword slashed to the left, killing the knife-wielding girl quickly. Nemesio swung his blade back to his opponent in time to slash the man's sword arm even as the girl hit the floor with a sickening thud.

Devon winced. Nemesio's move was necessary, but Devon could not help being shocked and sickened by what he had witnessed.

And ashamed that he had caused it. The southern elf had barely given his unseen attacker a glance. One well-placed slice to the left and he was back in the fight. But as he raised his sword to block his opponent's next blow, he afforded a glance in Devon's direction. A look of extreme puzzlement crossed his features, not the nod of thanks Devon had expected. The mage was unsure what to make of it.

He decided to stop hiding. He had only just started to stand when an icy hand clamped down on his shoulder.

It was all Devon could do to keep from screaming. He jerked his head around and came nose to nose with the ice elf.

At this range he saw something he had not noticed before. The ice elf had no lines on his face. Most elves were devoid of wrinkles, but even one who is near ageless would have some marks of the world on his face. Some laugh lines around the eyes, perhaps, or a crease at the corners of the mouth. Talesin had none of these blemishes and the effect was eerie. His skin looked like smooth stone.

"Come quickly," Talesin commanded. He turned away without waiting for a reply. Devon followed him out the back door, moving on shaking hands and knees and trying to reestablish a normal breathing pattern. The ice elf made his way around a battered water trough that was currently being used as a garbage disposal. It stank so badly that Devon wanted to crawl back inside but Talesin turned on him.

He reached down to give the mage a hand up but Devon backed away, unable to bear the elf's icy grip again.

Talesin seemed to understand this and turned away as Devon hauled himself to his feet.

Dagmar waited a few feet away, already seated on her horse and holding the reins to Panas's white horse, Spiro. They looked prepared to leave. As Devon stepped toward them Dagmar motioned for him to hurry. "Come, Devon, we must go."

Devon stopped his advance. "But the others," he stammered, pointing back to the pub. "They are still battling inside and hard pressed to win. We cannot leave them."

The ice elf swung himself into his saddle. "I assure you, they are more than capable of holding their own."

"But..."

"You are our top priority now, Devon," Dagmar said. "Jinin thinks you're dead. It is important you are not seen and that you deliver the key, correct?"

"Yes, but..."

"Then let us depart quickly. The others will catch up when they can."

Dagmar's swirling gray eyes investigated Devon's brown ones. She was calm and collected, but Devon was miserable. "*If* they can," he muttered. He didn't much care for the way things were going, him stealing away while the others risked their lives to cover him.

"What if the Watch comes?" He took a tentative step toward them. "What if Jinin has more men lurking somewhere? What if..."

"What if lightning strikes us all dead right now!" Talesin hissed. His black eyes bored into the mage, promising death. "Get on the horse now, mage, or I'll put you on it myself."

Devon saw that Talesin was barely containing his rage. He knew he shouldn't push the volatile elf, but he could not help himself. "Cowards," he snarled, "Is this how you always work, then? Every elf for himself? Split your number and make sure at least two of you have the means to escape?"

Talesin was glaring at him and fingering his sword dangerously but Devon did not care. "It must be very easy to keep the authorities constantly guessing at your number when you never seem to fight together or for one another."

"Devon..."

"Were there more of you at one point?" the mage overrode the wild elf. "Because I can see the mortality rate being rather high if you constantly abandon your teammates."

Devon expected anger from the wild elf, but she continued to smile at him as if nothing at all were amiss. "Devon, your ire on behalf of our comrades is noble, but you do not understand…"

"I'd rather go back in there and fight than sneak away into the night," Devon interrupted her. "You don't care about me. You might as well kill me and take the key for yourselves." He turned his rage back onto Talesin. "Or maybe that is what you intended to do all along!"

"Enough!" Talesin dismounted and took several steps toward Devon.

The mage backed away from those blazing eyes and reached for his pocket recalling the first defensive spell he could think of.

"Talesin!" Dagmar caught the ice elf's black eyes and shook her head. Devon was surprised he even acknowledged her.

But Talesin backed off a step, crossing his arms and scowling. Dagmar turned back to the mage. "You do not know what you are talking about, Devon Bane. Kiernan himself ordered us to take you out of here as soon as we could find an opening. Jinin wants the key, and if he can take Tain out in the process he will, but the rest of us are simply in the way." She opened her long arms and gestured about. "I assure you: the rest of our group will catch up to us."

Devon looked from Dagmar's soft gray eyes to Talesin's hardened black ones and swallowed. He was being foolish, he knew, and he felt suddenly guilty. As mysterious as they were, they had yet to harm him or give him reason that they would. They were trying to help, and he could think of nothing better to do than insult them.

Without a word, he walked toward the wild elf and took the reins of the horse she held for him, pointedly avoiding Talesin's heavy gaze. He mounted and the three rode off into the night, leaving behind them the sound of clashing swords.

24~Friends or Enemies

The road before them was flat and wide open, obviously well traveled, with not a scrap of foliage in sight. Low, brownish fields stretched out for miles on either side of the trail, providing little or no cover for any potential attackers. Talesin and Dagmar had slowed their pace a bit, giving their companions time to catch up.

Less than two hours later, they did. The stillness of the air allowed the three escapees to hear pounding hooves long before they caught sight of the riders racing towards them.

Galloping by at top speed and roaring with laughter, Tain overtook them first, Panas clinging to her cloak and screaming for her to slow down. She obeyed and pushed her horse alongside Spiro. Devon watched in awe as Panas stood on the back of Tain's saddle and, before Devon could protest, made a graceful leap right at the mage.

The light elf landed on the back of his own horse and bowed dramatically.

Devon reined in the white horse, amazed by the move, and turned around in the saddle to look up at the light elf.

Panas squatted down and stared into Devon's face. "What do you say, handsome—mind if I take my horse back?"

Devon didn't mind at all. He scrambled off. "It's a beautiful animal," he stammered as he moved to Tain's horse.

"Takes after me, doesn't she?" Panas said, stroking Spiro's neck.

"Yes, big teeth and loud snort," teased Nemesio, who had ridden up behind.

Panas glared at him. "Anyway, I'm certainly glad to have him back. Devon, my boy, much luck to you, continuing your ride with that one," he said, nodding to Tain.

Tain was now lying on her stomach, draped across Algoryn's saddle. Her legs dangled down one side of the animal and her chin rested on the other.

"What," she said, in protest to Panas's comment.

"How did it go?" Dagmar asked.

Tain sighed dramatically, "Not at all well. I believe Jinin may actually be angry with me."

"Ha!' Panas breathed, crossing his arms.

"Shut up, Panas! Jinin likes me!" Tain protested.

Panas rolled his eyes. "The Wisia Watch finally came," he said. "Sabon covered for us. Jinin was passed out at a table. We've bought ourselves at least a day while Jinin recovers and his group answers some questions."

"Any casualties?" Dagmar asked with some concern.

"Just one."

Devon turned as Kiernan and Nemesio made their way toward him, their faces unsmiling. "And I'm betting our new friend can explain that one to us."

Devon looked up into the light elf's green eyes and swallowed. "What are you talking about?" he asked.

Kiernan Nightwing scanned Devon's face. The mage wanted to close his eyes against the elf's scrutiny, but he settled for squinting slightly instead. "You have the key?" Kiernan now said.

Devon nodded, determined to hang on to it even if the elf demanded it.

But to his surprise, he did not. Instead Kiernan turned to Nemesio, whom Devon had just noticed seemed extremely agitated, his normally congenial features now hard and closed. He pointed one long brown finger at Devon. "Back in the Washbin," he began, "when you warned me…" He shook his head slightly, trying to clear it. He could not seem to vocalize his thoughts. "I don't know how you did it. I mean… how could you?"

Devon was confused. This was hardly the thanks he had expected for saving someone's life. "I don't know what you mean," he said. "I saw the girl with the knife. You didn't, so I called out to you."

But Nemesio was shaking his head vehemently and holding up a hand. "No, you don't understand," he said. "You never opened your mouth."

The silence following Nemesio's words was deafening. Devon couldn't even be sure he had heard the southern elf correctly. "What…?" his voice, barely a whisper, echoed in the circle surrounding him. He could sense them staring at him, but he could only look at Nemesio's intense violet eyes.

The southern elf took a step forward. "I heard you in here," he said, pointing at his head. "You screamed your warning in my mind but you never… opened…your…mouth."

Nemesio was deadly serious and clearly suspicious. But before Devon could respond, he heard the distinct ring of metal. Nemesio was suddenly pushed out of the way and Talesin's smooth face filled the void, his double-bladed sword swinging up to Devon's throat.

"*Mind-reader*," he spat at the mage, as if the word left a bad taste in his mouth. Talesin's black eyes were blazing. Devon felt sure he was about to be killed. His knees started to crumple under him. But then Nemesio and Kiernan grabbed at Talesin's arms.

Tain and Panas appeared at Devon's side and he clutched at them for support while Kiernan, Nemesio and Dagmar wrestled Talesin backwards.

"Wait, Talesin!" Kiernan was saying to the enraged ice elf. "Let him explain!"

But Talesin was on fire. His face was flushed blue and he struggled fiercely against the arms of his friends. If he wasn't going to kill Devon before, he surely looked as though he would now.

"Explain what?" Talesin growled. "You know what he is! What if he has been reading our minds all along? He could have told Jinin where to run, why else would he have insisted on going directly to Preliona? For all we know he has been in contact with Odin as well. The princess could have been right all along!"

"Princess Kalliroestria?" Devon asked. He immediately regretted it when Talesin lunged forward again. Kiernan and Nemesio almost lost him and Dagmar slipped in front of Devon and pushed him back a step. "I am not in league with Jinin!" Devon shouted over Dagmar's shoulder. "And I don't even know who this Odin is!"

"Prove it," Talesin snarled.

"Back off, Talesin!" Kiernan commanded, yanking the ice elf backwards. It was the first time Devon had seen the light elf speak harshly to any of his group. Talesin glared at him but he did not protest. He shrugged off the arms that held him and sheathed his sword. With a final glare in Devon's direction he stormed away.

Kiernan watched him go. Then he turned to Dagmar and nodded. The wild elf moved off silently in the direction Talesin had taken.

Kiernan faced the mage fully. Nemesio crossed his arms and studied Devon over his leader's shoulder. "Well, can you prove your innocence, mage?"

Devon threw up his arms. "I don't even know what the charge is!" he shouted. He was aware of the danger he was in now. Somehow, he had gotten on the wrong side of the outlaws and he was suddenly unsure of his status among them. His stomach churned and his forehead was sweating. "What does this have to do with Kalliroestria?"

Kiernan raised an eyebrow. "Do you know her?"

"Of course I know her!" Devon shouted. "She is an alumna of Lorcan DeCresler's school. She's famous all over Tearlach." The mage paced back and forth, frustrated. He stopped suddenly and locked eyes with Kiernan. "Oh, and one more thing—she hates me."

Kiernan exchanged a shocked look with Nemesio, who shook his head and rolled his violet eyes.

Devon looked back and forth between the two of them. "What?!" He exclaimed.

Kiernan took a step towards him. "It was Princess Kalliroestria who hired us to come after you, mage."

Devon found he was gritting his teeth as he turned away and shook his head. "Unbelievable," he hissed.

"You do not seem surprised." Kiernan said.

Devon sighed, remembering last semester's studies at DeCresler's Institute. "Last year the princess brought some students from the SLS over to DI and…"

"Wait, L.S. and what?" Kiernan asked, sounding thoroughly confused.

"Sorry," Devon said, "*The School of Light and Sorcery* and *DeCresler's Institute of Magic*. The students of each school have taken to shortening the titles into initials. Anyway, Lorcan and Kalliroestria sponsor a competition between the schools each year. Last year I was in it. The two headmasters serve as judges. They can give or take away points or disqualify where they see cause. In the same respect, students can contest those decisions if they can prove they were right in the actions they took."

"Go on." Kiernan said.

Devon grimaced. "I won the final competition under questionable circumstances."

"You mean you cheated." Panas smirked.

"No!" Devon protested, then frowned sheepishly. "But I did use a series of spells that were technically illegal in such a competition. Kalliroestria wanted to disqualify me, and I contested the decision."

"On what grounds?" Kiernan asked.

"Well, you see, the student I won against was an elf. She used spells that only an elf could know. In the competition one can only use spells that your opponent also would know."

"So, because she cheated, you did too," Panas said.

"Well that's just it," Devon explained. "Kalliroestria didn't think her student was cheating. She felt that Lorcan should have included elven spells in our curriculum and therefore her student was right to use the spells she did. I argued that I couldn't be expected to contend against spells I had never learned. I needed to defend myself, and I did so by using spells that would counter the elf's, even though they had never before been used in competition."

"So, what happened?" Kiernan asked.

"Well, in the end a special committee of graduate students from both schools voted and the decision went in my favor. I won." Devon shrugged feebly. "The princess was not too happy with me."

Kiernan closed his eyes and let out a long breath of air.

Nemesio was pacing behind Kiernan throughout this story. Now he held up one long finger as if he were looking for clarification. "It sounds as though you are at the top of your class, Devon."

Devon shrugged. "Only students with top marks are allowed to compete, so I guess you could say that."

"*Mediocre mage,* indeed," Panas snorted. "Sounds like we are taking care of an old grudge for the princess, if you ask me."

Kiernan nodded. "Maybe. But right now, I want to discuss that little episode back in the Washbin."

Devon swallowed as Nemesio stopped his pacing and moved to stand behind Kiernan again, his massive arms crossed over his chest.

"Can you offer me any proof that you are not what Talesin says you are?" Kiernan asked. "Can you give me any concrete evidence that you are not the ringleader behind all of this?"

Devon looked from Kiernan to Nemesio. Finally, he lowered his head and stared at his feet. He dropped his shaking hands and sighed. "No," he admitted quietly. "No, I can't."

Kiernan scanned the mage's confused features. "I believe you," he said.

"Kiernan…" Nemesio began to protest.

But the light elf held up a hand. "He admits he cannot defend himself," he said. "Why would he do that if it were not the truth?"

"Then explain what happened back in Wisia," Nemesio demanded.

But he couldn't. Devon hadn't even realized his warning to Nemesio had been telepathic until the elf had told him just now. Devon held out his arms in frustration.

Nemesio rolled his eyes. "Don't tell me you've conveniently forgotten how to do it."

"I've never done it before," Devon retorted.

But that wasn't true. Now that he thought about it, that wasn't true at all. He had suspected Jinin Aurek of ill deeds all along and he had been right. He had known exactly where Panas was in the tree and where to aim his fingers when Nemesio appeared at the battle site. He had even known what type of room Jinin would be in at the Washbin. All of these things could have easily been passed off as instinct, intuition, or even luck, but Devon didn't think that was the case. There was something more.

He looked up at Kiernan Nightwing. The light elf's face remained impassive, yet he did not seem to blame Devon for the night's events. He was not angry or afraid of Nemesio's discovery as Talesin seemed to be, but simply curious and willing to give Devon the benefit of the doubt.

Devon suddenly swayed on his feet and touched his head. Something clicked for him. There was no way he could have known these things about the elven leader just by looking at him. The light elf's face was an unreadable mask.

"Talk to me, Devon," he said.

Devon held up a finger. He looked into the elf's eyes and concentrated again. He felt himself opening, a light, floating sensation that prickled his fingertips. Pictures came to him. An image of the princess Kalliroestria, her red hair flying and her pale green eyes piercing him with their usual hardness. The familiarity he felt was undeniable. "*Kelina,*" he whispered, as he felt himself pulling back. He was still staring into green eyes, but their shade had darkened. The resemblance was too close to be coincidental.

"*You're her brother,*" he said.

"Yes," Kiernan confirmed.

"Kiernan..." Devon heard Tain protest from beside him.

But Devon ignored her. "And that means you're the..." Devon could not finish. He realized he now faced the elusive younger prince of the light elves.

And he was a criminal.

Yet more important than this discovery was the fact that Devon had pulled it from the prince's mind, yanked it out all by himself. And the feeling left him wanting more. He forgot all about Nemesio's anger and Talesin's accusations. Like a moth drawn to a flame, Devon pushed his mind forward again, hungry for the feeling he had discovered.

The same light sensation came to him again. He heard Kiernan saying something to him, but he ignored it. This was far more interesting.

An unseen barrier suddenly stopped him. A door slammed in his face; a window shut him out. Like an invisible wall, an imaginary force field not only stopped him but pushed him back. Devon found himself on solid ground again, his pounding head in his hands. Kiernan held him by the shoulders.

"Are you all right, mage?" he asked, looking concerned.

Devon shook his head. "What happened?"

"You tried to read my mind and I blocked you," Kiernan replied evenly. "All elves and fairies are able to do this. Most keep a wall up at all times."

Devon found he was shaking. "But just a moment ago..."

"I let you," Kiernan replied. "In Nemesio's case you caught him at a very tense moment. You planted a warning in his head at a moment when his life was in danger. The message was so strong that you broke through his wall and probably saved his life."

Devon turned to Nemesio, who was now, after things had been cleared up, nodding his thanks.

"What happened in the pub was a reaction that you had no power over," Kiernan explained. "And this changes things a bit."

Nemesio narrowed his eyes. "What do you mean?"

Panas took a step forward. "What are you thinking, Kiernan?"

Kiernan spoke to the whole group, but he kept his green eyes trained on Devon as if he knew it was the mage he had to win over. "We don't have time to get to Kalli's school. Her deadline is less than twenty-four hours away."

"What deadline?" Devon asked.

"The princess has threatened to expose us to Prelionan authorities if we do not deliver the key to her by tomorrow night," Nemesio explained.

Devon stared at Kiernan. "But she is your sister."

"Yes," Kiernan admitted sourly. "Devon, I think we can solve both our problems at once. Kalli lied to us about you. Perhaps she thought she could get rid of you through us; perhaps taking the key from you was all the revenge she needed. At the very least, she intends to hurt your reputation with Lorcan as she intends to hurt us in Preliona if we do not follow her orders. If she can prove to him that you stole his precious key, then she can say that she was right about you all along. Well, this time she is not going to get what she wants. Not exactly."

"We're going to Preliona." Nemesio stated.

Kiernan nodded. "Yes. Kalli may not be able to hold the key, but she will see that we have it." He turned to Devon. "Cornelius can decide what to do with you from there."

Anger flared in Devon's head for a moment. "No one has to *do* anything with me, Your Highness."

Kiernan spun about and glared at the mage. "*Do not call me that,*" he hissed. "I did not give you that information so you could use it against me."

Devon softened somewhat. "I only meant that once Cornelius has the key, I intend to return to DeCresler's Institute. No one need be responsible for me. Either way, I assure you, your secret is safe with me."

Kiernan nodded. "Let us hope so, mage. I would truly hate for our newfound relationship to come to an unhealthy end."

25~Passing the Torch

The white dragon was cornered, and knew it. It was all the seven companions could do to stay out of the way of its frosty breath. Back and forth the creature paced, snaking its head side to side to get a lock on its attackers. Already the landscape around them was slippery with ice and it was becoming increasingly difficult to make any type of stand against the dragon.

Cornelius had created a small sphere of magic about himself and was currently floating above the White, raining bolts of electricity down on the lizard. This only served to irritate the dragon and Cornelius was now trying to avoid its swinging tail.

Althea was on the ground, fighting viciously side by side with Cassian and Cade, the twin warriors from LaTourlamine. Each one darted around the legs of the White, too close for the animal to get off an ice blast. The three warriors had already cut the dragon deeply in several places, leaving its left hind leg unusable.

Finella, the dwarven healer, and Barrett, the half-elven thief, were hanging off to the sides, both with weapons drawn, pacing and looking for an opening to join the fight. But they were unable to do much more than watch their friends take on the dragon.

Lorcan had disappeared. Cornelius figured the other mage had gone around behind, perhaps to surprise the dragon from the back while the others deterred it from the front.

Cornelius turned his eyes back to the fight.

Althea was mesmerizing. Her gleaming sword sailed through the air with a grace that suggested the weapon was a part of its mistress. Her long hair, pale blonde then, streamed out behind her as wild and free as the dragon, yet it never once touched her face or got in her way. He could have watched her forever. But instead he pushed his bubble in a circle around the dragon, again searching for a weak spot.

What he saw surprised him more than he wanted to admit. Lorcan, red cloak whipping in the wind, was snooping around the ledge where the dragon had made its final stand. He was ignoring the battle behind him, instead searching the pile of snow and ice for the damned box.

Cornelius was stunned. Here they were, facing one of the most intense menaces they had ever encountered— a white dragon who had led them on a hellish journey to the borders of Serenia—and now that victory was nearly at hand, Lorcan chose this time to continue the fruitless search for a treasure they were unsure even existed!

Damn the scrawny little gold digger, Cornelius cursed. Even Barrett the thief was fighting the dragon—not searching in the snow for treasure!

Cornelius was about to head down and blast the red mage himself when things suddenly got worse on the ground below. The dragon made a lunge and all three warriors were forced to dive aside or be crushed in its massive jaws.

Cassian and Cade both rolled and stood, each one taking a stab at the White as it skidded by them. Finella managed to take a swing at the dragon's maw with her mace, cutting it deeply.

Althea was not so lucky. Forced to dive in the opposite direction, their leader went sliding toward the ledge at an alarming rate. Here the ice pitched downward, aiming at the cliff and certain death. With a tremendous effort Althea plunged her sword into the thick ice and brought her slide to an abrupt halt.

Cornelius pushed his sphere in her direction.

"Cornelius!" Althea yelled. "Help the twins!"

Cornelius hesitated. Though she had saved herself for the moment, he could see that Althea would never be able to make it back up the steep incline without help.

Cassian and Cade were in trouble as well, however. The dragon had bought itself some room and was flapping its great wings to get at the twins. Torn,

Cornelius searched the ground again for Lorcan. He spotted him in nearly the same place he had been a moment before. Only this time he had something in his arms. The chest.

At that moment Cornelius did not care if the other sorcerer had a blue ice diamond in his hands. "Lorcan!" he shouted. "Althea is in trouble!"

But Lorcan could not hear him above the wind caused by the dragon's wings. Now Cornelius had a truly difficult decision to make. Disobey a direct order and snag his leader before she slid off the edge of the world, or go to the aid of the other two warriors.

Hoping he would have time to do both, Cornelius turned to the dragon. Summoning one of the most complex attack spells he could think of, the wizard focused his entire being on the worm.

His words came quickly and sharply but still it took several seconds to recite the entire spell. All the while Cornelius could feel the hold on his sphere slipping. A tremendous amount of heat was building inside the sphere. Beads of sweat were trickling down his temples, and he could feel his clothes sticking to his body.

Cornelius dropped the sphere spell. At the same time, he loosed a massive heat spell. A blanket of fire enveloped the dragon, circling its white form and scorching it black. The giant let out one last howl of pain, stretching its head to the sky. It did not bring it back down. Its body, crisp and charred unrecognizable, frozen in place, was a hideous statue of ashes.

Weakened from the effort, Cornelius plummeted to the ground. The impact broke his foot, but he hardly noticed. He was too exhausted to feel anything but a growing numbness. He could barely lift his head.

He found the strength to move when Cassian and Cade screamed Althea's name.

The Malhurian sorcerer used the last ounce of his power to turn his head. Barrett was running toward Althea, skating across the ice with the grace of a dancer. But he would not make it in time. Fast as the thief was, he would never make it. Cornelius rolled to his knees just as Althea slipped over the edge of the cliff.

Cornelius Pav woke with a start, grasping the arms of his chair and breathing hard. Terrified, he swung his head to the side.

Althea slept in the bed beside him—alive—covered in white bandages and blankets.

Cornelius was bathed in sweat, his knuckles pale from gripping the chair. She had never gone over the edge. That was an extra addition to his nightmare, the only part that had been untrue.

Cornelius wiped a hand across his sweaty brow and leaned back in his chair, exhausted. Until the last few moments, he had not slept in three days. Yesterday he had overseen the hours of work the clerics had spent healing Althea's scorched back. The skin there had been nearly seared away by the fireball blast. It had taken him and four clerics fourteen hours of intensive work to repair the damage. There would be scars, but she would probably live.

Now the biggest risk was that she would die of infection.

Technically, he had been there in a magical capacity only. The healers required a completely sterile environment to work in. Cornelius, the inventor of the *Breathing Sphere*, was the one to provide it. Emotionally, he could not tear himself from his friend's side, terrified that if he turned his head for a moment she would slip away.

Perhaps that was why the dream came to him tonight, he thought, that strange memory of a decades-old battle; one among countless others, and hardly the most memorable. Still, they had nearly lost Althea that day. The warrior had managed to crawl halfway up the icy incline, using her sword for leverage, before Barrett and the others reached her. By the time Lorcan had realized what was going on, Althea was safe. Cornelius had nearly killed the other mage in his fury.

He shook his head at the memory. He was tired and afraid. Yes, that was the feeling in the pit of his stomach. Fear. And the only other time he had really felt it was that day on the cliff thirty years ago, when they were young.

But they were not young now. Cornelius was exhausted and drained by the spell he had invented. Lorcan DeCresler was headmaster of a school he was too old to run. And Althea, their fearless leader, was laid low by a fire spell that might yet kill her.

Something else nagged at him, some other clue was dancing right at the edge of his recollection. For a bare moment he tried to figure it out, but the effort made his vision blur and he finally dropped his head in his hands, rubbing his smooth face.

The door creaked ever so slightly. Cornelius sat up straight and glared. "Gregory," he said, softening when he saw who it was.

"Hello, sir," the half-elf replied. The young scribe was as worn out as the wizard and he leaned on the doorframe, letting it support him. "Alistair sent me. He wants to see you."

Cornelius checked on his friend a final time and stood. "Where is he?" he asked, moving toward the scholar.

"Weapons Hall," Gregory replied.

The wizard nodded and put a hand on Gregory's shoulder. "Have you slept at all, my friend?"

Gregory shrugged. "Other than during useless meetings? No."

"Why don't we get one of the clerics to relieve me, eh? You are no good to her in this state."

But Gregory waved him away. "I couldn't sleep now if I tried. I've made it past some bizarre sleep threshold." He moved to the chair Cornelius had just vacated. "I'll be fine and so will Althea. Go on."

Cornelius decided not to argue and made for the door. "If anything changes, you send for me."

Gregory smiled weakly. "Of course."

"Thank you, Gregory." And he dashed around the corner.

Cornelius was over six feet tall and had a long, purposeful stride. He sailed down the marble halls past startled scholars and councilors who scurried out of his way. The five-minute trip to the Weapons hall took him three. Tired as he was, he did not even break a sweat.

He ducked under the frame of a small door at the back of Nimbus and into a circular room about fifty feet around. Iron bars encircled the room, fixed to the stone with metal bracers jutting out at different lengths into makeshift racks that each held hundreds of weapons. Swords, bows large and small, thousands of stacks of arrows, and a slew of other artillery.

Althea had always been a connoisseur of strange weapons. Over the years she had amassed quite a collection. A good quarter of the racks in the room were devoted to these prizes, and to Cornelius's knowledge were never used. A black saber from Malhuria shone a dark light from a rack high up. A gigantic claymore sheathed in a blood-red scabbard, which could only have belonged to the Crimson Guard, leaned precariously against a lower rack. Twin golden swords from LaTourlamine, an ancient Dwarven Halberd, and several wicked looking scimitars… all these Cornelius recognized from one place or another. He had been with Althea when she had acquired them. But hundreds of others he had never seen. It had been years since Cornelius had entered this room. He was surprised by how vast Althea's collection had grown.

Alistair stood in the dead center of the room, straight and unwavering as usual. Beside him stood a woman Cornelius did not recognize. She wore a gray Watch uniform and stood as immobile and unwavering as her commanding officer. Cornelius's eyes flicked to the sleeve of her gray tunic, which was marked with three silver lines. He smiled. She was a commander, one of only three in the city. Cornelius nodded his approval.

"How is she?" Alistair asked suddenly.

Cornelius raised an eyebrow, pleased that the chief put his concern for the governor over introductions. "She is stable. The next few hours will be critical, however."

Alistair nodded and turned to the woman beside him. "Cornelius, this is Commander Gabrielle March. I have asked her to head the investigation."

She was quite tall. Cornelius only had her by an inch or two and she was not thin. Her arms were sculpted so that the muscles under her uniform were well defined. She looked to be about twenty years old and quite attractive despite her intimidating size. Her brown hair was cut short and her dark eyes gleamed with intelligence. She had a square face, but her cheekbones were high and sharp.

Cornelius extended his hand. "Good to meet you, Commander," he said as she took his hand in hers. Her grip was strong, and she met his eyes without fear.

"Sir," she said. "It is my pleasure."

"And mine," Cornelius replied, intrigued by the young woman before him. "But Alistair, if you might indulge me, why aren't you conducting the investigation yourself?"

Alistair sighed. "I believe my hesitancy toward Odin's claims yesterday put me in a position to be criticized as unobjective. I think it's in everyone's best interest to put the job in the hands of an unbiased party."

"I see," Cornelius said, clearing his throat. "Do not take this the wrong way, either of you, but doesn't Lord Darweshi have a problem with high-ranking female officers?"

Alistair grinned. "Indeed he does." He looked so much happier than he had in weeks that Cornelius had to laugh. The commander too cracked a small smile.

Cornelius turned to her. "Have you found anything yet, Commander?" he asked, almost afraid to hear the answer.

Gabrielle March sighed. "Unfortunately, no. The scene of the attack on the governor has long since been trampled over. Besides, Alistair himself went over the evidence there, and I sincerely doubt he missed anything."

Cornelius smiled inwardly. The woman was not trying to score points with the old man—she was serious.

"I have also interviewed Edmee S'Trobenue's cousins again on the subject of her husband's disappearance. They volunteered plenty of information, almost all of which was false. Still, though their stories of that night vary, their description of a red-haired elf is consistent, and their insistence on the presence of the imp thief does not waver in the slightest. They believe what they saw."

Cornelius frowned. Here was the part where the wizard was supposed to speak up and throw the commander off the trail. This was the point at which Cornelius would supply the officers with a description of the decoy, thereby keeping the Watch Chief from discovering the identity of *Duak-Thenal's* leader.

But Preliona's wizard hesitated. For some reason he could not fathom, Cornelius wanted to see what the commander would do with her information. "Are you sure they were not all drunk?"

Commander March gave him a wry smile. "Now, or at the time of the incident?"

"Either," Cornelius chuckled.

She shrugged. "Offhand, I would say that today they seemed pretty well put together, though I wouldn't doubt Darweshi had something to do with that. He would not want his star witnesses messing up his show. At the time of Raymond's disappearance, though, I could not say. My guess would be yes, they were drunk, but since their story is consistent the question of their inebriation won't matter."

"Unless they are all lying," Cornelius suggested.

"Then they are doing an excellent job," March replied. "I can usually catch someone in a lie. And I interviewed each of them separately so they wouldn't be able to hear what the others said."

Cornelius scanned the commander's face. He decided that she was older than he had first surmised, perhaps mid-twenties. It was her eyes that gave her away. Her tanned skin was smooth except for a crease at the edge of each eye. Those brown orbs spoke of a calculating type of intelligence. She was observant and understanding and exceedingly studious.

He had liked her instantly. He was positive that Althea had had a hand in training her. She had the same tenacious and straightforward manner Althea possessed. She would do her job to perfection and without fail.

Exactly what Cornelius was afraid of.

"So, what are your conclusions?" he asked cautiously.

She sighed. "Such as they are? Unofficially, I would rule out kidnapping. By all accounts, Raymond S'Trobenue was extremely unhappy with his wife's family, and I do not doubt they made his life miserable. It is very possible he was escaping them. If Captain Tain Elire was involved, I cannot think for what purpose, but I don't imagine it being anything malicious. The small profile we have on her does not suggest that she is famous for anything untoward, other than thievery. I cannot say the same for the elf—the group has been accused of kidnapping before."

Cornelius swallowed. "And the rest of the attacks?"

"The robbery of Darweshi's architect certainly points in *Duak-Thenal's* direction. Two elves stole blueprints and money. As both these incidents happened on the same night, I believe they were connected somehow."

Cornelius was almost afraid to ask. "And Edmee?"

She opened her arms. "We know from the wounds that Edmee S'Trobenue sustained she was killed by a dagger with an unusual serrated blade. Up until this point we have always assumed her death was the result of a random robbery."

Alistair interrupted. "Now, however, it does not seem such a coincidence that the original architect of the Opal Bridge is killed, and a few months later her husband disappears and the plans for the bridge she designed are stolen."

Cornelius was wary now. Alistair and Gabrielle March were far more on track than Cornelius would have expected. "Still, it is hard to imagine elves murdering an unarmed woman in the open streets," he suggested.

Alistair crossed his arms and wandered about, "True, my friend, but as of right now, they are our only suspects."

The commander went on. "But as far as Althea goes, my guess would be that the elves are not responsible."

"I am inclined to agree with you," Cornelius replied with relief.

"Also, if what you say is true, then the attack bespeaks a wizard's involvement."

Cornelius nodded at the commander, thankful for this small insight. "What do you think, Alistair?" he asked.

The Watch Chief stroked his gray whiskers and walked slowly toward them. "Cornelius," he said, "I have had enough thinking for one day, which is why I've turned this investigation over to Commander March here. As far as I am concerned, she is in charge. I would like your public support on that. It's why I called you down here."

Cornelius raised an eyebrow. "Of course," he said. "But what will you be doing if not heading the investigation?"

"I have my hands full increasing security in the city. I am ashamed to admit that things have been rather lax lately. Perhaps if I had noticed sooner, Althea would not be lying in that bed back there."

"You mustn't blame yourself…" Cornelius began.

Alistair raised a hand. "Please," he said. "It is I who have the authority to place said blame, and I give it to myself freely." He paced about and ran a wrinkled hand through his gray hair. "Ultimately *everything* is my fault. So until further notice, I am doubling the guard shifts. No one will get in or out of this city without my knowing about it. We will catch *Duak-Thenal*, and we will get to the bottom of this," Alistair said to him. "Do I have your support, Cornelius?"

The intensity of Alistair's words gave the wizard pause. It was not revenge he was looking for, but redemption. He blamed himself for recent happenings and he needed to capture the Exiles to make up for it. In that moment, Cornelius wanted to tell him everything. For a split second he thought he could get the old man to put down his sword and listen. If anyone could understand the predicament Cornelius found himself in, it should be Alistair.

But in the end, he simply shook Alistair's hand. He was in too deep. Spilling his secrets now would only complicate matters. "Of course, you have my support," he heard himself saying. "And you, Commander. Please call on me if you need any help."

"I may do that, sir. I doubt Darweshi will be happy with Alistair's decision to put me in charge."

"Really?" Cornelius grinned. "I find that hard to believe."

Gabrielle March laughed lightly. Cornelius again decided he really liked the woman. He sincerely hoped that the next few days would not change his mind.

26~The Key to the City

Lieutenant Bergeron Tellen, one of twelve night watchmen at the Dawn gate, was on the lookout for disguised elves trying to enter the city. *Du-ak-Thenal* was expected to show up, and he was under express orders to detain all suspicious looking travelers.

So far this night, the over-eager Bergeron had mistaken several half-elven merchants, an extremely wealthy family from Villuna, and a band of dwarves for the elven rogues. All had been outraged—the dwarves had been especially angry. All six of them had gone so far as to threaten to press charges against the Watch, and Bergeron personally, for even suggesting their resemblance to a gang of elves. The lieutenant had poured forth apologies to the dwarves and promised them a full night of free room and board at The Mercy Inn. They accepted with no small amount of grumbling.

Bergeron had since allowed nearly everyone entering Preliona to pass without question. And why not? It was thought among the ranks that the Exiles had been using more unconventional methods of penetrating the city than the front gate. In weaker spots, the Watch Chief had even tripled forces. In the unlikely event that the rogues decided to sneak in at the front, Bergeron felt more than confident in his ability to spot them. After all, how well could a group of skinny elves disguise themselves?

So it was that when a ragtag group of weary travelers stumbled through the Dawn, Bergeron barely gave them a glance.

All the travelers were hooded, and they staggered along, as though they had walked for days. Bergeron assumed they were beggars—seven in all.

He moved from the guardhouse door and into the group's path, holding up a hand and motioning for them to stop. At the head of the group were two young men. Humans, Bergeron could see, for enough of their faces showed under their cowls to make out a few features. Square jaws and full cheekbones were in plain view. "State your business in Preliona," Bergeron sighed, without much effort.

The front man raised his head ever so slightly, but Bergeron could easily see human eyes peering out at him. "Study, sir," the man said in an accent Bergeron could not place. He raised an eyebrow and took a closer look at the speaker.

The man did not flinch or back away under Bergeron's best intimidating glare. "What type of study?" Bergeron asked.

"We are scholars from Wisia," the man went on. "We have some business at the library, and we intend to see some sights when our work is done."

Bergeron nodded, still struggling to recognize the accent, for it certainly was not of Wisia. "Let's see some identification."

Without hesitation all seven party members unrolled similar pieces of parchment. Bergeron only bothered to look at those of the two men before him, and those only briefly. Everything seemed to be in order. "All right then, *Mr. Wisia*," he said. "Library's straight ahead, opposite side of the square. But I suspect you already know that."

"Aye, sir. But I thank you anyway."

Bergeron nodded and began to motion the party past. "On your way, folks. There's a curfew tonight, so you may wish to wait until tomorrow to begin your research."

The whole group stopped. "Curfew?" the front man asked. "What for?"

Bergeron shook his head. "Standard procedure. Nothing to worry about, I assure you. Ten o'clock, everyone off the streets."

Bergeron was about to hustle them along when the lead scholar turned to him. "Thank you for the warning, sir," the visitor from Wisia said. Then he tipped his head in an odd sort of way and winked, "Have a good night."

Bergeron opened his mouth and froze. He was certain the lead man's eyes had changed to gold. He reached out and grabbed the speaker of the group by the arm.

The man stiffened and turned back to him sharply. But Bergeron wanted a better look at the face under the cowl and he leaned in.

A gruff and un-shaven man peered out at him. Normal ears and plain brown eyes set amid rather puffy features all but erased Bergeron's thoughts of stopping an illegal elf on his watch.

He closed his mouth with an audible snap and released the man. "My apologies, sir," he stammered. The man nodded and shuffled quickly away.

Bergeron Tellen shook his head and passed the exchange off as a trick of the moonlight. He went back to his post and looked up at the large clock tower to his right, silently wishing the minute hand would move along.

— ✷ ✷ ✷ —

Halfway across the square and out of sight of the Watch, the seven companions ducked into the alley between the library and Nimbus.

"That was amazing!" Panas said throwing back his cowl. He could barely contain his glee. "I told you it could be done." He turned to Devon, who had his hands on his knees, breathing hard and looking as though his eyes might roll back into his head any moment. Panas clapped the mage on the back and Devon tumbled forward. Nemesio grabbed him before he could fall on his face.

"Brilliant job, mage," Panas said, ignoring Devon's woozy state and turning to the scowling ice elf. "You see, Talesin, mind readers can come in handy sometimes." He pointed back toward the gate. "That guard never suspected a thing!"

Talesin glared at the light elf and turned away. "I'll check the square," he mumbled, and moved away without waiting for a response.

Kiernan started to follow him, but Dagmar put a hand on his arm and slid past him. "I'll go with him," she said.

Kiernan glanced at her, then stared at the retreating form of his friend. He sighed. "We'll wait for you here."

Dagmar nodded and trotted off after the ice elf. Kiernan turned back to the remaining members of his crew. Panas was still spouting praises to himself as quietly as his excited voice would allow. He fairly danced about on the sidewalk. "Best performance I ever gave!" he sang.

Tain, leaning against the wall beside Nemesio and Devon, shook her head and laughed, "And the smallest! You didn't speak more than a dozen, mumbled words. And what was that accent?"

Panas opened his mouth to object, but Nemesio cut him off. "Did you see the look on that poor watchman's face? He suspected you right from the start. We were lucky to get past him!"

"Now, now, my critics," Panas said, holding up his hands. "Do not let your jealousy get the better of you."

"Jealous of what?" Nemesio said, keeping his voice low and even. "An actor with a bad accent, whose ego gets in the way of his performance?"

Panas scowled, aware for the first time that his friends were doing more than simply teasing him. His gold eyes flickered from Nemesio to Tain and back again. "What are you talking about?"

"Panas, you winked at him!" Tain nearly shouted. "Poor Devon can only do so much with his mind-bending abilities. The guard looked right into your eyes. Why do you think he stopped you?"

Panas waved her away. "Oh really, Captain, you should talk. Who nearly fell from the top of the balustrade a few minutes ago?"

Tain set her jaw and suddenly looked stony. "I slipped, Panas." The imp had scaled one of the city walls, something she had done countless times before. She had been unprepared for the unusual number of guards patrolling the upper walls of the city. She slipped and fell only seconds before being spotted. Talesin had caught her, but the imp was embarrassed. Panas was taking ample advantage of the situation to get the spotlight off himself.

Panas turned his back on the imp. "Well, my dear, if I were you, I'd have those pointed ears checked. Your balance seems a bit off."

The imp exploded and lunged for Panas, leaping onto the light elf's back and latching onto his golden locks.

Panas cried out in pain and twirled around, trying to throw the imp off. Kiernan surged forward and wrapped one arm about her waist, using the other to pry her tiny hands from Panas's hair. Nemesio grabbed at her other arm and together they managed to remove the enraged imp from Panas' back.

But the elf continued to taunt her. "Temper, temper, Captain," he said, waggling one long finger in her face.

With a growl of anger Tain lunged again. This time the two elves nearly lost their hold on her.

"Enough you, two!" Kiernan hissed, no longer having the patience to hold everyone together. "Panas, the Captain's right. You and Devon pulled off a great trick, but that is all you did. The guard here has at least doubled, and that no doubt has something to do with us. Now is not the time for experimenting with magic tricks…"

"Magic tricks!" Devon protested, pushing himself from the wall. "Do you have any idea how difficult…?"

Kiernan rounded on him. "Yes, I do. And I applaud what you did, but I do not want to see that particular maneuver ever again. It is risky, and we cannot afford to take chances of that kind. Find another use for your talents if the need arises."

He let go of Tain and moved toward the entrance of the alley. "Let us get to Cornelius quickly and do what we came to do. We can argue about our tactics later." He turned back to them and his green eyes flashed dangerously, daring anyone to oppose him. "Understood?"

No one answered, so the prince turned his back on them and scanned the square. It was not quite eight-thirty and the night was relatively mild, yet the large square was close to empty. The Guild Hall was dark. The white marble stairs of the library, usually teeming with people late into the night, were deserted. Even Nimbus, which was well lit and still contained a few men and women milling about, had a strained feeling. Instead of scholars and council members engaged in friendly parley, the leaders of the city stood on the steps looking solemnly out on the square. Arms were crossed, brows were furrowed, and feet were planted.

There was more going on here than a few extra guards out to apprehend a band of outlaws. As much as Kiernan liked to believe his merry band of cohorts struck fear into people's hearts, he knew their reputation alone could hardly drive an entire city from the streets.

He wanted to talk to Cornelius immediately, but sneaking the group across the square without the cover of crowds of people was going to be extremely difficult. The glow from Nimbus lit up most of the square. The group would have to skirt the perimeter, and that meant slipping past the guard again—something Kiernan did not wish to chance.

The lengthening of a shadow at the base of the library stair caught his attention. Kiernan watched as two dark shapes slid effortlessly across the square, completely undetected by the guard at the gate. Talesin and Dagmar rejoined them in the alley. They threw off their hoods and it was immediately obvious to everyone that they did not have good news.

Dagmar scanned their faces and blew a thin stream of air from her lips. "The governor has been attacked."

"What!?" Panas, Nemesio and Tain shouted together.

Kiernan held up a hand, silencing them. "How?" the prince asked.

"We don't know," Talesin admitted. "The few people that were around to talk with did not know much. Dirt Alley has been shut down."

"Shut down?" Kiernan said.

Dagmar nodded. "Apparently that is where she was attacked. But we have no idea if any arrests have been made. There is no word on the governor's condition."

Kiernan ran a hand across his brow, hoping that his mounting headache would pass. He needed a minute to think, but all that came to mind was the raging conversation he intended to have with his sister.

He leaned back against the wall.

His crew waited patiently near him, not encroaching on his space but lurking in the shadows. He marveled at their relative calm and patience. The Captain, never overwhelmed by a challenge and rarely rattled by anyone but the enigmatic Panas, had apparently already made up with the light elf. The two stood guard at the alley entrance, quiet for once, tossing one of Tain's gilded daggers back and forth between them.

Devon and Nemesio leaned opposite each other against the alley walls and spoke in hushed tones. In fact, Kiernan could not even be sure the mage was speaking at all. He suspected Nemesio was allowing the mage to read his thoughts. Of all of them, Nemesio was probably the most open to having his thoughts probed. The elven court in Malhuria employed dozens of mind readers for a variety of jobs. The most prominent of these was spying on the Court of Lilies, the human power at the opposite end of the desert city. The two large households were in a perpetual state of rivalry. Nemesio had become quite used to filtering his thoughts so that mind readers picked up only what he wanted them to.

Talesin could not be seen, but Kiernan knew where he was. He skulked about at the far end of their hiding place, scraping one black booted foot along the wall, scrounging for who knew what. The ice elf was hurting, Kiernan knew. Traveling with the mage had been difficult for him, bringing up memories he would much rather have forgotten. And Kiernan had done little to placate his friend these last few hours.

Dagmar alone stood near him. She leaned against the wall and stared at a spot on the ground. She did not look up at him, even though she must have felt his gaze. He knew she would not look either, not until he decided.

If Kiernan had a second in command, it was Dagmar Coal. Yet in a time like this she rarely offered her opinion even though she most certainly had one. In a way, her silence was the best thing for him. It forced the prince to make a decision unhampered by the view of others, to go with his first instinct, which was almost unerringly the right one. He knew all this, but it did not make her ignoring him any easier.

Kiernan dropped his head against the granite behind him, hit it several times and closed his eyes. "Tain?" he called, finally breaking the silence. He heard the light step of the imp and knew she was beside him. Without opening his eyes, he spoke, "Can you navigate us to the other side of Cornelius' tower without getting us caught?"

"Yes," she replied firmly, without the least bit of sarcasm.

Kiernan was grateful for small favors. He opened his emerald eyes to scan the group. "Let's go, then. I fear the wizard will be the only one who can lend us some insight. I did not want to involve him too deeply this time, but it seems we have no choice. Lead on, Captain."

Without a word, the Captain turned about and headed not to the entrance of the alley but toward the back of it. The puzzled group hesitated but it was Panas who spoke up.

"Ummm, Captain? Perhaps you didn't notice but our exit is that way," Panas said, pointing over his shoulder.

Tain rounded on him, eyes blazing. "Did Kiernan assign you to navigational duties, oh great thespian?" She spun on her heel without waiting for an answer and continued toward the back of the alley. The tight space between the two buildings was unlit, and it got darker the farther back they went. The alley was longer than Kiernan had expected and the street under them began to slant downward. Devon, nearly blind in the darkness, slipped. Dagmar caught his elbow before he could hit the ground.

Several long minutes passed, and the prince was about to question Tain's guidance himself when she stopped. They had come to the end of the alley, but Kiernan saw no sign of an exit. The Captain was bending down over something in the ground. Kiernan stepped forward as Tain hooked her tiny fingers under a round metal plate in the middle of the alley. The prince grinned as he watched Tain struggle to pull up the sewer grate. She could not budge it and Talesin and Nemesio bent down to take over. The grate came up with a hollow scrape and Tain stood, smiling confidently, and brushing off her hands.

Kiernan nodded his approval at his ever-resourceful friend.

"Oh, I *know* you don't expect me to slop around in the underbelly of this overstuffed city!" Panas protested. He stepped forward and peered over the edge. The light elf pulled back, holding his nose, and waving his hand before his face. "Really, Kiernan—there *has* to be a better way."

"It's the shortest way, Panas," Tain growled. "And it isn't that bad. Preliona's the only city that employs street sweepers—the sewers are clean."

Panas curled his lip at the imp. "I'm sure our definitions of clean differ drastically," he muttered.

Tain chose to ignore the light elf and made to climb into the hole in the street. Talesin pulled her back, however, and before she could protest, dropped into the sewer first. The others followed suit, with Kiernan and Panas bringing up the rear.

But before Kiernan could squat down Panas grabbed at his arm. "How did she know?" Panas whispered.

"Know what?" Kiernan asked.

"How did she know where to find the grate? How does she plan to navigate underground in a city she has only visited with us?"

Kiernan turned to face Panas fully, then looked back toward the hole into which Tain had disappeared. How, indeed? The Captain had a photographic memory when it came to mapping a city. Even based on the few times she had been in Preliona, he was confident she could get them to Cornelius the quickest way. But the sewer had surprised him. He had never seen the underground of this city.

Therefore, neither had Tain.

This meant one of two things. Either she had heard about the sewer system and was now relying on someone else's description, or...

"She's been here without us." Panas finished his thought for him.

For what seemed like the hundredth time in the last few moments, Kiernan Nightwing closed his eyes in vexation. "Damn her," he hissed.

Tain had sworn up and down to all who would listen that she had never stolen anything from Preliona. If it turned out now that she had been lying—if she had committed a crime in Preliona—then the Watch Chief would have more authority to pursue her. She would have successfully doubled the odds against herself.

And all of them.

He opened his eyes and pointed one long finger at Panas. "Not a word about this," he said. "I'll deal with it later."

Panas nodded. The two of them stepped onto the ledge of the grate. "She didn't have to tell, you know."

Kiernan turned back to look at his friend. "What?"

"She could have taken another path to Cornelius. I wish she had. But she picked the quickest, safest route even if it meant you'd find out she'd been here before." Panas shrugged his shoulders. "Who knows, maybe she didn't steal anything. Maybe she just likes sewers."

He knew Panas was right, of course. He silently promised himself not to kill the imp once he reached her. He would talk to her later, when this whole business with the key was over. The prince of the light elves dropped into the hole.

Kiernan had braced himself to land in several inches of murky water. He was wholly surprised then when his booted feet hit dry rock. His eyes adjusted quickly to the dark as he sized up the gray tunnel before him. It was larger and better lit than most sewers; not that roaming about the garbage systems of human cities was a favorite pastime of his. Though there was a distinct rancid odor in the air, it was not nearly as bad as he had expected. There was murky water in the tunnel, but the companions were standing to the right of it. The dark stream was about ten feet across and sloshed around inches from their boots, dawdling away from them. Along the walls every fifty feet or so, metal sconces burned a low yellow light.

It was a well-kept and obviously frequented sewer. Kiernan had to wonder at their chances of encountering someone down here. Though at this hour he doubted it. At least if they crossed swords with anyone it would be unheard by the Watch. Unless Alistair had begun stationing guards for garbage detail, too.

Panas landed lightly by his side. "*Ziyad's blood!* These sewers are clean."

Tain was already at the head of the group, motioning them along the small walkway. She was pointedly avoiding the prince's gaze, all but proving her guilt.

For the next half hour, *Duak-Thenal* silently trooped through the sewers of Preliona. Whenever they came to a place where they could go one of two ways, the Captain never hesitated. She knew these tunnels. Knew them too damned well.

Finally, after what seemed like forever and long after Kiernan had completely lost track of his whereabouts, Tain came up short, stopping the crew in their tracks. She stood in a tiny pool of light, much like several others they had passed, and pointed upward. "This one is right outside the front gate," she said.

Without waiting for approval, the Captain started to climb the metal ladder that clung to the wall. Once again, she was pulled back by Talesin, who always insisted on going first. Tain, who had long since stopped complaining about the ice elf's chivalry, simply stood back, and waited for Talesin to give a thumbs up.

Kiernan stared hard at the imp while they waited. But Tain would not look up and did not return his gaze, though she surely must have felt it. She was guilty, no doubt about it. More than anything, Kiernan wanted to have it out with her.

But what was he supposed to do? Berate her for doing what she did best? For essentially practicing the art that Venk and *Duak-Thenal* relied on her for?

When Talesin called down to them, Tain scooted up the ladder as fast as a mouse, before Kiernan could say anything. He waited for the others, then followed slowly, still fuming.

The street above was dimly lit, but that was nothing unusual on this side of town. Dirt Alley, now deserted, spread out before them.

The group moved silently down the alley, flitting in and out of shadows, dragging the clumsy mage with them.

Tain stopped under the awning of the last shop on the street and waited.

Cornelius's pale tower was quiet and still. The gates that blocked it were strictly for show. No locks barred their entrance. Simply an enormous wrought iron fence with an ancient snake-like design preceded the white walkway to the tower.

Cornelius had no need for locks. No one in the city of Preliona would have dared enter here without permission. But Cornelius had to protect himself from those from outside the city limits: foolish thieves who did not know or care about the reputation of the great white wizard. Those who risked crossing the borders of the white tower uninvited regretted it. Always.

Fortunately, Kiernan and his crew knew the secret for entering the most mysterious building in Preliona.

Talesin and Tain went first, slipping across the gravel like ghosts, barely touching the ground. Kiernan watched them go, confirmed that they were not being watched, and turned to Devon. "Look carefully," he said to the mage. Devon looked up at him and Kiernan pointed to Talesin and Tain.

The imp was feeling about the pale stone to the side of the gate. It appeared she was searching for an opening, but Kiernan knew she was not. After a moment she found what she was looking for. She placed her tiny hand over one brick and pressed in. Nothing changed that the eye could see, but Talesin and Tain walked straight through the gate.

"A mirage?" Devon gasped.

Kiernan nodded and grabbed the mage's arm, propelling him across the street. "Yes. Now you do the same thing. I will go with you. But once we are inside you must be even more careful. Stay on the white stones. They form a path. Do not step off even an inch."

"Why?" Devon asked.

Kiernan grinned but it was not a friendly one. "Step off the stones and you become visible to the creatures of Cornelius' garden—who would not hesitate to have you for a snack."

Devon swallowed and reached for his spell bag.

Kiernan grabbed his wrist. "Do not bother, mage—it won't help. You are walking into the den of one of the most powerful wizards in Tearlach. I doubt your spells will protect you here. No offense."

Devon dropped his arm. "None taken."

"If you do as I tell you, you will not need any spells."

Devon sighed and turned back to watch Dagmar and Panas step through the gate.

"Your turn," Kiernan said, pushing the young mage forward.

— ✳ ✳ ✳ —

Stepping through a portal, especially one you cannot see, was like convincing yourself to walk through glass. Your body knows it is not possible and resists the action.

Devon believed in the portal. Did not doubt the validity of the prince's statement or of what his eyes had seen, but his body simply would not allow him to press on. In a way he wasn't really surprised when the elf pushed him. He was almost glad. With an oof of surprise, Devon stumbled through the gate and landed in an orange heap in the garden.

And what a garden it was.

Green grass covered the entire expanse, but the color was not the normal hue one might expect in a garden. It was several shades darker, more the color of fir trees, and it looked soft and smelled fragrant. Huge aqua-leaved trees bordered the garden and several saplings dotted the lawn. There were other trees, but Devon was unable to name any of them. The one closest to him had a blood red trunk and its leaves were jet black. It was an ominous specimen, but certainly not the most bizarre.

Statues and sculptures, a multitude of types, were scattered about the garden in no particular design or order. The statue closest to him was a gargoyle. A particularly ugly piece and one that Devon did recognize from an old picture he'd seen of a Malhurian castle. Only in the picture the gargoyle had been resting atop the castle, not being used as a lawn decoration.

Devon slowly stood and brushed himself off. He was just beginning to wonder what all the fuss was about. Cornelius' menagerie was eclectic and a bit bizarre, but certainly not at all terrifying.

And suddenly the air to his right turned cold. A low sort of hum filled his ears. Time seemed to slow to a crawl. Very slowly Devon Bane turned his head.

Hanging in the air, mere inches from his face, was a head. Just a head—one whose soul had long since left its body. Its languid blue eyes lolled about in its skull, focusing on nothing. Its mouth hung open at an odd angle and what might have been blood but was now a sickly black substance was oozing from it. One ear was completely gone, and its nose appeared to have been partially eaten away. Devon thought the head belonged to a male, but he could not be certain.

Now he was repulsed beyond the capacity for rational thought.

The face moved. For the first time, Devon saw that it did not float but in fact was held. Two grimy hands, both missing a finger or two, were holding the head up to Devon's eye level. Devon swore he heard his own neck creak as he forced himself to look down.

The hands were attached to obscenely long arms that shot out from the shoulders of a squat, stunted body. Rags no longer recognizable as clothing hung from the pasty white frame. Its gnarled feet were attached to legs so short they could barely be seen.

As Devon stared transfixed, the creature slammed its own head back onto its neck with a sickening crunch, spun about and waddled away.

Sound came back for the mage with a pop, and the world, which had begun to fray at the edges, slammed back into focus with startling clarity. He spun about, careful to stay on the white stones.

Squinting into the shadows, he could now see other creatures lurking. Whether they were ghosts or some other form of undead creature, Devon could not tell. And whether they were tangible or made purely of magic Devon did not know—but they were truly frightening and a definite deterrent.

"Devon, come on."

Devon shook himself and looked ahead. Tain and the others were at the door. He turned and saw that Kiernan and Nemesio had followed him through the gate and were motioning for him to go on. Heaving a shuddering sigh, the mage moved forward. It did not much surprise him that his legs were shaking as he traversed the white stones. He was exceedingly pleased when he made it to the door, and he leaned heavily against the huge frame, waiting for the others to catch up.

He had not yet caught his breath when he noticed the Captain bent over and inserting one of her many tools into the keyhole of the door.

Devon jerked himself upright. "What are you doing?"

Tain did not look up at him. "What does it look like?"

"Well, it looks like breaking and entering," Devon began, not attempting to hide his disapproval. "But I know that couldn't be what you're doing—because why would you want to break into a wizard's castle?!"

Tain Elire stood and placed her hands on her hips. "Because he isn't answering the door and I for one do not want to spend another second in this garden. Do you?"

Devon didn't have an answer for that one, so the thief went back to her task.

"Careful, Captain," Kiernan cautioned. It was the first time the prince had seemed even remotely unnerved by the imp's actions. Devon suddenly became more concerned.

She pushed a twisted white tool further into the keyhole and bent down so her eyes were level with the doorknob. She then bent the flexible tool downward and began to twirl it in a clockwise circle.

Outwardly the imp showed no signs of tension. Her hands were steady, her eyes focused. She did not even break a sweat. But Devon was still nervous. He wasn't sure if it was his newfound telepathy, but somehow, he got the feeling that the Captain was uneasy as well.

After a long moment there was a small audible click and the Captain stood up straight.

"Got it," she announced to a relieved group. She replaced the tiny white lock pick into her belt and reached for the doorknob with a grin.

She had no sooner grasped it than the door was quite suddenly ripped from her hand. A huge, muscled arm shot out from the shadowy tower depths and latched onto the Captain's collar. Tain barreled her arms backward, but she did not escape.

Devon stumbled backward with a cry as the Captain disappeared off the step.

27~Unwelcome Guests

All around him the ring of swords coming free of their sheaths could be heard. Devon himself instinctively reached into the pockets of his robes.

"WHAT ARE YOU DOING?" A booming voice floated out of the darkness, stopping the Exiles in their tracks. "Get in, here the rest of you, before someone sees you!"

Devon turned about and saw that all weapons had been lowered and the elves were sighing with relief. Dagmar, who was closest to him, patted the mage on the shoulder and strode forward, motioning for Devon to follow. Devon hesitated and peered into the gloom. If there was even a shred of light inside, the mage did not see it.

He was about to question the shrewdness of entering when Panas gave him a nudge. "It's all right, Devon," he said. "Cornelius appears to be home, after all."

Devon swallowed and followed Panas and the others across the threshold.

It turned out that he could see rather well on the other side of the door. Sconces hung on pale granite walls, giving off more light than the moon outside did. They were standing in a large foyer, though nothing resembling furniture could be seen. It was simply a big empty white room.

As for the wizard of the tower, well… between the man and the tower, he was by far the more impressive of the two.

He was from Malhuria, so Devon expected him to resemble Nemesio, in skin tone at least. There his expectations came to a grinding halt.

Where Devon had imagined a wizened white-haired old man, there stood a robust bald sixty-something gentleman. Instead of the colored robes common to mages and wizards, Cornelius Pav donned huge ballooning black pants gathered at his ankles, brown sandals criss-crossed his feet, a black shift stretched across his massive chest, and a deep purple vest that flowed past his ankles and fluttered on the floor. He wore no jewelry, but Devon could just see the edges of the swirling black tattoos that marked his arms.

Dangling from the end of one of those arms, held by her collar and pressed against the wall, was the Captain.

Cornelius was furious with her.

"Tain Elire, if you *ever* try to break into my tower again, I will personally see you hanged by your stunted little fingers!"

Tain was struggling to get away from the wizard and failing miserably. "Then maybe you should answer your door when friends come calling!" she objected.

Cornelius leaned into her and glared. "You did not knock, Captain."

"I did, too!" Tain squirmed and smiled sheepishly. "Once... maybe."

Cornelius looked as though he might throw the imp back out the door, but Tain kept talking. "And there was no *trying* about it, Cornelius!" she exclaimed. "I *did* break into your tower, and it's my professional opinion that your security system is in need of improvement."

Instead of arguing, the wizard surprised Devon by smiling sweetly and laughing at the imp. Then he abruptly loosed her from his grasp. Tain fell to the floor, landing hard on her backside. Talesin and Nemesio immediately reached down to pick her up, but she shook them off harshly and rounded on Cornelius.

The wizard stood as before. His huge arms were crossed, and he glared straight down at the imp, who was forced to look up over a foot and a half to meet his gaze. Tain opened her mouth, prepared to unleash a torrent of sarcastic remarks.

But whatever scathing words had been on the imp's tongue were swallowed when she looked into Cornelius' face. The wizard's black eyes were swirling with anger, his square jaw set and foreboding. Tain gulped and took a step back. Devon guessed this was not the first time the Captain had been admonished by the wizard.

Cornelius Pav raised one finger and pointed it at the Captain. "Don't. Touch. Anything," he warned.

Tain crossed her arms over her chest and stuck out her chin. "Fine," she pouted, and stormed past him, disappearing down the hall and into the darkness.

Cornelius did not turn to watch her go but instead called over his shoulder. "I mean it, Tain! More eyes than mine guard this tower."

"I said *fine*!" Tain's angry voice floated back to them.

The wizard sighed and turned to Talesin and Panas. "Go on," he nodded, "See that she doesn't get herself killed, will you?"

Panas slipped lightly by them and began walking backward in the direction Tain had taken. "You've made her angry now, Cornelius. You'll be lucky if she doesn't try to steal anything she can carry."

The light elf trotted away, followed by Talesin. Cornelius Pav turned back to Kiernan and the remainder of the group. "Well?" he demanded.

"Sorry, Neil," Kiernan said, stepping forward. "We were in a hurry."

"I gathered," the mage replied. He then turned his heavy gaze on Devon. "So, this is Kalli's thief?"

Kiernan nodded. "Devon Bane, meet Cornelius Pav."

Devon was at a complete loss for words. Before him stood a man he had dreamed of meeting, though certainly not under these circumstances. He did not know much about the wizard. Lorcan had always been rather tight-lipped about Tearlach's other infamous mage. But what he did know filled him with wonder and dread.

Cornelius was one of the three most famous mages in Tearlach, Lorcan DeCresler and the princess Kalliroestria being the other two. Lorcan and Cornelius had both been members of an infamous band of heroes called *Glory*. It was said in some books that Cornelius, always the darker of the two mages, was responsible for some of the most dangerous spells and curses invented in the last several decades.

Cornelius stuck his hand out and Devon took it with only slight hesitation. "A pleasure, young man," the wizard said. "Lorcan tells me you are one of the most talented students he has ever had."

Devon blinked in surprise. Lorcan had never said any such thing to him. Without taking his eyes off the man, Devon quickly rummaged in one of his voluminous pockets and brought forth the key.

Cornelius plucked the silver and blue piece from Devon's palm, turned it over once in his hand, and took off down the hall.

Devon and the others followed quickly.

"What are you going to do with it?" Devon called after the wizard.

"Don't know yet," Cornelius admitted. "I'm not even sure what it is, or if it was worth you stealing it, young man."

Nemesio laughed.

But Devon was still nervous. "If you don't mind me asking, sir," Devon said, running to catch up with the long-legged wizard, "How is it that I came by the title of thief in the first place, when Lorcan himself sent me here with the key?"

Cornelius did not stop or even slow his pace. "I must say, Devon, that little piece of information has me puzzled as well. Only a day after he told me you were coming, the princess Kalliroestria informed me that Lorcan had reported his key stolen. I have not been able to contact Lorcan since then."

The wizard rounded one dark corner after another until Devon was so turned around he thought he would be lost forever. "But you must know how befuddled he has been of late. My guess is that he simply forgot he had sent you. It is a good thing Kiernan found you before his sister did."

Devon swallowed.

"Yes, I think this will do," Cornelius said, stopping outside an open door. The room before them was completely devoid of furniture, large and windowless, made of the same pale granite as the rest of the structure.

Without warning the wizard waved his hand above his head.

...and the room began to change. Before Devon's stunned eyes the pale walls wavered and seemed to slide down as if they were melting. Devon felt his stomach do a flip flop as deep cherry wood materialized before him. A large desk, several cushioned chairs, and a fireplace began to develop out of thin air. In seconds, the once blank room had become an elegant study.

"I hate it when he does that."

Devon jumped and stepped back, nearly falling over Nemesio. Panas had magically appeared and stood in a corner of the room. He was shaking his head as if to clear it. "You could at least warn us, Cornelius," the light elf complained.

"That would take all the fun out of it now, wouldn't it?" The wizard smiled and glanced around. "Where is the Captain?"

"Up the hall checking out the view from the turret," Panas said. He grabbed onto the desk before him to steady himself. "I feel like I left my stomach up there, Cornelius. Don't you ever use the stairs?"

"No," Cornelius replied.

"What happened?" Devon asked.

Nemesio came to stand at the mage's side. "Cornelius can move the rooms of his tower whenever he wishes. It is a wonderful trick as long as you don't happen to be in the room that is being moved," he commented, nodding to Panas.

"Where is Talesin?" Cornelius asked.

"Scouting, no doubt," Panas said.

Cornelius raised an eyebrow and turned to Kiernan. "Expecting company?"

"Yes, actually," the elf replied. "But that story will keep. Tell us what is going on here. Is the governor all right?"

Cornelius sighed. "Sit down, all of you," he said, and motioned to the large chairs near the fire. Devon waited until everyone else was seated before choosing a chair next to Dagmar.

The wizard stood before the fire and folded his hands in front of him. "Althea was attacked in Dirt Alley two nights ago. She was very gravely injured, and she will survive, but the situation may be touch and go for some time. The problem at hand is this: *you* are the prime suspects in the attack."

Shocked silence reigned for all of two seconds before everyone spoke at once. The elves were beside themselves, but Cornelius held up his hands. "I have been in meetings with the Watch Chief and the Council all day!" he shouted. "Alistair has given the case over to his first commander. She has been over the area a dozen times and found next to nothing."

"*Next* to nothing?" Nemesio asked.

Cornelius frowned and reached into his robe. He placed a gold piece on the small table before him. Kiernan immediately reached for it, but Devon could already see what it was. The same type of coin they had found near the dead merchants.

Without a word Kiernan produced the twin coin and handed it to Cornelius.

"Neither is one of ours," Dagmar explained.

"I suspected as much," Cornelius nodded.

Kiernan blew out a stream of air. "Someone is trying to frame us."

"It seems a possibility," Cornelius admitted. "At the moment, however, your more immediate problem is Odin Darweshi. He will be only too happy to use your current tribulations as fodder against you."

"While the Council ignores the fact that he builds a bridge with faulty materials?" Nemesio shot back.

"Believe me, the Council wants nothing more than to find fault with Darweshi. Unfortunately, he has been remarkably successful at keeping the attention off himself and placing it on you."

"But what purpose does it serve Darweshi to turn the city against us?" Panas asked.

"Really, Panas. You've shot a hole clear through his plans. You stole the blueprints for his bridge and the money funding it, you have disrupted half a dozen Barexium shipments to Preliona and Malhuria. The Council, and most especially Althea, suspects him of wrongdoing. What better way to throw them off the track than to blame everything on invisible rogues who terrify architects in the night?" Cornelius sat down.

"And with Althea out of the way, he'd have little trouble convincing the rest of the Council to back him." Kiernan had dropped his head in his hands.

"Wait a minute, what about Xanith Creese?" Dagmar asked, "And Alistair? Surely they were not so quick to jump on Odin's wagon?"

"Xanith is gone," Cornelius said. "Althea sent him to Lasairian to look for information concerning you. Alistair, to his credit, held out as long as he could. He is no friend of Odin's, but the merchant made another powerful case against you this afternoon."

"Now what?" Panas asked.

Cornelius cleared his throat. To Devon it looked as though the mage did not want to say more. "Alistair has re-opened the case of Edmee S'Trobenue."

Kiernan looked puzzled. "What case? Raymond is gone, there is no one left to blame."

Cornelius looked down at his hands. "Except you."

Kiernan leaned forward, green eyes going wide. "*We* are now suspects in Edmee S'Trobenue's death?!"

Cornelius nodded. "And in the disappearance of Raymond. Odin paraded Edmee's cousins before the Council, and all they had to do was mention the Captain… Alistair was won over."

Dagmar shook her head. "Surely Alistair does not really believe…."

"Of course he does not, my dear, but the truth is he has very little control here. The Council voted in Odin's favor. Now, it is Alistair's choice as to how he handles all of this. And I believe he has made a good choice."

"How so?" Nemesio asked.

Cornelius took a breath. "This commander of his, Gabrielle March -- she is thorough, extremely so, and that could bode ill for you. However, she has the instincts of Lady Althea herself. She will not jump to conclusions or close the case simply to please her superior officer. Most of all, Odin hates her. I think Alistair put her in charge on purpose."

Cornelius was smiling slightly but the others were not. "What do you propose we do?" asked Kiernan, clearly frustrated.

"Nothing," Cornelius replied. "Lay low until March has exhausted her possibilities. No one will bother you here. Stay until things calm down."

"I don't think that's going to happen."

Everyone turned to the door where the Captain stood.

"What is it, Tain?" Panas asked.

She looked solemn and serious as her wide blue eyes settled on Kiernan. "Jinin is here."

28~Using the Stairs

"Jinin who?" Cornelius asked, narrowing his eyes.

Tain stepped into the room and crossed to the chair. She paced behind them, "Master thief, sometime assassin, blonde streaked black hair. Ring a bell?"

Cornelius maintained his serious look but turned his raised eyebrows toward Kiernan.

"He took the key from Devon—and Tain took it back from him," Kiernan affirmed.

"And he followed you here?" Cornelius was still serious.

Kiernan inclined his head.

Cornelius's black eyes shifted back to Tain. He stared hard at the imp, who squirmed slightly under his gaze. "Is there more to this story, Your Highness?"

"There is. He is responsible for the death of about a dozen merchants Devon was traveling with. Devon was supposed to be among the deceased."

"And does this thief work for Odin?" The news of the dead merchants apparently did not even faze the wizard.

"We don't know. But we found these all around the wagons." Kiernan pointed to the two coins on the table.

Cornelius scanned the group, "Two questions. How long did Jinin have the key in his possession, and how much does he know?"

Kiernan turned to Devon, who shrugged. "He had it for more than twenty-four hours."

Cornelius looked back to Tain, "And how much does he know about all of you?"

Tain bit her lip. "Enough to do some damage."

Kiernan winced. He had not expected her to admit as much, for all her insistence on Jinin's warm feelings for her.

Cornelius was standing now. "All right. I am going back to Nimbus to see what I can find out. Find the ice elf and stay here," he said, pointing a finger at them. "I will return shortly."

Cornelius handed the key back to Devon. "Better hold this for now, Devon." He moved to the door, then thought of something and turned back to them. "Do not leave this building," he commanded, pointing at them all in turn.

There was no puff of smoke or flash of lightning at the wizard's exit. He simply winked out of existence.

Talesin moved into the room just as Cornelius was leaving it. "We should have taken care of them," he said, obviously having heard the conversation.

Kiernan shook his head. "There were too many of them, Talesin. Besides, Jinin's presence would have been missed. The Council would have had one more reason to pin something on us."

"The Council would not have missed him. But I'll bet my horse Odin would have," Panas said.

Nemesio stood and paced. "I can't stand here and do nothing."

Kiernan quietly shuffled past them all, brow furrowed. "I am going to talk to Kalli," he announced, and made for the door.

Devon stood and moved after him. "How do you plan to accomplish that?" he asked.

Kiernan turned back to him. "Cornelius has a scrying pool. Kalli has access to it. I can call her whenever I wish." He began to walk away again. "Whether or not she'll answer is a different story."

Devon followed him out. "I want to go with you."

Kiernan stopped outside the door and turned to face the mage. "I don't think that is a good idea."

Devon threw up his arms in frustration as his unruly blonde hair fell into his eyes. "Well, why the abyss not?! You intend to tell her about me, right? She'd have an easier time believing my innocence if I were standing there beside you."

Kiernan rolled his eyes. "Or she could simply kill you before I had a chance to explain your presence."

Devon backed down. "She couldn't do that. Not in an incorporeal form."

Kiernan smiled wryly. "Actually, she could. And likely, she would."

Devon swallowed hard. "I am coming with you."

Kiernan Nightwing blinked once and glanced over Devon's shoulder at his crew. Four elves and one imp stared back at him with mixed emotions. But not one expression gave him the answer he needed. Would the princess accept Devon, or would she simply eliminate him?

Kiernan sighed. "All right, Devon. If you insist on coming, let's go. I want to be back before Cornelius returns."

"Good. You go talk to *Her Royal Grumpiness* and I—" Tain said, slipping past them, "I will see what I can see from the tower."

"I already did that!" Talesin called from inside the room.

Kiernan glared at the imp and took a threatening step toward her. "Tain…."

"Oh, really, Your Highness," the imp said, dancing away. "You know I have to take *some*thing."

Kiernan frowned severely. "One of these days Cornelius is going to carry through on one of his threats, Captain."

The imp grinned and scampered off down the hall. "I'll be back before you are. Give my best to the red-haired fury."

Kiernan shook his head and turned on his heel, cursing several times under his breath. He stalked down the hall in the opposite direction, leaving Devon to catch up on his own.

"Umm, am I to understand that the Captain has stolen from the wizard before?" Devon asked from behind him.

"She tries every time, but Cornelius always catches her."

Devon was perplexed. "Then why does she continue?"

"Tain has proven herself nearly invincible when it comes to thievery. As far as I know the wizard is her only failure." He smiled thinly. "She has a hard time accepting that."

"So, it is a game to her," Devon reasoned.

"Probably," Kiernan replied, losing interest in the conversation.

"But it doesn't make sense. Why would she…."

"Devon, if you don't mind, I would rather not talk about the Captain at this moment. I have other things to think about."

Devon went silent immediately and Kiernan felt a pang of guilt. The mage was curious and most likely nervous. He was about to meet the most powerful sorceress in Tearlach, who also had a vested interest in seeing him dead.

Over a key. Ridiculous.

"You and your sister do not exactly see eye to eye on most issues, do you?"

Apparently, the mage was not going to give up on conversation. "No, we don't."

"But the princess works for the same goal as you do, correct?"

Kiernan grimaced. "Yes, but our methods are slightly different."

"How so?"

"My sister is a purist mage. She does not like humans."

"She accepts humans into her school," Devon pointed out.

"But she does not teach them."

He could see that Devon was dismayed. "I fail to see how blatant racism could be favorable to the three other elven kingdoms. I would think the princess's opinions would be unsettling to members of the other races."

"And you would be wrong," Kiernan said flatly.

Devon frowned. "How so?"

Kiernan sighed, "Because, for the most part, the other kingdoms share her opinion."

Devon stopped. "What?"

The prince did not pause, and Devon had to run to catch up with him. "For some time Kalli has been in contact with royalty from Jathaharwel and Malhuria. She has had no luck with Serenia, of course, but she has not given up."

"And has she made any progress?" Devon asked.

Kiernan shrugged. "That depends on how you see it. As far as contacting the other kingdoms and discussing the possibility of reunion, Kalli has far outdone *Duak-Thenal*, I'm afraid."

"But that's wonderful," Devon argued. "You should be working together."

Kiernan laughed. "You don't understand, Devon. They will not do it. The other kingdoms won't reunite as long as humans occupy the land at the center of the realms."

"Oh," Devon said, slowing. Kiernan could hear the disappointment in the mage's voice. "So, you are saying that the rest of the elves are just as bigoted as your sister."

Now Kiernan did stop. "Yes," he said, spinning about to face the mage. "Yes, they are. But let us examine your words for a moment, shall we?" Kiernan said icily. "Yes, the elves dislike humans as much as dwarves and fairies—and they even find it difficult to get on with members of other kingdoms. But they do at least have some respect for each other."

Devon crossed his arms and stuck out his chin. "And what is that supposed to mean? Humans have no respect?"

"Not nearly enough." Devon started to object, but Kiernan held up a hand. "Humans are always claiming what is not theirs and then killing each other over it."

Devon snorted. "Now you want me to believe that the elves did not ever war among themselves?"

Kiernan shook his head. "Never. Why do you think they moved farther and farther away?"

"Just because the elves moved away to keep from warring with each other does not mean they never engaged another kingdom." Devon raised his voice. "What about the Goblin wars?"

"Elves were coming to the aid of their neighbors," the prince replied. "No territory was claimed. No one was killed for gold or treasure."

Devon seemed perplexed. "But there has not been a human war in years."

"Twenty, to be exact," Kiernan replied, picturing a giant forest and the fairies who lived in it. "To you it has been years. To me it seems like yesterday that I watched the Crimson Guard burn three miles of forest floor in the Shelkelar. The human king of Graxton wanted that land and he was willing to destroy it and everyone in it to get it."

Devon hung his head. "Then why help us at all?" he asked, sounding defeated. "If we are such primitive, warlike creatures, why bother with us? You could wipe us out and be done with it."

Kiernan caught himself, realizing how anti-human his diatribe had become. And from him, the one elf who consistently defended humans from his mostly bigoted sister, he even startled himself. This was not going at all the way he had intended.

He lowered his voice. "Because we aren't like you. Kalli will never convince the other kingdoms to do away with you, no matter what she thinks. Besides," Kiernan smiled and laid a hand on Devon's shoulder, "On a personal level, you aren't that bad."

Devon was silent again, but Kiernan did not think the mage was done. He was not surprised when Devon piped up again. "You and your sister are twins, correct?"

The prince nodded.

"Interesting," Devon mused.

Kiernan frowned. "What is?"

Devon dragged a foot along the wall. "Well, I guess I just assumed that being twins, you would think much on the same level." He brushed off his robes, still not looking at the elf.

Kiernan understood, "We used to think very much alike, actually. As children, we barely had to speak to know what the other was thinking."

"What happened?"

Kiernan hesitated, trying to decide how much he wanted to tell the mage. "I don't know, really. I hardly remember myself."

Devon did not pressure the prince. He was silent, humble, with his head down and his booted feet shuffling. He sensed the mage hoped he would reveal something important and dramatic. The truth was dramatic—he could certainly admit to that. But it wasn't important. Just a terrible footnote in time, no more. And Kiernan hated being reminded of it.

"When we were young," Kiernan began, "and it was time for Kalli to go to school, I went with her to see her off. It was our first trip without the company of our parents or our brother. A dozen guards were sent with us for protection, but really it was unnecessary. By then Kalli was the best defense we could have had."

Devon's eyes widened. "She was already performing spells? How old was she?"

"We had just crested one hundred years, which in human age would be…"

"Around ten!" Devon blurted. "You are telling me that your sister was exhibiting her powers at ten years old?"

Kiernan shot the mage a superior look. "Are you really that surprised? Halfway to the DeCresler's Institute we passed through a small village called Elk Bay." Kiernan put a hand to his head and rubbed his temples. "I don't remember much, but I believe the village had been attacked somehow. The culprits were still there. About three dozen or so." Kiernan stopped again and shook his head. "My sister killed them all."

Devon froze, shocked. "How?"

Kiernan squinted his eyes, struggling to remember. "Fire," he said. "She vaporized them."

Devon was shocked. "With a spell?"

"I can only assume," Kiernan replied.

"Impossible," he breathed, his voice barely rising above a whisper.

But the prince was at a loss himself for an explanation, and he did not add more.

Instead he watched as Devon paced. "She killed forty people in a blink. No experience, no schooling. Practically a child, for an elf." He stopped and looked at Kiernan. "Impossible," Devon said again.

"I saw it with my own eyes, Devon," Kiernan insisted calmly. He could understand Devon's shock. It was hardly a believable claim.

Devon ran a hand through his hair. "You must be mistaken. You said yourself you couldn't remember much."

"That much I remember," Kiernan said. "But how she did it, or why… no, that part is gone from my mind."

Devon suddenly licked his lips and took a tentative step toward the elf. "Do you think…? I mean… I could try to find out for myself?"

Kiernan's brow furrowed and he stiffened slightly. "I don't suppose you would find much. It is an event I have apparently chosen to bury. If I cannot find it, how will you?"

Devon did not have an answer for that, but he was certain there was way.

"Come," Kiernan beckoned. "Let's get this over with."

They had come to the end of a hall, where a circular ramp pitched them toward a set of stone steps. The stairs took them down to the bottom of the tower and even further below it. For several seconds they continued downward in a seemingly never-ending spiral that probably dizzied the human mage behind him. Kiernan took the steps quickly, sometimes skipping a stair or two.

"How many levels are there in this tower?" Devon asked, looking about and breathing hard.

"I have no idea," Kiernan replied. "Cornelius keeps changing and adding on. I lost track somewhere at around a hundred."

Kiernan stepped through a low door at the bottom of the stairs.

They entered a large room, made even more spacious by the almost complete lack of furniture in it. The walls here were darker and smoother than those of the stairway they had just left. There was only one item in the room: a stone pool about eight feet in diameter, with black, flat water that seemed to have no bottom.

This was a scrying pool. A rare device used by enormously powerful sorcerers to contact other-worldly creatures… and each other.

Kiernan blew out a stream of air. "This would be much easier if Cornelius were with us," he said.

"Kiernan, how can you do this?" Devon asked, his voice laced with concern. "You have no magical powers. You can't control the pool."

Kiernan placed his thin hands on the edge of the pool and did not look at Devon. Instead he concentrated on the water. "I don't have to. Kalli does all the work for me." He put an arm out. "Stand back, Devon. I don't want your face to be the first one she sees."

Devon did as he was told and moved away from the serene water. In fact, he backed himself right into the wall.

Kiernan stood straight, closed his eyes, and thought of his sister.

Instantly the water of the scrying pool began to slosh about violently. Kiernan had seen this process a dozen times before, enough to know that the behavior of the water matched the mood of the one being called.

The prince took several steps back as the water splashed out of the pool and onto the floor. A tall, thin form slowly took shape above the black water—a shimmering blue outline, pale strawberry hair and sparkling sea-foam eyes.

Even before her image solidified, the sorceress's eyes swept the room. They instantly fell on her brother.

She frowned at him, immediately angry. Then in slow motion Kalliroestria turned toward Devon. Her green eyes widened in anger and recognition. Only then did he realize he had made a grave error in coming with Kiernan. His breath caught in his throat. She raised her hand to strike.

Devon remained frozen to his spot. He could not have moved to defend himself if he had wanted to.

"Kalli, no!" Kiernan shouted.

Her green eyes ignored him. "Thief," the princess hissed, as a bright stream of blue fire shot from her hand.

Aimed right at Devon's eyes.

29~The Thief is to Blame

Cornelius arrived in the main hall of Nimbus just in time to witness Jinin Aurek whispering to Alistair, Commander March, and Odin Darweshi.

He was exactly as Tain had described him. The man oozed an air of indifference that even Cornelius found frightening. It was obvious he was a thief, for he had the same fluid grace that seemed to come naturally to the Captain. But this man had another underlying quality that Tain did not. There was a soullessness about him, a calculating coldness Tain would never possess. He moved about his small circle of listeners like an actor, speaking quickly and with fervor, more than pleased to have an audience to hear his tale. Even though Cornelius could not hear him, he knew by the expression on Alistair's face that the words Jinin spoke were important.

And just as Jinin finished, Odin exploded.

"I told you, Alistair!" he hollered. "That nasty little imp thief has been playing you all along! Why in Tearlach a bunch of elves would want to follow her is beyond me. But here you have it from one who knows her."

Cornelius closed his eyes and sighed. "Oh, no," he breathed to himself. He stepped forward. "Something new, Alistair?"

Alistair had his arms crossed when he turned to Cornelius. He only barely extended his hand to grasp the wizard's before folding it back in place. "It seems as though we have identified *Duak-Thenal's* leader after all," he said, his brow furrowing.

"Really?" Cornelius asked, feigning surprise. "Who is it?"

"The damned imp, of course!" Odin shouted. The merchant's face was so red that Cornelius almost took a step back for fear he would erupt. "Jinin here saw her!"

"That's right," Jinin continued, smooth as silk. "She broke into my room at the Washbin. I caught her in the act, but she had the elves with her. They attacked me and my group on her command."

"Right," Odin jumped in. "Before that she attacked the caravan Jinin was guarding."

Alistair turned to Jinin. "Is this true?"

Jinin nodded solemnly. "Yes. And all the defenseless merchants were killed at their hands. Tragic." He shook his head. "Truly tragic."

The commander shifted and cleared her throat. "And yet you managed to escape alive with *your* crew intact."

Commander March spoke the words that were on the tip of Cornelius' tongue. He smiled despite himself.

"Barely," Jinin's eyes flashed. "They crept up on us. Killed half the merchants before we knew what had happened. I lost three fighters there and another at Wisia." Jinin pulled a handful of coins from his pocket and held them out for all to see. "Does this give you proof enough? They were all over the bar at the Washbin. I'll bet you'll find several more where we left the caravan."

Alistair rubbed his chin. "And where are they now?"

"Here, of course!" Odin shouted. "Jinin followed them right to the front gate."

Alistair's eyes widened. "Impossible," he breathed.

"Don't believe me?" Jinin suddenly pointed one long finger at Cornelius. "Ask him, why don't you? He knows all about it."

Alistair turned to Cornelius with a raised eyebrow, but Cornelius did not look at him. He stayed focused on Jinin and did his best to look disgusted with the dangerous man before him. "Why would I harbor thieves and murderers like you?"

Jinin's eyes widened in anger, but he did not miss a beat. "Perhaps it is for you that they steal and murder."

Alistair immediately rounded on Jinin. "Do you know who this is?!" he thundered. "How would you like to spend the night in a jail cell?!"

Odin slid in front of Jinin, a sly smile spreading across his face. "I don't think so, Alistair. I have just as much cause to accuse Cornelius as Jinin does. If *Duak-Thenal* did sneak into town this night right under your nose, what better place for them to hide than in his impenetrable tower?"

"It certainly would explain why the elves have had such an easy time entering and exiting the city," Jinin said from behind the relative safety of Odin Darweshi.

Cornelius' outer mien remained impassive but inside his blood was boiling. Whoever this Jinin was, he certainly knew much. Too much. And the wizard had the sinking feeling he had lost the battle before it had even begun.

He said nothing, however. As if this confirmed his guilt, Jinin and Odin both smiled identical sneers of triumph.

"All right, that's enough," Commander March said, stepping forward. "Aurek, you may take your people and get them cleaned up. I will call you when I have need of you."

Jinin opened his mouth to say something, but Odin shoved him aside. He must have figured he had done enough damage.

Odin gave Alistair and Cornelius one final, knowing look and stormed away.

Commander March followed them out, somehow knowing the two older men would need a moment alone.

Cornelius sighed. He wanted to say something to Alistair, but the damage had been done.

The chief paced away. He did not look up at him. "Cornelius," he began, "I hate to accuse you of anything, but..."

Cornelius shook his head and turned away. "I know how this must look, Alistair. But I cannot give you the answer you seek."

Alistair held up a hand. "I am unsure I want to hear it." The Chief moved past the wizard. "Neil, I would like to pretend I did not hear what Odin said just now. He has no way of knowing the comings and goings at your tower any more than I do." Alistair turned to him. "You realize, however, what kind of position this puts me in. Can you give me any proof that Odin is lying to me?"

Cornelius lowered his voice. "I cannot," he said. "I'm sorry."

Alistair rubbed his face in his hands. "Neil, this could be very bad. You realize that, don't you? And without Althea and Xanith here I will be hard pressed to protect you."

Cornelius laid a hand on Alistair's shoulder, finally looking his friend in the eye. "I would never think of asking you to protect me, old friend—but I am asking you to trust me. At least for the night."

The Watch Chief scanned the face of the taller man for a full three seconds before he nodded curtly. "All right, Cornelius, you have your night. But know this—I am giving the commander as much leeway as she needs. If the elves or the imp venture out this night, be sure that she will catch them. And I doubt you will have any say in what happens after that."

Cornelius nodded his thanks and began to turn away. Things had not gone at all the way Cornelius had hoped. He had just been forced to confess his involvement with *Duak-Thenal* to the one man he had tried hardest to keep that information from. It was a turn of events he could have done without, not to mention how badly he felt deceiving Alistair. He only hoped the Watch Chief could find the will to forgive him eventually.

"Cornelius!" Alistair called out to him.

Cornelius stopped and turned to face Alistair's tired blue eyes. He looked drained and sad, but he managed a wry smile for the wizard. "Whatever you are trying to prove, old friend, you had best do it tonight. Come morning I will be knocking on your door. Garden or no garden."

"I understand." Cornelius bowed his head, silently thanking the Watch Chief for his warning. And the wizard of Preliona, more troubled than when he had arrived, disappeared.

30~Kicked Out and Helped In

Jinin dismissed his crew as he was asked, but Odin continued to complain. "When is he going to do something, March? By the time he makes a move, the thieves will be long gone."

"If anything happens, Darweshi, I am sure you will be the first to know."

Commander Gabrielle March escorted Jinin and Odin to the back of the main hall. Here the white marble of the back wall, which bowed outward at its center, converged with the deep wooden sidewalls. Between them stood a small door that was only opened for guests. Those who came seeking audience with the Council could wait in the anteroom. Odin entered through this door almost daily. Now Commander March was about to kick him out of it.

Both men stopped short of the door and looked at each other. "You can't be serious," Odin balked.

The commander reached past them and opened the door. "Gentlemen," she said sweetly. "May I suggest you wait here until Alistair calls for you?"

Odin glanced sidelong at Jinin. The thief leaned against the wall, picking the dirt from under his nails with his curved dagger. He looked up at Odin from under black eyelashes. He shrugged his shoulders, not caring about Odin's need to oppose the woman standing before him.

The merchant snorted out a laugh and turned back to the commander. "We'll stay here for a bit, I think," he pressed.

The commander did not flinch. She looked at the two men with conviction and her stoic features remained unchanged. "I am sure you will be more comfortable out here," she insisted.

Odin took a threatening step toward the commander. "I enter Nimbus almost every day, March," he hissed. "What makes you think I would be uncomfortable in it now?"

Gabrielle March raised an eyebrow and smiled. "I know of your activities here, Darweshi...."

"*Lord* Darweshi thank you," Odin corrected.

The commander ignored him. "... and I know how comfortable you are in this room. Which is precisely why I am asking you to leave it."

"I am staying," Odin said. "I have every right to be here."

Again, the smile from the commander, "Actually, you don't. Alistair has ordered all unnecessary personnel out of the main hall. Believe it or not, that includes you." She put her hand on her sword. "Now get out or I will have you thrown out." She said all of this without ever raising her voice. She did not have to. The White Watch had seen the confrontation and several soldiers were now making their way toward them.

Odin instantly backed down. He held up his hands defensively. "No need to be pushy, March."

Commander March did not answer. She just kept smiling as she watched them go through the door to the outer chamber.

Jinin went first, uninterested in the exchange. Odin followed, sparing one last look at the commander. Her expression remained unchanged. Odin looked as if he wanted to kill her, plunge his dagger into her sneering face.

"You handled that well, I'd say," Jinin commented as Odin shut the door. The thief sheathed his curved dagger and seated himself at the nearest window ledge. "She suspects something, you know."

"Of course she does," Odin hissed. "She was trained by Althea herself." Odin tore at the clasp of his cloak. "I'll bet the old hag told her a whole slew of lies about me."

"Oh, I doubt that."

Jinin and Odin spun about, weapons in hand, startled by the voice behind them.

At the far corner of the room stood a small writing desk with two chairs. A mage sat in one of these, his red hood covering most of his face. "I suspect much of what Althea says about you is true, Odin. I have never known the woman to lie."

Odin sheathed his sword and took several quick steps into the room. He grasped the back of a green sofa. "What are *you* doing here? Alistair is on the other side of that door! If he catches you…"

The mage was shaking his head and chuckling softly. "Calm yourself, Odin. Alistair cannot hear us. He is at the opposite end of the room, and Commander March has already joined him."

"How do you know all of that?" Jinin asked, remaining near the window. His reed-thin body tensed drastically.

The Red Mage shrugged. "Magic," he said. "By the way, excellent performance out there, Jinin."

Jinin glanced at Odin. Now he took a tentative step forward. "Thank you," the thief replied hesitantly. "May I ask who I'm thanking?"

The mage did not move. "Oh, come now, Jinin. You're a smart man. I was sure you'd have that figured out by now."

Jinin nodded. "I guess I have. Nice to finally meet you… LaRante?"

Odin stood up straight. "LaRante, Jinin. Jinin, LaRante." Odin waved his arms about in a lame attempt at introductions. He came around to the front of the large green sofa and plopped himself into it. "What the abyss *are* you doing here, LaRante?"

LaRante ignored Odin and kept eye contact with Jinin, who had not moved. "I would not have expected Alistair to buy your story."

Jinin shrugged. "Nothing to buy. I told the truth. The imp captain is their leader. The rest I heard from Odin. I assume you told him that *Duak-Thenal* hides out in Cornelius's tower?"

"I did," LaRante said. "And you are quite sure the imp is leading them?"

"I saw her with my own eyes," Jinin affirmed.

LaRante chuckled. "Drugged as those eyes were."

Jinin gripped the cloth of the sofa, his emotions betraying him for the first time. "Something Tain Elire will die for, I assure you."

LaRante placed his long fingers under his chin and smiled, enjoying the thief's discomfort. "After you reclaim the key?"

"Is it still mine to take?"

"That all depends," LaRante drawled.

Jinin's cold eyes narrowed and his fingers danced across the hilt of his sword, "On what?" he asked.

"On whether you finish the job you're being paid for," LaRante teased.

Jinin blinked but Odin leaned forward. "What are you talking about, mage?"

The red-robed wizard did not look at the merchant. "Devon Bane is still alive, Jinin."

Odin stood and rounded on the thief. "You said he was *dead*, damn you!" he barked.

Jinin slid by Odin with the grace of a dancer. He completely ignored the merchant's red face as he came around the front of the sofa and sat down slowly. The thief leaned forward and tried in vain to peer into the gloom under the mage's cowl. He could see nothing but the gray beard curling beneath it. "That is not possible."

"I assure you, dear thief, it is. For all your thieving talents and your cutting words, your assassin skills are sorely lacking."

Jinin stayed very still. "How?"

"Did you see the body fall?"

Jinin shook his head slowly. "And the two men I sent to kill the boy made it back to the fight… but…"

"But they were dispatched by *Duak-Thenal* before they could inform you of their failure," LaRante finished.

Jinin seethed in silence. He felt certain that his men had succeeded in killing all the merchants, including Devon Bane, before they were attacked. Tain must have interrupted things. He would kill the imp now, for certain. And as many of her comrades as he could take down with her.

"I see this revelation does not please you," LaRante goaded.

"It does not," Jinin hissed.

"Good. Then finish the job. The boy hides inside the wizard's tower. Take care of him and the key and the imp are yours."

"How do I get in?"

Odin rolled his eyes. "You're the thief. You figure it out!"

LaRante put up a hand to silence the merchant. "You won't have to break in."

Jinin looked at the mage quizzically, but LaRante did not elaborate.

Odin meanwhile was near to bursting from lack of attention. He began pacing. "Great!" he shouted. "So Jinin gets his key and the little pointy-eared thief. What about the damned elves?!" Odin pounded the arm of his chair.

"If we are lucky, Cornelius will go back to his tower and send the elves out into the night," LaRante said.

"Why would he do that?" Jinin asked. "I mean, obviously the wizard will tell *Duak-Thenal* all about what happened out there. Wouldn't it make more sense for them to stay hidden?"

"No. Because thanks to you, Alistair is onto them. Sooner or later he will want to check out the tower, regardless of how much he trusts Cornelius. No, I think we can expect an excursion from our friends sometime this evening," LaRante said.

"But can they be caught?" Jinin began looking from Odin to LaRante. "Tain Elire leads a band of the fiercest elves I have ever seen."

LaRante stood. "I am counting on Commander March to help us with that."

Odin snorted. "She hates me, LaRante. We should keep her away from this whole thing."

LaRante laughed at Odin's unease. "I suspect her loyalty to Alistair and Althea far outweighs her suspicions of you, Odin. In fact, I don't think she has much use for you at all."

Odin lunged for the mage, but Jinin grabbed the merchant's arm and pulled him back to the sofa as LaRante chuckled. "Can the commander catch them?" Jinin asked, once he had Odin under control. "You may be underestimating *Duak-Thenal*. They made it into this city right under Alistair's nose. What makes you think March can sniff them out?"

LaRante opened his hands and smiled, "Perhaps we will need to lend the good commander a hand."

31 ~ Judgment from the Pool

Devon had stopped breathing altogether.

He was certain his heart had stopped, or at the very least skipped enough beats to kill him. He was staring down the pointed edge of the brightest blue flame he had ever seen a magic user produce. And it was hot.

Princess Kalliroestria had brought the arrow of flame to a grinding halt dangerously close to Devon's right eye. Now he could hear nothing but his own desperate attempts at breathing, ragged as they were.

"You have three seconds to explain why this boy is with you, Kiernan, or I will end his life and you can tell me while we watch his carcass burn," the sorceress spat.

Devon felt himself begin to shake. Over the tip of the flame he could just make out Kiernan Nightwing. He stood near his sister's feet, his arms held out as though they could somehow stop her, and he looked at Devon with more fear than the mage cared to see at that moment.

"Kalli, he is innocent," the elf said quickly.

"Not true," Kalli said. "I spoke to Lorcan this morning. He is still missing one silver and blue key and this one is to blame for it, I believe. Venk tells me there are some dead merchants to account for, as well. Three seconds are up, dear brother." Kalliroestria drew her hand back to strike. Devon closed his eyes.

"Kalli, wait!" The prince threw himself between his sister and Devon. "He was bringing the key to Cornelius! Lorcan himself sent the boy!"

Kalli curled her lip. "Lies," she hissed.

"No!" Kiernan shouted. "No, Kalli, I don't think so. Cornelius spoke to Lorcan too. He was told to expect Devon."

Kalliroestria's arm lowered an inch.

"Cornelius thinks the old man is confused," Kiernan went on in a rush. "He believes that he doesn't remember he sent Devon with the key in the first place."

Kalliroestria's form floated several inches above her brother. She stared down at Kiernan, then back at Devon, clearly weighing her options.

"Come on, Kal," Kiernan pressed. "Isn't it possible that Lorcan simply forgot?"

"And the merchants?" she asked.

"Killed," Kiernan replied. "By the thieves who took the key from Devon here."

The sorceress slowly dropped her arm and the blue arrow disappeared.

Devon's trembling legs gave out suddenly and deposited him in a shivering puddle onto the ground.

As one, Kiernan and Kalli turned their attention on him. "Does Cornelius believe him?" Kalli asked, not taking her eyes off the mage.

"Yes," Kiernan replied. "But the key itself should be proof enough."

Devon knew that was his cue, but he seemed unable to pull himself from the floor. He brought one shaking hand up to his forehead. His sleeve came away drenched with sweat.

"Get up, Devon Bane," Kalli said, her voice softening somewhat. "I swear I will not set you ablaze until after I have seen the key."

Devon didn't hold out much hope for his survival anyway. If the princess felt like it, she would make him into a scorch mark on Cornelius' basement floor. He pressed his back against the stone wall and pushed himself to his shaking feet.

Slowly, trying not to make any sudden moves, he reached into his pocket. He grasped the silk ribbon at the end of the key and pulled it from his robes. It dangled in the air for a moment, spinning and shimmering in the light of the princess's incorporeal form. Devon stretched out his hand for the princess to see. The key was cold against his skin and made a long shadow on his palm.

She showed no sign that she even recognized the artifact. She turned to her brother. "How long did it take you to get it back?"

"Almost two days," Kiernan admitted.

"And I assume that is why you are now here and not in my chambers?"

Kiernan licked his lips. "Just trying to make your deadline, Kalli."

She scowled at him. "Bring it here," she commanded.

Devon risked a glance at Kiernan. The elf nodded and Devon took a tentative step forward. He could not have been more than five steps from the sorceress, but to his eyes he was a mile away. The headmistress of SLS was fiercely intimidating and eerily powerful. She was as tall as her brother, thin and sharp. Her pale strawberry hair was pulled back from her angular features and spilled down the back of her blue robes. Her sea-green eyes stabbed through his defenses like ice. It took all of Devon's nerve to take another step toward her.

Kalliroestria turned all her attention to the key that glowed in his hand. She studied it for a moment, then her eyes flickered to Devon's. "Have you used it?" she asked.

Devon blinked and shook his head quickly. "No. No, I would never…"

"Of course you would," the sorceress cut him off. "You are a mage. At some point your curiosity will overwhelm you. The question is what would you use it *for*?"

Devon felt his anger mounting. "I wouldn't use the key. It does not belong to me."

The princess smirked. "Well that hardly matters, does it? It did not belong to Lorcan either, but do not fool yourself into thinking he has never used it."

Devon swallowed. She was talking about his mentor as though he were a thief and not a celebrated wizard of the Northern Realms. "Headmaster

DeCresler only charged me with taking the key to Cornelius Pav in Preliona. I had no reason to use it."

The princess smiled slyly now. "But if you had a reason, what would you do with it?"

Devon hesitated. He didn't know what she wanted him to say.

Kalliroestria would not back down. "Come now, Master Bane. It cannot be so hard to think of something. The key can open any door. It can teleport you to any room. There must be something you want, something that this piece of ancient magic could get for you."

There were plenty of things Devon wanted that he could not have. There were places he would love to visit, not the least of which was his own home. How easy it would be to simply transport himself to his parent's house whenever he wished! No traveling, just a simple thought and he would be there.

And all the doors he could open! There were several locked rooms in the DeCresler Institute that Devon was itching to have a look at, places old Lorcan had warned the students against entering.

But he wouldn't. He knew it even before he answered the princess. He would not betray Lorcan that way. He would not use a tool of magic that was so old that its intended use was lost, and Devon had not become so reckless that he was willing to disobey a direct order from his mentor.

"You are trying to trick me into betraying my teacher," he said, the tension in his voice rising. "It won't work. I have not used the key. I have no reason to use it."

Devon thought perhaps he had gone too far, that the princess would make good on her threat to kill him now. But Kalliroestria only shrugged as if she never actually cared about the answer to her question—as if his mere presence were simply an inconvenience to her.

"It does not matter, Devon Bane. Whether or not your intent was to use it, I could care less. I want to know where your allegiance lies now." Her green eyes narrowed. "With Odin Darweshi, perhaps? Though my brother speaks for you and would never lie, it is very possible that you have deceived him."

"Oh, for *Kelina's* sake, Kalli, what more do you need?" Kiernan growled. He moved to stand beside Devon in an unusual show of support. "He is not in league with Odin Darweshi. He does not even know who he is! If there is a mage involved in Odin's endeavors, Kal, then it is not Devon Bane. Gods forbid you would admit you might have made a mistake!"

Kalliroestria glared down at her brother. "Are you finished?" she asked.

Devon glanced sideways at Kiernan. The prince appeared to be out of answers.

But then he suddenly straightened, brightened even. "Wait." Kiernan held up a hand and stepped back toward the pool. "There is nothing Devon can say that will convince you of his innocence, and you have yet to trust my opinion. Why not try another way?"

"I am listening," she replied.

Kiernan took a breath. "Devon is a mystic, Kal, a mind reader. It is a power he has only just discovered but I believe he is strong enough for an exchange."

The sorceress turned to Devon. There was a new look on her chiseled features. Devon couldn't be sure, but he thought it was interest. "Is this true?" she asked.

The mage nodded and swallowed.

Kalli blinked and looked at him thoughtfully. "And would you permit me to search *your* mind?" She phrased it as a question, but it was obvious she was expecting only one answer.

"How—how can you?" Devon stammered. "Are you a mind reader as well?"

"No," she replied. "But because you are, I should be able to access your thoughts." She drew herself up taller, if that was possible. "Enter my mind, I will allow it, but stay at the outer edge. I will search your thoughts as you do mine. It will be a strange sensation but not painful. Do not resist it."

Devon blew a thin stream of air out of his mouth. Again, he looked to the prince. This time Kiernan made no move. Devon understood he had to do this, or the sorceress would never trust or take him seriously. He would become the object of another argument between the twins, and Kiernan would lose. "All right," he said. "I'll give it a try." Devon closed his eyes.

"Good," the princess said, "Oh, and Master Bane."

Devon opened his eyes.

"Go any further than the outer layer of my mind, and I will kill you."

Devon flinched slightly. By his count, the sorceress had now threatened his life twice. He didn't think he could take a third.

The sorceress took a deep breath. "Whenever you are ready, Devon Bane."

Devon risked one final glance at Kiernan, who was staring at him intently. This was his chance to win the elf princess over. There would not be another.

Devon swallowed and focused his eyes on the elf before him. He wasn't sure his power would work on an incorporeal form. He was about to mention this when he felt that familiar floating feeling pull at his senses. His feet drifted off the floor, though he knew this was quite impossible. His forehead tingled as he looked at the elf princess… he found himself falling straight into those sea-foam eyes.

And suddenly the sky was green.

A soft rose-colored tower with a petal-like top sailed high above the main structure of the school. It was made of pink granite imported from the Breezeway, designed after a Malhurian castle. In some ways it resembled a larger version of Cornelius's tower. But while a true Malhurian structure would be full of archways and openings, Kalli's tower was studded with windows—so many windows, in fact, that the building appeared to be in danger of collapse.

Devon's eyes followed the line of the structure to its base, where a throng of students milled about the entrance. All elves, Devon noted. The main structure, which held living quarters, the library, and several classrooms was built in a horseshoe shape rather than a traditional square. Its opening faced a crystal green lake. The stunning view allowed one to glimpse the elven city of Lasairian on the opposite shore.

Devon had never seen the School of Light and Sorcery, but he seemed to know all about it at a glance. He could even name one or two of the students on the grounds.

These were Kalliroestria's memories, he knew. It would not occur to him until later to wonder how the princess had accomplished this feat, for she had never really been in the basement. She was at her school looking out a window at her students… the same window Devon was seeing out of now, while the sorceress combed his mind for the truth.

And then it was gone.

The beautiful image of SLS. The pictures of the pink granite tower and the lake zoomed away from him as if he were sucked backward through a tunnel. His feet slammed onto the floor of the basement with teeth-rattling suddenness. He was left looking at the almost transparent form of the sorceress again.

She was neither smiling nor frowning. It was impossible to tell what she had found or how she now felt.

And then she blinked. "All right, Devon Bane," she said. "I believe you."

Devon thought this admission was likely the closest thing to an apology he would be getting from the princess. "Thank you, Your Highness," he said with a small bow.

"Mm-hmmm," the princess mused and crossed her suntanned arms. "Were you planning on handing that key over to Cornelius anytime soon?"

"He can keep it for all I care!"

— ✵ ✵ ✵ —

Kiernan jerked his head about. Cornelius and the remainder of *Du-ak-Thenal* stood in the room. The door to the basement had never opened and the room had never changed. Cornelius had managed to teleport himself and the five others into the room without disturbing the air.

"With all due respect, Your Highness," he said with a small bow, "We have much larger problems on our hands."

The wizard stepped out of the shadows toward his scrying pool. He looked worried and slightly older than he had an hour ago, when Kiernan had last laid eyes on him.

"Have we straightened everything out, you two?" Cornelius asked, eyeing the twins.

"Yes," Kiernan replied, shooting his sister a cautionary glance.

"Good." He circled the pool to stand on the same side as the prince, while the rest of the group spread out around the room.

"I have just come from Nimbus," Cornelius announced. "Jinin Aurek has indeed arrived in Preliona, and Odin Darweshi is screaming from the rooftops that Tain is the leader of *Duak-Thenal*."

The imp, who hung near the wall with Talesin, let her mouth drop open, clearly stunned.

"What!?" Panas said.

Nemesio stepped in the imp's direction, concern writ on his face. "Where did he get that idea?"

Cornelius held open his arms. "She orchestrated the retrieval of the key from Jinin. Naturally, he assumes her to be the leader."

"Damn it," Kiernan hissed, holding his head.

"Relax, dear brother," Kalli said. "This new development at least throws Alistair off the track. Does it really matter what they believe?"

"It does if the Captain gets caught!" Kiernan snapped.

"Which is unlikely," Kalli countered. "Let them think the imp your leader. If you want to keep your identity a secret, this is the way to do it."

That comment was meant to cut, and Kiernan felt his anger mounting.

"We have another problem." Cornelius was saying.

The others focused on the wizard. He was standing in the shadows of the room, leaning against the wall with his arms crossed over his massive chest, looking seriously troubled.

Kiernan took a step toward him. "What is it?"

Cornelius' black eyes flickered to each of them. His gaze at last fell on the princess. Kalli stood above them all, hardly a part of the group, but Cornelius seemed to address her most of all. "Odin is receiving information from another source," he began.

"What do you mean?" Dagmar asked. "Is there a spy?"

"Sort of," the wizard continued, still staring at the princess. "Your Highness, you may have been misinformed about Devon here, but in another way, you were quite right. There *is* another mage involved."

Kalli's pale eyes blazed in triumph. "Who?" she hissed.

"I don't know. Jinin just accused me of harboring *Duak-Thenal,* and I am sure this was not a coincidence. He *knew.* He was given that information, and knew exactly when it would be most effective to reveal it. Right in front of Alistair and Commander March."

"Well, Alistair is not taking him seriously, is he?" Nemesio asked. "He would not listen to Jinin."

"He did not have to," Cornelius replied with a grimace. "He read the truth in *my* face."

Silence.

Things had gone from bad to worse.

Talesin whistled. "What now?" he asked.

Cornelius sighed and slowly sat on the edge of the pool. "Well, you have very few options left," he said. "Surrendering is one. Chances are strong that Alistair would take your side."

This suggestion was not met with much enthusiasm. The elves shifted about and looked to Kiernan for a decision. His ensuing scowl was enough of an answer.

Cornelius went on. "Or you could simply leave. You have completed your mission. It would be difficult to get you past the Watch now, but I am sure we could pull it off. Of course, that would cement your guilt in the eyes of Preliona." He sighed. "Regardless of what you do, Alistair will be here come morning, looking for you."

"So, we have one night to prove our innocence," Panas concluded sourly.

Kalli rolled her eyes in Panas' direction. "I hate to break it to you, Panas darling, but you are hardly innocent."

"But we did not attack Althea!" Nemesio protested. "And we certainly did not kill any merchants."

"And these are not our coins," Dagmar finished, placing three of the gold pieces on the edge of the pool.

"Then maybe we should find out whose they are."

Everyone turned to look at Tain, who now spoke for the first time since Cornelius had brought them down here. Slightly shaken by Jinin's accusations, she was still and quiet for once. Kiernan was suddenly worried for her.

"She's right," Kalli said, surprisingly taking the imp's side. "The only way to clear yourself is to find out who has been framing you."

"Well, it is obviously Jinin," Panas said.

"And Jinin works for Odin," Talesin offered.

"So, it comes back to him."

"But how is he doing it, and why?" Dagmar asked.

"And where do we start?" Kiernan asked.

"May I suggest Odin's warehouse."

Everyone looked to the princess, surprised at her interest, and seemingly pleased at her suggestion.

Kiernan looked to Dagmar. The wild elf shrugged. "It is as good a place to start as any," she said.

The others nodded in agreement, a new glint in their eyes.

"Wait a minute," Cornelius's deep voice cut in. "You do all understand that the White Watch is looking for you." The wizard moved to the center of the room to better address them all. "And I'm sure Odin and Jinin have their own people on the street."

"So?" Tain said.

He took a step in her direction. "So, Captain, if they catch you, that is the end. I will be unable to help you. Do you really think they will listen to a criminal?" He swung his arms about, indicating the others. "Oh, the rest of you may go free on the word of King Gilleece. But you, dear Captain, will rot in jail."

Tain Elire moved close to the wizard and looked up at him, her wide blue eyes full of mischief, not fear. "Alistair could never find a cell to hold me, and you know it," she said. Then she turned to the others with a smile. "Besides, we'll be in and out of Odin's warehouse before anyone knows we've flown our cage."

"That's just what I am trying to tell you." Cornelius latched onto the imp's arm and turned her back to him. "The Watch is going to be out full force tonight. They will have a guard on every corner." He lowered his voice and brought his smooth face down to hers. "Do not underestimate them, Tain. You will not get out of here without being seen."

The imp smiled at him. "I'm sure you can cover our escape, Neil," she said, wiggling out of his grasp.

"Yes," he admitted. "I can help with that, but if there is another mage involved…"

"How do you know that for sure, Cornelius?" Kiernan asked.

The wizard turned. "There is no other way Jinin could have the information he used against me tonight. He and Odin were far too sure of themselves. Jinin and his band were hours behind you with no way to trace you to my doorstep. No one saw you enter this building. Someone with at least as much power as I have has been spying on you."

"So, it is very possible this mysterious mage could be listening to us right now," Panas said.

Cornelius shook his head. "No. Inside these walls you are protected by my magic. It would take a direct attack to challenge my authority here, and our friend would have to expose himself to do that. But whoever it is knows you are in here, and as soon as you leave…"

"Then I suggest you get moving," Kalli concluded.

Kiernan scowled at her. "And how do you suggest we get there? Should we go stumbling through the city until this wizard tracks us down?"

"You could try a map," Kalli sneered at him.

"Which still doesn't keep us hidden, Kal! How do you expect us…"

"I know a way."

Kiernan turned sharply to look at the Captain. Tain met his eyes, but barely. She stood near Talesin, shoulders slumped, head bowed, trying to look abashed, but Kiernan's anger was not abated.

Cornelius slid in front of him. "Do tell us your plan, Captain."

"The sewers," she replied quickly. "There is one that comes up under the walkway of the Darweshi warehouse. It is well hidden and near a set of basement windows."

There was silence for what seemed a long time. Everyone in the room now knew without a doubt that the Captain had been frequenting the city without *Duak-Thenal's* knowledge.

Kiernan crossed his arms and glared. Honestly, he did not know why he was so upset. After all—Tain Elire was doing what she did best. He had often said so. It was not as though she could damage her reputation further.

But of course, that was not the point.

"Right, then," Kalli said, breaking the uncomfortable silence. "Cornelius can help with your exit from the tower. I will monitor your progress from here for as long as I am able. But you must move *now*."

"I suggest we take a look at a map anyway," Cornelius suggested. "Have an alternative in case you are separated.

The wizard produced a map from the air and they crowded around it. Kiernan hung back and leaned into his sister. "Being awfully helpful, aren't you Kal?"

His sarcastic tone was not lost on the princess, and she smirked. "Are you saying you do not need my help?"

Kiernan shrugged. "I only wonder at your motives. You must admit you have been rather uncooperative these past few months. Why help us now?"

"You wound me, brother," she said, though her voice betrayed no emotion. "I am only concerned for your safety."

"But not theirs?" Kiernan challenged. "Not Talesin's?"

Kalli gritted her teeth and faced him fully. "Do you want my help or not, Kiernan? I will not offer it again."

"That's just it, Kal! I can't tell if you're helping me or just pushing me in the direction you want me to go."

If Kalli was going to counter that argument, Kiernan did not find out. He spun on his heel and moved to the others. "Where do we stand?"

"We are nearly ready," Cornelius said rocking back and forth on his heels. "But there is the matter of who is to lead this mission."

Kiernan's brow furrowed. "I will, of course."

But Cornelius was shaking his head "Not this time, Your Highness. Your name is at stake here. If they are caught it will mean nothing. They are not known in this part of Tearlach. *You* are, however."

Kiernan took a step forward, confident in his case. "They will not know me. No one in this city knows my face."

"Don't bank on that, Your Highness. You underestimate the resources of the city's Council. One of them is in Lasairian as we speak. It will only be a matter of time before they discover your identity."

Kiernan started to object, but Cornelius overrode him. "If you are caught, then *Duak-Thenal* is finished. The secrecy you have fought to maintain will end." Cornelius opened his palms. "Unless you are ready for that."

Kiernan's sigh was long and heavy. He rubbed his hands through his red hair and clasped them at the back of his neck. Then he shook his head and turned back to his sister. She was smiling. Kiernan fumed. "Fine," he hissed. "Dagmar is in charge." He turned on the imp. "And I mean *only* Dagmar."

Tain raised her hands defensively and tried to look innocent.

"Now go, before I change my mind."

Duak-Thenal nodded as one and quickly filed out.

First Talesin, then Nemesio and Panas. Tain he did not even see leave. Cornelius clapped him on the shoulder and Devon backed away, following the wizard up the stairs and leaving Dagmar alone with Kiernan.

She shifted from side to side, her gray eyes looking first at her feet and then at his face. She was searching for something to say. Kiernan licked his lips, as much at a loss for words as she.

"Any final words of wisdom, chief?" she asked finally.

Kiernan laughed softly and took her hand. It was cold. He could feel her heart beating in her fingertips. "Be careful," he said, and leaning forward, he brushed her lips with his.

The wild elf squeezed his hand and turned away. She slipped out without looking back at him.

Kiernan made to follow her up the stairs, but Kalli's voice stopped him. "Leaving me so soon, Kiernan? I thought we could watch your merry little band together."

Kiernan placed his hands on the walls to either side of the stairs, tired suddenly, unable to argue anymore. "Our conversation is finished, Kalli," he said. "I have nothing more to say to you."

"Oh, now we both know that's a lie." Her voice drifted over to him, shooting through his nerves like lightning. "You came down here with more on your mind than silver keys and thieving mages, didn't you? Why not have your say, now that we are truly alone?"

Kiernan turned slowly to face his sister. He wanted this. Desperately wanted the confrontation he had been waiting years to have—and thanks to his twin, he now had the time. "Fine," he hissed, "Have it your way."

Fists clenched and jaw set, he stepped up to the pool.

32 ~ Tale of the Twins

The prince of the light elves stared at his twin in silence. Kalli looked back at him with the same cool indifference he had come to expect from her. It took all his considerable patience not to scream at her, or at the very least throw something through her shimmering form. But this was how it was with his sister. She was frosty, aloof, and totally fearless.

That, of course, was the problem.

Princess Kalliroestria had little to fear.

"I know what you're thinking," she said suddenly.

Kiernan raised an eyebrow and looked up at her. "Do you?"

"Of course. Your anger is pouring from your ears. Come on, let us have it out. There is no one left to overhear you. There will never be a better time." Kalli's eyes were now thin slits. She set her teeth as she glared at her brother down the length of her thin nose. "Spare your little crew the ugly sight of seeing their leader finally lose his temper," she taunted. "Do it!"

And how he wanted to.

She was pushing all the right buttons.

Kiernan now reflected that she had gone out of her way to make the recent years of his life as difficult as she could. On the few occasions *Du-ak-Thenal* had truly succeeded in advancing their cause, Kalli had taken the credit. She told half-truths and misled them whenever she could. Several of the jobs she had thrown at them seemed designed to keep them out of her way or get them killed. She hated Tain, tolerated Nemesio and Dagmar, ignored Panas and shared a secret relationship with Talesin that Kiernan found strangest of all.

He did love her. Always had. But he also hated her.

There was so much to say, and very little time to say it. He felt his anger coming to a boil, creeping up from his stomach and threatening to explode from his throat. But at the last second, he swallowed. The torrent of obscenities with which he wished to drown her did not come.

Kiernan laughed. For the first time in several weeks, the prince laughed. It may not have been a wise move, considering his current company, but he could not stop himself. He shook his head in defeat and plopped himself down at the edge of the pool. He opened his mouth to speak, looked up at his sister and laughed again.

Kalli glared down at him, perplexed. "Oh, for *Kelina's* sake," she grumbled.

"I'm sorry, Kalli," he said, getting hold of himself. "I just can't do it."

Kalli shook her head in disgust. "You're ridiculous," she spat at him. This only made Kiernan laugh harder.

She rolled her eyes. "What does it take to get a rise out of you?"

Kiernan stopped laughing and wiped his eyes. "What happened to us, Kalli?" he asked suddenly.

"We grew up," she replied.

Kiernan stood. "Did we? Did you?" he asked. "In the eyes of our parents we are children yet."

"In the eyes our parents we will always be children, Kiernan."

"Fine, then, in the eyes of the elven people we are children." Kiernan said.

Kalli leaned into him as much as her astral self would allow. "How old do you feel, brother? Tell me, do feel like a child when you plunge your sword through the heart of a man?" She tilted her head slightly. "How old do have to be to handle something like that? *Kelina,* Kiernan, do you not remember what happened to our childhood?! Do you not recall that day of days when we saw our brethren murdered?"

Kiernan hung his head. He had been waiting for this. He had expected it. "Of course I remember, Kalli," he whispered. "But do you?"

He looked up. Kalliroestria's eyes stared down at him through slits of hard pale green. "*Absolutely*," she whispered back. "Every detail."

Kiernan blinked. This surprised him because he remembered so little. Honestly, he had trouble piecing together much at all. He held out his arms. "Tell me about it then, Kalli."

"Now?" she sneered. "I thought you wished to watch your precious minions do their dirty work."

Kiernan sighed. "I trust them. Please, Kalli, we have never talked about it before."

Kalli stared at him for what seemed like an eternity. He thought she might be softening to the notion. "I have a better idea," she said at last. "*Let's relive it*."

The sorceress closed her eyes.

"Kalli, wait!"

An explosion of blue light blinded him. He felt himself floating straight up. He could not stop himself. His ears were ringing, and his skin tingled madly. He wanted to pull back, but he could not. He could not even move his arms.

And then the scene began to blur. The deep gloom of the basement faded into the colors of the outside world, whipping past him at a sickening speed. Cities and forests flew by, all tinted in a blue that blended with the sky. Kiernan tried to identify the monuments he passed, but they were moving too quickly.

When his feet touched solid ground, the world came sharply into focus. The prince lowered his arms and let his eyes adjust. Cornelius's basement had disappeared. Kalliroestria had yanked his consciousness right out of his body and dragged him into an incredibly solid world she had created from her memory. He found himself in a familiar green countryside, nearly untouched by civilization. At his feet, a narrow wagon trail cut into the grass. To his right was a hillock studded by trees in full bloom. To his left, a village.

The village.

His limbs felt languid, as though he were moving through water. A peal of laughter brought his head slowly around. It seemed difficult to go any faster. Then the prince saw the source of the laughter.

He froze.

Kalli rode pell-mell along the path. Her pale red hair streaming out behind her, she pushed her gray horse hard.

This was not the Kalliroestria of the present. It was the young elven mage of forty years ago. To the untrained eye, the princess appeared to have changed not at all. Forty years was not a long time in the life of an elf. It would be almost three hundred years before either twin showed any sign of age.

Still, Kiernan knew his sister, and he could see the difference in her right away. She was laughing, for one thing, a beautiful sound, one Kiernan had rarely heard since that day.

He only had to wait another moment before the next rider came barreling around the bend. The stallion he rode seemed adamant about throwing him off—it was all he could do to hang onto the reins. Prince Kiernatrialis Aila on a pale horse, his face free of stress, twenty years before *Duak-Thenal* had taken over his life.

Both elves completely ignored the shouting guard behind them. They kept riding, laughing wildly, headed for the small town in the distance.

That town was burning, but the two young elves had not yet seen that. They were too intent upon racing their horses across the field, seeing how long they could outstrip the guards their father had sent with them.

"Kalli, stop!" young Kiernan called out. "We have lost them. Shimron will kill us for sure this time."

Kalli laughed again and brought her horse about and charged back toward her brother. They had been on the road for two days, and Kalli and Kiernan had managed to lose their escort a total of four times. They were like human teenagers, rebelling against authority and enjoying the chaos they left in their wake.

"Oh, I don't care. Shimron has no authority over me anymore. Neither does our father, Kiernan. Let them be angry."

Kiernan grinned. "Are you scared?"

"Of what?" Kalli scoffed. "I have been personally invited to attend DeCresler's Institute of Magic. It will be the first time an elf has gone there. Why should I be afraid?" Kalli glared down at him, daring him to argue with her.

But the Kiernan of the present could see a small flicker of uncertainty in his sister's misty green eyes. He stood on the side of the road watching his younger self. He could barely breathe. He kept glancing at the burning village, waiting for the two riders to notice. They would in a few moments. Then the really bad memories would start.

Young Kalli looked over his shoulder and smiled. "Here they come."

Kiernan turned as the elven guard finally caught up with their wild charges. The leader circled his white horse about them and shook a long finger in their faces. "When your father hears of this, you will both be lucky to live long enough to go anywhere ever again!"

"It was just a race, Shimron," Kalli complained, trying to hide her laughter.

"For which I did *not* give permission, Your Highness. You forget, if anything happens to you, your mother will kill me first and ask questions later. The Captain of the Guard was furious, but the two younger elves were not listening. They had finally caught sight of the cloud of smoke blackening the sky above the village. "Now, for my sake…"

"What is happening?" Kalli interrupted, staring over the captain's shoulder. *How young and innocent her voice sounded.* Kiernan Nightwing knew it was only a matter of hours before that voice would be lost forever.

Shimron stopped his scolding and turned. "It is Elk Bay," he said with a frown. "It is burning."

Kiernan saw himself look at his sister. The two of them locked green eyes. In a single, unspoken moment they had decided what to do.

Ignoring Shimron's call to stop, they pushed their horses down the hill and into the burning town. Fearless and stupid. Had anyone been standing in the smoke-shrouded towers the two elves would have been shot down before they could come anywhere close to the gates.

The elder Kiernan watched his younger self and his sister fly through the front gate, black smoke covering their path. He hoped Kalli would leave it at that. He did not want to see.

But his sister was relentless. The scene shifted and Kiernan found himself in the town square, though he had not moved his feet.

He tried to turn away and erase the images from his memory, but he could not. He focused instead on the two newcomers on the scene. Both young elves slid from their horses, scanning the hideous sight before them. They were stunned, Kiernan could see. Neither had seen anything remotely like this before, and it was taking their fragile young minds a moment to catch up with reality.

At least two dozen bodies, broken, bloodied, burned and most decidedly dead, were clumped together in a morbid sort of circle. It was impossible to tell which were human, elven or both -- but all of them still clutched weapons in their hands. They most certainly had been fighting each other when they died.

The younger Kiernan took a step toward one of the dead elves, but his sister grabbed him by the arm and pulled him back. He looked at her, but she did not return his gaze. Instead her sea-foam eyes scanned the empty expanse of the square. She heard something.

A millisecond later, Kiernan did as well.

It was the sound of movement being stifled, voices being hushed. Someone did not want to be heard. Kiernan knew instinctively that they were being watched. Feeling suddenly very exposed in the square, the twins slowly backed up, looking for cover.

At that same moment, the elven guard rode into the town.

"Dammit, you two!" Shimron was yelling, before he had taken in his surroundings. It took him only a beat, however, to see the carnage and recognize the danger. He slid from his horse and unsheathed his weapon. The rest of the guard followed suit. "Fan out," Shimron whispered, already sensing the forced stillness Kiernan and Kalli had noted.

"Walk your horses to the gate, Your Highnesses," he said with finality. "Wait for me there." But the young royals had no intention of moving. They were still looking around, trying to figure where the danger would come from. The elven captain reached out and grasped the reins of Kiernan's horse and began pulling the animal toward the burnt gate.

A whistle pierced the air. As one, Kalli and Kiernan whipped their heads about. "Too late," Kalli said.

The first arrow tore through Shimron's neck and clear out the other side. The ensuing spout of blood splattered Kalli's tunic. The captain was dead before he hit the ground.

The sight rocked Kiernan Nightwing's head badly. He remembered Shimron well, but he had blocked out this moment and it pained him to see it again. Of more interest to the present-day Kiernan at that moment, though, was the look on his sister's face. At the time he had been too concerned with finding the source of the attack, as flaming arrows rained down upon them from all sides.

From his new perspective he could see Kalli's reaction that day. She was staring at Shimron's dead face. Was she shocked? Afraid? Yes, she was both of those things. It was the last time Kiernan remembered witnessing these emotions on his sister's face. Almost instantly they melted away, revealing something far more disturbing.

What consumed her features was revenge.

The fledgling sorceress turned. Kiernan watched her raise one thin hand. Three harsh, arcane words escaped her lips and a blue fireball streaked across the square. It hit a parapet at the far side. By now Kiernan had also discovered that this was the source of the arrow fire. The parapet exploded.

But now, teeming from the buildings, came a mob. Forty or so in all, and every face was twisted in anger and bent on death. They ran at the remaining elves with a fury Kiernan had never seen.

They were mad. Every one of them completely insane. Most disturbing of all were the children in the throng.

Kiernan had precious few seconds to wonder what had happened here to turn these people into the enraged mob barreling down on them. Citizens of a town who had little or no fighting skills, but who attacked with abandon.

Kiernan did not wish to kill them, but he had no choice. He found his sword in his hand and in seconds he had cut down half a dozen citizens of Elk Bay. It happened quickly, and Kiernan was so horrified he nearly dropped his sword. He backed away and tripped over a burned body. He went down on his back but was quickly hauled to his feet by two other elves.

Kalli turned when Kiernan fell. She stopped and an arrow sliced open her thigh. A second plunged into the chest of one of the guards and then the screaming mob was upon them.

"Run," the remaining guard yelled. Kiernan grabbed at his sister's arm, but she shook him off and raised both her hands.

Kiernan Nightwing in his astral form truly wished he could close his eyes now. This was the part he *did* remember. He did not think he could stand to see it again.

Princess Kalliroestria, her face completely devoid of any feeling, spoke the magic words that Kiernan would never understand. The air in the square became suddenly still, while the space around the princess sprang to life. Her hair whipped about her face, though there was not a breath of wind. The villagers slowed as though time was coming to a standstill. They looked confused, as if realizing their peril for the first time.

At first, the young Kiernan thought his sister merely meant to put a sleeping spell on the town. It was one she knew well. Kiernan only hoped it would work on this many people. But when sparks began to jump around Kalli's hands, Kiernan became concerned.

The air close to his sister became dangerously hot. As if she were building up a volcano of energy. One crazed man did not wait to see what the elf would do next. He raised his bow to strike, but he was too late. Kalli's hands, which now held an enormous amount of blue power between them, flew apart. At the same time a giant explosion rocked the area.

Kiernan was thrown back by the force of the detonation. He cracked his head hard on the ground and it was several seconds before he could reorient himself. When he did, he quickly pushed himself up onto his elbows, intending to leap back to his feet.

He froze where he was. His sister did not need his help.

They were gone. Where the angry mob had once stood, there was now nothing but a pile of ash.

Kiernan rose to his feet on legs that felt like lead and stumbled to his sister. She had not moved but had folded her arms about herself as if she were suddenly cold.

Kiernan moved to her slowly and gently touched her shoulder. "Kalli," he said. "What happened?"

"Did you see that?" she whispered, not looking at him. "Did you see what I did?" Kiernan listened to her voice carefully, looking for some sign of shock. She was not scared. She was excited about her power. That revelation frightened him.

Kiernan Nightwing watched it all. In Kalli's odd astral world, he had been able to observe the scene from all angles. Now, as what was left of their group moved to retrieve their horses, he was pulled back. The scene before him stretched and blurred until he could no longer make out the characters. Wind swept by his face and he heard a loud popping sound as he came back to himself.

His vision sharpened as the world of the living came back into focus. The basement walls of Cornelius' tower swam in front of his eyes, his own heartbeat filled his ears and his legs shook uncontrollably. He sat slowly on the edge of the pool, holding his aching head in his hands.

"You didn't have to do that, Kal," he whispered.

"Didn't I?" Kalli answered quietly. "You have forgotten, Kiernan. You choose to block out that day because you are afraid of it."

Kiernan looked up at her and cocked his head. "Of course I am. Why aren't you?"

She looked smaller now, hunched over slightly. And she was not as tangible as she had been when she first appeared in the pool. She was fading. The spell had taken its toll. "What would you have had me do, Kiernan? We would have all been killed had I not acted as I did."

Kiernan laughed ironically. "You tell yourself that every night, don't you? Tell me, how many times have you replayed that little scene for yourself?"

"I did what I had to do," Kalli said, ignoring his question.

Kiernan shook his head sadly. "Kalli, I don't fault you for what you did. You protected us. You saved our lives, along with dozens of others still hiding in the town."

She clenched her fists. "That's right—protected *you* from the humans."

Kiernan shook his head. "Kal, Elk Bay was not a war between humans and elves. It was magic that destroyed the town, a curse probably cast by one of their own that affected the minds of the citizens. They turned on each other because they had gone insane with paranoia and fear."

Kalli glared at him. "And who were the ones left standing, my darling brother? *Humans, nearly all.*"

"The elves had weapons too."

"Most of the elves were dead. None were left standing to tell the tale," she hissed at him.

Kiernan hauled himself to his feet. "And now we will never know their tale at all."

Kalli flinched, but Kiernan did not back down. He walked slowly about the scrying pool, trying to pull some emotion other than anger from his sister. "No one has ever questioned you about that day and no one ever will. But why do you continue to torture yourself with it? Why do you choose to live your life trying to make up for people you knew nothing about? Elk Bay was a tragedy. Good folk who have lived together in harmony struck down by an amateur spell gone awry. You think you could have prevented that? Do you think that by getting rid of humans you can keep it from happening again?"

The sorceress rounded on him and the halo of blue around her body flared. "Is that what you think I am doing?! Trying to expunge humans from the world?"

"No," he said holding up his hands. "No, I don't. But I do think that on some level you hope they will leave the Northern Realms. That if you can reunite the Kingdoms, perhaps the other elves will simply push the humans out of the way." He put his hands at the pool's ledge and looked up at her. "Am I right?"

Kalli dropped her eyes and turned away, unable to hold his gaze.

Kiernan knew he had the advantage and he pressed it. "Or are you afraid of what you could do to them on your own?"

Kalli's head snapped up her green eyes going wide with anger. "I killed forty people with a thought, Kiernan! Tell me you would not be afraid of that kind of power. You think I replay that scene day after day to remind myself of what those people did to *each other*? I relive it to remember what *I* did. So, I will never forget what I could have become." She held out her long hands to him and tightened them into fists. "Do you have any idea how it felt to have that much power coursing through me?" She closed her eyes, savoring the moment she described. "It was terrifying. It was exhilarating. It was the most incredible thing I had ever felt or will ever feel again." Slowly she opened her eyes, and now the sea-foam orbs fell directly on him. "And I will make sure no one else feels it, either."

Kiernan stared up at his sister, relieved by her honest revelation. She was swaying slightly on her feet now, and Kiernan became slightly concerned. But he had one last question. "You destroyed the spell, didn't you? The one you used that day."

She nodded slowly. "Of course. And anything of its like that I come across. To my knowledge, only Cornelius and I know of the spell's existence at all. Not even Lorcan has heard of it."

Kiernan suddenly understood something. "You intended to destroy the key, didn't you?"

Again, she nodded in affirmation. "It comes from a group of powerful human artifacts. It is one of three that has recently resurfaced. All of them are highly dangerous."

"Where are the others?"

"We have not found them yet. But we are looking—Cornelius and I."

Kiernan pursed his lips, ready to challenge her again. "You have no claim to them, Kalli."

"No, I don't," the princess agreed. "But regardless, I will find them and I will destroy them. Lorcan sent the key here because he knew that Cornelius or I would be able to identify it. Now I will ask his permission to destroy it."

"Will he give it?"

Kalli sighed. "I don't know."

There was a long silence then. Kiernan was tired, and he knew Kalli was as well. His head still throbbed, and he could not quite shake the image of that fierce blue light enveloping a throng of people. Still, he felt he may have made some awkward sort of peace with his twin tonight. Their relationship was far from healed, but he at least understood her better. And hopefully she him.

"I will not harm your precious humans, Kiernan," Kalli said suddenly, breaking the silence. "And they will never harm us. Ever again."

She glanced past him suddenly, as if she were hearing some distant conversation he was not privy to. "Your friends have reached the warehouse," she said. "If you wish to watch their progress, I must leave you."

Kiernan nodded and backed away from the pool.

Princess Kalliroestria's form was disappearing. She was barely recognizable now. There was a light outline of blue and Kiernan could almost make out her eyes, but she was fading fast.

"Promise me one thing," he said quickly, afraid she would disappear before he could say more. "Forget that day. Please, Kal. Your purpose will remain intact without that memory. Do not torture yourself any longer."

The outline of the sorceress nodded and her voice echoed throughout the basement. "I will try. *Kelina* be with you, my brother."

33~The New Leader

Kinnard was bored. Spending the last hour circling the perimeter of the Darweshi warehouse was not how he had planned to spend his evening. Three times he had passed by the front door, and he was now on his fourth round. Truly this was the biggest waste of time in his long tenure as chief of security for the Darweshi household. Seven others stood guard tonight, and Kinnard deemed that unnecessary as well. The White Watch was out in full; two of their patrols had already stopped by. *Duak-Thenal* would not dare hit the warehouse. Even if they managed to overcome the guards—something Kinnard seriously doubted—another Watch patrol would be by in less than half an hour.

Kinnard turned a corner. Here the ground sloped downward abruptly and spilled out onto a path that pitched down toward the water of Opal lake. Overhead hung a small footbridge that connected the warehouse to the boathouse. This was Halver's post.

And he was not there.

Kinnard peered into the darkness. Perhaps the older man had fallen asleep. Kinnard would not blame him if he had. "Halver?" he called out. The guard stepped further into the gloomy shadows under the suspended bridge. "Come on, Hal, wake up." Kinnard's booted toe caught on something soft and heavy. He toppled forward onto his hands with a cry of surprise. Unhurt, he rolled over and quickly got to his knees to see what he had tripped over.

It was Halver.

Kinnard shot to his feet, sword drawn and ready to call out to his associates, when a dark form dropped from above.

Kinnard stumbled backward and fell into the stone wall below the bridge. The creature landed in a crouch and then rose slowly, drawing an enormous double-bladed sword as he did. With one midnight blue-draped arm, the figure reached for his hood. Kinnard was quite sure of what he would see when that hood was pulled back. Still, he was unprepared for the sharp icy features and hard black eyes that now glared at him.

"Do not bother calling out to your brethren," the ice elf warned. "They cannot hear you."

Kinnard knew he should attack, but he could not make his sword arm move. It hung limply at his side. His vision had gone slightly fuzzy about the edges.

Talesin caught the fainting guard as he fell and gently lowered him to the ground. This was the second guard who had passed out at the sight of him. He was unsure how to feel about the situation.

Talesin placed the guard next to his companion and put two fingers to his lips. Dagmar and Tain emerged from the shadows, each from a different direction.

The wild elf reached him first. "We have to hurry."

Talesin nodded. "We have about twenty minutes."

"Tain, where do you want to go in?"

The imp had moved past them both and was crouching near a basement window. She already had it open, though Talesin had not heard her pick the lock. "This will do," she said.

Talesin and Dagmar bent over the imp and peered into the darkness of the warehouse basement. "Which door?" Dagmar asked.

Tain looked up. "On the bridge. Meet me up there."

Dagmar followed the imp's gaze and frowned at the small bridge above their heads. "That is two floors, Tain. Are you sure you want to go that far?" Dagmar asked. "We don't have a lot of time here."

Tain nodded. "I know—but if the Watch comes by again, they are less likely to notice you above their heads."

Dagmar studied the imp's sharp features. It was almost always easy to decipher the fairy's thoughts by gazing into her eyes. She was not a particularly good liar and those enormous orbs always gave her away. At least to those who knew her.

And Dagmar did know her. Maybe not as well as Kiernan, but she knew her. Well enough to catch the flicker of concern reflected in those depths of blue. This knowledge did not give Dagmar pause about the imp's plan, however. In fact, she embraced it even more. Self-confidence regularly got the imp in trouble. But she was not confident now—she was concerned. Concern meant caution, and Dagmar welcomed that.

Dagmar nodded. "All right."

But Talesin stepped forward. "I'm going with you."

Tain turned to the ice elf. "I have to go alone."

"Absolutely not," Talesin said with finality.

"You'll slow me down," Tain argued.

Talesin started for the window. "I'm going with you, Tain. You know the rules."

Tain grabbed at his shoulder and pulled him back. "Rules don't apply here, Talesin. The rules ceased to exist as soon as we were framed for murder!"

Talesin growled and opened his mouth to berate the Captain, but Dagmar put a hand on the ice elf's shoulder. She knew he was conflicted, trying always to protect the little Captain—especially now, in Kiernan's absence. "She's right. Let her go."

Talesin gaped at her, surprised that she took the imp's side. He dropped his head. "Kiernan would never allow it," he muttered.

Tain crossed her arms. "Kiernan would know when it was time to let me do my job."

Dagmar looked at Talesin then back at Tain. "Five minutes," she warned. "Or we're coming in after you."

Tain grinned. "Three minutes. Time me." She slipped through the window feet first and disappeared.

Talesin closed the window behind her and the two elves stood and moved silently under the suspension bridge. It was only about ten feet above the ground, and the two nimble elves had no trouble leaping up and grabbing the wood in their hands. With barely a sound, they hoisted themselves up and over the rail.

Talesin leaned out over the edge, trying to get a look at the street. They would have heard the White Watch a mile away, but Dagmar knew he felt better having a visual.

Dagmar meanwhile put a hand to her lips and took a breath. From her mouth issued the signal that would bring Nemesio and Panas from hiding.

Seconds later Panas dropped from above and Nemesio climbed the bridge as Dagmar and Talesin had.

"Time?" Dagmar asked.

Talesin shrugged. "I lost track," he said. "It cannot have been five minutes."

Dagmar drummed her fingers against the rail. "She said three, and it feels like ten."

"You're not timing her?" Panas scolded. "Ooh, she is going to be angry."

"We are a little busy here, Panas," Dagmar shot back.

A light audible click caused them all to turn. The door on the bridge opened a crack and Tain peered out at them. "Well?" she said.

"Two minutes and fifty-four seconds," Panas answered, shooting them all a warning glance.

Tain grinned and motioned them to follow her inside.

The outside of the warehouse was nothing impressive. Two wooden buildings set by the lake, a small boathouse connected to a larger structure by a suspension bridge—their entry point to the main structure.

Up until that point, none of them had seen the inside of the Darweshi Empire. Dagmar was willing to wager that even Tain did not know exactly what was produced here.

Most townsfolk were under the impression that the boats at the docks carried supplies back and forth across the lake. It made sense, then, that Odin would be sponsoring the construction of a bridge that would speed up his father's endeavors. The inside of the warehouse offered nothing that disputed this belief.

The five members of *Duak-Thenal* spread themselves out along the rail of the second floor balcony and stared down at the floor of the warehouse. It was empty save for the rows and rows of wooden benches and tables heaped with tools and aprons. The floor was covered with a thin layer of sawdust left unswept by the day's last workers.

Without a word, Dagmar swung a leg over the banister and gracefully lowered herself to ground level. She did not wait for the others to follow, but stepped lightly across the dimly lit floor, cautious but sure of her surroundings.

She made it to the far end of the floor first and peered around the corner. A hallway greeted her, and she caught the attention of her comrades with a wave of her hand. Talesin appeared at her shoulder and the wild elf pointed at a closed door at the end of the hall.

The ice elf nodded and moved ahead of his surrogate leader. The others followed cautiously, moving briskly in and out of the other rooms, finding nothing but offices and other small workrooms. Talesin slid down the hall and positioned himself just to the side of the closed door. He drew his sword and with a nod from Dagmar, he turned the doorknob.

What greeted them was difficult to describe. Dagmar had never seen anything like it before. This room had the same high ceilings as the main floor of the warehouse. Shadowy moonlight shot through three huge windows high above the floor, casting light on the only piece of furniture in the room. It seemed to be a machine of sorts.

And it was enormous. Easily twenty feet in height, the massive concoction of metal reached the windows that now lit it. The mechanism had chutes and trays, funnels and buckets, and whole shelves full of what looked like small rectangular plates. Dagmar could just make out the shape of a circle carved twice into each plate.

It was working. It shifted and groaned under its own weight; the sound of the screeching metal bruised her sensitive ears.

"What is it?" Panas asked from beside her.

Nemesio was the closest. He was now poking and prodding it like a healer examining a patient. "I believe this thing holds the answer to our current dilemma." He reached under one long tray and pulled out a small gold coin. "Take a look," he said, tossing it to Dagmar.

The wild elf caught the flying gold piece and held her palm open for Panas to see.

It was indeed a gold coin, but the piece was smooth and completely blank. It had no impression on it whatsoever—no image, no words, nothing. At least not yet.

"You must be joking," Panas said, looking up at Nemesio and walking cautiously toward the hulking machine.

"It appears not," Nemesio replied.

Dagmar followed. "I do not understand," she said. "What is this?"

Nemesio peered at them from the opposite side of the machine. "This," he said patting the giant contraption, "is designed to create, or recreate, money."

Tain suddenly appeared above them, dangling by her knees from a rather flimsy looking piece of metal. "Great!" she said. "I could use one of these."

Dagmar ignored the imp. "How does it work?" she asked.

Nemesio looked around. "As far as I can tell," he began, "when you release this lever, water comes in from the lake, spins that flap about, dumping that large cauldron onto this tray which then rolls into this section where—and here I'm a little unsure—another piece of metal imprints the soft gold with its brand."

Dagmar was almost afraid to ask the next question. She ran a hand through her tangled hair. "And what brand might that be?"

Nemesio smiled mirthlessly and held open his other hand. In it he held a gold piece marked with an X. "Any kind at all, I'm afraid."

Dagmar closed her eyes and felt her heart pounding in her chest as she grasped the full ramifications of their discovery. She scooped up some metal plates and several gold coins and shoved them into one of Tain's black bags. She thrust the pouch into the imp's hands and turned to go. "Let's get out of here," she said.

She led the way out of the room quickly, itching to get back to the tower and dump their findings into Cornelius' lap. They were stealing across the main floor when a whistle suddenly cut through the stale air.

Dagmar stopped dead.

"What?" Panas asked.

She held up a hand. "Someone's here."

"Dagmar, it was a bird," the light elf insisted.

But Dagmar, an expert at signals, shook her head. "No, it wasn't."

Taking the wild elf at her word, Talesin turned to investigate, taking a step toward the front door. At the same moment, it flew open with an echoing crash. Talesin danced backwards and searched for another exit as the White Watch filed in fast.

They began backing away but behind them another door crashed open and more men and women poured in.

In seconds they were surrounded. At least two dozen soldiers pointed their weapons at them. Talesin drew his sword but Dagmar stayed his hand.

"How could we not have heard them?" Nemesio hissed beside her.

"No one moves until I give the order." Dagmar commanded. "Understand?"

They all nodded.

Her gray eyes flickered back and forth, scanning the large group around them, searching for a weak spot. There was none. They could not hope to escape this situation without a serious fight—and Dagmar, for one, was not about to kill any of Althea's soldiers. Still, someone had to get the coins and the plates back to Cornelius.

"Surrender!"

Dagmar whipped her head about, searching the faces before her, looking for the owner of the voice.

The front door, where the bulk of the soldiers had entered, was covered by the walkway of the second level. The four feet of shadow it produced obscured the entryway so that even the keen-eyed elves had to squint to see there. Four soldiers stood abreast blocking the entrance, but now they stepped aside, and a new figure moved forward.

Out of the shadows stepped an extremely tall young woman. Dagmar herself was about five foot ten and this woman had at least an inch on her. She had short rusty hair and penetrating brown eyes. Even before she looked at the arm of her uniform, Dagmar knew this woman was in charge. Her gray uniform bore three white horizontal stripes, the mark of a commander. She did not draw her sword and she did not have to. She was intimidating enough without it.

"I am Commander Gabrielle March," she said. "You are under arrest. Put up your weapons and come quietly."

"What is the charge?" Panas piped up.

The commander raised an eyebrow and opened her arms to the room around them. "I should think that would be obvious."

"We broke in here with a purpose," Nemesio objected. "Odin Darweshi has been trying to frame us. There is a machine back there that melts gold and creates coins." He raised his hands and took a tentative step forward. "Do you understand? He can make *any* coin he likes."

The commander took in everything Nemesio said with a congenial nod. "I understand you perfectly," she said. "But it is not my job to hear confessions or explanations. You may explain your actions to the Council. I am only under orders to take you into custody. Now please put up your weapons."

"I am afraid we cannot do that, Commander," Dagmar said cautiously. "We have as important a mission here as you do, and we intend to carry it out."

The commander inclined her head slightly, acknowledging the challenge. She then shifted her stance and looked at her patrol. "Take them," she said.

Dagmar sucked in a breath, realizing she had to act fast. At least one of them had to make it back to Cornelius. "Back to the machine!" Dagmar hissed. "Go!"

Duak-Thenal backed away in a rush as the White Watch surged forward. Dagmar drew her crossbow and ran backwards as Panas shot a volley of metal balls into their midst.

"Well, this is a nice surprise," Panas quipped under his breath. "And the trip has been just lovely so far."

"Shut up, Panas," Dagmar hissed over her shoulder.

"Move!" Nemesio yelled, leading the way and letting loose one arrow as he did. Tain followed, throwing one of her daggers and catching the raised arm of one soldier.

The man stumbled and cried out.

"Do not kill them," Dagmar hissed and let loose an arrow. The tip sank itself into the thigh of the closest soldier, putting him out of the fight. The rest came on, however, silent and determined. They rounded the corner as the Watch gained on them. Dagmar dumped her crossbow and drew her sword in time to meet the downward arc of a giant blade that forced her to back through the doorway in a shower of sparks.

The room that hid the machine was not large. They could barely find space to swing their weapons. They stayed close, fought side by side and back to back as they heard their own weapons clattering along with the sounds of the metal machine near them. They saw the surprise in the eyes of the soldiers who fought them. The Watch had not expected this bulky monstrosity to be there, but their shock and awe did not hinder their fighting ability in the slightest. The elves were hard pressed to keep the soldiers at bay.

Dagmar glanced at her companions. The companions she had led into this mess. None of them looked at her with reproach, but she felt guilty all the same.

Dagmar took a chance and looked up at the top of the machine. The moon peered through the clouds, barely lighting the tall windows on the second level. The windows were a long shot, but it might be the best chance they had.

"Tain," Dagmar called, "If I clear a path for you, can you get that stuff back to Cornelius?"

Tain stared at her. She looked like she about to argue, but Dagmar shook her head. "We can't all make it out of here, and you know it. You're the quickest and you know the city the best."

Tain sighed unhappily. "All right, Dagmar," she said. "Just find me an opening."

Dagmar nodded and turned to Talesin. The Watch was slowly closing in, tightening their circle and the ice elf was busy. "Talesin, you are going with her."

"What!" Talesin nearly stopped the fight he was involved in to stare at her.

"You heard me," she said.

Talesin twirled the ice sword over and knocked his opponent off his feet. "No way," he said.

Dagmar beat back two soldiers with her whippet thin blade, but they were persistent. Talesin joined her and together they fought and argued. "A half hour ago you wanted to shadow the Captain," Dagmar complained. "Now you refuse?"

"That was before you asked me to abandon you to the Watch," Talesin pointed out.

With a growl of frustration, Dagmar pushed back her enemy and slashed at the next to fill the space. *"I'm not asking you, Talesin!"*

The ice elf looked at her sharply, then turned back to the two-dozen soldiers before them. "Dagmar, I don't think…"

"That's right Talesin, you don't think," Dagmar said, a little too harshly. "Because I am calling the shots, not you. You and Tain get that stuff back to the tower and let me worry about the rest. That's an order!"

Talesin nodded, spit at the ground and cursed. Then he held up his sword. "Fine," he hissed.

"Great, O brilliant leader!" Panas shouted. "But do you have a plan for their escape while the rest of us fight for our lives?" He had pocketed the slingshot and had just deflected the first of many White Watch swords with his own.

"The windows above the machine…" Dagmar had no time to explain more, for the ranks of the White Watch were closing in fast. She could only hope Talesin and Tain understood and would make it to the window before the group was completely overwhelmed.

But swords were coming at her so quickly that Dagmar had no time to check on her teammates. The soldiers of the White Watch were excellent fighters. It was difficult to hold them off without seriously injuring any of them. She ducked under two separate sword slashes then pushed her shoulder into the nearest body and shoved them back. Two soldiers went stumbling away, but were immediately replaced by two more.

She realized, however, that she wasn't really fighting for her life—simply to hang onto her sword. Her opponents kept trying to push her sword arm wide and grab onto her arms. Dagmar yanked her arm out of the grasp of the nearest soldier and danced away from the group she fought.

Three men and one woman dashed after her as she pulled herself away from the circle, aiming to distract the soldiers away from Talesin and Tain and make some room to swing her golden sword.

Dagmar backed away, risking a glance at her friends. Nemesio had removed his bow and quiver and tossed them aside, but the large elf was keeping his opponents terribly busy. His long arms held all swords at bay with his own. As he pulled away from the circle, Panas followed, leaving Talesin and Tain at the base of the machine, the latter already scaling the huge metal thing.

But the soldiers were not stupid. They saw immediately what the imp intended to do, and several shouts rang out through the warehouse. Dagmar shot a quick glance at the commander, who was making her way to the machine and drawing her sword. Dagmar did not really want to see this woman fight. She felt their chances of escape would all but evaporate if the commander started swinging. The wild elf began fiercely swinging her sword, pushing the soldiers back and trying to intercept Gabrielle March.

Talesin was on the machine now and Tain was nearing the top. "Stop!" The commander yelled. She pointed her weapon and ordered her soldiers up onto the machine. "Cut them off!" she called to her patrol.

The soldiers moved quickly to get to the imp and the ice elf.

"Captain, move!" Dagmar yelled, lunging forward.

Commander Gabrielle March whipped her head about and stared at Dagmar as if she had just realized something. She turned back to the two figures climbing the machine and focused on Tain. Her eyes widened in recognition and Dagmar cursed herself for drawing attention to the imp. The commander had not really noticed her before, but she did now.

The wild elf grabbed at the back of one climbing soldier and pulled him off the machine. Then she shoved him aside and moved to block the commander. March came to a halt and brought her sword up, barely giving her elven opponent an appraising glance. Dagmar swung her sword about and stabbed at the larger woman, with every intention of pushing her back.

But March did not move. Instead she brought her sword down at a fierce angle. Dagmar barely managed to dive to the side. She came up and stabbed sharply toward the commander's shoulder.

But the commander's sword was larger and her arm more powerful than the slight elf's. March blocked the move with a speed and accuracy that defied her size, and pressed Dagmar back. The wild elf tried to sidestep again, but she barely gained any ground. March simply would not budge. Dagmar was fast, but the commander was immovable. Her weapon came down hard and strong, pushing Dagmar's blade to the ground.

The wild elf yanked it free and spun about, narrowly avoiding the commander's vicious plunge. She brought her sword about and moved to meet March's sideways swing, but Dagmar's back suddenly came up against the machine. Some sharp point of the damnable thing poked her back and pierced her skin. She jumped to the side in surprise and pain, lowering her sword just enough for the commander to get inside.

Her sword was up and at Dagmar's throat before the wild elf could call to the others.

At that same moment, Panas broke away from the group that surrounded him. He pulled his slingshot from his pocket as he ran to the center of the room. Two of the soldiers had made it up the machine and were fast closing in on Tain and Talesin. The imp was at the window, but Talesin would not get out before the Watch got to him.

Dagmar held her breath as Panas got off two quick shots. The two soldiers cried out one after the other, each holding injured body parts with one hand and their tenuous perch with the other. At the same instant, Tain opened the window.

They were gone before March could issue another order.

Panas, having dropped his sword in favor of the slingshot, was now left unprotected. He had no time to get off another shot before he was grabbed from behind by several pairs of hands and forced to his knees, at least four swords at his throat.

Once Nemesio saw that his friends had escaped and Panas and Dagmar were compromised, he threw down his sword and raised his hands.

Commander March stared at Dagmar as she sheathed her sword. The wild elf held her gaze, trying to discern what she would do next.

March stepped back, her brow creasing with suspicion. "We were told the imp was in charge, and yet it was you who gave the orders," the commander mused. "I wonder why that is?"

Dagmar swallowed hard. It was bad for Tain, unbelievably bad… if these people thought her the leader of *Duak-Thenal*… and yet, for the moment, it was as good a cover as any.

This woman clearly did not believe it, however.

"Where did you send them?"

Dagmar did not answer. She kept her face a complete mask and waited. The commander did not seem fazed. "We will catch up to them."

"Doubtful." Dagmar returned.

March raised an eyebrow, clearly not expecting any response from the wild elf. "How do you think we caught up with you?"

"Luck," Panas the Hawk said from beside her.

Dagmar saw a tiny flicker of anger in the commander's brown eyes when she turned to glare at Panas. But just as quickly it was gone. "Alex," the commander called to a young man near Nemesio. "Choose six officers and take these three back to Nimbus." She looked pointedly at Dagmar. "They will not give you any trouble."

Dagmar wanted to say something, but the commander did not give her a chance. She spun on her heel and headed for the door. "The rest of you come with me."

Dagmar bit her lip, suddenly worried. The commander seemed very sure of her next move, even though Tain and Talesin had a considerable lead. She could not possibly have guessed their destination.

Still, she left Dagmar with the sense that she knew exactly where the fugitives were going.

34~Unwanted Help~

Talesin Darken and Tain Elire ran for close to half an hour before they began to tire. Talesin's clothes were stuck to his body and soaked straight through. His black hair was matted to his forehead and his face was flushed, not pink, but pale blue. The ice elf, used to almost sub-zero temperatures, was sweltering in the spring air.

Tain, on the other hand, was shivering uncontrollably. It had started to rain some time during the night, and the cool water splashing onto the imp's perspiring skin was an unhealthy combination.

Neither was in the best of shape to be tearing through the city, but they had little choice.

Talesin was sick about leaving the others behind, and he knew Tain, who had been strangely quiet, was feeling just as guilty.

But Dagmar had been right. Getting the evidence back to Cornelius and Kiernan was imperative.

A rendezvous was becoming increasingly difficult, however, while the resilient White Watch remained steadfast in their attempts to capture them. Twice after their escape from the warehouse, Talesin and Tain had come face to face with nearly a dozen of the well-trained men and women. Both times the elf and the imp had managed to escape without injury to themselves or the soldiers, but Talesin feared they would not be able to keep this up much longer. Curbing their fighting skills to keep from injuring any of the soldiers was fast wearing on both the elf and the imp.

Even more disturbing was how adept the White Watch was at intercepting them in the first place. Both times they had faced off, the Watch had been expecting them. Talesin and Tain would slip around a corner, certain they were safe, and then come face to face with the gray-garbed soldiers. Talesin figured the Watch knew the city better than he did, but there was no way they could simply guess where their quarry would be next. How they had managed to catch them so off-guard at the warehouse in the first place was still baffling to the ice elf.

"If I'm right… we should be in a position to hit the rooftops… around the next corner," Tain panted beside him.

Tain had wanted to use the sewers again, but Talesin feared their previous luck with that route would not hold. He did not want to get stuck down there in a fight.

Talesin nodded his assent and both sped up as they rounded the corner.

A half dozen Watch soldiers blocked the alleyway.

Talesin came to a screeching halt, barreling his arms to keep from plowing into the six drawn swords that were pointed at him.

Tain had a much more difficult time stopping. Talesin snagged her collar and yanked her back before she could impale herself on the extended swords.

Stark and imposing, the six figures did not move. Each face was an unreadable mask, solely focused on the job at hand.

In a swift graceful move that belied her exhaustion, Tain turned about quickly and pressed her back against his. "More this way," she hissed.

Talesin glanced over his shoulder and counted four more soldiers advancing on them. He glanced up and counted three archers overhead. This was not possible. There was no way that a dozen armed men and women could get the drop on them like this. Elves and imps moved almost without sound when they wanted to. Humans did not. Yet here they were acting as if they had been waiting for hours, hardly out of breath.

He knew instantly that they could not win against this adversary. Were it not for the imp beside him he may very well have surrendered.

The Captain opened her staff as Talesin drew his double-bladed sword. Instantly the mood in the alleyway tensed as the soldiers surrounding them readied for action.

And then the same young woman who had led the group at the warehouse slid gracefully through the ranks of her soldiers. "Your friends have been taken. Put up your weapons and I assure you, no harm will come to you."

The commander had a deep and resonant voice that managed to convey respect for those she spoke to. Talesin surveyed her face, wondering if he should chance a conversation with her, if it would make any difference whatsoever. March seemed extremely rigid—the type of soldier who followed rules and liked all things orderly.

Talesin lowered his sword ever so slightly and licked his lips. "You seem awfully determined to catch up with us, Commander. I hope you do not think we have harmed anyone in your city."

Commander March did not blink. "It does not matter what I think. Please lower your weapons and come quietly."

But Talesin sensed that things mattered to the commander quite a bit. "Perhaps you would give us a chance to explain."

March shook her head stubbornly. "You will have more than enough time to explain at Nimbus," she replied curtly.

Behind him Tain shifted slightly. "Talesin…" she warned. Talesin could hear the nervousness in his friend's voice. He knew he could not let the imp be taken.

"This is your final warning," Commander March announced. "Lower your weapons now or we will take them from you."

But Talesin was no longer listening. He had just seen something that had lifted his hopes. Trusting in the commander's honorable showing so far, the elf whispered to his tiny partner. "Tain, up and to my right," He felt the imp shift behind him. "Turn and face me. I'm going to boost you up onto the roof."

"Did you happen to see the archers up there?" she whispered incredulously.

Talesin ignored her sarcasm. "There are three soldiers covering us, but there is a large gap between two of them. Do you see it?"

"Yes, but…"

"You can make it," he assured her.

"I'm not leaving you," Tain hissed urgently.

"All right, take their weapons!" the commander ordered.

"Now, Captain!" The imp turned to face him as the soldiers surged forward. Talesin clasped his hands together. He heard shouts of protest from all around them, but he did not stop. He bent his knees and hoisted the lightweight imp into the air. Tain Elire flew up and over the stunned faces of the White Watch, flipped once and landed like a cat on the rooftop above.

The three archers fired.

Talesin winced as he saw the imp spin about, duck out of the way and disappear. He could not see if she had been hit, and he had no time to think on it as the soldiers surged forward and knocked his weapon from his hands.

The commander was hollering. "Hold, dammit! Hold your fire!" She pointed to the three men above, "Is she hit?"

One of the archers put a hand to his head, trying to see ahead. "I don't know. She disappeared over the next building."

"You three get after her!" The commander ordered. "And do *not* shoot her!"

The three archers complied and dashed off after the imp Captain. The commander then turned her attention to the ice elf before her.

Talesin had given up without a fight, but the first two men who had grabbed his arms had been treated to a stinging cold on the palms of their hands. Two more had donned gloves and had managed to shackle the elf's arms behind him without further incident. The ice sword was still presenting a problem – even through their thick gloves, the humans were feeling the sting of its cold.

Talesin watched March closely and calculated his next move. There were about to be questions Talesin did not wish to answer. But he also did not want to lie to this young woman. There was something decent about the commander, something that he liked despite himself. She seemed to know much more than she let on, and though she was obviously intent on completing her mission, she was patient in accomplishing her goal. She had already demonstrated a surprising measure of control here, despite the impulsive volleys of her jittery archers.

Talesin could see that the soldiers surrounding him were eager to listen to the commander as well, though many were far older than she was. Talesin felt a healthy respect for that.

March looked him up and down, taking his measure. She gazed directly into his eyes, something few humans were able to do. Talesin's esteem for her grew even more.

As she approached him, the soldiers around Talesin grew tense. Several swords came up to his throat and chest, filling the space between him and the commander protectively.

"I don't suppose you'd like to tell me where she's gotten off to?" March asked in a tone that suggested she did not expect an answer.

Talesin shook his head slowly, careful to keep his eyes trained on hers. "I'm sorry," he replied.

The commander nodded. She was not angry. Her features remained stern but incredibly calm. "You make my task more difficult and the case against you more damning, you realize."

Talesin nodded in the direction Tain had taken. "No offense, commander, but if the Captain succeeds in her task, then I hope you will not have a case at all."

Gabrielle March sighed and paced before him for a moment. Talesin watched her with interest. She closed her eyes and rubbed the back of her neck. Something was clearly bothering the human, and she was trying to decide how much to share with Talesin.

She turned suddenly and walked back to him, locking eyes again with the ice elf and leaning toward him. "Look, I realize you wish to protect the thief, but I cannot vouch for her safety," she whispered. "The Watch is under my command…but we are not the only ones out here looking for you this evening."

Talesin did not answer this time. He was quite worried about the imp's safety himself.

March stared at the ice elf for another moment, scanning his frosty features for anything she could use. Finding nothing, she spun on her heel and began to walk down the alley. "Bring him," she called over her shoulder.

Talesin was pushed forward, but a voice suddenly stopped the Watch's advance.

"Excellent job, Commander March—excellent indeed."

Talesin saw the commander tense as Odin Darweshi emerged from the shadows. The ice elf glanced around, aware that the entire group had frozen. There was a collective grimace of disgust on the faces of all the White Watch soldiers. None of them seemed happy at the new arrival.

— ✸ ✸ ✸ —

Gabrielle March was least happy of all. She was nearly sick at having had to take advice from the merchant in the first place. For the life of her, she could not figure out why Alistair had suddenly chosen to do so.

Now Odin sidled up to her, positively beaming. "We expected to have the most trouble with this one… but of course I knew you were the man, er, woman for the job."

Gabrielle's lip curled. "Yes," she replied shortly. "We have all four elves in custody and are bringing them to Nimbus for questioning." March began to move past the merchant, but he slid in front of her, blocking her path.

"Ummm… one moment, Commander. You don't mind if we ask the prisoner a few questions, do you?" Odin motioned to his companion hiding in the shadows behind him.

It was Jinin Aurek.

"Actually, Lord Darweshi, I do mind," March replied tightly, watching with mounting concern as Odin's men spread out around the alley, surrounding her patrol.

Odin smiled a sickly sweet smile and crossed his arms before him. "You say you caught all of the elves, but I see no sign of the imp."

March hesitated, unsure of where he was going with this. "She escaped," she admitted with caution.

Odin nodded to Jinin, who slipped into the shadows again.

"I have already sent soldiers after her, Lord Darweshi," she protested.

But Odin was shaking his head in mock sadness. "Their efforts will not be enough, I assure you, Commander. The imp is far too clever for three soldiers to handle." And he brushed past her and moved to the ice elf.

Gabrielle followed his progress, ready to intervene should the need arise.

Darweshi began circling the ice elf as though he had found a long-lost toy. "So," he hissed. "Help your little Captain escape, did you? Sacrifice yourself for your leader?"

To his credit, the ice elf remained completely impassive. He did not even blink.

"She won't get too far. Not with Jinin on her tail," Odin snarled in his ear.

Still no reaction.

Odin moved in front of the elf. "Where is she going?" he growled.

Nothing. Gabrielle was unsure the elf even saw the merchant. He seemed to look past Odin, or through him.

Then, before the commander could stop him, Odin drew back his fist and connected with the elf's jaw, rocking his head to the side with an audible crack.

"Darweshi!" Gabrielle shouted, diving forward.

Odin reached out and snagged the elf by the collar pulling him back up, impervious to the stinging cold emanating from the ice elf. He put his large square face close to the elf's smaller one. "Tell me, you cold-hearted freak!"

Odin hit the elf again, this time in the stomach, doubling him over and knocking the wind out of him. The two men gripping the ice elf's arms held him up but were looking to Gabrielle for support.

The commander saw herself fast losing control of the situation. She launched herself forward and grabbed Darweshi's shoulder turning him about. "That's enough!" she growled at him.

Darweshi shrugged off her arm and rounded on her. Standing toe to toe, they were nearly the same height. "I don't think he has had enough, Commander! He could very well be responsible for the condition of your dear matriarch, and you insist on treating him like a guest?"

Gabrielle stepped closer to him, bringing her voice up several notches. "I was only sent to retrieve him, Darweshi! It is neither of our jobs to interrogate him!"

Odin opened his mouth, presumably to yell at her further, when the ice elf chose that moment to take advantage of Odin's lack of attention. Using his captors as levers, the nimble elf raised both feet into the air and launched his heels at Darweshi. The elf's feet landed in the center of Odin's back driving him several feet forward so that he fell into his own crowd of jeering men.

The commander stared at the elf in shock. She motioned to the two soldiers who held him, and they yanked him back, away from the fuming merchant as she silently cursed him for making her job a whole lot harder.

Odin's men were in an uproar. The man himself came barreling back at the elf, ready to do serious damage. Gabrielle quickly inserted herself between the two.

"Stay back, Darweshi," she said, placing a hand on his chest. "And the rest of you, shut up! You'll wake the whole city with this clamor."

Darweshi gaped at her but recovered quickly. "Really March, I was simply trying to get some much-needed information out of him sooner rather than later."

"He is *my* prisoner, Darweshi," she growled, pointing a finger at him. "You have no authority whatever in these arrests!"

"On the contrary, my dear Commander," he oozed as he took a threatening step forward. "I have all the authority I need."

March shoved him back. This time Odin's temper finally did blow. He reached for his sword, as did the rest of his crew. The ring of metal echoed through the alley as the two groups prepared to face off.

March knew her soldiers were better trained than Darweshi's. If he were stupid enough to challenge her in the streets, he would lose. But she could not fight Darweshi and at the same time protect the ice elf, who had just made himself a target for Darweshi's volatile temper.

"Get out of here, Darweshi," she said, her voice low and threatening. "Or I will tell Alistair all about your *help* this evening."

"He accepted it," Odin hissed back at her.

March backed off a step, feeling more in control again. "He accepted your advice, not your interviewing skills. As usual, you have overstepped your bounds."

Odin smiled thinly and crossed his arms. "I don't recall Alistair drawing any lines."

"But I have," March spat. "And if Alistair finds out that you have tried to take matters into your own hands this night, he will have you arrested."

Odin laughed, but he had lost some of his bluster. "I have hardly done anything close to what you say."

March shrugged. "And who do you think Alistair will believe?"

Odin's eyes widened, clearly not expecting this much backlash from her. "You wouldn't dare," Odin hissed, any pretense of friendliness completely gone now.

She did not answer.

Odin backed up. "You wouldn't lie, March. Not to the old man."

"Wouldn't I?" Gabrielle shot back. "My orders are to bring in *Duak-Thenal*, unharmed. Interrogations will take place at Nimbus—and you will have nothing to do with them, I assure you. You will have your say at the hearing. Until then, take your filthy lynch mob and get out of my way."

There was a long uncomfortable silence during which Odin alternately clenched and unclenched his hands about his sword hilt. For a moment Gabrielle feared she would have to fight her way through after all. But Odin must have realized he had played out his hand, because finally he sheathed his sword and began backing away.

"Very well, March, have it your way," Odin sang, straightening his purple cloak and brushing his black hair from his face. His sweet good-boy act had returned, and he was grinning from ear to ear in a way that made the commander instantly suspicious. "In the end, I always get mine."

He motioned for his men to follow him and sauntered out of the alley.

Commander Gabrielle March closed her eyes and breathed deeply. She turned around and surveyed her patrol and her prisoner. The ice elf was standing, but he was bent over slightly, and a line of blood was trickling from his lip.

Gabrielle frowned and approached him. She was trying to decide who she was angrier at, Darweshi for causing such chaos, or the elf for making it worse. "Are you all right?" she asked him.

The ice elf looked up at her with his depthless black eyes and nodded.

"I apologize for that," she said sincerely. "It shouldn't have happened."

Surprisingly, the ice elf smiled. "No apologies necessary, Commander. I only did what you could not. It was my pleasure."

March scowled. She cleared her throat and glanced at her patrol, most of whom shifted their feet and looked away. They all knew how much she and Odin hated each other, but only the ice elf had the courage to voice this opinion.

"Yes… well. Let's try to keep our hands… and feet… to ourselves from now on, shall we?"

She did not give the elf a chance to answer. Instead she turned and walked briskly from the alley, not speaking to or looking at the elf again.

35~Thieves in the Garden

Tain scampered across the rooftops with as much care and stealth as she could muster. The thatch of the buildings was slippery with mud and slime, made more unmanageable by the pelting rain. Her black hair had come undone from its braid and was now plastered to her thin face.

She was drenched. Wetter than she could ever remember being and colder than she cared to ever be again. And that was the least of her problems.

Her left arm hung limp at her side, thanks to a well-placed arrow that had narrowly missed her chest. She had seen the White Watch soldier loose his weapon. Her catlike reflexes had enabled her to turn out of the way enough to save her own life. But the arrow had still taken a chunk out of her upper arm.

For a time, she had tried to cradle the injured limb, but the action interfered with her balance. She had settled for simply trying not to jostle it, for every time she did electric shocks of pain ripped through her shoulder and down her fingertips. She did not have time to look at the wound and was only dimly aware of the steady stream of wetness that trickled down the inside of her cloak.

She had lost the three soldiers who had so successfully kept her on the run, but there was no telling how long it would take them to catch up to her again. Tain had been to Preliona many times. She had contacts with jewelers and merchants here; visited several private businesses in the jewelers' district—always in disguise, of course. She snooped around the small shops in

Dirt Alley, keeping an eye out for thieving tools and an ear to the ground for new information from the alley's less than savory denizens.

So, she knew Preliona. Better than she should.

But the well-trained White Watch seemed to know every dirt-encrusted recess, from the sewers to the highest towers. They now displayed an uncanny knack for tracking the injured Captain. She made a mental note to compliment Commander March on their prowess the next time she saw her.

If she lived that long. Her vision had started to become fuzzy around the edges and balancing on the rooftops was becoming more and more difficult.

A shout from behind her startled the imp so badly that she nearly pitched right over the edge onto the cobblestones below. As it was, she had to barrel her arms wildly to hang onto her perch, sending fresh waves of pain coursing through her left side.

Tain glanced behind her and caught sight of one archer bobbing over the top of a roof two buildings away from her.

A surge of untapped energy swelled in her and Tain thought she might have one last run left. The Captain had never been caught, and she was not about to break her flawless record this day.

She righted herself, and then crouched low, her head swimming. She toed the edge of the roof and jumped ten feet to the street below.

She landed in a crouch but immediately tipped forward, losing her balance entirely and catching herself on her good hand. For a moment she closed her eyes, willing the world to stop spinning. Then she stood slowly and flattened herself against the wall.

The voices and footsteps of her pursuers passed right over her head, never even stopping to consider the ten-foot leap she had made. With every ounce of her effort, the Captain heaved herself away from the wall and sprinted around the building she had hidden behind.

The alley here was much darker than the rest of the city. For a moment Tain feared she had taken a wrong turn and landed herself in some impoverished part of town. When she glanced down, however, she noticed the pink cobblestones were fading away, replaced by dirt and stone.

Tain sighed in relief.

Without realizing it, the Captain had managed to land in Dirt Alley and the back door of Cornelius' tower.

But Dirt Alley, for all its darkness and secrets, was no place to hide. The buildings on either side of her provided no cover. Literally hundreds of shadowy corners lurked along the fifty-yard expanse. Dark curtained windows offered no light. She would have been better off on the roof. On the ground she was a moving target.

Tain drew her staff from its back holster and clicked it open. She crept along the narrow street, careful to hug one side of the alley as she peered into the gloom of each grimy storefront. Any movement in the surrounding area would have been heard by the keen imp…and yet she could not shake the feeling that she was being watched. She made herself move faster. By the time she was halfway down the street she was too exhausted to care if she was heard and she began to sprint the last few yards to the tower gate. Twenty feet from the end of the alley, nearly home free, a dark form emerged from the end of the street.

Tain came up short, skidding to a halt and swallowing hard when she saw who blocked her path to safety.

Dressed all in black, the thin figure would have been unrecognizable to anyone who lacked the shrewd eyesight of the fairy. As it was, the pounding rain blurred her vision, but not so much that she could not make out the badly died hair and hawk nose of Jinin Aurek.

Tain glared through the rain and the darkness at the man who was about to delay her. "Hello, Jinin," she said.

The other thief grinned. "Almost made it, Tain."

The imp captain sighed heavily and weighed her options. She could call for help, but the chances of anyone in the tower hearing her over the driving rain were slim. Her only other option was to fight the thief and in her current condition, she did not hold out much hope for victory. She needed to stall. "All alone, Jinin?" she quipped. "I didn't think you would venture out without your loyal crew."

Jinin lifted his chin and sat back on one hip casually. "How do you know they are not lurking about this alley right now?" he said.

"Because I would have heard the bumbling oafs," Tain smirked. "You're taking a chance being alone and unprotected, aren't you?"

Jinin laughed. "I could say the same about you."

Tain swallowed. He knew she was alone too, so he must have known that the elves were taken. "What do you want, Jinin?" she asked.

"I think it's time we settled a few things, *Captain*." Jinin Aurek drew both his weapons—a short sword and a wicked serrated dagger—and advanced on the injured imp, stalking forward hard and fast. Tain tensed but stayed where she was, still unable to believe her sour luck and unsure if she would be able to move if she wanted to.

Jinin stopped a few feet from his foe. Tain could have touched him with her staff. But she did not raise a finger to defend herself, forcing the other thief to make the first move.

"Your crew is dead," he said evenly. "Or they will be soon."

Tain knew he was lying, even though his trained features gave nothing away.

"I'd ask for your surrender, but I know you won't give it. So, I figured I'd just save the people of Preliona the trouble and kill you myself."

"Very noble of you," Tain sneered. "But I don't think your efforts will be appreciated by the governor or her Council."

"The governor will not make it through the night and the rest of the Council will believe me when I tell them I acted in self-defense."

Tain raised an eyebrow. "Really. Since when does the Council take the advice of cutthroats and petty thieves like you?"

"Since I brought them proof of your guilt. And since Odin and I took over for Alistair," Jinin hissed.

Tain laughed. She did not want to provoke the volatile human, but she could not help herself. "Ha! The day you take over anything…"

"It's true!" Jinin interrupted, gripping his weapons tightly.

Tain gritted her teeth. "I'll believe it when I see it."

Jinin leaned into her and Tain could feel his breath on her face. "You won't live that long."

With a fierce growl, Jinin Aurek swung his short sword down and across, forcing the Captain backward before she could raise her staff.

The imp took two quick steps back, crouched low, and somersaulted backwards. She came up in a squat just in time to raise her staff and block a sword swipe and a dagger plunge before slashing her staff horizontally across the ground to take out Jinin's legs.

Jinin jumped straight into the air, narrowly avoiding the sharp blade on Tain's staff. He landed gracefully but took a step back to reposition himself.

Tain pressed the advantage. She assailed her opponent with a series of stabs and swings that kept Jinin on the defensive for several seconds. But the imp was in a world of pain and as strong as her attack was, she knew she could not hope to finish this fight quickly.

All too soon, Jinin managed to slip under one of Tain's vicious swings. He glided past the imp, slashing at her exposed side on the way by. Tain was forced to throw her body to the left to avoid the blade, barely managing to spin about in time to block yet another stab of Jinin's oddly shaped dagger.

But the Captain's last move had forced her staff vertical, the blunt end facing the ground and Jinin's attack had been a low one. As he dove for her, Tain swung her staff straight up. The harsh move caught the unsuspecting thief under the chin, throwing him back several feet. Jinin hit the alley wall hard, cracking his head soundly on the brick wall behind him. He pushed himself up with a shake of his head and swiped at her with his knife.

Tain easily knocked the dagger out of his hand. The knife clattered to the ground and Tain kicked it out of reach. Then she swung her staff into

Jinin's unprotected stomach. The man doubled over. This time Tain heard the wind go out of him.

She expected him to go down then, but the wiry thief surprised her by cutting toward her with his sword. Tain spun out of the way, arching her back and sucking in a startled breath.

Out of the corner of her eye, she saw Jinin recover and reach for her with his free hand. He latched onto the center of her staff with an iron grip. Tain pulled, trying to wrench the weapon away but at this point Jinin was by far the stronger. He yanked on the staff, nearly pulling her arms from their sockets, and spiraled her into the alley wall with dizzying speed.

Her bleeding shoulder connected harshly with the brick and stone. Pure white pain erupted along her whole left side and sparks of light veered in and out of her vision. Tain felt herself start to sink to the ground and she bit her tongue to keep from passing out.

Jinin was holding Tain's staff up under her chin and it was taking the last vestige of her strength to keep Jinin from choking her with her own weapon. Jinin was unable to press his advantage, however, because he was forced to hold his remaining weapon in one hand while he held the imp against the wall with the other. If he dropped his sword, Tain knew that the thief would crush her windpipe and she would be too weak to stop him.

Both fighters were breathing hard now. Tain knew she looked a mess, but she was oddly pleased to see that their little tiff had taken its toll on Jinin too. His long blonde streaked hair was matted to his face. A fine line of blood trickled down his temple and he was bent over so much so that his head was currently hanging at Tain's level. Tain suspected she had cracked a couple of his ribs in that last attack.

But his injuries did not seem to be affecting his will.

"Checkmate, Captain," Jinin gasped.

Tain smirked. "You mean stalemate."

"How do you figure?" Jinin laughed at her. "I've got you, imp. Give up."

Tain forced her pain-filled features into a condescending smile. "Now what kind of respect would you have for me if I let you win, Jinin?"

Jinin snorted. "You think I have any respect for you now?"

"Yes!" Tain countered. "Why else would you have chased me all the way through this city? You want revenge? Getting rid of me won't take away that feeling, you know."

Jinin's eyes widened in anger, "Squashing you like the bug you are, Tain, has *nothing* to do with revenge."

"Of course it does," Tain teased. "You think I don't remember what you said to me the day Breccan drummed you out of the *Black Bloods*?"

Jinin's eyes suddenly softened. They went slightly out of focus as he remembered that long-ago day. "I said the next time we met, I would come out on top."

Tain smiled thinly. "That's right. But you haven't come out on top, have you, Jinin?" she pressed. "I am still beating you—just like old times. Tell me, how did it feel to lose that key after you only had it for a few hours?"

Tain knew she had hit a nerve by the way Jinin's temple throbbed. "You *cheated*," he hissed, pressing the staff into the Captain's neck and making her gasp. Jinin grinned, "But I bet you don't have any of those sleep-inducing drugs on you today—do you, Captain?"

"I drugged you because I didn't want to kill you," Tain gasped.

Jinin gritted his teeth. "Because you're weak."

"No," the imp insisted. "Because I had some respect for you. Even though I knew you had those merchants killed, I still respected you for the thief you were."

Jinin's eyes narrowed. Two slits of pale blue, almost closed. "And now?"

Tain dropped her voice. The sound that came out of her mouth was low, adult, and extremely harsh. "Now I feel nothing for you. You have become what you set out to be. A lackey for someone with the money and power you were too cowardly to earn on your own."

With a growl Jinin yanked the imp toward him and slammed her viciously back into the wall. Tain cried out. Her head spun threateningly and for a moment she thought her knees were going to give out.

"Coward!?" Jinin screamed in her face. "*I'm* not the one who stabbed the Prince of Graxton in the back, Tain!"

Tain felt her grip on her staff tighten. She had been accused of this crime a thousand times before. She had stopped being offended by it long ago. But her patience with Jinin had reached its end.

Tain brought up her knee and slammed her heeled boot into Jinin's shin. Jinin howled in pain, but his hold on her staff did not loosen. Instead as the thief fell away, he dragged the imp with him.

Tain let go and Jinin stumbled to the ground, favoring his leg, and cursing violently. Tain reached for her remaining dagger. But when she crouched over, her equilibrium finally failed her, and she tumbled to her knees.

Jinin, also down and dangerously close, threw Tain's staff. It clattered into the opposite wall, well out of reach. He tried to stand, failed, and settled for scrambling toward her on his knees.

Tain finally grasped the hilt of her dagger in time for Jinin to slash at her with his own weapon. She deflected his sword once, twice, a third time. And then they both fell forward on their hands, splaying mud and water into their own faces.

"Where's the key, Tain?" Jinin gritted his teeth and dove for her again.

Tain fell back. Kicking out, she connected with Jinin's sword arm, throwing it wide. She brought her foot up again desperately. This time she thrust it straight forward and heard a sickening crunch as Jinin's nose flattened under her heel.

Tain winced, but Jinin barely registered the impact. He lunged forward on hands and knees, slashing at the imp, who scrambled backward to keep away from his sword. Blood was streaming down Jinin's chin and more blood from his temple had flooded his right eye. But he kept coming.

Tain's left arm gave out on her and she landed on her back. She managed to roll aside a spilt second before Jinin's blade would have struck her shin. The imp sat up quickly, grasped the blade of her dagger between two fingers and threw. The dagger connected with Jinin's shoulder and embedded itself to the hilt. The thief was thrown back by the force of it, landing on his back with a wet thud.

Tain didn't wait for her opponent to recover. She skidded backward with her feet, trying to gain some ground. But when she felt something cold and hard against her back, she stopped and looked up. A gate. A huge black metal gate with a curving cobra fixed in the center. Cornelius' crest. The two had carried their fight to the wizard's front door.

Tain was about to cry out—surely someone would hear her from this distance—when a hand closed around her throat. Her shout, and most of her air, was cut off and Jinin's blood-stained face loomed in front of her. The hilt of her dagger still protruded from his shoulder, but Jinin seemed not to notice. Tain's fingers danced across the wet ground until they closed on a large rock. She swung it at Jinin's face, but the thief grabbed her wrist with his other hand and smashed it into the metal gate behind her. When Tain did not let go, Jinin hit it again, bloodying her fingers and forcing them open. The stone dropped to the ground and Jinin kicked it away.

"It's in there, isn't it?" Jinin said, nodding toward the tower.

Tain could not have answered him if she wanted to, but Jinin did not seem to need an answer. He knew. This was the real reason he had come after her alone this night. The key called to him, and he knew the imp would lead him to it.

Jinin hauled her to her feet and dragged her to the lock on the huge iron gate. Tain tried to pry his fingers from her throat but Jinin would not budge. "Open it," he hissed at her.

Tain shook her head. "I can't," she gasped.

Jinin's hold on her tightened and Tain squeezed her eyes shut, waiting for him to crush her windpipe. "Yes, you can," he said calmly, and eased his hold.

Tain breathed easier and glared up at the man. "There is no lock," she told him.

Jinin glared at her from beneath dark lids, his blue eyes glowing brighter by the minute. "How do I get in?"

Tain swallowed, "To your right. Odd-shaped brick seven up from the ground and third from the gate. Push it."

Jinin glanced to his right. He saw the brick immediately. He shifted his hold on the imp and dragged her with him to the bricks next to the gate. "This better not be a trick, Tain."

In slow motion she watched Jinin reach for the brick. His long thin fingers barely brushed the stone surface and Tain felt the metal behind her waver. She knew the gate had disappeared, leaving a holographic image in its place.

But to Jinin's eyes, nothing happened. The gate stayed closed. The thief howled in anger and frustration, and once again tightened his grip on Tain's neck. Tain tried not to panic. Instead, she latched onto Jinin's arm and threw herself backward. They both fell through the gate and onto the white stones of Cornelius' garden.

Jinin toppled to the ground on top of the Captain. But he did not fall away from her as Tain had hoped. Instead the thief gripped her collar and rolled away from the stones dragging Tain with him. Tain landed on her back, hitting her head as Jinin hovered above her.

"Cheat!" he howled, and raised his hand to strike her. Tain moved her arms to block his fist when Jinin froze. A high-pitched chattering to the right, a spine-tingling squeal from the trees above, and bushes swayed, shadows lengthened. Jinin cocked his head and turned.

Tain did not. She knew what Jinin had heard—Cornelius' garden was coming to life.

Tain stayed very still, terrified and intensely curious at the same time. She had never seen what happened when an intruder strayed from Cornelius' white walkway.

Jinin glanced about nervously, his eyes darting from side to side. He pushed himself away from the imp and stood peering into the darkness. There was a loud ripping sound, like fabric being torn, and a long black shadow pulled itself away from the wall of the tower. A gigantic specter, monstrously tall and thin, slipped across the garden right into Jinin's path. It looked down at the thief as though challenging Jinin to a duel.

Tain tried to sit up, but somehow her body would not quite obey. For a moment Jinin only stared at the apparition, dumbfounded, unwilling to believe in it. Then he slashed out with his sword. The blade passed harmlessly through the specter, but Jinin's sword turned black and crumbled in his hands.

Crazed and obsessed as he had become, Jinin still had the presence of mind to know when he had lost a fight. He turned to run, reaching for Tain as he made for the gate.

His way was blocked by what Tain could only describe as an ogre. It wasn't, but Tain had no other word in her vocabulary to describe this creature. It was squat, only about two feet in height with arms so long that they dragged on the ground. They might have been borrowed from a larger creature and grafted onto this one. Its skin was a mottled blue. It had three fingers on each hand and no nose, but its mouth took up the entire lower half of its face.

That mouth was open now. Its grin revealed rows of rotten teeth that, for all their discoloration, seemed extremely sharp. Jinin tried to back up, but those abnormally long arms wrapped themselves around the thief's knees. Tain scrambled backwards as Jinin lost his balance and fell backward himself. The ogre kept hold of Jinin's lower half and shook him fiercely. The thief's legs snapped like twigs.

Jinin screamed. A loud, long, ear-piercing sound that finally unglued Tain from her position on the ground. She gained her knees, ignoring her numb left arm, and began crawling toward the stone path, glancing over her shoulder as she did.

The creature now sank its teeth into Jinin's side, bit down and pulled away, leaving an impossibly wide hole in the thief's body. Tain turned away, horrified by the sight. But she could not tune out the sound of Jinin's anguished screams.

She made it to the stoop of the wizard's door and collapsed onto it. Then she swung her head to look at Jinin. She was just in time to see the ogre's hideous teeth close over Jinin's throat, silencing his horrible cries forever. When at last the door opened, and a large black hand reached for her, she barely noticed.

36~Meeting His Match

Alistair Kellen Keane, Watch Chief for Preliona and its surrounding towns, sat alone awaiting the arrival of his prisoners. He had lit several lamps, but in this dark and musty place the fires seemed of little use.

The prison of Preliona was split into six long hallways, all of which spilled into the large circular cavern in which Alistair now waited. Each tunnel housed a different class of prisoner. The three at the south kept men, and the opposite three women. Out of those three, one on each side held violent criminals, murderers, and thieves; the second held non-violent criminals; and the third kept those who had been charged with crimes but had not as yet been convicted.

The dungeon was the underbelly of Nimbus, interspersed with more than a few secret entrances—not all of which were known to the soldiers of the Watch. It was through one of these that Commander March had earlier escorted her prisoners, hoping to keep the capture of *Duak-Thenal* under wraps and question them without drawing unwanted attention.

Alistair had not dared to use the Great Hall of Nimbus or any of its conference rooms, for fear of being overheard by Odin's cronies. They were everywhere, it seemed, and no matter how many soldiers he placed around the building, he still did not feel safe from the prying eyes of Jinin Aurik.

A cell door on the upper level yielded a groan. Alistair craned his neck to see who had entered. The upper level was only about six yards away, but in the gloom, Alistair couldn't make out which soldier stood in the cell door.

"Yes," he said.

"We are ready, sir," the young man said.

Alistair nodded. "As am I. Send them in."

"Sir," the soldier acknowledged, and turned to go.

Alistair stood and straightened his uniform. He was tired, in no mood for interrogations. He could have left this job to March, she was more than capable, but considering the strangeness of the situation he felt he had better deal with this one himself.

The Commander had informed him of the trouble she had encountered with Odin and his gang. Alistair was not surprised. He had taken a chance listening to the merchant's son at all. After Cornelius left Nimbus, Darweshi had apologized for his rudeness and presented Alistair with a suggestion. He asked if Jinin Aurek could accompany the White Watch on their rounds. Having seen the members of *Duak-Thenal* firsthand, Jinin would be better equipped to identify them.

Much as Alistair hated to give in, he could not argue with this logic. But he had wondered what else Odin wanted from this barter. He had certainly proven overzealous in giving his help. Gabrielle said that Odin and Jinin had kept one uncanny step ahead of *Duak-Thenal* the entire night. They had successfully led the White Watch around the city, directing and giving them the edge they needed to corner the elves.

Alistair was bothered by this, as was March. Pointing out the elves to the Watch was one thing, but how exactly had Jinin known where *Duak-Thenal* would be next?

The sound of steel-toed boots echoed in the upper hall. Alistair started to turn to get a look at the newcomers but caught himself. He did not want to appear too eager.

He did not know what he expected, really. Gabrielle had warned him that these were not normal elves. Alistair shook his head. That wasn't right, he knew. It was not that they were abnormal; it was that several of them transcended the commander's view of elves in general.

Preliona was the geographic center of the Northern Realms and was thus surrounded by three out of the four elven territories. Yet the only elves the seventy-something-year-old general had seen were the gold-skinned, light-haired type. So, when the commander had informed him that they had captured only one elf that met that description, he had been a bit surprised.

The upper gate opened. Alistair turned and watched two guards enter from the third hall, followed by three elves and four more guards.

Alistair felt his heart race at the sight of them. They were all tall and thin. The light elf was what Alistair expected. Gold hair and eyes to match, he looked around the room and took in his surroundings long before his golden eyes fell on the Watch Chief. He studied every dark recess and watched each movement of the guards around him, as if searching for a weak spot. He was cunning, this one. He looked innocent, angelic almost, but Alistair had the feeling the light elf was anything but.

The second elf was Malhurian, surely. His skin was as deep a brown and sable smooth as Cornelius', and he was just as tall. His eyes, however, were purple. Alistair had never seen such a color. He also looked as though he could take on the six guards that surrounded him single-handed. Alistair was accustomed to seeing elves as lithe and quick creatures. But this elf was wide and muscular. He, too, took in his surroundings first before letting his eyes settle on Alistair— and then, only for a second. Alistair saw that he was focused on the doors at the other end of the room, perhaps also looking for an escape.

Last came the ice elf. Alistair, who had seen almost everything in this world, shivered visibly despite himself. This one looked at Alistair first before he did anything else. His black, depthless eyes blasted through Alistair like a sharp icicle. It was difficult for Alistair to move after the ice elf entered the room. He could see his soldiers were having the same problem. It was as if the elf brought along his own special air—and the rest of them could choke on it, for all he cared.

They were angry, these three elves. Gabrielle said they had been no trouble at all, but Alistair sensed that was all about to change.

"Gentlemen," Alistair began. "Please sit down."

The three elves now stood in a line before him. None moved toward the chairs he had offered them.

Alistair glanced at the guards, who were now inching their hands toward their swords. But Alistair held up one finger, signaling them to hold back.

The Watch Chief crossed his arms before him. They were intimidating, to be sure, but they were noticeably young, even by elven standards. Alistair would be damned if these children would get the better of him. "Is there a problem with my chairs?"

"Where is Dagmar?" The southern elf spoke up.

Alistair raised an eyebrow. Understanding lit his features. "Ah. The wild elf," he said. "She is in a different set of cells. She should be arriving any minute now."

The light elf stepped forward. The guards shifted, but again Alistair held them back. In a voice that belied his good looks, the light elf said, "If anything has happened to her…"

Alistair held up his hands, amused but not quite daring to laugh. "I assure you, gentlemen, she is fine. We separate women from men here, that is all. This is Preliona, not Graxton."

This seemed to calm them a bit. Except for the ice elf. His features did not change a bit. Alistair again motioned them to the small table. "Please have a seat."

They hesitated. It was only a second, but to Alistair it seemed that the young elves took his measure several times over before they made a move for the chairs.

They glided more than walked, melted into their seats more than sat. Their grace made him feel older than he had ever felt in his life. He watched them without moving himself, afraid that they would see the arthritis that riddled his body, though he took great pains to hide it. *They will see it,* he thought. *They will, though no one else can.*

At that moment one of the cell doors at the opposite end of the room opened and Commander March entered. She was followed by the most ethereal creature Alistair had ever seen.

Dagmar, that is what the others had called her, was almost as tall as the commander -- and that was saying a lot. Still, she was only about half as wide. She walked with all the trained force of a warrior and at the same time managed to make Gabrielle look like an ungraceful child. She was not beautiful in a traditional sense, but she was intriguing. The guards were as transfixed by her as they were fearful of the ice elf. And Dagmar did not seem to notice or care. It was as if, with a look, she made them all forget what a dangerous specimen she was. Alistair understood why Gabrielle suspected her to be the leader.

The other three elves stood again at her entrance, obviously looking to see if she was all right. But the wild elf glared at them until they all got back into their seats. Alistair checked the urge to laugh. It was something Althea would have done. The female was their equal, and the males were treating her like their little sister. The wild elf was obviously not pleased. It was nice to know that things were not all that different in elven circles than they were in his own.

She turned to Alistair then and the old man's breath caught in his throat. He had heard that it was the eyes of an elf, not the ears that were the telltale sign of their race. Goblins and imps had pointed ears. Most half-breeds had pointed ears. No, it was the eyes that made an elf, he believed, and he had not been disappointed this day. Dagmar's eyes were gray. But they were not a flat, stone color. Ghostly, misty, clouded, and as calm and placid as a lake the morning after a storm. The light elf's eyes were mischievous and sharply cunning. The southern elf's were eerie and full of the mystery of desert-dwelling people. The ice elf's were nothing short of terrifying... But the wild elf's? Dagmar's eyes held all the secrets to an untouched natural world.

Alistair nodded to the wild elf and extended a hand to the empty chair at the opposite end of the table. She nodded in return and took the chair without a word.

Gabrielle dispatched some of her guards and sent one of them to each end of the room. That left only Alistair and the commander to deal with the power of these four unique elves. Alistair knew that these elves—*Duak-Thenal*—were terribly dangerous, but somehow he wasn't worried.

He took a breath and looked at the report Gabrielle had written.

He took another breath and spoke. "I know that you represent some of the members of *Duak-Thenal*," Alistair began. "Before I ask you any more questions, I would like to ask your names." He leaned on the table and looked them all in their vastly different eyes. "Your real names."

There was a long moment of silence. Alistair was afraid he would be conducting a one-ended interrogation when Dagmar finally spoke up. Her face was calm, her voice free of any malice, but her words were sharp and forceful. "We can give you the names we know each other by. They are real to us, though they may not be to you. The names we were born with, and the ones I am sure you seek, ceased to exist the day we banded together. We will not give them, and it will take more time than you have in this life to find them."

That last comment stung, as it was meant to. For a moment Alistair hated the wild elf for the hundreds of years she would outlive him. "Fine," he said, for he saw no point in arguing about this. "Give me the names you are known by."

"Dagmar Coal."

"Nemesio Firebrand."

"Panas the Hawk."

"Talesin Darken."

Alistair nodded. "And along with Captain Tain Elire, you are *Duak-Thenal*."

Dagmar Coal leaned forward. Her eyes flashed silver in the light of the lamp. "*We* are *Duak-Thenal*," she said, "Those of us here in this room. We count no other in our number."

Alistair did not believe this for one moment, but he decided to let that line of questioning alone for now. He scanned all their faces. There had been a shift in attitude as soon as he had mentioned the Captain. Almost as if they had expected the question and had a rote answer for it.

Alistair stood straight and put on his glasses. "Right, then. These are the charges against you." He cleared his throat and read from the paper in his hands. "The hijacking of three shipments of barexium out of Graxton in the last two months. The breaking and entering of Odin Darweshi's barge and the stealing of money and papers intended for the bridge. The suspected kidnapping of Raymond S'Trobenue and his child. The murder of Sigmund S'Trobenue. The suspected murder of two dozen merchants on Hunter's Heights. The murder of Edmee S'Trobenue. And the attack on Althea Gaenor, Governor of Preliona."

"What!" The light elf was on his feet before Alistair could lay down his papers, but the ice elf and the Malhurian managed to drag him back down.

"You have something to say to these charges, Master Hawk?" Alistair asked, removing his glasses.

It was obvious he did, but the others were glaring at the fiery golden-haired elf and he got himself under control.

Alistair narrowed his eyes. "Lady, and gentlemen, if you are innocent of these charges, then you must speak."

Silence.

Alistair sat down and laid his glasses on the table. "Will you say nothing in your defense? Can it be that you are responsible for all these actions? Or are you guilty of only some of the charges?"

"You are wasting your time," Dagmar said suddenly. "We will not speak either way."

Alistair sighed. "Miss, you are making a mistake. If you do not speak on your own behalf, who will speak for you?"

She said nothing, only stared back at him with those strange, misted eyes.

Alistair leaned back. "All right," he said. "Have it your way." He looked back at his papers and then at the elves again. They remained impassive as before, but as Alistair swept his eyes over their faces, he realized something. Something he had missed before. "Commander," he said. "I thought one of them had red hair."

"I'm sorry, sir?" Gabrielle moved to his side and looked over his shoulder at the small stack of papers.

Alistair looked back to the elves and pointed at his papers. "We have a description of an elf with red hair and green eyes."

It was the light elf who spoke up and this time, in a completely different tone of voice. "That would be me," he said, grinning from ear to pointed ear.

Alistair scowled and stood. He moved in front of Panas the Hawk and leaned forward narrowing his eyes and scanning the angular face before him. He raised one knarled finger. "I may be an old man, elf, but I am not blind. "*That*," he said, pointing to Panas' sheaf of blonde locks, "is not red."

"Ah, but it does appear that way in the right light." Panas' grin widened, if that was possible. The glint in his golden hawk-like eyes sparkled with a mischief that made Alistair wary. "Anyone seeing me from a distance might mistake me for a redhead. I've often thought of changing my natural color just to avoid confusion."

Alistair did not believe Panas the Hawk, and knew the light elf was stalling. But the war-hardened, worldly chief had never dealt with anyone quite like Panas the Hawk before. He found himself nearly at a loss for words.

Gabrielle intercepted smoothly and leaned toward the light elf. "Our witness was fighting hand to hand with a red-haired elf. There could be no mistake."

"Did your witness say he fought in the dark?" Panas asked.

Alistair did not see what relevance this had, but he answered, "It was night."

Panas opened his hands to Alistair and Gabrielle as if to say, *See? I told you so.* "Well, you see, at night and by the light of the moon, my hair is much darker. Besides, anyone who was fighting me would have been too busy defending himself to get a good look at my hair."

It was all Alistair could do to control himself. He turned to look at Gabrielle, who seemed about to say something. Then she closed her mouth with an audible snap. For his part, Alistair would have liked to shake the golden-haired elf until his golden eyes rolled from his head.

Which led to another thought. "The eyes," he said. "Explain the green eyes, for we can all see yours are plainly not green."

"Take a closer look, Chief," Panas said, pulling at the lids of his eyes. "You see my eyes are gold. But they have green flecks in them, and I am sure that in the right…"

"The right *light*," Alistair finished for him.

Panas the Hawk nodded with a smile. Alistair pursed his lips as he decided to drop this subject for the time being, as well. "Fine," he said, moving down the line. "So, there are four of you. Then which of you is the leader?"

The four elves stared straight ahead.

"Then I suppose it would be the imp Captain whom we have failed to capture."

Still no answer, but Alistair could detect a small change in the air about the elves. It was odd, really. Their faces gave away absolutely nothing. It was the air about them that seemed to shift slightly just then. As if these creatures, who were so adept at detecting the slightest smell and the smallest sound, were incapable of controlling their own very intense energies.

He had hit a nerve, and this was a subject he had no intention of dropping.

He shifted his focus to Dagmar. "She was seen with you this evening," he said. "Was it she who got you into the warehouse?"

Nothing. The wild elf did not even blink.

Alistair moved to Talesin, even though his arthritis seemed to flare up just being near him. "She traveled with you. The Commander says you helped her escape. Where has she gone?"

No answer.

Alistair stood back and surveyed the group before him. There was a connection here, he knew. But not the one that Odin had described. Gabrielle had the strong suspicion that the wild elf was the leader, and from what he had observed thus far Alistair was inclined to agree. The question was, how far would the other three go to protect her identity? How close were they to the imp, and would they further damn her reputation to keep up appearances?

Alistair decided to push a little further.

"Look, we know the imp is your leader," Alistair lied. "And I know you think you are protecting her—but you're not. Tell me where she is, and I promise you she will get a fair trial."

They did not move, they did not speak, and they did not breathe. This last was the most important fact, for up until the last few seconds they had been breathing. He knew he would never get the Captain's whereabouts from them, but he still harbored hope that he or Gabrielle would find her on their own. No, he was simply hoping to get them to admit that the imp was *not* their leader, after all.

"I assure you I will get the thief with or without your help." He knelt, with some effort, before Dagmar, looked her straight in the eye. "I must say, however, things will go better for you and for her the sooner we locate her."

So far Dagmar had remained frozen to her place, her eyes locked with his. Which was exactly where he wanted them. "Miss Coal, I am going to see Cornelius in the morning. I have the papers. If she is there, I will find her."

She blinked.

"You cannot protect her, but you can at least help me keep her presence a secret. If I take her tonight, there will be no one around to see. If we wait until morning, everyone will know. The charges she faces here will triple once the people of Preliona find out we have her."

"She hasn't stolen anything in Preliona."

Alistair knew it was the southern elf who had spoken even before he turned to look at him. He could not be sure, but he thought Dagmar looked relieved as he tore his gaze from her and focused on the large Malhurian.

He placed his hands on the edge of the table and pushed himself up as gracefully as possible. "That may be true, Master Firebrand, but considering her reputation, there are literally hundreds of complaints filed against her here. All would have to be investigated. And there are enough warrants for her arrest in the surrounding towns to convict her for an exceedingly long time." Now he looked back to Dagmar, "Especially if she turns out to be your leader. Though I must confess I find that extremely hard to believe."

There was still silence, but it was a new kind of silence. They were all thinking on what he had said, and their silence meant they believed him.

"She isn't."

Dagmar.

Alistair moved to her as fast as his screaming joints would allow. "What?" he hissed.

She blinked slowly, opened her misty eyes, and let them drift past him. "She isn't our leader."

He had her.

He knew it without looking at the others. "Look in my eyes and say that, my dear."

She brought her gray eyes back to his blue ones with a snap of her head. "Captain Tain Elire is not the leader of *Duak-Thenal*."

Alistair nodded. "And who is the leader, Dagmar?"

Dagmar Coal took a short deep breath. "I am," she replied.

"Dagmar!" Panas hissed.

Alistair glared and pointed a finger at the light elf. "Quiet," he snarled, and turned back to Dagmar. "And what is the Captain's place in your ranks?"

"She doesn't have one," Dagmar replied. Without knowing quite why, Alistair knew she was lying.

Alistair shook his head. "I don't believe you."

Dagmar's gray eyes flared. "I don't care."

Alistair pointed his crooked finger in her face. "You had better care. The only way you can prove your innocence right now is to implicate her."

"How do you figure that?" Panas asked in a rather tired, almost broken voice.

"Could you have broken into the warehouse without her?" Alistair asked.

He heard a chair scrape and turned in time to see Dagmar rise quickly and angrily to her feet. She was seething. Alistair had backed her into a corner, never considering that the placid, cool elf would come out fighting. "Do you honestly believe any one of us is incapable of entering that building without a key?" she shouted. "One does not need the master thief of the Northern Realms to pick a lock!"

Gabrielle was behind the elf in a second. She placed a hand on Dagmar's shoulder, but the furious elf shook her off. The commander grasped the hilt of her sword and nodded to the two remaining guards in the room. They immediately left for reinforcements.

The elves were now inching to their feet. As the commander was occupied with Dagmar, the other three elves took full advantage of the situation. Alistair was far from alarmed, but he was smart enough to know when the situation was fast approaching dangerous.

Nemesio, the closest to Dagmar, was on his feet first and now Gabrielle did draw her sword. With lightning speed, she placed its tip at the southern elf's throat. "Stay back," she commanded.

Nemesio froze, but Talesin and Panas would not stand down. Panas moved to step around Nemesio so that Gabrielle was forced to keep two elves between her and Dagmar. Talesin got around the table and a step or two toward Alistair, who was backing up. "Call them off, Miss Coal," Alistair demanded.

But the wild elf did not move. In fact, she seemed not to hear him at all. March backed away from her and turned her attention to Nemesio and Panas. The two elves were splitting, trying to get the commander between them.

Talesin Darken was stalking toward Alistair, forcing the chief to draw his sword. "Dagmar!" Alistair shouted.

The ice elf was feet from Alistair when a dozen Watch members poured through each door. They instantly drew their swords and moved to surround the elves. But Alistair held both hands out to keep his soldiers back.

The three male elves had stopped their advance and were eyeing the Watch with apprehension but little fear. Each of them was close enough to Gabrielle and Alistair to do some serious damage and yet they did not move.

Alistair licked his lips. The White Watch soldiers were fingering their weapons tensely. He was playing with fire, he knew. He had no doubt his soldiers would obey him, but if the elves made another move toward Alistair, he knew he would have a fight on his hands.

He tore his eyes from Talesin and walked toward Dagmar slowly and sheathed his sword.

The wild elf was calming, regaining that cool, collected mien she had started out with. Still she gripped the edge of the table and gritted her teeth. Swords surrounded her but Dagmar did not seem to care. Alistair wondered how far she would have let the other elves go if the soldiers had not barged in.

"Let's try this again, shall we?" he asked. "What do you need the imp for, Dagmar?"

She spoke and her voice was deep and deadly. "I will entertain no questions regarding the imp Captain. Change your course or you will get nothing else from us."

"You cannot deny her existence and protect her at the same time," Alistair pressed.

Dagmar leaned forward, her posture positively menacing. In that moment, Alistair believed her truly capable of the crimes she was accused of. "You wanted the leader of *Duak-Thenal?*" she spat at him. "You've got me."

"Dagmar, don't..." Panas started to object.

"Shut up, Panas," she hissed, never taking her eyes from Alistair's. "You can use the information I have given you for whatever ends you need to or use none of it. Take your pick."

There was a long and uncomfortable silence. Alistair scanned the faces of the other elves.

Panas and Nemesio stared at Dagmar with deep concern. Talesin, however, glared at Alistair with something more resembling loathing.

Alistair had not wished things to progress so badly here, but the damage was done. He may have gotten some answers, but they had come at a cost.

Alistair tore his gaze from the ice elf and turned back to Dagmar. "What's it going to be?" he asked.

She had not moved, and her features had not melted a bit. "I will not bargain with you over the Captain thief. If you want her, then you are on your own—and *Kelina* help you if you succeed in that ridiculous quest."

Alistair nodded, giving in. "Will you answer to the charges?"

"To hijacking Barexium shipments, to entering Odin's barge and warehouse uninvited. These things only will I discuss with you. As for the rest, you will have to prove we were there with more than a scratched coin, for we will admit to none of those crimes."

Alistair knew he would get no more from her. He counted himself lucky to have gotten what he had. And perhaps it *was* folly to pursue the Captain this way. He had told Cornelius he would knock on his door come morning if *Duak-Thenal* did not show themselves. They had, and now he had no right to bother the mage. Imp thief or no.

Alistair nodded to the wild elf, and some of the hardness went out of her eyes. She sat down again, much to the guards' surprise.

Commander March took a step away from Dagmar, but she kept her sword trained on Nemesio and Panas. "Sit down," she told them.

Both elves glanced at Dagmar, who nodded. They sat slowly, very aware of the swords trained on their backs.

That left the ice elf. Alistair suddenly found he could not find the breath to command this one to back off. He was facing him, only feet from him. Waves of cold floated off the elf, freezing Alistair to his spot and making his voice creak.

Thankfully, Gabrielle stepped in. "Master Darken?" Commander March said.

He looked at her, then at Dagmar. She raised her head long enough to nod at him, then resumed staring straight ahead at the wall.

Talesin walked back to the table without a word and sat beside his friends.

To look at them now, one would never have guessed that only a moment ago they had been ready to attack. They were calm. Completely calm.

Gabrielle sheathed her sword and turned to Alistair for further direction.

He knew what she wanted. She wanted to be done with this. She wanted to lock her prisoners away before any of the Watch got antsier than they were already. Someone could make a mistake, and she did not want that to happen any more than he did. For though the elves had backed down, the Watch soldiers were now more tense than ever. Well trained as they were, they could not get past seeing their chief threatened.

He nodded. "I'm finished for now, Commander. Return them to their cells and meet me in my quarters when you are through."

Gabrielle visibly relaxed, as did the men and woman under her control. "You four, with this one," she said, pointing to Dagmar. "You," she said, pointing to a group of about eight large men, "With me."

Alistair left before Commander March got any further. He had too much to think about. And he did not care to see the elves escorted from the room—he was too shaken. He had seen his own reflection in Talesin's eyes, and he could not stop shivering at the image. For he had not seen the Alistair of the present day in the ice elf's onyx orbs. As old and crooked as he was, that at least would have been bearable.

No, what he had seen was the face of a dead man.

37~The Wizard's Plan

It was nearly dawn, only hours after the night's disastrous events.

Kiernan's head hurt. He had not slept.

Cornelius had magicked up a spread for the dining room table: breads and cheeses, fruit, milk, pastries, and ham. Kiernan had yet to touch a thing. He had not even looked at the food. He rested his elbows on his knees and held onto his head, as if to keep the contents from spilling out of it.

With his eyes closed, his other senses seemed to be working overtime. The scent of breakfast wafted past his nose, making his stomach growl and turn at the same time. He could feel the mage sitting across from him. Devon chewed his food in relative silence so as not to disturb the elf.

After Tain's return Cornelius had switched the floor plan around. The dining room door was currently bordering one of the wizard's guest rooms. Cornelius had carried the semi-conscious imp into that room and told Kiernan and Devon to wait outside for him. That had been over two hours ago.

For the first hour Kiernan had paced. Even after the dining room had magically arrived, complete with a feast, and the prince's stomach had flip-flopped, he had paced. Then a cramp in his calf had forced him to sit in a chair, where he suddenly realized he had a pounding headache. So, there he had remained ever since.

In a jumbled pile on the table beside him lay the metal plates the Captain had smuggled from the warehouse. The prince had been unable to make much sense of them, but Devon had grasped their significance right away. "They have been making your coins, Kiernan," he said. "Don't you see?"

The prince, furious and frustrated and more than a little frightened by the current situation, had taken it out on the observant mage. "Of course I see!" Kiernan had barked. "But the damned coins are not what has the Captain laid up in that room there! It's *your key* that's done that!"

A childish outburst, to be sure, and one he had instantly regretted—but he did not apologize to the mage. He could not find the words. Devon dropped the subject after that and ate in silence.

When the door to the guest room opened, Kiernan raised his head at last. Devon stood, but the elf prince simply could not. He was so sick with worry over Tain and the others that he was unsure his legs would support him.

He tried to judge the look on the wizard's face, but it was an unreadable mask.

"How is she?" Devon asked, voicing the thought Kiernan could not.

Cornelius quietly shut the door behind him and glided across the floor to take a chair at the head of the table. He did not reach for any food. Despite having had no more rest than Devon and Kiernan, the wizard did not look any different than he had the night before. "She's all right," Cornelius said at last. He rubbed his shiny head. "Or at least she will be."

Kiernan studied the wizard's face and saw that he was sincere. He felt himself breathe a bit easier.

"That left arm may give her some trouble for a week or two, but it will mend completely," Cornelius said with conviction.

"But the blood," Devon stated, looking thoroughly confused. "She lost so much. Her cloak was soaked with it. And the bruises on her throat."

Kiernan winced at that. He had very clearly seen the purple fingerprints surrounding the Captain's tiny neck. Jinin had done that to her. If the bastard had not already been dead, the prince would have killed him himself.

"You must remember that the Captain is not of human blood, but fairy," Cornelius was saying to Devon. "As such, her anatomy works quite differently from our own. A wound that could lay up a large man for several weeks will only set an imp back for a few days. The blood that runs through her veins moves like fire. Her arm was already beginning to heal when she came in."

Cornelius turned back to the prince. "Your Highness, she will live. She has escaped capture once again, and with nothing more lasting than the sight of a former friend's death to haunt her. I cannot, however, be as confident of the safety of the rest of *Duak-Thenal*."

Kiernan swallowed. "What did she say?"

Cornelius leaned back in his high-backed chair and slouched down. "She is in and out of consciousness; it is difficult to make sense of it all. It is certain that the others were taken at the warehouse. Dagmar ordered Talesin and Tain back here with what they confiscated, but the commander cut them off, more than once by the sound of it. The last time this happened, Talesin sacrificed himself so that Tain could escape. Her arm must have been hit then."

"Why do you say that?" Devon asked.

"It is an arrow wound. That is not one of Jinin's weapons," Cornelius replied.

"And Jinin caught up with her before she got here?" Kiernan asked.

Cornelius nodded. "Evidently."

"Well, where is he?" Devon asked.

Both Kiernan and Cornelius looked at the young mage. "In the garden," they said as one, leaving Devon to ponder the meaning of those words.

"By my count, we have about two hours to do something before Alistair comes knocking at my door." Cornelius said.

Kiernan stood. "Then we must move quickly. Cornelius, do you have a floor plan of Nimbus's prison cells?"

Cornelius crossed his arms. "I built it, your Highness. But it will hardly matter, since you alone will not be able to break them out."

Kiernan turned sharply back to the wizard, startled.

The wizard smiled. "Yes, of course I knew you would want to try that," Cornelius said. "But think it through, Your Highness. If the White Watch beat *Duak-Thenal* out in the open, what makes you think you can get by them on their own turf?"

Kiernan moved toward the elder mage and leaned into him. "Because it will be unexpected."

Cornelius stood. "Will it?"

Kiernan sighed heavily and turned away. Cornelius got up and followed him. "Be reasonable, Kiernan. Reckless behavior does not suit you. If our secret enemy continues on the same course, then he will know your intentions the instant you leave this tower."

Kiernan stopped halfway down the length of the large dining room table and faced the wizard. He opened his mouth to object, but Cornelius cut him off. "You know I am right," Cornelius said.

Kiernan swallowed whatever harsh words he might have had for his friend. He threw up his arms instead and spun about. He was so frustrated he could no longer pace—instead he made a complete circle, looking for the entire world like someone who wasn't sure where to go next.

Cornelius saw this and must have understood. He lowered his voice slightly. "You did not order them to go, Kiernan."

Kiernan felt a stab of anger and his eyes widened slightly. "I am responsible for them, Neil," he said.

Cornelius took a careful step toward him. "You don't really believe that, do you?"

Kiernan turned with a growl and made his way to the opposite side of the table. This time Cornelius did not follow. "They are in jail because of me!" he said, slamming his hands on the smooth surface of the table. Then he nodded to the door. "She almost died because of me!"

"But she didn't," Cornelius said calmly.

Kiernan scowled. *That was beside the point!*

"Do you have any confidence in them at all?" Cornelius said, raising his voice. "Or can you simply not stand the fact that they must do something without you?"

Kiernan glared at the wizard, shocked by the suggestion. He pushed himself away from the table and made his way to the head of it. "I am going there. If I move quickly enough, perhaps this secret mage will be unable to stop me."

Cornelius stormed after him, matching the prince's long strides and cutting him off at the door to the guestroom. He put a hand out to stop him, but Kiernan threw him off. Cornelius grabbed his collar in both huge hands and held onto him. "Show up there and you will ruin everything you have achieved!" Cornelius hissed. "Your treasured secrecy will be lost, and your friends will be in worse shape than they are already!"

Kiernan was too stunned to try and break free of the wizard's grasp and regarded him with a mixture of frustration and helplessness. "Are you going to help me, or not?" he breathed.

Cornelius frowned. "Help you get yourself captured along with them? I will not."

"You would have me leave them there?"

The wizard shook his head and slowly let go of Kiernan's collar. "They know how to cover for you, Kiernan. They have a plan. You have always had a plan! Let them use it."

Kiernan straightened his blue tunic and rolled his eyes. "Using Panas as a decoy was a precarious plan at best. Alistair will see through it, and you know it! I can clear them; I can prove our innocence."

"By running into Nimbus, sword held high and green eyes blazing?" Cornelius shouted. "Cutting down anyone who gets in your way will certainly go a long way toward proving your innocence." The scathing sarcasm set the elf back a pace.

"I wouldn't do that," Kiernan replied, dropping his eyes, and shifting slightly.

"It does not matter what you do," Cornelius pressed. "If one person bleeds by your sword, the Council will have all they need to convict you in the court of public opinion. They will believe everything anyone has ever said about you. Mystery will become truth. One hasty move on your part and news of your guilt will spread like wildfire."

Kiernan scowled at that. "They already think we are guilty, Cornelius!"

"And they can't prove it! But if you go on some crazed rescue mission and inadvertently kill some soldiers… well, Alistair and the Council won't need a scratched coin to convict you."

Kiernan bowed his head. The wizard was right, of course. He had no plan. He was allowing himself to be driven by a blinding sense of worry that would surely lead to a mistake. He sighed in defeat. "What do you want me to do, Cornelius? Call for my sister? My father, even? Well, I won't do it. I can't."

"Don't *do* anything," Cornelius begged, holding out his hands. "Let me go down to Nimbus and find out what is going on."

Kiernan started to shake his head, but the wizard cut him off. "Give me a half hour, Your Highness. Then we will make a plan."

Kiernan hesitated a moment, agitated and tense. Then he nodded begrudgingly.

Cornelius was gone in a flash of white light without so much as a goodbye.

"Now what?" Devon asked after a moment. Kiernan, having nearly forgotten the mage was there, started slightly at the sound of his voice.

Kiernan shrugged and sat down again. It was Devon's turn to pace. Kiernan watched the mage walk the length of the room half a dozen times. He stopped suddenly and leaned against the wall opposite the dining room table, chewing on his nails.

Kiernan rubbed his face in his hands and pushed his tangled hair away. He was calmer now that the wizard wasn't pressuring him, and his head was starting to clear. He was thinking of something the Captain had mumbled when they first pulled her through the front door.

Shivering uncontrollably and barely conscious, the imp's first rasping words were not about the man who had tried to kill her but about the woman Cornelius had put so much faith in. "She knew," Tain gasped. "The commander..." The rest was lost in a coughing fit that curled the tiny Captain into a ball on the floor and exposed her bloodied arm for the first time.

Kiernan had sucked in a gulp of air at the sight and looked to Cornelius. The wizard reached out and took hold of her injured limb. Tain hissed in pain at his touch. "Tain, what happened?" Kiernan asked.

She ignored him and instead spilled the soaking wet contents of her pockets onto the stone floor. She looked at Kiernan with all the seriousness of one who is completing her mission. "From the warehouse," she rasped, and fell to coughing again.

Cornelius patted her gingerly on the back, and Kiernan grasped her hand. The prince was worried. He had spent too much time with Kalli. By the time she had gone, *Duak-Thenal* had been out of the tower for over an hour. It took Kiernan another half hour to locate his friends using the pool. He saw a glimpse of Talesin, but it blurred and then the pool found Tain. She was the closest and had the strongest connection to the tower. As soon as he saw her struggling with Jinin, he raced up the stairs to find Cornelius.

Both had flown for the door to find Tain on the step and what was left of Jinin dead in the garden.

Kiernan took her face in his hands and lifted her head from the floor. She was barely conscious, her eyes only narrowly focused on his. "Tain, where are the others?"

"Taken," Tain swallowed. "Commander March. Kiernan, she *knew*. She knew our every move almost before we made it."

Kiernan wasn't sure at the time what the Captain had meant by that. Cornelius had swept her up off the floor and carried her away, so Kiernan had been unable to ask more. Now he was rehashing her words in his head.

Commander March.

How had she done it? How had she managed to blow such a huge hole in their plans? How had she managed to do what Alistair never could?

Kiernan was about to get up and check on the Captain. Perhaps she would be awake enough to answer his questions. But a twinkle of white light signaled Cornelius' return.

It happened quickly. First there was only space. Then a large oval began to fill with white dots of light. If you looked away, you missed it happening. The white dots melted together quickly and stretched into a human form. In another second the light faded, leaving the Malhurian wizard in its place.

The older mage began talking before his solid form had filled the void. "They are there," he announced. "Alistair is keeping them below Nimbus. Don't even think about it, Your Highness," he said, responding to Kiernan's sudden sharp movement. "They are having a hearing in front of the Council tonight."

"Did you speak to Alistair?" Devon asked.

"No, but I did speak to Althea's assistant. Gregory Sweep is as well informed as the governor most of the time. He knows much. The good news is that Alistair has no intention of coming here to investigate. So for the moment, the Captain is safe, and we have some time. Your Highness, I think if we…"

"Did you see the commander?" Kiernan asked suddenly.

Cornelius blinked, surprised at the interruption. "No. Why?"

"Cornelius," he mused. "Do you trust this Commander March?"

The elder mage nodded thoughtfully. "I do," he replied. "She is one of the most intelligent soldiers I have ever met. I have no doubt she is honorable and trustworthy. I believe she will replace Alistair one day."

Kiernan sat up straight in his chair. "The Captain was very adamant that the commander seemed to possess more information than she should have had."

"Be clear, Your Highness. I am not following you," Cornelius said.

Kiernan stood and began to pace furiously again, only barely noticing his cramped muscles. "Regardless of her qualifications, Cornelius, this woman should not have been able to so expertly corner four elves and one very slippery imp. We have been all over this city in the past, never alerting a single guard. Tonight, however, this woman manages to capture all four elves and severely injure the Captain."

Cornelius stared at him. "Go on."

Kiernan stopped. "What if the commander is getting some help?"

Cornelius sat down slowly. "And I suppose the help you refer to would be of a magical kind?"

Kiernan held his arms open. "You said yourself there was a mage involved."

"Yes," Cornelius said. "But I find it very hard to believe that the commander, and most especially Alistair, would take advice from such a mage."

Kiernan held up one long finger. "She wouldn't necessarily know she was receiving the help. Not if that help came through someone else. Someone who was not a mage."

"Like who?" Cornelius asked.

Kiernan smiled tartly, certain Cornelius already knew the answer to his own question. "Like Odin Darweshi."

Cornelius crossed his arms, looking skeptical. "Now what makes you think that Commander March—or her betters—would take the advice of the spoiled son of a merchant, any more than they would that of a mage?"

Kiernan resumed his pacing. "I know it seems far-fetched, but you agree it is possible. I mean... if Alistair ran out of options and some free information presented itself..."

"Well, yes, I suppose," Cornelius said, only half giving in. "A moment's pause would calm you, Your Highness. It would certainly give *my* head a rest. Please stop and share your thoughts with a human who is too old keep up with the rapid thoughts of an elf."

The prince stopped, only barely, and faced the wizard. He understood how he must have looked. His green eyes flared brightly. He had gone from unreasonable and frantic to absorbed and calculating, "If the commander was able to track the movements of *Duak-Thenal*," he reasoned, "then someone is able to follow our every move the instant we exit your tower."

"A point I made well before last night's disaster, I might add," Cornelius said.

Kiernan ignored him. "However, we have hardly been behaving in an unexpected manner. Even without a mage's influence, Alistair could have concluded that we would hit the warehouse."

"Yes," Devon spoke up. "But what is impressive is how long the commander was able to keep up with creatures who could easily outrun her and her troops."

"Still," Kiernan went on, "Talesin and Tain's movements were not altogether unpredictable either, even after escaping the warehouse. Cornelius, you said yourself that Alistair suspected something. He would have known that anyone who escaped the commander's troops would have made straight for this tower."

"Yet Tain says they were cut off," Devon added. "Did she say where?"

"No. But judging by how much blood she lost, I'd say it wasn't very close by," Cornelius said.

"Take into account how long she spent fighting Jinin in the street before they entered the garden," Devon added.

But Cornelius was shaking his head. "They were not close. Talesin and Tain were cut off at least halfway across town."

"Did Tain say anything else in there? How much of a lead did she and Talesin have, I wonder?" Devon asked.

"She did not say much. And what she did say is jumbled, at best. Jinin takes up much of her thoughts, and what's left is random and out of order. A night's sleep will do much for her memory, I am sure," Cornelius said.

"And that is time we do not have," Devon mused.

Kiernan reached for a pastry, finally finding his appetite. "It doesn't matter. We have all the information we need."

Cornelius raised an eyebrow. "Really? It seems to me we have nothing at all."

"Then we have all we are going to get." The prince licked his fingers. "And it still doesn't matter, because the underlying truth is that someone helped the commander last night— whether she wanted their help or not."

— ✻ ✻ ✻ —

Half an hour later Cornelius was closing the door to Tain's room. Kiernan was standing at the window, arms crossed. He looked at the wizard when he came out. "Still asleep," the wizard said.

Kiernan sighed.

Cornelius came to stand by him. He glanced back at Devon, who was nodding off in one of the overstuffed chairs at the table. "What do you want to do, Your Highness?"

Kiernan rolled his eyes and snorted. "You know what *I* want to do. What do *you* suggest?"

The wizard looked at his feet and licked his lips. "Alistair may not believe Panas's cover story, but he will be perfectly willing to accept the Captain as your leader. I say let him."

Kiernan was shaking his head. "You don't really believe that, Neil." He pressed one long hand onto the glass pane. "And I am tired of this game. I am tired of the Captain taking the fall... and I am tired of hiding."

Cornelius smiled. "Then don't. Stop hiding."

There was an unspoken suggestion in Cornelius' voice. The elf searched the wizard's features. Cornelius was trying to tell him something, to get him to see something. Kiernan knew what it was, but that did not make his decision any easier.

Cornelius opened his arms. "Consider it a show of good faith."

Kiernan laughed mirthlessly. "To whom? The Council? Alistair? Somehow, I doubt they will see it that way. If Althea and Xanith were there, then maybe—but they are both out of commission. And what's left of the Council blames us for their absence."

Cornelius stared out the window for a moment. "Do you see any other way, Your Highness?"

Kiernan shook his head. "No." Then he looked at the wizard sharply, suddenly realizing something. "This was your plan all along, wasn't it?"

The wizard laughed and shook his head. "Not at all, Your Highness." He wandered back to the table, his long purple vest trailing behind him. With a wave of his hand the food upon it disappeared. He sat down across from the young mage and stared at the prince. "An opportunity has presented itself. If you are tired of hiding, of playing the mysterious spy for your sister, then perhaps now is the time to stop. There may not be another moment as perfect and public as this one."

The prince was silent. All these years he had led *Duak-Thenal* in their secret missions, and he had never once come close to reuniting the Elves. Instead, he had taken jobs from his sister and Cornelius and Venk. He was merely a hired sword, an adventurer. And though he was proud of his crew and their noble deeds, what had he really accomplished? All that their secrecy had achieved was to get them blamed for crimes they had not committed. For a while, that fact had kept the populace of the Northern Realms on edge and afraid of their very name. But now it had become a dangerous inconvenience. The Captain was a wanted criminal in practically every town they traversed. The others, though nobles in their own kingdoms, were unknown here. Their real names would not win them any favor in Preliona's court.

But his might.

"Your Highness," Cornelius interrupted his thoughts. "Ultimately this is your decision. But you cannot prove their innocence any other way."

Kiernan nodded and sat down. He leaned heavily on the table, almost relieved at what he was about to do. "You realize that by my doing this, *Duak-Thenal* is finished?" he asked. "How does that sit with you? We leave the fate of reunification in the hands of my sister."

"Is that all bad, Your Highness?" Cornelius asked, shrugging. "Kalli has always wanted it more than you did. And who knows, she may surprise us yet."

Kiernan sat back and laughed. "Oh, of that I have no doubt."

Devon suddenly woke with a start. "Wha... wha-happened?" he asked, rubbing his eyes.

Kiernan stood. "Come, Devon Bane, you can now be of help."

Devon shook his head and stood in confusion. "Help with what?"

Kiernan glanced at Cornelius. "We need proof."

Cornelius nodded. "Devon, would you be so good as to go and collect Jinin Aurek?"

Devon blinked. "You said Jinin Aurek was in the garden."

Cornelius smiled grimly. "And so he is."

38~Alistair Makes his Point

Ten out of twelve Council members filed into Nimbus's main hall.

It was dark and empty, save for a couple of dozen armed Watch soldiers. Gregory Sweep was busy lighting lamps and instructing two soldiers to light the sconces along the curved wall. Soon the hall was bathed in warm yellow light. It was not the glorious daylight they were accustomed to, but it would do for this one meeting.

Alistair glanced at his empty seat at the far right of the half-circle table—empty like the two at the center of the table. Althea and Xanith, absent only temporarily, he hoped, were sorely missed. This would be difficult, at best, without them. At least Laothist had relinquished control of the Council to Alistair. He would be able to run this inquiry as he saw fit... Odin Darweshi be damned.

The Council had started to take their seats, various levels of displeasure writ upon their faces.

Fale Copperhand glared and huffed, extremely unhappy that he had been dragged away from his nightly card game at the Mercy Inn. An axe with a curved blade hung from the dwarf's belt and he fingered it now. He was technically not allowed to carry a weapon in Nimbus, but no one had ever moved to stop him before, and Alistair was not about to start now.

Iris, in contrast to the dwarf, fairly skipped to her chair in anticipation of the coming inquiry. Gregory appeared serious, Laothist nervous. Judith Mercy looked amused and Poorez seemed annoyed... but not one man or woman voiced a single objection as they took their high-backed seats. For this Alistair was extremely glad.

Alistair looked to Gregory to see if he was ready with pen and paper. The half-elf caught his eye and nodded. Alistair turned to face the entire group. "Ladies and gentlemen, before we begin, I must lay down some ground rules." Mild grumbles came from the group, but Alistair ignored them and continued. "First, know that I am, with my staff, solely in charge of this inquiry. That means that while you may ask questions and confer on the answers, I ultimately will decide how things go and whether or not they will continue."

Poorez rolled his eyes. "Alistair, I hardly think…"

Alistair glared at the jeweler. Poorez immediately stopped speaking. The Watch Chief took a breath, clasped his hands behind his back and began to pace before the group. "Understand something," he began. "This meeting is happening only because I am allowing it. Under normal circumstances you would not be granted this privilege." He sighed and stopped pacing. "Under normal circumstances Althea herself would be by my side conducting the interview."

Alistair lowered his voice a bit. They were listening to him more intently than they ever had before. He did not need to yell over them tonight. "I realize this situation is anything but normal. Since Althea cannot be here—and given the unusual nature of the accusations—I feel it only fair that you all be allowed an audience with these prisoners."

Alistair scanned their faces, noting their expressions. They were unnerved by what he had said, and that was good. He wanted the seriousness of this inquiry to weigh heavily upon them.

"Now," Alistair went on. "Let me give you some background information." Alistair told the Council of his brief encounter with *Duak-Thenal*. He told them of his suspicions concerning the leadership of the group. He had all but dismissed the idea of the imp Captain as its leader, and he had not bothered Cornelius this morning. He even told them of his ideas on the extent of the group's guilt or innocence. "We are not looking for a scapegoat here," he warned them. "Keep your personal feelings in check, my friends. The only thing they are guilty of thus far is breaking into the Darweshi warehouse. I am not even sure they will speak to you at all."

"Then what is the point of all this?" Poorez burst out.

And what *was* the point? Alistair was not sure himself. He could have simply handed the Council a report and held *Duak-Thenal* until a trial could be set. But a trial for what, exactly? Was he really going to detain four of the most incredible creatures he had ever met for an undisclosed amount of time—just for breaking and entering?

He knew they had nothing to do with Althea's *accident*. Knew they had not killed those merchants. Alistair was positive of this. There was no rational explanation for his feelings, and he had no evidence.

And maybe that was the point.

He wanted the Council to see what he saw, to come to their own conclusions about the elves. To see if they felt as he did: that these creatures were simply not capable of committing the crimes of which they were accused. "The point, Poorez," Alistair finally replied, "is to discover what we know."

Quinlan wrinkled his wide brow. "You mean what *they* know."

Alistair shook his head. "I believe I have ascertained all on that account." He smiled thinly. "At least all that they will speak of. It is now up to us to put the pieces together."

Alistair did not wait for them to reply. He did not think he had the patience. Instead, he turned to the guard at the side door and nodded. The door opened and Commander March entered, followed by her four charges.

Alistair had meant to watch the faces of the Council members. He wanted to see their reaction to the elves when they walked into the hall, to see if they were as impressed as he had been. However, once the elves entered, so striking was their presence that Alistair could not tear his eyes from them.

They walked straight and tall, brave and proud—and this was no act. They wore chains, but their movements did not seem hindered in the slightest. Grace and poise emanated from them, intrigue and mystery pulsed from their bodies, impossible not to detect.

The southern elf led the way. He was so large for an elf, so opposite from the human idea of elves, that he commanded instant attention. He was followed by the light elf, cool and mischievous, stepping lightly into the room. Dagmar Coal, serene and calculating, scanned the room quickly and then stared straight ahead as if she had taken in everything she needed to in that one second. Finally came the ice elf. If the room had felt warm before, it was tangibly chilled by his entrance.

As they took their place behind the long table, Alistair finally managed to tear his eyes from them and look to the Council.

He was not disappointed. They were all slack-jawed and stunned. Judith was appraising, Ranabee deeply impressed, Halberth mesmerized and Poorez dumbfounded. Only Gregory looked on with anything resembling normalcy. He was part elf, after all. But even the half-elven scholar could not help but raise an eyebrow at the extraordinary group before him.

Alistair smiled and approached his four charges. He winced inwardly at the chains about their wrists. It was something he had been loath to do, but Gabrielle had insisted. It was then that he had begun to realize how affected he was by the elves. Though he knew they were far from the killers they were accused of being, they were still incarcerated thieves who would try to escape if they could—even kill if need be. So transfixed was he by their very presence that he let his guard down now, when he needed it most.

And so, thanks to Commander March, the elves looked, at least to the Council, safely subdued. Though Alistair knew better.

He came as close to them as he dared. He wanted a private moment out of earshot of the Council. "All right, then," he began, "This is a hearing of sorts. An extension of the inquiry we began last night. Do you understand that this is not a trial?"

They stared straight ahead. Only Dagmar would meet his eyes. A slight nod of acknowledgment from her was all he received.

He sighed. "You have made it abundantly clear that you do not accept responsibility for even half of what you have been accused of. Defend yourselves. Prove your innocence."

"I thought you said this was not a trial," Dagmar argued.

Alistair shook his head. "It isn't, but…"

"Then we have nothing to prove," the wild elf concluded, and turned away.

Alistair winced and leaned into her. "You must speak to these accusations. You must answer their questions."

She would not look at him.

Alistair shook his head and smiled mirthlessly. "Suit yourself."

He turned from them, determined to wash his hands of their stubbornness. He looked to Gregory, who nodded and stood. The half-elf turned to the group of elves before him and spoke. "Will you please state your names?"

Silence met the scholar's query. Alistair did not have to look at *Duak-Thenal* to know that they kept their gazes forward and did not focus on the members of the Council.

The Watch Chief took a step to the side of the table and began to point out the prisoners. "Nemesio Firebrand, Panas the Hawk, Dagmar Coal and Talesin Darken." He said their names quickly and without bravado. It hardly mattered what their names were; no one in the room knew about anything remotely connected to them, anyhow.

Gregory sat down, writing furiously as Alistair made his way back to the center of the room. He tucked his hands behind his back and rocked on his heels. "So, ladies and gentlemen, questions?"

The silence that met him was soothing. Alistair knew the Council was impressed, surprised even, at the presence of *Duak-Thenal*. They could not help themselves. No one on the Council had ever seen elves such as these before. It was as if they were in the presence of royalty—and the common folk of Preliona's governing body did not know how to react.

It was several minutes before Poorez leaned forward, elbows on the table. He was intrigued, and more sincere than Alistair had ever seen him. All sense of arrogance had left him. "Where are you from?" he asked simply.

Alistair glanced at the elves and was surprised to see Dagmar turn her misty-clouded eyes on Poorez. The jeweler, who might normally look down his nose at anyone, flinched. "I should think that our appearances alone would dictate the answer to your question, sir," the wild elf answered.

Alistair stifled a smile. From anyone else's lips that comment would have gotten a harsh response from those assembled.

As it was, Poorez seemed less than pleased with the answer. But if he had any intention of objecting to it, he did not. Instead, he glanced at his colleagues in the hopes that another would take up the questioning and let him off the hook.

Judith rested her chin on one calloused hand. She was the only member of the Council with the gall to look amused. "Do you mean to say, my dear, that you are come from the surrounding elven kingdoms?"

"We are," Dagmar answered.

Alistair could not have been more pleased. He had not expected the elves to speak at all.

Judith leaned forward, her eyes sparkling with interest. "And do your actions represent your kingdoms? Is Jathaharwel, for instance, in the business of thievery?"

Dagmar's gray eyes fell on Judith. The woman blinked. "The place of our birth affects our appearances and our beliefs. We are exiles in Tearlach. We hold some allegiance to our homelands, but we do not carry out our secret orders on their behalf."

"Then who might you be taking those secret orders from?" Ranabee asked.

But Dagmar only smiled and turned away from the Council, facing forward again.

The councilors looked at each other, grumbling and whispering. But Quinlan remained unfazed. "Who are you?" he asked finally.

"I believe the good Watch Chief has already told you that," Dagmar replied, barely giving the Guild Master a glance.

"Who *were* you, then?" Fale pushed. "Who were you before all of this started?" Fale waved his stubby arms to emphasize his point.

Dagmar slowly scanned the faces of the Council members. Alistair noted that not one of them could hold her gaze for long. Then she turned to her companions. Her eyes fell on Panas and she nodded to him ever so slightly.

Alistair saw the light elf grin and knew that the small thread of truth they had so far enjoyed was about to end.

Before Alistair could protest, Panas the Hawk began to speak. "My dear dwarven friend, before all of *what* started?" The twinkle in the light elf's golden eye was unmistakable. Alistair started to make his way to the table, to try to stop Panas before he brought this somewhat quiet and thus far truthful meeting to a screeching halt.

Ranabee answered. "Before you became *Duak-Thenal*. Who were you?"

Panas flashed a bright smile at Ranabee. Alistair couldn't believe it, but he actually saw her blush.

"Why, my dear, we have *always* been *Duak-Thenal*." Panas tossed his blonde hair out of his tanned face and opened his hands as much as the chains would allow. "Orphans forced from our own kingdoms, exiles, we have traveled far and wide, looking for a place to be accepted. The world is such a judgmental one that we are forced to commit heinous crimes to survive the cold place we live in. Truly we are guilty of nothing more than…"

Alistair grabbed the light elf's roaming arms and pressed them down to the table. "That will do, Master Hawk," he cautioned.

Panas looked at him in mock surprise. "But sir, I was only answering their questions. Isn't that what you wanted us to do?"

Alistair frowned up at the golden-haired elf. "Truthfully? I would much prefer your silence to your lies, Hawk."

He turned back to the Council and motioned for them to continue.

Most of the councilors sat in their carved chairs behind the gleaming white table still unsure what to make of the proceedings. But Quinlan stood now and raised a finger. Alistair nodded to the Guild Master. "Are you responsible for the deaths of the merchants on Hunter Heights?" he asked.

Dagmar Coal gave Quinlan only the briefest of glances before she replied. "No."

Quinlan brushed his black hair from his face, mildly perturbed at the wild elf's lack of attention. "Can you prove it?" he asked, undeterred.

This time Dagmar gave him her full attention. Her gray eyes blinked only once as they scanned the young Guild Master's features. "No," she said again.

Quinlan stared at the wild elf for a long moment, as if he were suddenly lost in thought. He could not seem to tear his eyes from hers.

"Quinlan?" Alistair prompted. "Anything else?"

Slowly the Guild Master turned from Dagmar. He looked at Alistair and shook his head.

"Fine," Alistair concluded with a smile. "Next."

Laothist cleared his throat. Alistair rolled his eyes but motioned for him to go ahead.

"Did you attack Darweshi's architect, Calen Jase?"

"No." Nemesio this time.

Alistair shot the southern elf a look, but Nemesio did not return it. He rested his purple gaze on the merchant, and Laothist was having a hard time standing still under that heavy stare.

"Let's rephrase that question, shall we?" Ranabee said, taking over. "Did you steal from Calen Jase?"

Panas the Hawk smiled knowingly and shrugged. "Perhaps."

"Have you attacked Darweshi interests before?" Ranabee continued.

Panas the hawk's grin widened. "Perhaps."

The rest of the Council grumbled at the light elf's opacity. But Iris raised her hand. Alistair pointed to her and motioned for the others to be silent.

Iris swallowed, determined to ask her question, but too nervous to speak. "Why…" she began, and looked to Alistair. The old man nodded to her encouragingly. Iris swallowed again and looked at the elves. "Why did you attack the governor?"

The entire Council leaned forward, eager to hear what the rogues might say.

Dagmar scanned their faces and shook her head. "We did not," she said. "We had not even arrived when your governor was attacked. We are not responsible for her injuries."

Judith rested her chin in her hand. "Can anyone vouch for your whereabouts?"

This time there was no answer.

Poorez ignored their silence and jumped to his next question. "Where is Raymond S'Trobenue?"

This time Dagmar smiled. "That we cannot tell you."

"Cannot or will not?" Fale snarled at them.

Dagmar shrugged.

That was a mistake.

The Council became quite agitated now. Clearly the elves knew Raymond and perhaps where he was. The knowing look on the wild elf's face frightened them, Alistair could see.

"What have you done with him?" Laothist spat.

"And his child?" Quinlan added.

Nemesio raised his hands. "He is absolutely safe, we assure you."

But Nemesio's assurances were not calming the Council, who were now talking all at once, certain that Raymond S'Trobenue had perhaps met the same fate as his late wife's.

"What proof can you give us besides your word?" Poorez shouted at them.

Nemesio looked at Poorez and frowned. "I'm afraid we can give you none. Their safety depends on the secrecy of their whereabouts."

"Too bad," Judith said. "It seems he is the only one who could give evidence on your behalf."

The room went silent and many of the councilors turned to look at Judith, who had hit the nail on the head. For while it was more than plain that the elves did not accept responsibility for many of the crimes they were accused of, there was simply no way to prove otherwise without a reliable witness.

Alistair smiled wryly. He had gotten what he wanted; more in fact, for he never expected the elves to answer so many questions. But it was difficult to know what to do next. The elves remained quiet and still, resigned to the fact that they could not or would not defend themselves.

The Watch Chief moved back toward the center of the room. He glanced from the calm collected faces of the elves to the confused and awed faces of the councilors and cleared his throat. "Well," he began. "If there is nothing else…"

The door behind him blasted open before he could finish. Odin Darweshi blew into the room, practically bowling over the guards near the door in his bravado. "Dammit, Alistair, how long did you think you could keep me waiting?!"

Alistair closed his eyes and sighed. He had expected this interruption.

Alistair unfolded his hands from his chest and clasped them behind his back. Only then did he turn to face the merchant's son. "My, my, Lord Darweshi, it has only been a few hours since last we spoke. Can't get along without me for any longer?"

The youngest Darweshi came to a halt a few feet from Alistair rolling his eyes and chuckling mirthlessly. "Very amusing, Alistair."

Odin had brought with him a small contingent of the same men who always hung about him. The three surviving S'Trobenue cousins, along with several other drunken brutes who presented an ongoing headache for the Watch. But after a quick head count, Alistair realized someone was missing, someone who had been at Odin's side almost continually since yesterday.

"And where might the elusive, partially blond-haired Jinin Aurek be?" Alistair asked.

Odin held his arms wide and sneered at Alistair. "You tell me." He glared at Commander March. "Or ask your commander here. I suspect she has something to do with his disappearance."

Alistair walked slowly past Odin. "According to the commander and the rest of the Watch, Master Aurek slipped away of his own accord. If he met with foul play, it was not by our hand."

Odin followed Alistair with a flourish of his red cape. Leaning forward, head protruding and eyes narrowing, he poked one finger toward the Watch Chief, bringing several Watch members forward a step.

"I suppose you believe every breath that emanates from that one's mouth," Odin hissed, pointing at Gabrielle.

Alistair smirked. "You don't really expect that I should believe anything that comes from *yours*?"

Odin stood up straight, took a step back, and touched his fingers to his velvet-covered chest. His eyes suddenly became shrewd again. Alistair could practically see the gears working in the man's head. The Watch Chief was suddenly wary.

Odin raised his voice so that it filled the entire room. "Did you ask your commander who else they chased last night? The one they failed to capture?"

Alistair froze. At that point he would have very much liked to punch Odin Darweshi in the face. Octavius Darweshi's youngest son was a volatile brute, to say the least, but he also possessed a keen perception that was positively frightening. Somehow, he knew exactly which switch would throw the Council off track. Alistair had not told the Council of the near capture of the imp Captain. He had only told them that he had dismissed her as leader of *Duak-Thenal*. If the Council knew that she had been spotted last night, it would force their focus on her once again. Which was exactly what Darweshi wanted.

"What is he talking about, Alistair?" Poorez asked.

Alistair glared at Odin as he turned to face the Council. "Captain Tain Elire was spotted last night," he began.

"*With* the elves," Odin interrupted.

"Yes," Alistair growled. "With the elves. And as I have already said, I have dismissed her as the possible leader of *Duak-Thenal*."

"Well, I haven't," Odin said, brushing past the Watch Chief. "Ladies and gentlemen, I believe that the imp is responsible for my missing comrade.

Not only is she the leader of this group, but she is being protected by your very own house wizard, Cornelius Pav!"

That was all it took. The main hall erupted into shouts of anger and disbelief. The councilors all stood, most of them pointing fingers straight at Alistair.

Looking smug and satisfied, Odin Darweshi folded his arms, gave Alistair a slight bow of his head, and backed into the shadows to watch the fireworks.

A sharp sliver of pain was working its way up the side of Alistair's head and sneaking its way into his right eye. He plunged his thumb and forefinger into the corner of it and pulled at the skin around his eyebrow. Then he held up his other hand and calmly called for quiet.

He did not get it this time. "Why didn't you tell us about this, Alistair?" Quinlan asked sternly.

"I can't believe you knew about this and didn't say a word," Fale hissed.

"Perhaps he doesn't want us to know about his failure to catch her, eh, Alistair?" Judith said with a playful wave of her hand.

"Yes, Alistair," continued Laothist. "Didn't you think we should have this information?"

"OF COURSE, I DIDN'T!" Alistair finally shouted. The hall immediately quieted, shocked into silence by a man who, though easily angered, never lost control. Alistair saw how taken aback they all were. He took the moment to get ahold of himself. He would not let Odin get the better of him again. "Believe it or not, ladies and gentlemen," he said calmly, "There are some things you simply do not need to know."

"And what makes you think that this was one of those things?" Halberth dared.

Alistair leveled his gaze at the street cleaner. "Precisely because of the reaction you just had. Can't you accept that I have dismissed the imp as a suspect?"

"No," Fale growled.

"We want to speak with her," demanded Ranabee.

"I am afraid that would be quite impossible."

Once again, every head in the hall turned toward the door.

Only the door had never opened. Two figures had materialized just inside the archway, startling the guards into drawing their swords. But just as quickly they lowered them when they saw who had entered the hall.

White robes billowing about him, Cornelius Pav stepped into the room. He had changed for this visit, but in flowing white robes Cornelius was no less intimidating than usual. He walked with heavy forceful steps, yet he carried himself with the air and confidence of one with vast intelligence. If his demeanor was dark and somewhat dominating, his eyes were calm and friendly. If one could hold his gaze for a small period, he would find himself unafraid of the large wizard, for his black orbs were inviting and kind.

Many of the Council members had never allowed themselves to do this, however. To them, Cornelius Pav remained, at best, a mystery, and at worst a menace.

Cornelius nodded his bald head to the soldiers at the door, who immediately let him pass. The boy beside him was not so lucky. Three swords came up to catch the sandy-haired, orange-robed mage's neck. "Who's your friend, Cornelius?" one guard asked.

Cornelius did not even turn. "A witness to current events. You will want to hear what this one has to say, Alistair. He will shed much light on these proceedings, I assure you."

"Your name, young sir?" Alistair asked.

"Devon Bane," the mage answered nervously, eyeing the sharp swords drawn about him.

Alistair nodded to the guards and the swords were lowered. He immediately dismissed the boy and turned his steely blue eyes on Cornelius. He moved close to the dark-skinned mage and spoke low, so the others could not hear. "What are you doing here?"

Cornelius smiled wryly. "I thought you could use a little help."

Alistair shook his head. "You place yourself in the center of the fire here, I'm afraid. You would be better off out of sight."

Cornelius risked a glance at the councilors, who were fervently looking on. "It seems your contemporaries will not let certain matters rest." He looked to Alistair. "You need me."

Alistair frowned. "I chose not to seek you out this morning, Neil. Do not make me regret that decision."

Cornelius' visage became serious. He nodded in acquiescence. Alistair motioned for him to go ahead and the wizard faced the Council.

Judith Mercy was the first to find her tongue and pick up the conversation. "So, Cornelius," she began, still standing and leaning across the long table. "Why can't we speak to the elusive fairy Captain?"

"Because she is gone."

"Where?" Laothist piped up.

"I do not keep track of her, sir," Cornelius replied calmly. "Even if I had the inclination, I could not possibly keep track of her movements."

"Then you do not deny her affiliation with these elves," Poorez said.

Cornelius smiled. "Nor can I confirm it."

Odin stepped forward, shoving Devon aside. "But she was here last night, seen with these rogues."

"Which hardly means she was working with them, Master Darweshi," Cornelius kept his demeanor calm in the face of the merchant's ire.

Odin was starting to fume. "*He* helped her escape!" he hollered, pointing to Talesin. "A dozen guards do not lie, wizard. Where is she?"

Cornelius shrugged. "I do not know. She has not appeared to me this night, nor do I expect her to." Alistair knew instantly that his friend was lying, but for some reason he kept quiet.

"But you know who she is," Fale pressed.

Cornelius turned to him. "Everyone knows who she is."

Poorez slammed his hand on the table. "Come, come, Cornelius, stop playing games! We need answers."

"And I am here to give you some. Captain Tain Elire is not the leader of *Duak-Thenal*."

Alistair grinned, pleased to finally have his intuitions confirmed. "And do you know who is?"

Cornelius nodded. "I do."

"Why should we believe you?" Quinlan drummed his fingers on the table, his dark eyes shifting from Alistair to Cornelius.

Gregory cleared his throat and shot Quinlan an embarrassed look. "Have some respect, please."

Quinlan ignored him and pressed on. "Can you produce him?"

"Or her," Judith added, a twinkle in her green eyes.

Cornelius scanned their confused faces. "I can," he said.

Halberth, who had been quiet throughout the proceedings, suddenly raised his callused hand.

Both Alistair and Cornelius raised an eyebrow. "Yes, Halberth," they said together.

The street cleaner stood. "Excuse me if I'm being rude, Cornelius, but before you go revealing this big secret, I'd like a question answered."

Cornelius glanced at Alistair, who did not object. He simply nodded to the street cleaner, as surprised as the rest that the most silent member of the Council chose this most tense of moments to speak.

Halberth, who treated everyone as if they were the street cleaner from the next block over, cleared his throat. "Well, I been wondering: how is it that you know this mysterious leader? How do you even know *them*?" he gestured to the elves.

Alistair watched as Cornelius licked his lips and swallowed. Leave it to the street cleaner to hit upon the one subject the wizard seemed unprepared to discuss. Cornelius turned to Alistair again, an almost apologetic look crossing his features. Alistair narrowed his eyes, confused. But before he could clarify, the wizard turned quickly back to the Council.

"Because," Cornelius said, "I hired them."

39~And Then There Were Five

Alistair closed his eyes as the whole room erupted. The entire Council was on its feet. Some shouted at him, some at each other, and still others at the wizard.

Above them all, Odin screeched in triumph. He might have even launched himself at Cornelius if Gabrielle and her guards had not blocked his advance. "I told you!" he howled, jumping up and down. "I told you! Arrest him, Alistair! Arrest the wizard! Do it!"

Alistair pushed himself away from the wall, where he had been leaning with his arms folded across his chest. He moved to the center of the room, nearer to Cornelius, and held his hands up for silence.

It was some time before he got it. Most Council members were clearly furious at having been duped for so long by the wizard, whom they barely trusted to begin with. The loudest of his accusers were Fale and Poorez. Quinlan and Ranabee were a close second. Halberth and Laothist were desperately trying to calm their co-councilors. Judith stood off to the side, laughing to herself at the spectacle and giving neither negative nor positive support. Only Gregory remained relatively calm throughout.

At least, thought Alistair, everyone in the room remained predictable.

Through it all, the wizard never moved. Alistair was unsure he even breathed. When he met Alistair's eyes he blinked. Alistair knew instantly Cornelius wished to apologize.

Alistair sighed and shook his head at the wizard. He was angry and felt betrayed, but he would not hold a grudge against his old friend. Cornelius would have his reasons, and he would or would not recount them to Alistair in his own good time. The Watch Chief moved in front of the wizard. "Please, ladies and gentlemen, sit down! I do believe Cornelius has some sort of explanation. We owe him at least our ears."

Thankfully, the din finally died down. The members of the Council sat, grumbling and complaining.

"This had better be good," Poorez said as he took his seat.

Alistair frowned at the jeweler but said nothing. He turned instead to Cornelius and nodded for the man to continue.

Cornelius cleared his throat. "As I said, I hired *Duak-Thenal*."

"For what, for *Kelina's* sake?!" Fale burst out.

Cornelius held up a hand. "Two weeks ago, Raymond S'Trobenue came to my door begging me to help him escape from Preliona."

"Why would he do that?" Ranabee asked, clearly perplexed.

Cornelius turned his heavy gaze on the noblewoman. "Would you wish to remain in a household where every other member blamed you for the death of its matriarch?"

Quinlan was shaking his head. "But he had been cleared of all charges. We declared that Raymond had nothing to do with Edmee's death."

Cornelius shrugged. "Edmee's cousins did not agree with this Council's decision. Raymond feared for his life."

Laothist drummed shaking fingers on the table before him. "Being a bit paranoid, wasn't he?"

Cornelius fixed Laothist with a stern glare, which the chubby man shied away from. "You have met Edmee's cousins," the wizard said, pointing now to the three blonde men. "What do *you* think?"

Laothist was saved from answering by the ensuing outburst from the indignant cousins. "What's *that* supposed to mean?" Vincent howled, lunging forward.

With one hand Gabrielle grabbed his shirt and shoved him backward into the arms of his brothers. He shook them off and took a threatening step toward the commander. Gabrielle unsheathed her sword and swung its tip up to Vincent's throat before he could take another breath.

He stopped with a snarl as Alistair calmly sauntered over to stand behind his commander. "What do you *think* it means, you fool?" He looked from the frozen Vincent to his angry brothers and shook his head. "You wanted Raymond gone because Edmee had left everything to him." He curled his lip at the most vocal S'Trobenue cousin. "I cannot imagine how horrible his life must have been."

Vincent clearly wished to respond, most likely with a string of obscenities, but as he took a breath Gabrielle pressed the silver tip of her sword deeper into the groove of his throat. Vincent swallowed hard, breathing heavily through his nose, and glaring so that his eyes swelled from their sockets.

"But Alistair, why didn't Raymond lodge a complaint with you?"

Alistair turned to address Poorez. "My guess is that Raymond knew there was nothing I could charge them with at the time." The Watch Chief turned back to the cousins. "Believe it or not, the S'Trobenue boys have been very careful up until now. Isn't that right, Vincent?"

Despite the commander's biting sword tip, Vincent managed to smile. "You can't prove a thing."

Alistair looked to the other two men. Both seemed to be taking their cues from their brother. Their eyes darted nervously between Alistair and Vincent, waiting to see what would happen next. Alistair leaned into them all. "You are right, I cannot. Not now, anyway. But I will find something—and when I do, rest assured that inheritance you so desperately want won't amount to a bucket of sand by the time I am finished with you."

Alistair turned away before Vincent could respond. He clasped his hands behind his back and crossed in front of the wizard. "Continue, Cornelius," he said as he passed.

The wizard nodded. "I hired *Duak-Thenal* to take Raymond away."

"Did you pay them?" Halberth asked.

"Not in the traditional sense, no," the wizard replied. "I pay them with information."

"What kind of information?" Poorez asked.

The wizard shrugged. "Knowledge of lost artifacts, protection with magical wards, contacts in surrounding towns." Cornelius glanced at Alistair with a sheepish grin. "You see, I am their contact here in Preliona. If someone like Raymond is looking for them, that someone comes to me."

"They have other contacts?" asked Ranabee.

"Of course."

"Who?" Poorez asked.

Cornelius smirked. "I won't be naming names today, Mr. Montalbosh. There are plenty of you in this room who know the value of secrets." Cornelius winked at Judith, who snorted and rolled her eyes. "Suffice it to say there is very little illegality in what I do for them."

"Except that you harbor them and assist them in illegal activities," Fale grunted.

Quinlan nodded in agreement. "Not the least of which is helping them enter this town."

Cornelius dropped his head. "That, I am afraid, is true."

"So why?" Ranabee asked, "Why all the secrecy?"

Cornelius smiled. "I believe that question can best be answered by the leader of *Duak-Thenal*."

Alistair noticed the wizard's sudden change in demeanor, and stiffened. He scanned the room in suspicion.

Judith Mercy leaned forward. "You mean he or she is not currently among us?"

"I have kept their secrets at the request of their leader, and it is by his command that I now reveal them." Cornelius paused, waiting for further interruptions. There were none. "Ladies and Gentlemen, may I present the leader of *Duak-Thenal*."

Slipping gracefully from the ranks of the White Watch came an elf with deep red hair. How long he had been here, hiding in their midst, listening to their arguments, Alistair could not know. He watched the elf glide across the floor and found himself planted to his spot.

His red hair hung in loose waves about his shoulders. His angular features were set and determined. His shining emerald eyes swept the room, briefly lighting on all assembled. No one could deny the shiver that ran down their spines as the elf's orbs passed over them. He was a stunning and almost frightening sight. It was difficult to hold his gaze and at the same time impossible to turn away from the air of overwhelming power flowing from him.

No one moved, so transfixed were they by the vision before them. It was not until he raised an arm that the White Watch finally awoke.

The whisper of swords being drawn from their sheaths broke everyone's reverie. The elf stopped dead as the Watch surrounded him.

Alistair breathed deeply, aware that he had been holding his breath, and walked forward on pained but determined legs. He pushed aside several swords. For the first time the leader of *Duak-Thenal* and the Watch Chief beheld one another.

Alistair scanned the elf's face, taking in every aspect of him. He was tall and lithe and extremely young, if one could guess the age of an elf. He looked no older than Iris, whom Alistair knew to be only nineteen or so. His features were strong and sharp, but he was not the beauty that Panas the Hawk was. His face was too square and pale, not as angular and tanned as Panas's. But he held himself straight, with confidence. He looked Alistair in the eye, and did not seem to fear the swords surrounding him.

Alistair nodded finally, as if this turn of events was not totally unexpected. "So, you are not a figment of our imagination after all, are you?"

The leader of *Duak-Thenal* smiled wryly. "No, I am afraid I am real enough."

The elf's voice was as musical and mysterious as his friends'. Alistair was silent a moment, thinking. How well this one's friends had covered for him! Especially Dagmar, who had implicated herself to protect him and the imp Captain.

Gabrielle suddenly and smoothly appeared at Alistair's side. "Do you mind putting your hands where I can see them, sir," she said.

The elf did as he was told.

The Watch Chief was staring at the prince curiously. He was nodding his head, as if he had just realized something that had been close to obvious for some time. He turned to look at Panas the Hawk, whose golden hair and eyes were nothing like the red-haired, green-eyed elf before him. Panas now waggled his fingers at Alistair and gave him a wink.

Alistair scowled.

"The hair, Alistair! Do you see the hair?!"

Alistair rolled his eyes and glared at Vincent S'Trobenue. "I have eyes, Vincent," he hissed.

The Watch Chief turned his attention back to the elf. Alistair was pleased to see the green eyes focused completely on him. He had not let Vincent's outburst affect him at all. "You see that these men recognize you?"

The elf nodded solemnly.

"Did you meet swords with them several nights ago?"

Again, the nod.

Alistair pursed his lips and blew air through his nose. He hesitated to ask his next question. "Did you kill his brother?"

The elf did not hesitate. "I did."

Alistair frowned. "In defense of yourself?"

"No."

"In defense of another, then?"

The elf nodded.

"Who?" Alistair asked.

"Raymond S'Trobenue."

Alistair swallowed. "May I have your name?"

The red-haired elf took a breath. "My name is Prince Kiernatrialis Aila."

The Council collectively gasped. Alistair heard his own heart pounding in his chest.

The prince ignored them and continued. "Son of King Gilleece and Queen Galena-Ena Aila, brother to Crown Prince and Lasairian ambassador Emrys Emindar, and twin brother to princess Kalliroestria, sorceress and mistress of the School of Light and Sorcery."

No one spoke. The prince of the light elves had the complete attention of all assembled. If there had been any doubt of his identity when he had first stated it, it was gone by the time he had finished rattling off the names and ranks of his relatives.

He scanned the faces before him. Alistair could tell the prince was trying to decide just how to continue. He lowered his voice and licked his lips. Alistair thought the elf appeared rather humble, despite his bloodline. "I do not speak of my family to threaten you. I only ask, in their name, that you listen to what I have to say."

They stared at him for a full ten seconds. They made no movement for so long that Alistair thought they had forgotten how to breathe.

And then, just when Alistair thought he would have to carry on alone, Judith Mercy leaned forward. "Well, I for one would love to hear this."

And then everyone was speaking at once. Councilors arguing and debating, curious, angry, and perplexed by this new problem before them.

Alistair turned his back on them and spoke quietly, unheard by the Council and the surrounding guards. "I want you to know, Your Highness, that though I respect your heritage, it does not matter one way or the other in light of the charges against you and your crew. I suspect you have a lot to lose by surrendering yourself here today. My question is, what have you got to gain?"

The prince did not answer.

Alistair shifted his stance. "You cannot possibly believe that I will release the others simply because you have surrendered."

The prince shook his head. "I expect nothing of you, sir. And you are correct. I have much to lose by surrendering. But I cannot allow my crew to remain here under false pretenses."

"Are you saying they are innocent?" Alistair challenged.

"Of the most detrimental charges? Yes. And since they will not defend themselves, I must."

Alistair sighed, some of the fight going out of him. "Because they protect you," he affirmed. "They will not defend themselves because of you."

"Of course," the prince replied without a touch of arrogance. His face was open and honest, unlike that of his golden-haired countryman.

The Watch Chief liked the prince instantly, just as he had liked the rest of *Duak-Thenal*. He could not help himself. The prince was cool and collected, at least on the surface. While he held himself straight and tall, Alistair got the impression that this was not always the case. In fact, the tone in which the prince had rattled off the names of his royal family betrayed him instantly. This elf was not used to being addressed as a prince, and even less accustomed to having to use his family or title as leverage. This alone would have convinced Alistair that the red-haired elf was indeed the elusive rogue leader of *Duak-Thenal*.

But there was more to it than that.

It was the way in which the elf had blended so easily into the ranks of the soldiers. The secretive slip of his eyes, flickering about the room faster than most could see, taking in every inch of his surroundings, pointedly avoided looking at his crew. Alistair suspected that he did this more for fear of seeing their disapproving looks than because he was their undisputed leader.

He really could not see the harm in letting the elf have his say. After all, this was no trial. They were looking for answers, and this one could certainly provide some.

The chief turned to face the clamoring councilors. He held up his hands for silence. But Odin had other plans. The merchant's son had been strangely quiet after the prince's entrance. No longer.

"Arrest him!" the merchant shouted.

Alistair shot him a warning glance and then nodded to Gabrielle.

Commander March came up behind Odin and grabbed him by the arm.

But Odin shook off the commander's grasp and went stumbling into his crowd of followers. "How dare you," he hissed at her. "Alistair, you had better tell your dog to heel—or my father…"

Alistair turned and drew his own sword. He did not move as quickly as Gabrielle did, but Odin was still stunned into silence when the Watch Chief's long straight blade touched his chest. "Enough!" Alistair bellowed. "Be quiet. Or it will be you that I arrest."

Odin was looking mutinous. He held his arm where Gabrielle had pulled him and glared at the two of them as though he would like nothing better than to hurl obscenities at them. But with what seemed to be a tremendous effort, he remained quiet.

Alistair turned his back on Odin. "You may ask your questions, councilors."

Quinlan held out his hands in a gesture of exasperation. His usually well-groomed black hair now fell in thick sheaves about his face. He was clearly flustered. "I don't see how we can do that, Alistair. I do not believe that we can question the Prince of the Light Elves without some type of formal permission from Lasairian. There is no precedent for this."

Alistair turned to Gregory. "Well?" he asked the half-elf. "Is there?"

For his part, Gregory had barely moved since the Prince had entered. He remained frozen to his spot, his mouth open, staring wide-eyed at the prince.

"Gregory!" Alistair's stern voice cut through to the scholar.

The scholar jumped. "What?"

Alistair rolled his eyes. "Is there any precedent for questioning a prince?"

Gregory snapped back into scholarly mode. His long fingers began to flutter in the air as if he were counting or reading a script imprinted on his brain. His teal eyes went unfocused as he sorted through whatever system of historical references he held in his remarkable memory. "Yes," he concluded after only a moment. "Yes, there is." Then he paused, giving Alistair a bemused look. "Well, sort of. Eighty-seven years ago, Princess Calor, daughter of Cherene of LaTourlamine, was questioned while under house arrest for her involvement in the Tiara Incident."

Gregory finished his report and looked to Alistair for further instruction, but he could not help risking a glance at the prince.

"Well, there it is," Alistair concluded, apparently uninterested in any arguments that might follow Gregory's brief example. "There is precedent, so no need to worry."

"I don't know, Alistair…" Laothist mumbled. "Perhaps we should…"

"Should what?" Alistair snapped.

Laothist clamped his mouth shut with an audible snap, but Poorez spoke up. "Perhaps we should not be so hasty, Alistair. After all, his father is an ally of this city…"

Alistair threw up his arms and walked away.

"I am more than willing to answer your questions," the prince offered.

Alistair spun back around. "You see?" he said, as if the prince's cooperation solved all their problems.

Ranabee broke in. "With all due respect, Your Highness, you seem a bit eager. Forgive me for being suspicious, but why the sudden change of heart?"

The prince nodded to his friends. "I should think that would be obvious."

"So," Fale grumbled, tiring of the circular arguments and trying to get things moving. He sat down. "For the record, you are their leader."

The prince nodded. "I am."

"And will *you* answer the charges?" Judith asked. "We can get little from your compatriots."

"They keep silent to protect me," Kiernan explained.

"Do you need protection?" Halberth asked.

Kiernan rested his hard green eyes on the street cleaner. The man did not blink, and the prince nodded in approval. "Not anymore." He turned to the rest of the Council. "I will answer your questions."

Quinlan cleared his throat. "Alright, did you relieve the Darweshi architect of his plans and money?"

Kiernan nodded. "We did."

"Why?"

"We suspect the bridge is being purposely delayed."

Judith snorted. "So do we."

Kiernan smiled at her and went on. "We also have reason to believe that the bridge is being built with faulty materials."

"Liar!"

Alistair did not even turn. "Another outburst, Darweshi, and I will have you removed from this hall!"

The rest of the Council members were now eyeing Odin Darweshi with suspicion.

But Quinlan was still looking boldly at the prince. "What do *you* care about it?" he asked. "What does it matter to a prince how a bridge is being made?"

Kiernan raised an eyebrow. "I suppose it doesn't. But we were hired by someone who cares very much."

"Who?"

Kiernan shook his head. "That I cannot tell you."

Quinlan scowled and turned to converse with Fale.

Both seemed unimpressed by the elf's revelations. Alistair watched him closely. The elf licked his lips, looking as though he were scrambling for something that would get their attention. "You wish to know about Raymond S'Trobenue."

Quinlan and Fale stopped talking. The rest of the Council froze.

Kiernan paused, and glanced at the S'Trobenue cousins. "He is safe," he concluded.

"Where is he?" Iris asked.

"I will tell your Watch Chief his whereabouts in private. If he checks in on Raymond, he will find he is perfectly safe."

Alistair nodded his head. "That is a start, Your Highness. A show of good faith."

But Judith Mercy was not so complacent. "Why are you telling us this? What good does it do you?"

The prince lifted his head. "I wish to clear our name. *Duak-Thenal* has been framed."

There were new assorted grumbles, over which Judith Mercy continued to speak. "You have proof of this?"

The prince nodded. "I do."

Judith smiled and crossed her arms. "I can't wait to hear this," she said, giving Halberth a superior look. "Go on then, Your Highness. We wait with bated breath."

With a cautious look to the guards surrounding him, Kiernan Nightwing slowly reached for a pouch at his side.

"Hold!" Three swords immediately came up to the prince's throat as Commander March spoke. The elf froze before his fingers could disappear into the pouch.

Gabrielle stepped in front of the prince and held his eyes. "What is in the pouch, Your Highness?" she asked.

"Evidence," the prince replied evenly.

Gabrielle eyed his pouch. In all seriousness she asked, "Is this evidence able to be held by human hands?"

Kiernan smiled. "Since it was made by human hands, then I suppose so."

"Good," March continued. "Then why don't I relieve you of it."

The prince paused and for a moment Alistair thought the elf was going to defy the command.

The swords at his neck immediately tensed, as if those who held them were convinced he might lash out at their commander.

March seemed to sense this, and raised a hand for them to stand down. Alistair saw the prince take a breath once the swords were lowered.

Gabrielle produced a knife and reached for the elf. Once again, the guard surrounding the prince tensed, but Kiernan Nightwing did not move. He allowed Gabrielle to cut the strings of his pouch and take it from him without objection.

She quickly emptied the contents into her hand. She took only a moment to scan them and then looked back at the prince, raising both eyebrows. "Sir," she called to the Watch Chief.

Alistair crossed to his commanding officer and leaned over her shoulder to inspect the contents of the pouch. After a second, he too looked at the prince with newfound interest. "Are these what I think they are, Your Highness?"

"They are," the prince replied.

"Dare I ask where you got them?" Alistair asked.

Before the Prince could answer, Judith Mercy spoke up. "Anything you would care to share with us, Alistair?"

Alistair and Gabrielle eyed each other, an unspoken agreement between them, as they approached the Council. "It seems," Gabrielle said as she dumped several square hunks of metal on the table, "that we have a counterfeiter in town."

The Council members laid their collective eyes on three copper plates bearing the impressions of coins not only from Preliona, but from Malhuria and Graxton as well. The commander then set down one more plate before the wide-eyed Council members. This one was different. It had no heads of state or memorial birds carved into it. Only a single 'X' marked the copper.

"What are they?" asked Iris.

Quinlan sat down with an audible sigh, fingering one of the plates in one hand and rubbing his head with the other. "They are templates. Used to create fake coin."

"Where did you get these, Your Highness?" Alistair calmly asked.

He answered without hesitation. "The Darweshi warehouse."

"Liar!" Odin screamed from the corner and lunged across the room toward the prince. He was stopped by no less than four guards, who were hard pressed to wrestle the large man away from the light elf.

"Peace, Lord Darweshi!" Laothist hollered, for the first time trying to exercise some sort of control.

But Odin would not be silenced. "How dare you accuse my father of wrong-doing!" he hissed at the prince.

Kiernan Nightwing turned his head slowly to the raging merchant, his thin lips curling into a knowing smile. "I have accused your *father* of nothing, sir."

Odin opened his mouth to scream further obscenities, and then abruptly closed his jaw with an audible snap. There could be no mistaking the prince's insinuation.

Standing between the prince and the raging merchant, Alistair was drawing the same conclusion—realizing just what he had stepped into and how deep he had gone. The Watch Chief could not charge Odin Darweshi with counterfeiting without involving his father. Octavius Darweshi was about the wealthiest man in Preliona, and his contributions to the Council were numerous. It would have made his life a whole lot easier if *Duak-Thenal* were guilty.

"The templates were what your crew was after then, Your Highness, when they broke into the Darweshi warehouse?" Alistair asked not tearing his blue gaze from Odin's black one.

"Yes," the prince affirmed.

Alistair turned back to face him, a smirk glistening in his faded blue eyes. "And may I ask how they came into your hands, as they were gone from the warehouse by the time your crew was captured?"

The elf opened his mouth slowly, aware that Alistair was leading him into a trap. He would implicate the imp Captain if he told the truth, and Alistair knew it. He watched the prince swallow hard, as he no doubt scrambled to come up with some excuse.

But the Watch Chief held up a hand. "Do not answer that, Your Highness. I assume Master Darken stashed it away somewhere before Commander March caught up with him, yes?" Alistair was nodding slowly.

"Yes," the prince quickly agreed. He sighed, clearly relieved. Alistair nodded in acknowledgement.

The Council seemed to accept this explanation, forgetting that the prince had had no contact with *Duak-Thenal* since their capture. He would not have known where to find the hidden templates. Alistair was not quite sure why he had covered for the prince, but he was not sorry he had, if only to see Odin Darweshi squirm.

Laothist was busy twiddling his pudgy fingers as the templates were being passed around the table. "Well, this changes things considerably," he stammered.

Odin finally broke through the barrier of Watch members, who were now finding it difficult to hold back three drunken S'Trobenue cousins in addition to keeping swords trained on five different elves.

Odin made it to the table before anyone could stop him. By this time, he seemed to have lost a bit of his bluster. "You are not seriously considering believing this," he squeaked at them.

He seemed stunned. Alistair had to stifle a laugh.

It was Gregory who answered, much to Alistair's surprise. The usually soft-spoken half-elf stood sharply and slammed the templates onto the table right under Odin's nose. "We do not have to *believe* anything. We have proof!"

"Those could have come from anywhere!" Odin shrieked.

"But they did not," Dagmar announced coolly. "They came from your warehouse."

Odin spun about. "No!" He hissed, taking a step toward the wild elf.

"Then how do you explain that machine we found?" Commander March now asked, stopping the young lord in his tracks.

Odin whirled about again, eyes blazing. He was clearly hanging onto his story by a thread. "How would I know?" he stammered. "Ask my father!"

"We did," Alistair replied, taking a step toward the merchant. "He says that particular room belongs to you. He knows nothing of what you do in there, nor does he care."

Odin stopped speaking and clenched his jaw shut. Alistair could practically see the wheels turning in his head. Odin could no longer cover his tracks, and he knew it.

"I'm betting these coins were made there." Gregory was still standing and looking down the length of his angular nose. "But you didn't get the color quite right." He picked up one of the coins in front of him. "The coin that *Duak-Thenal* uses is Dwarven. You used melted Malhurian gold, didn't you? It's lighter than Dwarven gold. See?"

Gregory now held two coins up to the light, but Alistair only barely registered this. He was watching Odin, whose face had gone a disturbing shade of yellow.

"This one," Gregory continued, holding up the darker one, "was left at the bedside of your architect. This one, however," Gregory now held up the lighter coin for the Council to see, "was found at the side of Lady Althea's unconscious body." Gregory leaned forward on both his long hands. "I wonder who put it there."

For once, Odin was speechless. This was as much an admission of guilt to the Council as anything they had yet heard. Still, none of them moved to accuse the formidable man out loud. They too were stunned by the information and Gregory's none-too-subtle conclusions.

Alistair took a step toward Odin, thinking this was his moment to finally catch him off-guard, but Cornelius stopped his advance. "Before you accuse Mr. Darweshi of any wrongdoing, Alistair, might I remind you of the type of injuries the governor sustained."

Alistair grunted in defeat as he turned to the wizard, surprised at his sudden intervention on Odin's behalf.

The merchant too turned, and now grinned daringly at Alistair. "That's right. Burned, wasn't she? Hit with a fireball. Something only a wizard could do, eh, Cornelius?"

Cornelius leveled his gaze and smiled at the merchant. "Be careful, Odin. I have not absolved you of all guilt. You may not be physically responsible for the attack on the governor, but you supplied the coin that was left by her side, of that I am certain."

Odin crossed his arms, looking to the Council for support. "Even if I did make the coin, how can I be held responsible for how it was used?"

"What other reason could you have for making a fake *Duak-Thenal* coin than to use it against them?" Alistair asked.

Odin rounded on him. "You act as though they are innocent, and I am the one on trial here! So, what if I reproduced their coin and left a few here and there for you to find? I helped you! If it weren't for me, you would never have caught them at all!"

"Before you go patting yourself on the back, Darweshi, perhaps you should stop and think about what these elves have been charged with." It was Judith Mercy who spoke. Alistair could see that she was working herself into that state of scalding accusation she reserved for only the most inept of her employees. "You have just absolved them of the attack against Althea, and Cornelius says they only helped Raymond move to a new town—something the Prince, here, has corroborated and can prove. My guess is that your man Jinin, now mysteriously missing in action, has much more to do with the dead merchants than these five do… and I'll bet my horse Gregory can prove that the coins found in Hunter Heights match your melted Malhurian gold ones." She was standing now, her calloused hands pressing into the table. She beheld Odin Darweshi with sharp green eyes that had already made their judgment against the man she spoke to. "So, what does that leave us with?" she asked, her voice betraying the sarcasm she was so famous for. "Breaking and entering? And each time, it was *your* possessions they stole. It seems it is *you* who have a lot of explaining to do."

Odin remained silent, clearly shaken by Judith Mercy's tirade. Alistair watched him closely, suddenly leery of the man. The Watch Chief wanted to take him away before he could open his mouth and do more damage.

"Where is this Jinin, anyway?" Quinlan asked suddenly. "I think we ought to speak with him."

"He followed the imp to *his* tower!" Odin screeched, pointing at Cornelius.

"Then where is he now?" Fale asked.

"I think I can best answer that one," Cornelius said, and he nodded to the orange-clad mage who had appeared with him earlier. He was young, a child really, but one who clearly knew how to behave in a situation such as the one he currently observed. He had kept quiet throughout the proceedings and had managed to blend into the background of Nimbus. Alistair had forgotten that he was there.

Now, however, when he stepped forward, his sunset robes swirling about his feet, the Council members took notice.

He was nervous, but he held his head high and was sure to make eye contact with any who looked upon him. His sandy hair was cut short and neatly combed back from his face. There was not a trace of a beard on his smooth face, and his blue eyes sparkled with the brightness of youth.

In his hands he carried a rolled-up piece of canvas that he held gingerly, as if the contents threatened to spill from it.

"This is Devon Bane," Cornelius announced. "He traveled with the missing caravan and is its only survivor."

"Then you can tell us what you saw!" Poorez exclaimed.

"Sadly, I cannot." Devon's voice sounded very small. "I was in my cabin and saw nothing. However, I had been charged with bringing an enchanted key to Cornelius here in Preliona. Jinin stole that key from me, and *Duak-Thenal* helped me to retrieve it. Jinin came to Cornelius's tower tonight to try to get it back."

Devon began to open the rolled-up cloth he carried as Cornelius went on. "Jinin broke into my garden and attacked Devon here. Unfortunately, my guardians, in an effort to protect the mage…" Devon unrolled the cloth completely. A jumble of broken bones, splintered at the edges as if some animal had gnawed at them, were piled in the cloth. They were not clean of the gristle of muscle and blood left behind by whatever creatures Cornelius employed. "… killed him," Cornelius finished.

Several Council members gasped and averted their eyes. Little that was left was even recognizable as Jinin Aurek, save for a few bits of black cloth and several strands of black and blonde hair.

Odin was breathing very heavily as he looked upon the remains of his thief. "How do we know that… that… mess," he stammered, "is really Jinin Aurek?"

Devon Bane bent over the pile and pulled up one long ginger sleeve. He reached into the mess without flinching and pulled a large gilded dagger from it. He held it out for all to see. "Recognize this?" he said to Odin.

The young lord did not have to answer. His slack-jawed expression gave him away.

Cornelius lifted the blade from Devon's hands and tossed it to Alistair, who caught it easily. "It is an unusual blade, isn't it? Notice the jagged edge, the design of the blade. One large tooth and then two small. The pattern repeats all along the edge. Search the entire city, Alistair, and I assure you, you'll never find its like."

Alistair was staring at the edge of the blade with renewed interest. "Yet I have seen its markings before," he mused. Suddenly his head snapped up and his eyes met Cornelius's. "This was the blade used to kill Edmee S'Trobenue."

The Council stood in unison, barely able to contain their shock and rage. Several Watch members were closing in on Odin now, but Alistair still held them in check. "What do you know of this, Odin?" Alistair asked calmly.

Odin had now gone deadly pale. He did not lift his eyes from the remains of the thief. His fists were clenched at his side and his breath came in short gasps. Alistair moved cautiously closer, keeping his officers at bay with a nod of his head.

"Darweshi?" Alistair began as he approached. He held Jinin's dagger before him, hoping to get Odin to acknowledge its existence before the Council.

But Odin did not move. He did not seem to hear Alistair at all.

The Watch Chief inched closer, until he was only a foot away from the merchant. "Lord Darweshi," he began again. "Did you hire Jinin Aurek to kill Edmee S'Trobenue?"

Odin moved with lightening quickness. One second, he was absently staring at the floor, the next he had Jinin's serrated dagger in his hand. So drastic was this change that Alistair never saw it coming.

"YES!" he screeched, and plunged the knife into Alistair's neck.

Iris screamed and Gregory launched himself over the Council table, racing toward Alistair and Odin. Several other Council members fell over each other trying to get out from behind the table.

The pain was sharp and intense. Alistair felt his throat close and instantly flood with blood. Alistair latched onto Odin's arm thinking to push the man away, but instead he found himself sinking to the floor.

Odin ripped the dagger from the Watch Chief's neck and tore his arm from Alistair's grasp.

Then he ran.

Coward, Alistair thought.

Gregory and Devon tried to run after him, but the three S'Trobenue cousins, fighting furiously with the guards, got in their way.

Cornelius was running toward him, but Alistair barely saw him. Instead he watched as the red-haired elf flew out the door, unseen and unheard. His compatriots clearly wished to follow him. All four were moving, trying to get past the guards who were struggling to hold them back. As his head hit the marble floor, he locked eyes with the wild elf. Dagmar stared at him, would have moved to him were it not for the guards holding her back. Was it sadness he saw in her misty eyes? Sympathy? Respect even? Alistair appreciated the sentiment and he considered the wild elf generous to think of him before her friends.

He tried to smile at her, but then Cornelius was hovering above him, talking quickly, his hands covered in blood.

40~A New Watch Chief

As Commander Gabrielle March saw it, the knife moved exquisitely slow. So much so that she should have been able to reach him in time; should have been able to catch Odin's arm and wrench the knife from his hand before it made its hideous plunge.

It was not until much later that she realized how far away she had been and how many people had managed to get between her and Alistair as she ran to him. She had not even drawn her sword, something Alistair would surely have scolded her for. Instead she ran, trying to reach her mentor before his life's blood spread across the white marble of the hall.

How many people did she shove out of her way before she fell to her knees at his side? How many Council members and guards screamed her name? She did not know. Her hearing seemed to have taken leave of her. She could barely breathe as she assessed the damage.

It was great.

Cornelius was kneeling opposite her and holding Alistair's white head in his hands. He was whispering a spell and Gabrielle saw sparks of white magic twinkling about Alistair's body.

The Watch Chief grabbed at her hand, but he did not look at her. He focused instead on the wizard. "Forgive me, my friend," the Watch Chief whispered. "I should have come to you sooner."

Cornelius shook his head. "Do not speak," the wizard cautioned, desperately trying to keep more blood from spilling from the hole in Alistair's neck. Gabrielle saw that the Malhurian's hands were covered in it. She closed her eyes and felt hot tears stinging the insides of her lids.

She shook them away. She would not let Alistair see them.

"Althea... needs..." He was trying to speak again, but the blood that was flowing from his mouth garbled his words and choked him. Cornelius and Gabrielle held him until the coughing passed. Cornelius nodded his head at the Watch Chief, as if he knew what the man was trying to say.

Alistair then turned to his commander. She knew at once that he would be unable to speak to her. His mouth opened and closed but nothing came out. He stopped trying finally and settled instead on smiling at her. She had rarely seen the man smile, and that he bestowed this on her in his dying moment only made her love him more.

"Do not leave me," she blurted out.

He patted her hand, kept smiling that crinkled smile. "Protect," he whispered.

Gabrielle wanted to ask what he meant. Protect who? But at that moment Alistair Kellen Keane closed his eyes.

All the pain in his strained features melted away. His last breath flowed out of him like a cold draft down an empty hall.

He was gone, but Gabrielle was not ready. It had all happened too fast. "No," she hissed, and shook his hand. "*No, damn you!*"

She would have kept on shaking his hand, stayed there on the floor for who knows how long, if a darker hand had not landed on her shoulder. Gabrielle looked up into the deep eyes of the wizard. "Protect who?" she asked. "What does he mean?"

Cornelius squeezed her shoulder. "The city, my dear. You are the Watch Chief now."

And with that confirmation, hearing came plummeting back to her.

First a light pop, then a painful yet clarifying ring and above that, the roar of the crowded hall. Gabrielle could pick out each group of shouting people quite well now. It was as if those few moments of selective hearing had heightened her awareness tenfold.

The Council members had scattered. Most were standing near her, though she had not noticed them before. Judith Mercy was now kneeling in her place, the only one not yelling.

Quinlan and Poorez were standing on either side of her, predictably looking for action and hollering for vengeance. She wondered why Fale was not among them, but then she spotted him across the hall trying to get past one very large guard—intent on following Darweshi, apparently. Gabrielle silently blessed her crew for having the sense to close the doors and keep everyone in. She thought her soldiers could hold Fale for a few more minutes, at least.

She looked around, quickly scanning the room. Laothist, Ranabee and Iris were huddled behind the table. Halberth was making his way toward Judith, looking sad and serious. Gregory had disappeared altogether, but the commander was not worried about him.

No, those who most concerned her now were right in front of her. And they were more than anxious to speak with her.

Gabrielle made straight for the elves. She watched as relief flooded the faces of the guards who held them back—for though their wrists were chained, they were mobile enough. All four had managed to get around to the front of the table before being stopped by a large array of weaponry. But even a dozen or more swords seemed paltry protection in the face of the four elves.

One young and overzealous guard spoke to her. "Is he dead?"

Gabrielle did not look at him. She only had eyes for Dagmar. "Yes. He is."

The female elf lowered her eyes. Gabrielle saw her take in a deep breath before she looked up at the commander again. "I am sorry for your loss, Commander. He was a good man."

She was being genuine. March could hear it in her musical voice. But at that moment the commander was in no mood to acknowledge it. "You have no idea," she said flatly.

The wild elf ignored her comment and went on. "And you are in charge now?"

Gabrielle went rigid at the elf's assumption, but she managed a curt nod. Dagmar licked her lips, clearly hesitating. "You realize you must release us."

Gabrielle raised an eyebrow at the elf, "Must I? Give me one good reason."

"How about the death of your chief?" Panas blurted out.

Gabrielle shot out one arm and grabbed the light elf by the collar. She yanked him forward, pressing her face close to his. "Considering that I already know who the killer is and where to find him, you'll have to do better than that," she growled.

Dagmar did not even flinch at the danger her comrade was in. She kept her eyes trained on Gabrielle. "Our innocence has been proven, Commander."

Gabrielle shoved Panas away. "If you consider breaking into a warehouse innocent."

Dagmar's gray eyes flared. "Come, Commander. You waste time on minor details." The elf was becoming confrontational again, and the guards near her shifted nervously. "You must free us."

Gabrielle was gritting her teeth. She knew she should stay calm, but she had lost all patience. Every ear in the room was listening in on this conversation, but somehow the commander could not lower her voice. "And what will you do with your newfound freedom?" she challenged.

Dagmar started to respond, but March cut her off. "No, don't bother, I already know!" She came close to the elf and put a finger in her face. "*I* will bring Odin Darweshi to justice— *without* your help."

Dagmar shifted slightly and the guards moved with her, leery that the dangerous elf would strike out. "You mistake our intentions, Commander." She kept her voice steady, but Gabrielle could see the wild elf was seething with rage. The commander remembered their brief fight in the warehouse and saw that Dagmar would be only too happy for a rematch. "We wish only to find our leader, and leave," she said.

Gabrielle paused and looked around. She had completely forgotten about the Prince of the Light Elves. "Where is he?"

"Took off after Odin," one of the guards answered.

Gabrielle eyed Dagmar. "You mean to kill Darweshi, don't you?"

Dagmar shook her head. "No," she said with finality. "We mean only to protect our friend."

Gabrielle brushed a stray hair from her face, unaware of the bloody streak she left there. "He left on his own. He is not my concern."

"He is ours," Dagmar took a threatening step forward. The guards nearest to her latched onto her arms to pull her away from the commander, but Gabrielle held up her hand to stop them.

The wild elf instantly changed tactics, lowering her voice so the Council could not hear. "Commander, we can catch up to him faster. You know we can."

The commander wanted with all her heart to deny the elf's words. After all, *she* had caught them. "I have managed to keep up with you just fine so far."

"With Odin's help," came the light elf's quick response.

Gabrielle came close to stabbing Panas the Hawk at that moment, but Dagmar stopped her. "Please, Commander," she pleaded, a slight quake in her voice. "The Prince of the Light Elves is running after a crazed man with a dozen fanatic followers. Allow us to protect him and I assure you we will do our best to bring Odin Darweshi back to you. Alive, if possible."

Commander Gabrielle March, the youngest person ever to occupy the post of Watch Chief, turned away from her prisoners. A hurricane of anger was quickly replacing her grief. If she did manage to catch up to Darweshi she was unsure she would be able to control herself. It was easy to see herself severing the man's head from his neck.

Still, was she allowing her anger to cloud her judgment by holding these creatures?

She could feel the eyes of the guards boring into her back. They expected a decision from her, and it would have to be a strong one. She turned. "Release them," she said.

"Commander?"

Gabrielle did not look at the questioning guard. "You heard me," she said. "We have no cause to keep them."

Dagmar smiled as the guards unlocked the chains. "Thank you, Commander. You will not regret it."

Gabrielle became stoic again. "I regret the day I ever heard of you," she said, a slight break in her voice.

Dagmar nodded in understanding.

"Go," Gabrielle commanded them. "Do what you must do and get out of this city. I expect you will have to make a stop at Cornelius's tower first, but after that I want you gone."

Dagmar nodded and started to turn away, but Gabrielle grabbed her arm. "We will be right behind you," March announced. "Stay out of our way."

This time the wild elf did not answer. She only stared at Gabrielle, waiting for the commander to come to her senses and release her. Gabrielle suddenly felt foolish. She loosed the wild elf and began to walk away. Then she suddenly turned back. She wanted to wish them luck, and in an odd sort of way she meant it. But when she turned around, they were gone. She glanced about the room, searching for a fleeting glimpse of a cloak or a boot. There was none.

"Where are their weapons?" she asked the nearest guard.

The man shook his head in amazement. "In my hand only seconds ago. They took them before I could even hand them over."

Gabrielle nodded, not surprised. "We'd best go after them, though I doubt we will be much help at this point."

Lexi now came to her side. "We could just let them do the work for us, Commander," he offered.

The commander shook her head. "No. Whatever happens, I am sure there will be some sort of a mess for us to clean up."

Lexi let out a harsh laugh. "And that is what we do best, eh, Commander? Clean up the mess?"

He walked away. Gabrielle made to follow when someone behind her grabbed her arm. She knew who it was before she turned. The wizard had graciously hung back, letting her handle the situation with the elves. His cool dark eyes were clouded over. She did not know him well, had only been formally introduced a few days ago. But in her eyes, he suddenly looked more his age than Gabrielle had ever seen him.

He was about to speak. Gabrielle, not wanting to hear anything sentimental, cut him off. She was not ready to grieve. "Will you stay behind and take care of…"

Words failed her, but Cornelius was ready. He swallowed the words on his tongue and nodded to her. "Of course I will, Commander."

"Thank you, sir." She looked over her shoulder to the place where the elves had been. "I suspect you will have visitors again this night."

Cornelius raised an eyebrow, not entirely surprised that Gabrielle seemed to know the wizard kept the imp hidden in his tower.

"Will you be ready for them?" she asked.

Cornelius nodded sadly. "I will," he said. "I thank you for your discretion."

She nodded. "I give no more than Alistair would have given, sir. Your band has been absolved. I have no right to anything, or any*one* in your tower."

Cornelius licked his lips, bowing his head in thanks again. "Leave everything to me, Commander. All will be settled."

He released her arm with a pat and began to walk slowly back to Alistair's inert form. Gabrielle began to run the way Odin and the elves had gone. She motioned for several soldiers to follow.

She had wanted to thank Cornelius, but she could not find her voice. It was choked again with tears.

41 ~ The Other Side of Preliona

Kiernan Nightwing did not run after Odin Darweshi. He did not even jog. He glided.

He slipped from shadow to shadow, following the killer and his men through several back alleys he had never seen, and could easily have gotten turned around in. But he knew their destination. There could be only one spot for this battle to take place, and he intended to meet his quarry there.

He made for the lake and followed its edge until he was turned away from it by an oddly placed storefront that forced him to move north. He ran up through Wing Street and took the first left he encountered, trying to keep the bridge in his sights. Between a huddled mass of rundown shacks, the prince slowed and took in his surroundings.

This was a part of the city he had not known existed. It was well hidden from any eye that did not wish to see it. Like Dirt Alley, this was a place uncared for and all but forgotten by the shining light that was the largest and greatest city in the Northern Realms. Few people lived here, Kiernan could tell. And those who did would not care who passed among them.

The prince crouched in the crevice of a crumbled wall and listened intently to his surroundings. He was most certainly not alone. And it was not the tired homeless folk of this dead street that he heard.

It made sense that Odin would leave a few followers behind. That was fine with Kiernan.

He silently drew his black blade and held it two-handed before him. The metal shimmered liquid in the moonlight. Its reflection would likely give away his position, but he was beyond caring. He was feeling positively murderous and ready to lash out at the nearest body. It had been a long time since he had felt this way. His breath came hard and fast, but his hands were cool and unwavering.

Human footsteps, trying hard to be silent, pounded in his ears. There were six, three on either side of him, heavily armed and ready to fight.

Kiernan Nightwing stepped out of the shadows to meet them.

— ✳ ✳ ✳ —

Dagmar ran at top speed, splashing through puddles and slipping across rain-slicked cobblestones.

Talesin had wanted to split up, but Dagmar had refused. She did not want to divide their power. Besides, they knew where the prince and Odin were headed. All that remained was to find the quickest route there. The wild elf found herself sincerely wishing for the Captain's presence. She had a good idea of the bridge's location, Panas and Nemesio had both been there, but they had not reached it from this end of town.

What Dagmar wanted right now was a shortcut: the Captain would surely have known one. The prince had too much of a lead on them—and he was chasing a man who had a large ace up his sleeve—a mage who knew their every move before they did.

Tain had obviously made it back to the tower. She would have told the prince how easily the commander had been able to catch them, how Odin's secret mage had tracked *Duak-Thenal*, even with Cornelius covering them.

Dagmar also knew that Kiernan would take the risk, no matter what he had been told. A good man had died tonight, and the prince would likely blame himself for that. Kiernan would not stop now if the mysterious mage himself appeared before him.

Of course, that was exactly what Dagmar was afraid of. Now that the stakes had been raised and Odin's true nature revealed, she would not be at all surprised if the elusive sorcerer appeared.

"Where is Devon?" she panted.

"He could not keep up," Nemesio replied. "I suspect he will use the key to find us."

Dagmar shook her head. "He is safer with Cornelius."

"Wouldn't have to worry about him at all if you'd have let me kill him when I wanted to," Talesin quipped from in front of her.

Panas laughed behind them.

The wild elf turned a corner sharply and darted down Aft Street, only inches behind Talesin, who still maintained the lead. He was kidding, she hoped.

"The commander might have taken charge of him." Panas suggested.

"The commander has enough of her own to worry about right now, I'd say," Dagmar huffed. "Besides, he'll never catch up to us."

"Do not be so sure," Nemesio said. "With that key he could beat us. He could be at the bridge already."

Dagmar glanced at him with wide eyes. "Kiernan will not have made the bridge yet. If Devon shows up there now, he will be alone."

Talesin slowed, allowing Dagmar to catch up to him. "Or he will be greeting Odin Darweshi for us."

Dagmar suddenly found the strength to run faster.

— ✳ ✳ ✳ —

Two down, four to go. The Prince of the Light Elves fairly danced through this fight. Not that he was having an easy time of it. In fact, he was not even sure he was winning. Kiernan figured out quickly that the fighters laying in wait for him were part of Jinin's gang, not the drunken brutes of Odin's inner circle, as he had expected.

They fought intensely and with abandon, most likely looking to avenge the death of their leader. They had no fear, yet they maintained a quality of skill that belied their scruffy appearance. They were dangerous, possibly more than the elf himself. But the prince found he was ready to destroy them all if for no other reason than to put them out of the way of others who might encounter them.

He had already killed two of them. His blade now sliced neatly through the heart of a third. The man went down slowly, his body unable to completely collapse until Kiernan ripped his sword from it. In one precise move, Kiernan wiped the blade on the man's tunic as he fell and turned to face his next assailant before the last one had even touched the ground.

The three remaining stood together, determined to make a unified front against the blur of movement before them. Kiernan did not wait to see which of them would move first. He dove for them, swirling his dark sword at their collective faces and forcing them to back up or be shredded by his onslaught.

They did not stay on the defensive for long. Two broke loose and immediately made to surround him. Kiernan thrust his foot sideways, connecting squarely with one man's chest. The blow sent the man staggering into the alley wall as Kiernan continued pressing his advantage forward.

The man before him now was tiring; his parries were becoming sluggish. Kiernan made a stab forward and caught the man in the shoulder. He then turned in time to block a stunning blow from the third, whom he had ignored until now. A mistake, Kiernan discovered, as she was the strongest of the three remaining, evident from the power behind her strike. Kiernan threw his sword up in a horizontal arc, saving his own head, but the downward strike of the powerful woman sent the prince nearly to his knees.

He grabbed his sword in both hands and tried to push the attacker back. He failed and chose instead to dive to one side. The prince's opponent stumbled forward, unable to stop her momentum. Kiernan came up behind and shoved the woman in the back. She cracked her head on the alley wall and sank to the stones. She did not get up.

Kiernan turned. The man he had kicked in the chest was now the only one standing and he came at the prince with a sword in each hand. This man was shorter than Kiernan by a head, but the prince did not deign to think he had the advantage. There was a reason this dark-haired fighter was the last man standing.

He was good.

His two twirling swords were a blur of movement. As they came at the prince, Kiernan got a clear look at the man's brown eyes before he moved to defend himself. Both sword edges crossed and came down toward his head so fast that the prince felt the breeze lift his hair. The elf twisted to the right and brought his sword up in both hands, blocking his opponent's downward slashes. Kiernan swung his arms in an outward circle, forcing the two swords up and away from his body.

Kiernan spun about and made a powerful jab at the rogue. Amazingly, the man brought one sword up and the other down, catching the elf's sword between his own two. Surprised and slightly angered, Kiernan yanked his captive sword free and delivered a flurry of slashes and stabs, forcing the man to back away or be cut to ribbons.

But defend himself he did, and Kiernan was hard pressed to make a dent in the man's defenses. The prince did not want to prolong this fight any longer than he had to. If he did, he would lose Odin. But he could not finish the fight as quickly as he had with the others. The six fighters had been left to stall him, and this last was doing his job expertly.

Kiernan narrowed his eyes and forced himself to concentrate on any weakness in his opponent's fighting skills. At first, he saw nothing, only the blur of double swords and the quiet whir of the blades. But as the prince blocked blow after stinging blow, he began to see a pattern forming. The hired sword's offense was excellent, but his defense was one-sided. He kept his arms too close to his chest. He seemed loath too open them to any length, so his weapons were almost always crossing and cutting in diagonals.

He could not jab, and his sides were completely unguarded.

Kiernan took a calculated risk. Waiting until the man crossed his swords and slashed downward again, the prince stepped wildly to one side and spun about. He felt the bite of a blade slice his leg and at the same time let his sword arm fly and felt it connect with the neck of his opponent.

The elf watched the human grasp his neck and drop to the ground. He was dead before the first splash of blood soaked his tunic.

The prince sheathed his sword and glanced at his slashed thigh. It bled, but not profusely. He turned to go, but stopped suddenly and turned toward the alley entrance.

There was a slight change in temperature, he could swear it. His skin tingled and a layer of his hair began to float about his face. The very air was charged with energy.

Once again, he felt the presence of another, only this time it was no handful of swordsmen he was facing. There was something thick in the air. Something that smelled just this edge of burnt. Kiernan looked around sharply. Someone was watching him, making the air move with electricity.

He was about to give up the search when a clear voice above him spoke. "Well done, Your Highness."

Kiernan snapped his head up. There, standing atop one of the only stable buildings in the alley, was a red-robed mage. His face was shadowed under a large cowl, but Kiernan instantly knew that this was Odin's well-kept secret. This was the man who had led Commander March to his friends. Kiernan knew without a doubt that the mage had been here watching him the entire time.

"Who are you?" the prince asked.

The red mage laughed. The sound hurt the prince's ears. It was at once young and old, sick and healthy, completely sinister and totally pleasant. "If you don't mind, I would prefer to keep *my* identity secret awhile longer."

Kiernan really had not expected an answer. He was out of his league here. If this mage was as powerful as Kiernan had reason to believe he was, then there would be little the prince could do to overcome him. He was hoping to stall the man. "What do you want?"

The mage did not move. "From you?" he said. "Nothing. Nothing you can give me, anyway. Therefore, you have ceased to be of service to me."

Kiernan gripped the pommel of his sword in response to this threat. "And what service have I performed for you?"

Again the laugh, as the red mage's robes fluttered in the charged air. "Oh, hadn't you guessed? *Duak-Thenal* has been disbanded. You have drawn much attention to yourselves and therefore away from me."

Kiernan's mind scrambled, trying to decide what to say to this man. How much did he know already? "It doesn't really matter who you are," he stalled, "I have exposed *Duak-Thenal,* but we have not been destroyed."

"Ah, but there you've made your mistake," the mage snapped back. "Your power was all in your mystery. Your ability to instill fear and steal about unnoticed all these years dissipated the moment you gave the Council your identity."

Kiernan swallowed. He had convinced himself that exposing *Duak-Thenal* was the right thing to do. Now this nameless mage was making him doubt his decision. "Now that we are known to Preliona and the White Watch, we can share our information. Pool our resources. Together we can stop the likes of Odin Darweshi—and expose people like you."

The mage laughed harshly, throwing back his head and giving Kiernan a small glimpse of a face under the red cowl. "Odin Darweshi and I are not in the same category," the mage sneered.

"You didn't seem to mind associating yourself with him until now."

"Until now he has been useful," The mage countered. "But you still have not guessed who *I* am, have you? I, who have been standing behind Odin the entire time you have battled him."

Kiernan stared at the mage, desperately scratching at the back of his mind for some hint of recognition. The mage dropped his hooded head as he glared down the length of his unseen nose. "Come now, Your Highness, I had credited you with far more ability than simply wielding that magnificent sword of yours. You are your sister's twin, are you not?"

Kiernan froze. This wizard knew Kalli. "What gives you the right to even speak of her?" Kiernan found he was clenching his teeth. This was ridiculous. He had not felt a need to protect his sister in a long time. Kalliroestria was more capable of protecting herself than anyone else in Tearlach. Still, something about this mage made him extremely uneasy. For himself and for her.

"Your sister and I are known to each other," the mage replied. "I would tell you how, but it hardly matters, since you will not live to speak with her again."

Suddenly the air was sucked out of the alley. All moisture seemed to dissipate, and Kiernan immediately found it difficult to breathe. He looked up at the red-robed mage and his breath caught in his throat. In the mage's hand was a fireball the size of a carriage wheel. It floated above his hand, crackling, and sparkling with heat.

Realization hit him. This was the man who had dispatched Lady Althea.

"Goodnight to you, young prince. I'll be sure to tell your sister that you died bravely."

As the mage raised his hand to throw, Kiernan dove into the doorway of the nearest hovel. The fireball connected with the shack and Kiernan covered his head as the whole world turned to red.

— ✷ ✷ ✷ —

Dagmar came to a skidding halt, the explosion nearly rocking her from her feet.

"What in *Sherzak* was that?" Panas asked over Dagmar's shoulder.

The wild elf shook her head and immediately started to move toward the cloud of black smoke unfurling above the ramshackle houses at the end of the street. Something was not right. She glanced to the left of the alley and saw the moon shining off the lake. Work on the bridge had not progressed since the last time she had seen it. But when Nemesio and Panas had slashed the steel girders they had been on Opal Lake's eastern shore. Now *Duak-Thenal* stood near the shore of the West. Here, wooden platforms connected six of the girders to one another. Hanging from them were giant tarps that flapped about in the wind and light rain.

This was the side of the bridge that Odin would have headed toward. And the smoking alley before them presented a direct shot to its base.

"Kiernan," Dagmar whispered. The wild elf took off at a dead run for the alley.

"Dagmar!" Talesin called after her. "Dagmar, wait!"

She barely heard the ice elf. Dagmar tore through the alley like a terrible wind, moving fast and erratically. She swiveled her head back and forth, peering intently into the dark crevices of abandoned huts and biting the inside of her cheek to keep from shouting Kiernan's name.

She turned a corner too quickly, slid on the cobblestones, and went down on one knee. She hauled herself to her feet, ignoring the stab of pain there, and stopped dead.

Here the shacks were crammed so close together that one could not tell where one building left off and the next began. Clearly these dwellings had been vacant for some time, and it was just as well, for there was extraordinarily little left for any soul to live in.

The entire right side of the alley had collapsed. Many of the houses on the left side had been scorched black and looked about to fall in on themselves. Two small fires still burned weakly, one only a few feet from her, the other from under the pile of rubble that was several houses down. Littering the alley floor were six dead bodies. Three were partially covered by the collapsed wall.

Dagmar took a tentative step forward. She took a breath and immediately began to cough. Smoke burned her throat and stung her eyes. She doubled over, trying to catch her breath, and found she could not. She was starting to panic when she was rather violently whacked on the back several times by a cold hand.

"*Ziyad's blood!* Breathe, dammit!"

Dagmar sucked in air through her nose and tried to slow her panicked heart. Talesin took her shoulders and pulled her up straight. Dagmar wiped her watering eyes and glared at the ice elf. "I'm fine," she said, and immediately began choking again.

"Sure you are," the ice elf replied. Talesin thumped her back a few more times before Dagmar shook him off.

"Next time you plan on asphyxiating yourself, would you mind waiting for us?" Panas quipped from beside her.

Dagmar wanted to slap the light elf, but she was listening for something. A sort of hissing sound she had heard moments before.

Nemesio was kneeling beside one of the dead fighters and examining his wounds. "Kiernan did this," he said. "I am sure of it."

Dagmar held up her hand up for quiet and took a step forward. There was unearthly silence, but that was no comfort to her in the open alley. They were all easy targets from above. That is, if an assailant could stand on these crumbling structures.

Dagmar slid through the smoking ashes and embers, searching for a sound she hoped to hear again. A slight shifting of rock to her right made her freeze. The three elves behind her stopped as well, listening with animal instinct. There was something more in this alley than crackling fire and hissing smoke.

Dagmar cocked her head and held her breath. She lowered herself slowly into a crouch and bent forward, putting her face close to the ground. There, she picked up a subtle shift in the air, blowing out from underneath a downed abode. This shack had fallen in such a way as to leave a tiny triangular space inside it. Dagmar peered inside the dark crawl space, waiting.

When a puff of air brushed her face she nearly fell back in surprise. The breath was accompanied by a muffled grunt of pain. Dagmar flattened herself onto the ground, getting a face full of soot. Her three companions dove forward as the wild elf thrust her hand into the space beneath the fallen house.

"I've got him!" Dagmar called as Talesin skidded to his knees by her side.

"What!" Panas exclaimed. "Kiernan?"

"Is he alive?" the ice elf asked tentatively.

Dagmar nodded and strained to pull at the weight at the end of her arm. "I can't move him. Kiernan, can you hear me?"

Dagmar had to strain to hear the response, but she could still catch some of what the prince said. "The mage… protect yourself…"

Talesin shot to his feet and scanned what was left of the rooftops. "I am going up," he announced. Dagmar nodded without argument and continued to try and pull the prince free. "Panas," Talesin said to the light elf. "Come."

Panas had already unslung several weapons from his arsenal and was three steps ahead of the ice elf as they looked for a way to the top of the roofs.

Nemesio, meanwhile, was pushing Dagmar out of the way, trying to get a look at the hole the prince was in. He flattened himself onto the ground and peered into the gloom.

The building had caved in on three sides, leaving a space the size of a small child. Kiernan was wedged in this tiny pocket of air, curled in a ball, and using the hole to breathe through. Dagmar could not see how badly he was hurt, but was certain the prince would run out of air soon. Dagmar and Nemesio strained to see past the prince, and Dagmar was relieved to see a small flicker of light several feet behind Kiernan.

Nemesio stood quickly and ran around the corner. "Stay with him!" he called to Dagmar. "I am going in on the opposite side."

The wild elf barely heard him as she reached her long hand back through the triangular hole in the debris and grasped the prince's arm.

She was in up to her shoulder and could barely move left or right. She turned her head away from the wall as she felt along Kiernan's arm, searching for his hand. At the same time, she scanned the alley with her eyes at ground level. It was still empty. Neither could the sensitive wild elf feel the presence of any other than those she counted among her group.

That did not mean that whoever had destroyed this alley was not still lingering out of sight. Dagmar was relying heavily on Panas and Talesin to find that party, or at least cover her from above.

She saw the ice elf then, peering down at her from the top of the building directly in front of her. He gave her a barely perceptible nod, indicating that the rooftops were clear.

Dagmar turned back to her task. Her fingertips flittered across the pebbles of dirt and shards of glass and mortar. They were bleeding by the time she grasped the prince's hand.

He did not grasp hers back.

There was a moment of acute panic for Dagmar. A tiny second when her feelings for Kiernan surged far past anything she had ever felt before. She could not move. She could barely breathe. The air she took in hurt. Though she knew she was yelling, she could not hear her own words. "*Ziyad's blood, Nemy, hurry!*"

He's dead, she thought. So overwhelming was this thought that she did not immediately notice that her hand was being held. Firmly.

Her body suddenly unlocked itself from its frozen position and Dagmar found herself able to breathe again. She heard movement from inside and under the rubble. "Hang on, Kiernan," she said. A small squeeze of her hand was the response. Dagmar was about to speak again when the prince's hand was quite suddenly ripped from her grasp.

For a moment Dagmar froze, too shocked to move. Then, like the snap of a whip, she was on her feet and running around the building. She had her sword in her hand and was un-holstering her crossbow as she ran. Still she was as light and flowing on her feet as a stream. None would have heard her as she dashed around the corner, weapons ready to shred any who stood in her way.

None but another elf.

"Dagmar, stop!"

Nemesio's voice brought the wild elf's advance to a screeching halt, an instant before her blade would have cut into his arm.

Nemesio's violet eyes went wide and his arms clung protectively to the package he carried. Dangling limply from the southern elf's arms was the barely conscious from of the prince of the light elves.

Dagmar lowered her weapons immediately.

Blood was coursing down one side of his face, but Dagmar could see that this was not his most serious wound. Of more concern was the odd angle at which his right shoulder stuck out. It was twisted down and forward: dislocated. Even this could be fixed quickly, though it would be painful.

There were other bumps and bruises, small cuts, and gashes, but clearly the worst of his injuries, and those which gave Dagmar the most serious worry, were the burns.

The prince's entire right arm and much of his chest and back had been scorched. His tunic hung in tatters from his torso and had completely disintegrated from his arm. In its place there was bubbling, blackened flesh – and blood. His chest was disturbingly red, but his arm had received the worst of it. Clearly, he had shielded himself with this arm, saving his facial features but devastating his sword arm.

Dagmar placed her hands on either side of his head and turned his face to hers. The prince was struggling to open his eyes. Dagmar watched him carefully as she touched two fingers to the side of his throat. His heartbeat was fast, too fast perhaps, but Dagmar liked this better than the alternative.

Nemesio was breathing heavily and starting to kneel. "We have to get that arm covered up," he said. "If it gets infected, he will lose it for sure."

Dagmar nodded. She brushed Kiernan's soot-encrusted hair from his face. She examined his crooked shoulder and ravaged arm as Nemesio lowered him to the ground. Kiernan winced in pain and mumbled unintelligibly as Panas and Talesin rounded the corner.

Nemesio was already ripping his own tunic and handing the pieces to Dagmar when Panas lunged forward. "*Kelina!*" he gasped. "Is he all right?"

Talesin grabbed him by the collar and yanked him back. "Keep a lookout," he hissed at the light elf, and shoved him away. "Let them work."

Too concerned to argue, Panas slunk away and watched the alley.

Dagmar slowly lifted the prince's injured arm onto her knee. She held her breath as she did, unable to tear her eyes away from the damaged skin. Kiernan remained relatively still while Dagmar quickly wrapped the strips of cloth tightly about the burned arm. It was not until she grasped his dislocated shoulder and attempted to move it that they had a problem.

He screamed.

Dagmar and Nemesio both started violently. Talesin shot to the other end of the alley to scout for anyone who might have heard the awful sound.

Kiernan turned his face into Nemesio's tunic, trying to drown the sound of his own cries. He then clamped down on his teeth and shuddered violently.

Dagmar put a shaking hand on his forehead and leaned down to him. "I have to put it back," she whispered to him.

The prince clenched his eyes shut and nodded quickly. Dagmar looked to Nemesio, who seemed to be breathing as hard as the prince. The southern elf nodded to her, albeit nervously, to continue and grasped Kiernan's good hand with his free one. Trying to ignore the prince's gasps of agony, Dagmar placed the palm of her hand on the front of Kiernan's chest. The other she held to the back of his shoulder.

She took a breath and with a quick jerking motion, shifted her hands in opposite directions slamming the shoulder back into place with a sickening pop.

Dagmar remained frozen as the prince's entire body locked. He clamped his jaw shut this time to keep from screaming. Dagmar lamented that she had brought nothing with her that might ease the pain. But then again, the pain seemed to be keeping him from losing consciousness.

"Get me up," he said to them suddenly.

Nemesio and Dagmar did not argue. They stood and gently helped the prince to his feet as Talesin continued to pace at the head of the alley. He was quite steady—far steadier than Dagmar had expected him to be. "Are you all right?" she asked quietly as she deftly tucked a last strip of cloth under his elbow and up around his damaged shoulder.

He gripped Nemesio's arm and closed his eyes as she did. "I met the mage," he said.

Dagmar stopped and lowered her arms.

Kiernan opened his eyes. The emerald orbs fell on Dagmar and they were bright and clear, though he now wavered slightly on his feet. "I do not know who he is. He attacked me the same way he attacked the governor."

Talesin moved in closer. "What does he want?"

"I don't know," Kiernan said. "He has been using Odin to get to us all this time. But I think he means to abandon him now."

"Then the only way to find out what the mage is doing is to catch Odin," Nemesio said.

Kiernan nodded weakly. "He is heading for the bridge."

The prince took several shaky steps away from them, but Talesin stepped in front of him. "We are going after Odin Darweshi, Your Highness," Talesin said. "*You* are going back to the tower."

Talesin's tone was one that Dagmar had never heard him use with the prince. He was giving orders to one who never took them. Dagmar was not sure how the prince would take this turn of events. His green eyes scanned Talesin's black ones. "I can make it," Kiernan insisted.

Talesin nodded. "Maybe. But do you want to lose your arm finding out?"

Dagmar watched the two friends stare each other down. This was a confrontation she had never seen. The prince licked his lips, knowing that if Talesin intended to fight him on this issue, the ice elf would physically win out. Even had Kiernan been completely up to par, Talesin may still have beaten him in a fight.

Dagmar secretly hoped the prince would lay down his pride and give in. But the decision was quite suddenly taken out of their hands by the surprise arrival of another mage.

A flash of blue light momentarily blinded the group. Everyone threw up their arms to shield their eyes as Devon Bane appeared beside the prince and Talesin.

The young mage looked almost as shocked by his own appearance as the elves were. He stared at the key in his hand. "Well, it works better than I expected. I simply thought of all of you and, well… here I am!" He smiled at all of them. His blonde hair stood up in wild tufts and his dark eyes were wide with excitement. "Not too late, I hope," he breathed. "I went to the bridge, but I suspect I was too early. I figured the column of smoke must have something to do with you all. Did I miss the action?"

"Not yet," Kiernan shot out his arm and latched onto the mage. And before Talesin could move to stop him, the prince snatched the key from Devon's hand.

"Kiernan, no!" Dagmar shouted. Talesin dove for him, but the prince had already disappeared.

"Dammit!" Nemesio cursed.

"Where did he go?" Panas asked, finally catching up to them.

Dagmar shook her head as she ran to the end of the alleyway looking up and down the empty street.

Talesin, meanwhile, was glowering at the mage. "Perfect timing," he hissed. "As usual."

Devon plunged his hands into the sleeves of his robes, looking ashamed. "How was I supposed to know that the Prince of the Light Elves was as much of a thief as the Captain?!"

Talesin grabbed Devon by the collar and drove his back into the wall. "Why didn't you just read his mind and figure it out, eh?" Talesin sneered.

"I'm sorry!" Devon shouted.

Nemesio placed a hand on the ice elf's shoulder, and Talesin loosed the shaking mage.

Devon straightened himself. "If it helps any, I think I know where he is going."

Talesin rounded on Devon. "We know too, you fool," the ice elf hissed.

"The bridge. But why?" Panas finished.

Devon swallowed. "Well, if Odin knows he is finished, he will try to destroy anything else that could incriminate him."

Nemesio blew out a breath. "He means to take out the bridge."

Talesin's black eyes widened. He spun about to make a grab for the wild elf, already knowing he was too late. "Dagmar!" Talesin called to her.

But Dagmar was out of earshot. She was already running far ahead, hoping she would catch the prince before Odin Darweshi did.

42~Odin Undone

Kiernan Nightwing rematerialized at the base of the bridge.

It was dark here, the moon partially obscured by the gray clouds that had crept in. Kiernan suddenly felt very dizzy. That little jaunt through the magical airwaves with Devon's silver key had shaken his head badly. He could not quite clear the heavy feeling from it, and his vision had gone blue about the edges.

He put a hand on the metal piling before him to steady himself. His right arm had gone completely dead, but at least for the moment it was free of pain. It concerned the prince only slightly that he had lost feeling in that limb. His mind was now focused on how he would catch up to the slippery merchant without the use of his sword arm.

It now seemed ridiculous, to be here on his own. But his friends would waste time ensuring his safety while Odin escaped. Kiernan was too furious with himself to let that happen. He was going to stop Odin Darweshi even if it meant his own death. Or Odin's.

He looked up. Odin was right above him. He could see the man's feet shuffling about up there. It was not going to be easy climbing with one hand, but that would be the best way to sneak up on the merchant. In five minutes, Kiernan would be on the bridge. Then they would see who lived through the night.

Kiernan took a breath and started to climb.

— ✸ ✸ ✸ —

Odin Darweshi was sweating. He mopped his brow with one red sleeve and continued to drag the large box of black powder across the wooden scaffolding. There was no one left in the warehouse at this late hour. The remaining S'Trobenue idiots had run off as soon as they realized how much trouble they were in. Odin had been forced to push and pull four heavy boxes out to the bridge by himself.

Odin had lost a beat or two these last couple of hours. His normally well-groomed black hair had fallen in sweaty strands about his round face. His clothes, the red velvet tunic and leggings, were smeared with dirt and sweat. His cape had come off altogether. Odin could not remember where he had dropped it. A new look had come into Odin's eyes—a sort of crazed light that would not be dimmed by the current tribulations that assailed him.

The mage had deserted him, he knew. If LaRante had wanted to, he could have appeared at Nimbus. He could have magicked Odin away, saving him from the chaos that followed Kiernan Nightwing's entrance.

Darweshi had not expected that the Prince of the Light Elves would turn out to be the leader of *Duak-Thenal* any more than the Council had.

But LaRante had known.

The night Raymond had disappeared, the damned mage had known then. It was the prince who had joined the imp in spiriting away Edmee S'Trobenue's husband—and that bastard LaRante had known all along! That was one secret the mage had kept from Odin, something to hold over the merchant's head should something go wrong.

And things had gone wrong, hadn't they?

Odin hadn't meant to kill Alistair. He had given in to a brash response to an embarrassing situation—and he felt no remorse over it. Still, in retrospect, it had been a bad move. Had he exercised a little more self-restraint, Odin might have saved his endeavors. Now it was impossible. He had to destroy it all and get out of town before March could figure out where he had gone.

The entire smuggling ring was destroyed. Jinin was dead. The rest of his gang might as well be. Odin expected the elves had made short work of them, or he would have heard from them by now. No matter. At least there was no one left who could make things worse for him.

Odin sputtered and cursed all the way to the scaffolding. This was the last batch of black powder, the one thing LaRante had given Odin that would be of any use now. He was going to blow the bridge to the heavens of Ziyad, and he would take as much of his father's warehouse with it as he could.

Odin reached into his pocket and pulled out a piece of flint. He lifted one booted heel and smashed the wooden box at his feet. The crate cracked easily, and Odin Darweshi turned and struck the flint on the edge of the metal rail beside him. It caught immediately and he backed away from the boxes, raising his arm to throw it.

A stunning blow to his shoulder collapsed him to the wooden planks, the flame falling through the cracks and into the black water below.

Odin froze as a figure clambered up the side of the unfinished bridge, clumsy yet strangely silent. The merchant locked his fist around the hilt of his sword, but he did not get up, instead waiting for his silent attacker to show himself.

"Hello, murderer."

The voice was known to Odin, though he had only recently become acquainted with it. The merchant laughed mirthlessly. "Didn't think it would take you this long to find me." He watched the leather-booted feet of the light elf move around him.

"I was delayed by a friend of yours."

Odin raised an eyebrow and dared to look up. Bright green eyes glared down at him with fierce intensity, and for a moment Odin thought he was finished. This royal elf had most certainly come here to kill him.

Then Odin's eyes drifted downward. The elf's entire right side was severely burnt. His arm had been hastily wrapped in a brown cloth, but Odin could guess that the limb had been scorched as well. He was standing in a sort of stoop, leaning slightly to favor his right side.

The elf had indeed been delayed, and Odin quickly guessed by whom. His injuries had a wizard's touch about them.

So, the mage had not deserted him completely, after all.

Odin stood cautiously. "Yes, I see that you have met LaRante."

The elf raised one eyebrow. "Is that his name, then? He declined to give it to me."

Odin cursed himself for the slip. Still, giving the mage's name could not matter much now, as their relationship was about to be over.

Just as soon as Odin got rid of this last problem.

The merchant moved slowly, laying his hand on the hilt of his weapon. He froze again when the tip of an elven sword came free of its sheath and lay at his throat.

The elf was clearly right-handed, for his scabbard hung from his left side. It was his sword arm that was injured. Odin had not expected the elf to be able to use his opposite hand so deftly. He had not even seen the elf reach for his weapon.

"If you think I came to fight you, you are mistaken." The elf's green eyes were glassy with pain, but they held no less conviction. "There is to be no battle—only a quick execution."

Odin tried to think fast but the dark blade inching its way nearer his face hampered his brain. "You don't have the authority to carry out the rogue justice of which you speak!" Odin stammered. "Besides, do you think anyone back at Nimbus will thank you for what you've done?"

The elf prince hesitated, so Odin stumbled on. "You are still an outlaw here. Anything you do to me, no matter how right or wrong, will still be considered a crime in Preliona's eyes." The edge of the elf's blade dropped. "What will the Council say when they find you have taken the law into your own hands? What will Commander March say?"

The sword fell away completely. Odin found himself breathing again, though the hard eyes of the elf remained fixed on him. The merchant knew he was not out of danger yet.

"You will come back with me to Nimbus," he said.

Odin smiled and tried to look grateful. "Thank you, Your Highness, thank you. You won't regret this."

The elf did not return the smile. "I believe in this one instance you may be right, Darweshi. I will be doing the commander no favors by killing you this day." The elf leaned into him. "I believe she wants that honor for herself."

Odin flinched.

That reaction finally got a smile from the serious elf. "Move," he hissed.

Odin raised his hands away from his body as the prince's sword came near him again. He turned about slowly and began to walk from the bridge. "Nothing good will come of it, you know," Odin began reaching for his sleeve.

"Come of what?" the elf asked.

"My arrest, of course. The bridge will never be finished now," Odin said.

"You built it out of scrap metal, Odin," the elf sneered from behind him. "Even had you finished it, the structure would have collapsed."

"Perhaps," Odin shrugged. "But the town would have had its bridge, for better or worse. Now they have nothing, and they have you to blame for it." Odin closed his hand around another small piece of flint and drew it forth. Before the prince could answer him, Odin reached out and struck the piece against the rail.

— ✹ ✹ ✹ —

Too late, Kiernan saw the spark of flame in the merchant's palm. He lunged for him, sliced at Odin's arm. But the merchant had already thrown the fire.

The prince turned and dove for the sailing ball of flame. He reached up with his sword and knocked it from the air with the tip. It landed on the wood of the bridge, still burning and only a few feet from the box of black powder.

The prince landed on the bridge, sprawled on his stomach, and hissing in pain when the unforgiving wood chafed the length of his injured arm. Grimacing, he moved his free hand to flatten the flaming flint.

Odin's booted heel came down on the back of his hand.

Kiernan yanked his hand free, but not before Odin caught the elf's chin with his opposite foot. Kiernan rolled with the hit and came up, weaponless but ready to fight.

But Odin pressed hard when he had the advantage. He gave the prince no time to recover. He came at Kiernan with one meaty shoulder, barreling into him.

Kiernan fell back and grabbed onto a cable support with his injured hand. He could not help crying out, so blinding was the pain. Odin pressed into him, determined to squash the prince against the braces or force him over the side. Kiernan pushed the heel of his free hand into Odin's chin, forcing the man's head back, but Odin did not give an inch and instead dug his fingers into the charred flesh at the prince's shoulder.

Kiernan gritted his teeth to keep from screaming. He felt his grip on the merchant's jaw loosening. His eyes were rolling back into his head, despite his desperate attempts to hold onto consciousness. He felt the bite of the wooden crossbeams at the small of his back. Odin was pushing him right over the edge. Kiernan felt his last ounce of strength running out of him like water.

I'm dying, he thought, *squeezed to death by an oversized, corrupt, murderous merchant.* Kiernan kept pushing back, even as his focus on the man blurred around the edges. He felt his feet slipping and he scrambled to keep his balance.

"You make this too easy for me, Your Highness," Odin grunted. "I half expected your meddling crew to come around the corner."

Kiernan had expected their arrival before now himself. Perhaps they were angry at his actions and were at last abandoning him to his own foolishness. It would serve him right if they did. If he had not deigned to trust them to finish the job they had started, then perhaps he did not deserve to lead them at all.

Odin pressed forward again, intending to topple the prince. This time Kiernan went limp and sank to the floorboards, slipping out of Odin's grasp and forcing the merchant to fall forward, a victim of his own weight. Gasping for air, the prince dove to the side of Odin's stumbling legs and made a grab for his fallen sword. But the merchant spun about and hooked a foot under the prince's fleeing ankles kicking him onto his back.

Odin barreled toward him, arms outstretched, but the prince lifted both feet and landed them into the merchant's large stomach. Odin doubled over, cursing and sputtering, but he did not go down.

Kiernan dove left and pushed himself to his knees as Odin came at him again. He stumbled to his feet and stepped back. He let his right foot fly and felt it connect with the man's jaw. Odin fell back but recovered quickly. Kiernan had time to block Odin's oncoming fist, but with the use of only one hand the prince could not hit back, and he was not quick enough to avoid Odin's next attack.

The merchant clasped his hands together and landed a two-fisted blow to Kiernan's injured shoulder just as the prince kicked at the merchant's knees.

Both combatants fell away from each other, Odin howling in rage and Kiernan collapsing to the floorboards, again nearly losing consciousness despite his best efforts. He closed his eyes and clasped his shoulder with his left hand, biting his lip until it bled. The pain in his arm was so severe that Kiernan could focus on nothing else. He pressed his forehead into the cool wood of the bridge floor, forgetting for a moment that a murderous madman was still conscious and intent on killing him. For a moment he could not even remember where he was. He barely registered the two large hands digging into his back and it wasn't until he felt his own feet leave the ground that he was jolted into fighting back. By then it was too late.

Odin Darweshi threw the Prince of the Light Elves over the side of the bridge.

— ✵ ✵ ✵ —

Just as Dagmar was starting to think that there would be no end to the blackened buildings, the scorched alley pitched downward, heading toward the water at the base of the bridge.

Talesin was in the lead again. When he suddenly stopped, slipping on the muddy consistency of sand and dirt, Dagmar barreled into him. The two elves grabbed at each other, awkwardly trying to keep from falling. Dagmar hung onto Talesin's shoulder and looked up at his face, intending to apologize, but the ice elf was not looking at her.

Dagmar followed his upturned gaze and caught a flicker of movement above, on the floorboards of the unfinished bridge. She took a tentative step forward, trying to peer through the metal railings twenty feet above her head. A shuffling sound caught her ears. She waited with bated breath for another sign of movement from above.

She did not wait long.

A flash of red and Odin Darweshi's massive form came into view. She saw the merchant heave his arms. Her breath caught in her throat as Kiernan Nightwing was lifted into the air and thrown over the rail.

Dagmar surged forward, not knowing what she intended to do and half expecting the ice elf to hold her back. They both skidded down the sandy bottom of the embankment Dagmar reaching back with the other for her crossbow.

Even before Dagmar had shouldered her weapon, Kiernan saved himself from the deadly fall. He managed to latch onto the ledge with his left arm, the right hanging uselessly at his side. But Odin wasn't finished. He lifted his booted heel and brought it crashing down on the prince's knuckles.

Kiernan cried out and Dagmar fired her weapon.

The first arrow embedded itself into the metal support inches from Odin's ear. He jumped back. The second caught him in the shoulder. Darweshi howled as his black eyes fell on Dagmar. The wild elf felt a stab of fear. Odin Darweshi had killed Alistair. He was trying to kill the prince. And the way he looked at Dagmar now, it was clear he wanted to kill her too.

Dagmar kept her crossbow aimed at the merchant's head. If he lifted his boot again, she would kill him herself, Commander March be damned.

But Odin was apparently done for the moment. He ducked out of sight, cursing loudly.

She wanted to go after him, but the prince was losing his grip. Frantic, she turned to see that Talesin was already swimming out into the lake; ready to dive for Kiernan should he fall into the water. She looked over her shoulder at Panas and Nemesio, who were both standing at the bottom of the scaffolding looking up.

She caught their eyes and nodded to them. Without hesitation they began the climb.

Dagmar spun on her heel and ran up the embankment to cut off Darweshi.

With nothing but the life of the prince on her mind, she had completely forgotten about Devon Bane.

— ✻ ✻ ✻ —

The mage, never a fast runner and hindered even more by his lengthy robes, did not catch up to the elves until all four had begun making their respective ways to the prince.

Talesin was wading into the water up to his neck and would soon be treading. Devon did not know what the ice elf intended to do. If Kiernan lost his grip, the fall into the water below might well kill him, in the condition he was in. All Talesin would succeed in doing would be to retrieve a body to present to the King of the Light Elves.

Nemesio and Panas were scaling the scaffolding of the unfinished bridge as fast as they could, but they were not even halfway to the prince. He would surely fall before they reached him.

Dagmar seemed to have the best chance. She had already shimmied up the steep embankment and was running for the bridge. She was in the best position to deal with Odin, but Devon could already see a problem.

From his new vantage point directly under the scaffolding, Devon could see the merchant. Odin had given up on torturing the prince. He was focused on breaking several large wooden crates. Devon squinted his eyes and peered more intently. Odin's foot came down repeatedly on the crates, cracking them and spewing forth black swirling dust.

The young mage had no idea what the black dust was, but the sinking feeling in the pit of his stomach did not bode well. He felt the intense need to strike out at Odin, but he dared not hit him with magic until he was sure what the man was up to.

He could think of only one thing to do.

Devon Bane closed his eyes and relaxed his body. His arms went limp at his sides and he let his head drop back as the now familiar floating sensation came over him. His inner self soared up and away from his body quickly passing over Kiernan and the bridge railing. He watched Odin Darweshi continue to strike at the wooden crates, still not comprehending what they meant.

He focused instead on Darweshi himself and suddenly the scene around him went blank. He felt a fiery, uncontrollable rage combined with a fierce panic.

Devon felt the urgency that the merchant was feeling, and tried hard not to get caught up in it. He felt the regret that Odin felt—not at having killed Alistair, but at having lost all he had plotted and planned for.

The mage desperately fought to push these feelings aside. He worked instead at finding out Odin's plans for the crates.

The merchant was not being helpful, for while Odin's mind was extremely easy to enter in his scattered state, he was also fast losing his sanity. His thoughts were maniacal and unfocused. Devon understood that whatever the merchant was doing was simply a cover for his escape. The man clearly saw himself as able to get out of the alarming situation he had placed himself in. It was all he was focused on.

Odin shifted his position and reached into his pocket. The cracking of the crates had mercifully stopped for the moment. Devon tried to get a feel for what the merchant was up to now.

The object Odin had pulled from his pocket was cold and dark. To Devon it looked like a rock, but being inside Odin's mind gave him a whole new perspective on things. He knew what that rock was.

Flint.

Confused, Devon looked from the rock to the crates of black dust, and back again. At the very same moment one thought rang out clearly in Odin Darweshi's mind. *Light the crates.*

Devon felt his own heart skip a beat. He rapidly pulled himself free of Odin's mangled brain and rocked back into his own head, feeling like he had just been punched repeatedly. The mage reeled with the impact of his mind meeting his own body, but he did not give himself the chance to recover. He opened his eyes and looked to Dagmar, marking her progress.

She was inches from the bridge. "No! He's going to blow the bridge!" he screamed, "Dagmar, the crates! Get away from the crates!"

He saw her hesitate, saw her look to the prince, who still clung to the side of the bridge in a half-conscious state. He knew before she took her next step that she would not stop. Even when Odin's laughter stung their ears, she did not stop.

Devon watched in horror as Odin Darweshi raised the flint over his head, intending to dash it on the crate edge.

Devon Bane spoke the first arcane words that came into his head. A spell of great power, to be sure, and one that Devon had spent weeks perfecting. It was also a spell that did not directly address the problem at hand. What he needed was a water spell to douse the fire that Odin intended to create. Or a spell that would concentrate a small blast of wind to blow out the flames.

Instead Devon spoke the words to the most complex spell he had ever attempted.

The mage's blonde hair blew about his face, heat emanated from his body and his breathing became quick and erratic. A jumble of words poured from his mouth faster than the nonsense of a crazed man.

And then the breeze around Odin's box began to slow.

The mage's chant became more intense. As his arms widened a ring of orange translucency ballooned out from the boxes.

Odin smashed his hand through the box and the wavering ring of magic, and the connection of the flint with the wooden box shot an immediate spark into the air.

But the effect was sluggish. Odin stepped back as his spark of fire first flew upward and then slowed to a crawl. Undeterred, not yet understanding that a spell had been cast, Odin Darweshi ran.

The explosion that followed was muffled by Devon's spell. Fire that would normally have traveled at lightening speed was reduced to something more like the glide of a small bird. Odin Darweshi could not outrun the orange bubble. He found himself encased in Devon's spell, caught by the ring, and slowed by its effects. He could barely move. Nothing he tried could make him go any faster.

A sound like a runaway train rolled toward Odin and the ground shook. The merchant glanced over his shoulder and screamed as the fire ballooned toward him. Dagmar just outside the bubble was thrown clear, literally pushed away by the slow-motion spell. Devon saw her body sail twenty feet through the air. She crashed into the wall of the warehouse and crumpled at its base. She did not get up.

The bridge itself, shaken to its core by the rumble of powerful magic, threw off its three hangers-on, plunging them into the black waters below.

Odin meanwhile was stuck. He tried to push through the orange bubble, but he could not. The explosion engulfed him. The fire licked at his body and ate at him more slowly than was natural. His screams were horrific and lasted far too long.

Devon slammed his hands over his ears and closed his mouth, cutting short the spell. He turned his head away from the awful scene he had created.

Kiernan Nightwing, as Devon had feared, sank below the surface of the water, too weak to swim. Talesin dove for him, but Devon could see that the ice elf was too far away. Panas and Nemesio swam toward the prince, searching the water with their keen eyes for the spot where the elf had gone down.

As he dropped to his knees in exhaustion, he could not help but think he had, once again, only succeeded in making things worse.

— ✳✳✳ —

Asleep in his bed aboard his barge, Calen Jase awoke with a scream. An explosion rocked the water around him. The barge bounced about violently. The architect was thrown from his bed in a tangle of sheets. He staggered to his feet and threw open the shutters.

Smoke, heavy and black, assaulted him. The architect gasped and sputtered as he peered through the burnt air.

The bridge was on fire.

What was left of it, anyway. Much of the structure had already sunk below the surface of Opal Lake. Scraps of metal, thrown with violent force, had embedded themselves into the wood of his barge. Still more pieces were floating nearby.

Calen was close enough to see what had happened and feel the effects of it, but he was too far away to make out any details or see if anyone nearby had survived. He knew with some certainty that *someone* had set off the explosion. The architect found that he did not much care who that someone was. At that moment he was sublimely relieved that his part in building this accursed bridge was over.

Without a backward glance, Calen Jase climbed back into his bed and fell asleep, free from nightmares for the first time in months.

— ✳ ✳ ✳ —

Running at top speed through the scorched alley, Gabrielle March was violently thrown off balance by the force of the explosion. Her body teetered to the left and her shoulder slammed into the nearest brick wall. Several of her followers were hurled to the ground. Many more grabbed at the blackened walls for support.

It was the second explosion to reach the commander's ears this night. The White Watch was currently standing in the middle of the devastation of the first. By the sound of it, the second was not far away.

This one was different, however. This second blast had been drawn out—longer and slower than the first had been, if that was possible—pulsing through the city in waves. A rolling thunder floated over them, forcing them all to cover their ears.

"What was *that*?" asked a soldier beside her.

Gabrielle shook her head and pushed herself away from the wall. She strode to the nearest corner, already knowing what she would see.

The bridge was on fire. Flames and black smoke shot into the sky, blotting out the moon.

In all likelihood *Duak-Thenal* was there. The commander would not be at all surprised if the elves had had a hand in the destruction.

She sighed as she realized that she would be relegated to cleanup detail, after all.

There would be no revenge for her.

Odin Darweshi was dead, of that she was certain. She could not say how she knew it, but she was sure that the merchant was no more. Dagmar Coal and the rest of *Duak-Thenal* had not kept their promise.

In a way, Gabrielle supposed she should be thankful. Things had spiraled out of control at an astronomical speed. Even the slippery elves could not prevent the devastating descent of this night. *Duak-Thenal*, if they were still alive, had done her a favor. Had she gotten her hands on the merchant, the new Watch Chief did not know what she might have done. If the merchant were in fact dead, it would at least spare her soldiers from seeing their commanding officer dole out unprofessional and bloody vengeance. Faced with Alistair's murderer, Gabrielle could not guarantee anything having to do with self-control. She would destroy the man before anyone else could get to him—and she would lose herself in the process.

No, it was better that the choice was taken from her.

She moved away from the alley wall and broke into a run, motioning the others to follow her. If the elves had not been incinerated in the blast, then the new Watch Chief intended to give them all the help they needed.

— ✻ ✻ ✻ —

Cornelius jumped at the sound of the blast that shook the floor of Nimbus. The wizard had just seen his dead comrade carried from the room and he was leaning heavily on the Council table.

Chaos still reigned here.

Council members stood or sat in various states of shock and disbelief. The S'Trobenue cousins were being hastily and forcibly removed from the room by what was left of the Watch. Healers had been sent for, of course, but for Alistair it was too late. Now the robed clerics wandered aimlessly about, searching for someone in need of their services.

Cornelius blocked all of this out. The noise, the tears, the confusion—all of this he managed to push far from his ears in favor of his own thoughts. Their troubles seemed small to him at that moment. The wizard now needed to search for a way to tell Althea that Alistair had been killed while she slept.

The explosion shook him from his reverie. The red glow shining through the windows sent him running from the hall out onto the terrace. From Nimbus the bridge was not visible, but it was clear to the wizard what had happened.

A fire lit the night sky, burning the black clouds orange. There were shouts of surprise and confusion all around him. Cornelius took no notice. His heart was pounding in his ears. He suddenly felt the air go out of his lungs.

The wizard of Preliona sat on the edge of the terrace steps and silently prayed for the lives of his friends, hoping against hope that he would bury only one friend on the morrow.

43~The Key~

Kiernan Nightwing hit the water with a stinging slap.

He was under the surface before he could draw a breath to hold. Immediately he began to cough, and the cold lake water poured into his mouth. He flailed about wildly, panic setting in. The metal bar from which he had been dangling moments before had followed him into the freezing lake. The heavy beam, blown from its bracers by the explosion, was wedged against his abdomen, sinking the prince like a stone to the bottom of the lake. His injured arm was dead weight at his side, useless. The rest of his body could not find the strength to swim around the beam.

Kiernan looked up at the rays of moonlight shining down, fracturing the water. The white circle was receding; soon it would be gone altogether. With his good arm, he heaved at the metal weight bearing down on him, but it would not budge.

Suddenly he saw a pale hand loom from the gloom and reach for him. Kiernan started at the sight of Talesin Darken swimming down through the lake water with all his strength. His friend's face had turned alabaster white in the cold of the lake. Not the normal pale fawn color he was used to. He stretched his hand out and grasped the prince's torn tunic. The shirt ripped in his cold hands and slipped from the ice elf's fingers.

Then Kiernan felt his body collide with the sandy floor of the lake. The beam pinned him down. He couldn't move. Even as Talesin wrapped his icy fingers about the metal, the prince knew he would never be able to budge it.

Kiernan watched the ice elf struggle and vehemently shook his head. He motioned Talesin away, but the stubborn ice elf refused to leave. And he was out of air. He put a finger up to Kiernan's face, asking him to wait a minute then he swam for the surface.

Kiernan should have been panicked to see him go, but he was not. His body was relaxing against his will. The pain in his arm was diminishing and his head felt light. His eyes stayed open though his body was falling asleep. He was calm, watching small fish float above him -- bright little specks of color zipping through the waning light of the moon.

He was drowning. He knew this, but the confirmation did not upset him as badly as he might have thought it would. The lake bottom was soft, the pressure of the beam on his chest almost comforting.

Talesin would not make it back in time. And even if he did, what could he do?

He would miss the ice elf. He would miss them all, he thought drowsily, as water filled his lungs.

Especially Dagmar.

With a shock wave of renewed fear, he realized he had not seen what had happened to the wild elf. She had been close by when the explosion went off. Odin surely had been engulfed by the fire, but Dagmar had not been far away. What if she was hurt… or dead?

Kiernan wanted to move now but he no longer could. Talesin was not coming back. The prince's eyes were closing against his will. *He would not see her again.*

His arms drifted away from his body and just before his eyes closed, he caught sight of a bright flash of blue and silver dangling from his wrist.

The key.

In the commotion he had completely forgotten about it.

He focused all his attention on his hands and when they floated together and touched, he gripped the cold metal of the key between his fingers.

He touched the stone and thought of Dagmar.

― ❋ ❋ ❋ ―

Devon Bane was exhausted and terribly distraught. He watched through half-lidded eyes as Panas and Talesin repeatedly dived below the water in search of their fallen friend. Torn metal dangled from the charred remains of the bridge and flaming wood pilings floated all around them.

Devon could not help them. Even had he known a spell to lift a body from the water, he did not have the energy to cast it. He remained on his knees at the sandy base of the hill where he had landed minutes before. He could not move. He could scarcely breathe.

A movement from above gave him a start and he glanced up.

Nemesio was carrying an unconscious Dagmar down the incline. She was bleeding profusely from a nasty gash at her temple and her hair was matted to her face with the blood. Nemesio himself was struggling with fatigue. He was drenched and his cheek and left arm were cut and bleeding. He slipped as he reached the base of the hill and stumbled to his knees. He gripped the wild elf to him, careful not to let her fall.

Devon found the strength to move. He crawled forward as Nemesio laid Dagmar on the ground. She did not wake and Devon, suddenly afraid, reached out and pressed two fingers to the side of her neck.

He felt a strong beat under the pads of his fingers and bowed his head in relief.

Still, pleased as he was that Dagmar lived, he could not rejoice. He had not killed the wild elf with his spell, but he had certainly done some damage. And the prince…

Nearly three minutes had passed since the bridge had blown. The prince had not resurfaced. By his count, Talesin and Panas had each come to the surface twice now, without the prince in tow.

Devon hung his head in despair, rubbed his eyes with one hand. It was his fault. He should have tried something else.

The churning surface of the water broke as Panas' blonde head cut through the waves again. He was gasping for air, but he sank below the surface again, too tired to keep paddling. Talesin shot up beside him, took a giant gulp of air and dove back beneath the surface. Panas tried to do the same but he began to cough and sputter. Nemesio hauled himself to his feet and lumbered toward the water, ready to dive in after Panas the Hawk. Devon moved to follow him, wanting desperately to help, when a blinding blue flash of light went off near his head.

The mage hit the ground in a heap, covering his head and Dagmar's to protect the unconscious elf from whatever came next. His exhausted body tensed, and his frantic mind searched for the words to any spell that might come to mind. Surely Odin's secret mage had come at last to finish them off, and Devon did not have the strength to defeat him.

He uncovered his head, fully expecting to meet with a power greater than his own.

He was shocked to behold a very wet Kiernan Nightwing lying on the ground near him. His charred arm had gone white with cold. His face was paler than Talesin's. His hands were clenched together and folded near his chest, as if he held his own heart in its place.

And he was not moving.

Shocked as he was, Devon managed to find his voice. "Nemesio!" he yelled. "It's him! It's Kiernan, he's here!"

Devon did not know whether the southern elf heard him. He did not look up. He crawled instead toward the unconscious leader of *Duak-Thenal*.

He was not breathing. Devon could see that before he laid a hand on the prince's throat. Not waiting for the others to join him and unsure if he was doing the right thing; Devon Bane turned the unconscious elf onto his back, tilted his head back and offered up a prayer to *Ziyad* as he tried to breathe life into the prince's blue lips. Devon pushed all the air from his own lungs and sat back. He leaned into the prince's face, listening for some sign of life. There was none.

Nemesio raced back to the mage and stumbled to his side. He gripped Devon's shoulder as the mage sat back. Devon shook off the southern elf's hand and leaned over Kiernan's inert form again. "Breathe, dammit," he hissed as he took another breath.

Nemesio sat by his side, too exhausted and nervous to do anything but watch.

At the same time Talesin was dragging himself from the depths of Opal Lake, carrying a bedraggled Panas the Hawk with him. The two collapsed near Nemesio, watching intently as their young human friend worked to save their leader's life.

Devon ignored them all and clasped his hands together. He placed them on the prince's chest and pressed down violently. Again, and again he pushed down on the elf's sternum until his arms went numb and he felt his shoulders scream under the pressure.

Just when he thought his efforts might prove useless, that he had failed, Kiernan coughed.

The prince sucked in a giant gasp of air and sat up so quickly that Devon fell back into Nemesio with a cry of surprise. Kiernan fell into a coughing fit that doubled him over.

Nemesio patted Devon on the shoulder and crawled forward. Talesin joined him. Together they caught hold of Kiernan's shaking body, helped him to sit as he expelled the rest of the lake's water from his lungs. Finally, he leaned back, Talesin and Nemesio still supporting him. He gripped one hand in the other, holding onto something, it seemed. His eyes fluttered, open bright with shock and cold, focusing on the mage. "Dagmar?" he whispered.

Devon nodded his head. "She's fine. Fine." The mage shook off his outer robe and hastily wrapped it about the prince's shaking form as Nemesio gripped the prince's frigid hands in his own and began to rub them furiously, trying to restore some circulation.

"Your Highness, how did you…"

The prince unclenched his hands to reveal a dripping silver key on a fraying silken cord.

Devon mouth dropped open. He stared at the prince in astonishment. "*Ziyad's blood* -- the key," he whispered, closing his eyes and shaking his head. "Of course."

The prince coughed again and fell forward onto his hands. Nemesio hit him on the back a few times and Talesin held his shoulders to keep the prince from falling face first into the dirt.

Devon waited for Kiernan to get his breath. The light elf was fading fast. In the mage's estimation, he had been incredibly lucky to survive at all. He would be luckier still to keep the arm that now dangled uselessly at his side. Devon sighed in frustration. He hadn't caused the damage to the elf's arm and side, but he certainly felt responsible for his near death. Allowing the elf to steal the key from his hand had been foolish and naïve. But in the end, it had saved his life.

Devon crawled toward him on tentative hands. He reached out and took the prince's arm and gently, carefully removed the silken ribbon.

The prince looked up, freezing Devon in his tracks midway to returning the key to his pocket. Green eyes, shiny now with fever, locked onto Devon's and held them fast. For a brief moment the mage thought he was in danger. The elf was not himself. He seemed suddenly angry at Devon for taking the key from him.

Just as suddenly the flash of anger melted away. The prince blinked and rubbed at his tired eyes with his good hand.

Devon sighed in relief. "I'll just keep this safe for you, if you don't mind—Your Highness."

Kiernan nodded weakly. "I have no more need of it, mage," he breathed. "It saved my life once. I do not believe it will again. I would much rather rely on my friends." And now he looked pointedly at Devon.

"Me?" Devon was surprised. "Your Highness, I nearly killed you myself. I am the reason you had to use the key."

Kiernan shook his head. "No, Devon. If it were not for you, we would all have been killed. You saw what Odin was about to do… and, well… whatever you did, it saved us all."

Devon was stunned. He had expected the prince to be angry, at the very least indifferent. Surely Talesin would be itching to do some damage to him. Instead the ice elf gave him a nod of appreciation and continued to attend to the prince's wounds.

He wanted to express his thanks to the prince. He wanted to say something, anything. But at that moment a sharp shout from above caused them all to turn and look up the incline. Gabrielle March was sliding down the steep hill, followed by a dozen or so soldiers with their swords drawn.

Devon took one look at the commander's stern face and knew that *Duak-Thenal*'s excursion into the city of Preliona was over. Thank yous would have to wait.

44~The Blessing

The storm was slow in coming. Black and purple clouds drifted over the city. They lingered about, low and distended, for half a day until finally, bursting with moisture, they dumped their contents onto a city in mourning. Bloated drops of rain splattered the white and gray cobblestones, soaking everything in a matter of seconds. The citizens of the city hardly noticed. Windows remained open despite the howling wind, candles fought to stay alive. Animals found shelter on their own, forgotten by their masters.

The funeral was over before the worst of the storm started. Lingering mourners hung about the gravesite anyway, too overwhelmed with grief to leave. Alistair Kellen Keene was dead. The city he had protected for more than fifty years would never be the same.

Thousands had come to Breckenwreck Island for the service. At the center of Opal Lake, the graveyard was not overly spacious, and many had been turned away. Those who could afford to do so circled Breckenwreck in boats and barges. Hundreds more stood on the shore holding a myriad of candles, which had to be relit continually to keep pace with the blustery weather.

Governor Gaenor, recently revived from her devastating magical attack, gave the eulogy. It was short but reverent. All assembled agreed that the late Watch Chief would have approved. Alistair, the only name the dead man was truly known by, had lived as he died: with precision.

As many had already heard, the Watch Chief had used his last breaths to bequeath his title to Commander Gabrielle March. Alistair's second-in-command, though clearly grief-stricken by the death of her mentor and friend, had made the somber occasion a truly fitting memorial. Silvery flags draped the white granite headstone. Banks of white and silver lilies surrounded the shining black coffin. She had placed the Watch Chief's sword alongside his body before closing the coffin. Anyone standing near her may have heard the softest of sobs—but they would never tell.

Cornelius Pav was there, as well. He stood extremely near Preliona's recovered matriarch. Most funeral attendants would later attest that the mage had wiped his eyes more than once, even accepting a handkerchief from Althea herself.

Overall, it was a lovely service. Those who made it home before the downpour began were thankful. Those unfortunate enough to be caught in it shuttled their families along, but at no faster a pace than necessary. And any of Preliona's citizens still riding the barges, knowing that there was no shelter anywhere close by, made no attempt to keep dry. Instead they watched the island of Breckenwreck with welling eyes. Many saw the white robes of Althea Gaenor and Cornelius Pav. They saw the sorcerer look up to the sky—and possibly they followed his gaze.

Some may have even seen the small silver ray of light breaking through the black clouds, a light that magically shone upon the gravesite of Alistair Kellen Keene, catching it in a radiance that sparkled across the dark water of the lake.

Later, most would swear that it was a trick of the light. Still others could be counted on to lay blame on the wizard—a final spell cast by a mourning friend to memorialize Alistair's passing.

But one or two souls of Preliona, people who usually kept their thoughts to themselves, would speak of revelations. That day, they said, a day when the clouds in their hearts were as black as those in the sky, a ray of light had broken through from above. A goddess had smiled on their poor dead Watch Chief. A goddess of earthly warmth coaxed aside the stormy clouds, allowing the sun to shine down. This particular goddess rarely made her presence known to those in Tearlach. But when she did, it was counted as the greatest of blessings, and not to be taken lightly.

When those honored with the vision of the goddess spoke of the sight, none questioned them. From that day on, beloved Alistair was spoken of with as much reverence as the goddess who had chosen to honor him. And when the men and women of the Watch regaled each other with tales of his adventures, the story always ended with the same sentence. "*Abbelony smiled.*"

45~The Dwarf Lord Makes His Rounds

Venk Darkwater hated waiting.

And by his count this was the third time this day he had had to do so.

The first time was at the front gate, waiting to gain admittance to the bereaved city. The guards there were checking things more thoroughly than usual, and as a result the line was long and slow. Venk was hopping mad by the time it was his turn to have his cart, bags and papers examined.

"Took ya long enough, eh, boyos?" Venk barked at the two young men who examined his papers. Both ignored the dwarf, which only made him angrier. Without a confrontation, Venk had been forced to grumble to no one in particular as he made his way to Cornelius's tower.

After a brief meeting with the wizard and a look at the injured members of his team, the dwarf encountered his second wait of the day—at the front gate of Dawn Tower, for an audience with Watch Chief Gabrielle March.

Now in charge of the Watch, the young woman was charged with repairing much of the damage done by Odin Darweshi. Understandably, the new Watch Chief was under a lot of pressure. Venk could not fault her too much for the wait he had endured to see her.

He was not an impatient dwarf by nature. He could bide his time as well as an elf, if need be. But being brushed aside and put off more than once in a day was something the Lord of Breezeway was unaccustomed to.

So it was that he met the new Watch Chief with more bluster and less charm than he would normally afford such a personage.

Gabrielle March sat behind a battered and worn desk, hunched over a staggering pile of parchment. Had she been shorter, Venk may not have seen her at all.

He had been in this office only once before. Today's visit brought back memories of a time when burdens were lighter. Venk had gotten himself thrown out of no less than three bars in Preliona that night. A much younger Alistair had let him sleep it off under his black desk. The dwarf did not remember the incident fondly—the uncomfortable floor, even less.

Now the former Commander March sat in Alistair's place. Venk found himself wondering how this girl felt filling the old man's shoes.

"Afternoon, Commander," he huffed.

"One moment," came the brusque reply.

Hardly the welcome Venk had hoped for. It took all the control the oversized dwarf could muster to keep from howling curses to the gods. He sighed instead. "Forgive me for sayin' so, Commander, but I been waitin' o'er an hour now, an' one more minute is one too many."

March peeked over the top of her papers with a scowl. But she smoothed her features over when she saw who had barreled his way into her office. She stood quickly and Venk fought the urge to take a step back. Alistair's second in command was shockingly tall for a human girl, and lean for her considerable height—though not as willowy as Dagmar.

That she could wield the wide weapon strapped to her side Venk did not doubt, for he could easily see the curve of her muscles through the worn gray material of her uniform.

That uniform, he noticed, was still adorned with the triple white stripes of commander. Either the young woman had not had time to make the switch to the Watch Chief insignia, or she simply could not yet bring herself to.

Judging from the drawn and tired expression on her face, Venk suspected it was the latter. The dwarf knew the Commander to be less than thirty years of age, yet she appeared much older to him at this moment. He had the impression that she was indeed attractive. The brown wave of short hair normally combed back from her face was hanging unkempt in her dark eyes, eyes that were puffy and red-rimmed. Her uniform, though pressed and clean, was an old one. Venk suspected her usual attire was out being laundered, as by all reports it had been covered in Alistair's blood.

She was grieving, that much was obvious. But that did not stop her from going about her business with as much poise as she could muster.

"My apologies, Lord Darkwater," she said. "What can I do for you?"

Her tone suggested she wished to do nothing for anyone. Venk smiled briefly. "Don't mean ta bother ya, Commander. I know ya got a lot on yer mind right now."

She came around the desk, straightening her uniform and holding out one long-fingered, calloused hand to him. "Not at all, my Lord. Alistair spoke very highly of you. I am honored by your presence." She spoke with forced politeness. Little feeling accompanied her words. Though she was smiling, her expression did not extend to her eyes. They remained hard and flat.

Venk took the extended hand, impressed by her firm grip. "Ya might not feel all that honored when ya hear what I've come fer."

The ex-commander raised one brown eyebrow. "What might that be, sir?"

Venk cleared his throat, suddenly a bit nervous. "Right, then," he began. "I'll get right to it. The coins," he said simply. "I'll be needin' 'em back."

Gabrielle March leaned forward, her mouth dropping open. "I'm sorry?" she said.

Venk cleared his throat again. "Those gold pieces with the X's carved into 'em. I'd like 'em back."

March looked incredulous. She gazed at the dwarf as though he had just asked for her hand in marriage. "I am sorry, my Lord," she managed to say as she picked her way back to her desk. "The coins you speak of are evidence."

Venk followed her, moving to the front of her desk, and straining to see over the top. "If ya don't mind me askin', Commander—evidence of what?" Gabrielle snapped her head back to him but Venk went on. "*Duak-Thenal* has been disbanded and its members cleared of all charges. Yer case against 'em is closed. And those gold pieces belong ta me."

"I don't believe you understand proper procedure in this city, Lord Darkwater," March began, trying to override the dwarf.

"I understand all I need ta, Chief." The use of the new title made March flinch, but Venk pressed on, undeterred. "You got what belongs ta me, and ya got no cause ta hold it."

"My investigation is not over," she insisted.

"As far as *Duak-Thenal's* involvement goes, it is." Venk leaned forward and spoke more gently. "And I think you're holdin' on ta somethin' for the memory of a man ya held dear ta ya."

The dwarf watched in some alarm as the new chief's face went white with anger. She gritted her teeth and glared down at him over the end of her nose. She seemed about to explode. Again, Venk checked the urge to back up.

Slowly she got herself under control. She breathed deeply and closed her eyes. "I don't suppose you have a letter from Gregory Sweep with the governor's handwritten permission on it?"

Venk shook his head. "Nope. But if that's what ya want, then I'll be sure ta get it when I see her next."

March sighed and sank into her chair. "No," she said, defeated. "Do not bother her. She has enough to worry about."

Venk opened his arms in a gesture of complacency. "As do you."

March shot him a glare as she bent over her desk and reached into one of its many littered drawers. She pulled out two small cloth bags and tossed them across the desk.

Feeling slightly guilty, the dwarf lord emptied them into his hands. The contents of the first sack shone the dark honey color of dwarven gold. Venk held one up to the light and smiled. "Ah there ya are, my dears," he said, and stuffed them into his pockets. The second bag, which was much heavier, was filled to the brim with the lighter yellow gold of Malhuria. Venk rubbed at the scratched surface of one of the Malhurian coins and shook his head. That little piece of counterfeiting had caused a lot of trouble.

Venk closed the purse and tossed it back onto the desk. "Do what you want with the counterfeit ones," he said. "Perhaps if ya have not yet dismantled that machine of Darweshi's, you could use it ta melt these down."

"And start my own counterfeiting business?" March asked icily. "I think not."

Venk shrugged. "Oh I dunno… you couldn't do any worse a job then anyone else has."

March had her head in one hand and was looking at him sideways.

Venk backed away with a shrug. "Or perhaps a donation to a local charity?"

"Good day, my Lord," March said, dismissing him.

"Just a thought," he said. When he reached the door he turned back. "Nice to meet ya, Chief. Hope we can do business again soon."

"That day will be too soon for me, Lord Darkwater."

This made the dwarf chuckle. Venk let the door fall shut behind him. He felt sorry for the young woman, to be sure. But the gold was his, after all, and he certainly had more use for it than the former Commander of the White Watch did.

He reviewed the meeting now as he wandered the empty halls of Nimbus. Once again, he was kept waiting outside the main hall, this time by a nervous-looking young scribe who seemed more fit to be poring over tomes in the library than guarding a door.

Venk stopped pacing. The bells in the Coral District were ringing, reminding the dwarf that a full hour had passed. Growling under his breath, Venk unclasped his meaty hands from behind his back. Then, sizing up the youth at the door, he stormed across the marble floor and burst into the main hall of Nimbus, ignoring the cries of protest that followed him.

The main hall seemed to have lost some of its luster since Venk's last visit. Daylight shot through the skylights of the great white marble room.

But the glorious morning light could not burn away the deep anguish and oppressive emotions that lingered in the hall.

The dwarf did not possess the sensitive feelings of his elven friends, but it did not take an elf to sense the grief and sorrow emanating from the walls of Nimbus. The death of Alistair was a devastating blow to the city of Preliona. Venk understood that a few days' passage had done little to quell the misery that was universally felt.

The room was nearly empty of occupants, making the dwarf seethe afresh with resentment at the time he had wasted in the outer hall. Two people were seated at the marble moon-shaped table, both of whom Venk recognized, though he had never been introduced.

One was an elfish-looking male dressed in long gray robes, much like the scribe who had run in behind him. The other was a slouching older gentleman wearing an eclectic array of frayed black clothing that matched his rather rumpled appearance.

They stopped their heated whispering upon the dwarf's entrance.

Venk knew he was in the presence of Gregory Sweep, Althea's personal assistant and Council member. The other was Xanith Creese, Master of the Theatre Guild and ambassador to Lasairian. He had come by his knowledge through descriptions Cornelius and the members of *Duak-Thenal* had given over the years. He did not wish to appear too informed, so he feigned ignorance at the sight of them.

"Who the abyss are you?" he asked.

Xanith Creese dropped his feet onto the ground from the table they were resting on and regarded the dwarf with a raised eyebrow.

The elf, or more to the point the half-elf, as the young man was too short and had eyes much too round to be full-blooded anything, was more appropriately startled and backed up a step.

"Well, I usually know the answer to that question," Xanith said, leaning back and crossing his arms with a bemused smile. "But I must say in light of your rather surly and untimely entrance, I have quite forgotten my own name. Why don't you tell us yours while we collect ourselves?"

Venk was not amused. He bristled and took several heavy strides forward. "Name's Darkwater. One a you lot called me here, an' I been waitin' o'er an hour for an audience. Now, if nobody around here wants ta see me, that's fine—but I got better things ta do with my time than hang about yer shiny hallways."

The half-elf now came quickly around the table, fairly tripping over his robes to reach the dwarf. "My sincerest apologies, Lord Darkwater," he stammered, much to Venk's amusement. "I'm afraid I was unaware of your arrival. Things here have been rather hectic of late."

Venk eyed the young scribe. "I'll bet they have."

The half-elf smiled with some effort and stuck out a long, thin hand. "Gregory Sweep," he said. "This is Xanith Creese."

The elder councilmen did not get up at the introduction, only nodded politely and continued to smile at the angry dwarf.

"You all that's left of the Council?" Venk asked.

"I am afraid so," Gregory replied. "Everyone else has been sent home. I doubt we will meet again before the week is out. There is little enthusiasm after yesterday's funeral. Althea thinks we all need time to…"

Venk watched the half-elf's teal eyes glaze over slightly. There was a certain indifference in this one's features that helped to hide the grief he felt. Venk recognized it as an effect of the elven blood that flowed through the scholar's veins. But it was his eyes that gave him away. The blue-green orbs lacked the otherworldly jewel appearance exclusive to the elves. They were perhaps the most human thing about him.

"It was I who sent for you," Gregory said, clearing his throat. "Lady Althea wishes to speak with you. I can take you to her now if you wish."

"I do," Venk replied gruffly.

Gregory Sweep nodded and slipped past Xanith, who gave Venk a wink and a nod as he passed. "Hope your day goes better, Lord Darkwater."

"It'll be a mite better than yours after I'm done complainin' to the governor about *you*," Venk growled.

Xanith Creese chuckled. "I assure you My Lord, the governor is quite used to getting complaints about me. As I am sure many others are used to getting them about you."

Venk scowled at the man on his way past, but the look didn't hold much bluster behind it. The dwarf rather liked the sarcastic old man. Not many could hold their own in the face of the giant dwarf's ire.

He followed the scribe out the back door of Nimbus and into the more secluded halls of its council members' offices. Venk had been back here before, but never when the halls had been so empty. No arguing councilors, no scribes bustling about delivering documents—only dour-looking security guards and a servant or two.

The far end of Nimbus housed the governor's chambers. The hall ballooned out at the end and opened into a large alcove ringed by three doors. It was to the far-right door that Gregory motioned him. This surprised the dwarf. He had only ever met with the governor in her offices.

Gregory wrapped one pale hand about the doorknob and turned to Venk. "Wait here," he said, and quietly disappeared into the room.

Venk clasped his hands behind his back and rocked back on his heels. He considered himself a brave dwarf. He had faced his share of monsters and rogues. He had been on more than his share of dangerous adventures, and he had the scars to prove it. But the lady he was waiting to see was infamous, and he couldn't help feeling slightly anxious.

Venk had never had the pleasure of fighting alongside her, but Althea Gaenor, leader of the long-disbanded group *Glory*, was sung about in almost as many ballads as the original *Duak-Thenal* themselves. Her deeds and triumphs were endless, her strength and intelligence genuine, and her considerable charm and wit unhampered by age, he had heard. Her twenty-five years as Governor bespoke her administrative skills, and had cemented the undying loyalty of all those around her. It was no wonder, then, that the sudden violent exit of their leader had thrown the city and its councilors into turmoil.

The door opened a crack and Gregory slipped out, closing the door behind him.

Venk raised an eyebrow. "Is she well?" he asked, suddenly concerned that he would not get his audience.

"She will see you," the half-elf replied, raising a hand to quiet the dwarf. "But I warn you, the governor is still recovering. She is weak, though she would argue otherwise. I ask that you do not take too much of her time with your business." Gregory leaned into the dwarf conspiratorially. "But it must not be you who initiates the end of the meeting. She would surely suspect something—and that might spell the end of yours truly." The half-elf smiled wryly and Venk almost laughed at the young scribe's dry humor. "Anyway, try to keep it short."

He moved aside to let Venk pass. The dwarf nodded his thanks to Gregory Sweep and entered the private chambers of Althea Gaenor.

The first thing Venk noticed was how small the room was. He expected the governor of the largest city in the Northern Realms to have spacious accommodations, luxurious furnishings. But this was not the case. Not even close.

The room was entirely white and gray. The curtains at the single bay window were drawn tight, but the sun stubbornly pushed its way in, spattering yellow light across the white-carpeted floor. The rest of the room was covered in gray shadows, a modest room which held only the necessities of sleep and grooming. A long gray dressing table took up much of the space and hid a closet door to the right. The bed in the center was a rumpled mess, with white and gray covers thrown about as if its occupant were tired of it. Indeed, the room's only occupant looked as though she had neglected to climb into the unmade bed for several nights now. Althea Gaenor rested in the room's only seat, a soft white sofa that sat low to the ground.

She was not exactly dressed to receive visitors. She was in her dressing gown -- a long gray robe hanging about her shoulders. Someone had thrown a white lambskin blanket over her legs. A long-haired gray cat was curled up in her lap. Her hair, brushed and clean though it was, hung about her sharp features, partly obscuring her eyes. She made no attempt to brush it back.

For a moment Venk thought she was asleep. But when he cleared his throat, she lifted her head. He was encouraged to see her gleaming gray eyes focused on him.

"Lord Darkwater," she greeted him. "Do come in. I have been expecting you."

Venk bowed his way into the room, taking off his hat as he did. "Yer Excellency," he said when he was standing before her.

The governor waved away the formality and motioned to the empty space beside her on the couch. Venk sat, so deeply concerned about the lady next to him that he forgot all about his long and annoying wait.

"Are you well, Governor?" he asked in a tentative voice.

A small wry smile tugged at one corner of her mouth. She idly stroked the gray cat in her lap. "Physically or mentally, my dear Lord of the Breezeway?"

Venk hung his head and wrung his cap in his hands. "Dumb question. My apologies, Yer Excellency."

She shook her head, her long white hair flowing about her pointed shoulders. "Do not apologize," she said. "The truth is, I am neither well nor unwell. I am simply weary, my friend." She sighed. "And I am old. Ever so much more than fifty."

Venk, like most, had no idea of the governor's true age, but he guessed it to be considerable in human terms. Now, gazing into her saddened, misty eyes and taking in her slumped posture, Venk felt she looked whatever age she professed to be. He found himself sympathizing greatly with a human who quite clearly blamed herself for everything that had gone wrong in her absence.

"This whole business," she waved her hand about in a dismissive way, "has rather taken its toll on me—and I slept through all of it."

Venk nodded his understanding. "It is difficult to lose someone without the knowledge of it happening."

She took in a long breath and sighed deeply. "You know, I cannot help but think that, had I been there…"

Venk cut her off. "That things would be different? No, do not do that to yerself, Governor. Odin and his hidden mage's very purpose was ta get you outta of the way. They were after ya from the start. How could ya have seen that coming?"

"But if I had," she insisted, "Alistair might still be alive."

Venk grunted and shifted in his seat. "Maybe, maybe not." He glanced up at her from under heavy black eyebrows. She was not looking at him. Her eyes were glazing over as she stared at the opposite wall. Venk felt a moment of panic seize him. Althea Gaenor was sinking under the weight of her own guilty conscience, and he was here to witness it. He reached out suddenly and gripped her long pale hand.

"I believe in the fates," he said quickly. "And they got a funny way a makin' things happen, whether ya like it or not. If Odin's dagger hadn't found Alistair's throat that day, then it woulda been on another. By another hand, perhaps."

She was silent. She blinked once and her gray eyes drifted off again. But this time they remained focused. She was thinking over his logic. He knew she did not really believe she could have stopped Alistair's death. She just needed time to come to terms with the loss.

"Don't suppose anyone's heard from our red-robed friend, eh?" Venk broke the silence and loosed her hand.

Althea started and wiped her eyes with one hand. "No," she said, quickly composing herself. "In fact, the last one to see the mage was your young prince—and I'm afraid he was in no shape to dole out descriptions when he was brought to the infirmary."

Venk stiffened somewhat at the mention of the prince. This was a subject he wanted to avoid. He was partially responsible for *Duak-Thenal's* presence in Preliona, and he was just as guilty as Cornelius when it came right down to it. He hoped this was not what he had been called here to discuss, for he did not wish to deceive this lady any longer.

"How is he?" she asked, and her voice softened with the question.

Venk shrugged. "He'll live."

She nodded. "I have spoken to Gilleece. Cornelius lent me that scrying thing of his. I assured the king that his son was well, as were the members of his party. He expects them in his court within the week."

Venk raised his downcast eyes to hers in sudden realization.

She was understanding but stern. "I am sorry, Venk, but I want them gone. Tomorrow, if possible."

Venk nodded as if this had not been unexpected.

Althea shifted to face him more fully. "Please understand, my friend, that I do this only out of necessity. *Duak-Thenal* is disbanded, but that does not mean they are innocent in the eyes of this government. This city has suffered a heavy blow—lessened, I am sure, by *Duak-Thenal*'s intervention—but my people will not see it that way. Once their grief and shock has faded, they will look for vengeance. It has been denied them with Odin's death. They will be only too happy to turn on five mysterious elves and one infamous imp."

Venk cleared his throat. "Are you saying they are banned from Preliona?"

"As *Duak-Thenal*? Yes."

Venk winced.

"But I am not unreasonable." Althea scratched the gray cat behind his ears. The animal purred adoringly. "I am grateful for all they have done. They are welcome here, as far as I am concerned, separately or together. But as *Duak-Thenal*? Never again."

"And the Captain?" Venk asked.

Althea stared down the length of her long nose and raised one eyebrow. "Do you really have to ask?"

Venk nodded. "I'll do my best ta keep 'er away."

Althea laughed lightly. "And no offense to you, Venk, but I fear your best efforts will never be enough." She leaned into him and whispered, as if someone else were in the room to overhear. "A word of caution. You would do well to keep her out of sight when you leave. As I understand it, Cornelius has done his best to convince the Watch that the imp has already vacated the city."

Venk's eyebrows shot up.

Althea smiled. "Yes, you old fool—of course I know she is here. Between you and Cornelius, I am beginning to get a complex. You both take me for an idiot."

Venk bowed his head and chuckled. "Hardly, Yer Excellency. We simply underestimate you."

She nodded and laughed. "That you do, My Lord. That you do. And the two of you would do well to remember that in the future." She stood then, dropping the cat to the floor and, in a flourish of gray robes, headed for the door. Venk followed, understanding that he was being dismissed.

"Express my thanks to the prince and his crew," she said. Her countenance quickly became serious and a little melancholy. "I truly believe they have done some good here. It pains me not to be able to say so publicly, or in person."

Venk nodded. "Not ta worry. They will know."

"Good. Perhaps when things have calmed down some, we can set up an informal meeting." She put her hand on the door handle and turned it. But she did not open it and instead leaned down to the dwarf conspiratorially. "Oh, and Lord Darkwater… you may pretend that it was you who called an end to our little talk." And with a shake of her finger, the Governor of Preliona bade the Lord of the Breezeway good day.

Venk dropped his mouth and put a hand to his head as the door closed behind him. He didn't know why he was surprised that Althea had guessed at the deal he had struck with Gregory Sweep. The Governor missed absolutely nothing.

He then realized that with this meeting *Duak-Thenal*, and most especially the Captain, had been pardoned. Perhaps not officially, but certainly personally—and by the only person that Venk figured really mattered in Preliona. That was enough for him.

"How did it go?"

Venk turned to his right to see Gregory Sweep standing in the alcove inside Althea's office. The dwarf harrumphed and shrugged his shoulders, surly again. "As well as can be expected, I s'pose."

Gregory moved into the hall and began to lead the dwarf away. "Well, it was short, at least. I thank you for that—and for your discretion."

Venk stopped and laughed hard, clapping the dark-haired half-elf on the back and making him stumble. "*My* discretion? Boyo, how long have you been workin' fer that lady?"

Gregory raised both his dark eyebrows. "Six years. Why?"

Venk rolled his eyes. "Talk to me when you been around 'er fer twenty." He sailed past Gregory Sweep, shaking his head and laughing all the way. "You got a lot to learn, boyo," he called over his shoulder to the confused assistant. "You got no idea who you're dealin' with. And I'd say yer in fer just as much of a rude awakening as the rest of us!"

46~Leaving Preliona

The sun shone brightly over Preliona the day *Duak-Thenal* chose to leave.

A gigantic wagon was parked outside the gates of the wizard's tower, filled to overflowing with parcels and surrounded by an array of horses. The hustle and bustle was more than this benighted area of Preliona had ever seen.

Elves, four of them, busied themselves securing their horses and readying the cart, all oblivious to the human eyes carefully watching them.

Four White Watch officers stood guard around the wagon, seeming to do nothing more than observe. Sent by Althea herself, their presence was not threatening—but neither was it exactly friendly.

The two women and two men were there to make sure the *ex-Duak-Thenal* left town. They were a sort of escort, and were none too happy with their assignment. They'd received their share of scowls and curses from the dwarven owner of the wagon for more than an hour now. In fact, three of the four soldiers had taken to grasping the pommels of their swords each time Venk Darkwater passed them.

The dwarf lord reveled in their reaction. He made it a point to cross their paths much more often than was necessary. Venk understood that Althea had sent the White Watch as a formality only. The governor trusted the dwarf lord to keep his word and get the elves out of the city, but there were other Council members who did not. Althea, once again at the head of Preliona, was forced to play politics.

As she had predicted, a week's worth of gossip and grumbling had done much to arouse new suspicions concerning the elves. In no time at all, the Council had once again become skeptical of the elves and their intentions. It mattered not who spoke in their behalf—Cornelius, Watch Chief March, or anyone else. Regardless of their heroic deeds in the city's best interests, *Duak-Thenal* was still suspect, and the leaders of the city wanted them gone.

Since this was her wish as well, Althea had agreed. She would placate the Council and the citizens of Preliona by making it look as though *Duak-Thenal* was being forced from the city by an armed guard—exiles from Tearlach's largest city.

Venk was annoyed by this, but not surprised. Althea was only doing what she did best. Venk had to respect that.

He set the last bag of supplies high on top of the pile. The back of the wagon was near to bursting with a variety of goods not available in the Breezeway. Wine and other spirits had to be imported, as well as some spices and dried goods. Venk had stocked up while in town. This was nothing unusual, but today Venk was also carrying five elves, one imp and all their supplies.

Panas had also managed to do some shopping while in Preliona. How he had done it under the critical eye of the Watch, Venk would never know. The elf's purchases were now taking up a lot of space in the cart. There were three new weapons—a sword, a dagger, and a single golden arrow that supposedly gleamed through the darkest of nights. There was half a case of books, and a cache of new clothes. Venk honestly wondered when the elf would find the time to wear them all—and where.

Venk finished loading the cart and checked on the horses. He had hooked up Tain's enormous horse Algoryn and Talesin's steed Iromanthe to the heavy wagon and was now considering whether to add Kiernan's and Nemesio's horses as well.

He latched onto the reins of Firoz and led the animal to the front of the line, passing the horse's master on the way.

Kiernan Nightwing sat atop the wagon, his cloak wrapped tightly about him. It had been a week since his devastating injuries had nearly cost him his arm. Once again, Cornelius Pav had worked a miracle. The Prince of the Light Elves had survived with little more than a few scars to show for his encounter with the mysterious mage.

He was still weak and badly in need of more rest, but his green eyes were bright and focused. His angular mouth cracked the barest hint of a smile. He breathed deeply and closed his eyes as he took in the morning air. Venk had never seen the prince looking so contented. Such an air of calm surrounded the light elf that all lines of concern and worry had left his face. For the first time in a dozen years, Kiernan Nightwing looked relaxed.

Seated next to Kiernan, her hand curled in his, was Dagmar Coal. The large white bandage wrapped around her head did not quash the aura of peace that surrounded her as well. Neither elf spoke. The demise of *Du-ak-Thenal* seemed to have allowed the two elves to let down their guard, at least a little. Though they were still far from public declarations of love, they were at least able to stand near one another without acting as though a glass shield separated them.

"You two all set, up there?" Venk asked.

Dagmar and Kiernan looked down at him as one. "Ready to go?" Kiernan asked.

Venk nodded. "Just about. Nemesio!" Venk shouted across the wagon seat to the southern elf. "Wanna bring that animal of yours to the front of the line? I need a little more pull, thanks to the Hawk's extra weight."

"Oh really, Venk—it can't be *that* bad," Panas said from atop his white horse.

Venk scowled and shook a finger at Panas. "Listen here, Hawk…" he began.

But at that moment the door to Cornelius's tower opened.

Venk turned quickly and shot a glance in the direction of the Watch soldiers. They too had turned at the sound of the door. But if they suspected anything out of the ordinary, they did not show it.

Talesin and Cornelius Pav exited the tower carrying a long thin crate between them. Devon Bane held the door until they were clear, then ran ahead of the pair to open the iron gate. Venk watched with growing unease as the ice elf and the wizard carefully brought their package toward the wagon. He took a step forward, careful to keep his back between the Watch and the crate.

Blankets were thrown over the contents. Though the box was no more than wood and nails, Talesin and Cornelius carried it as though it contained something extremely fragile.

Venk leaned over the blankets and raised an eyebrow as one corner of the box's lid shifted slightly. "Stay still," he hissed through his teeth. "There's four unwanted pairs a eyes lookin' this way, Tain. Don't draw attention ta yerself."

The lump underneath the blankets cursed in dwarven, making Venk's face color dramatically. He raised pained eyes to the wizard. "Ya *sure* you don't want ta keep her for awhile, Neil?" he said, *sotto voce*.

Cornelius chuckled and shook his head. "Thank you, Venk, but I will pass on that magnanimous offer."

A growl emanated from the crate. "*You can both go to the abyss.*"

"Quick," Venk said. "Under the seat before she gets us all sent ta jail."

Talesin and Cornelius moved past the dwarf and lifted the Captain up to where Kiernan and Dagmar sat. Together they pushed the imp's container under the wagon seat, hoping that the Watch guards would fail to hear the thief's curses.

Cornelius moved to Venk's side and placed a hand on the dwarf's shoulder. "Better get going," he said. And then, under his breath, "You won't be able to keep her in there for long."

Venk harrumphed and turned to face the wizard fully. "How's her arm?"

"Nearly mended," the wizard replied. "Actually, she is in far better shape than she has any right to be."

"Just my luck," Venk said sourly. He turned to the younger mage at Cornelius's side. "Decided to stay, have ya, mage?" he asked.

Devon Bane smiled and nodded. "I have—for a few days, anyway."

Venk looked up at Cornelius and smiled. "Wanna pick his brain about that slow-motion spell he pulled at the bridge, eh?"

Cornelius shrugged and folded his hands in front of him. "Devon and I have many things to discuss. Slow motion spells are only the beginning. We will be spending some time discussing that key, I assure you."

Venk studied the wizard's smooth face a moment. "Ya gonna let Kalli destroy it?" he asked.

Cornelius' brown eyes lost their merriment. "In this case, I am inclined to agree with the princess. She is the expert in this field."

"And how will old Lorcan take the news? The key belongs ta him, don't it?"

"Lorcan will have to understand." Cornelius nodded in Devon's direction. "The way I hear it, DeCresler may not even miss the key." Cornelius took Venk by the shoulder and steered him away from Devon so the mage would be out of earshot. "Besides, if I know my former partner, the key was not even his to begin with."

Venk narrowed his eyes. "You think DeCresler stole it?"

Cornelius shook his head. "I have no idea. Lorcan stole a lot of things during our time together. Very often his thieving skills rivaled his magical ones. The blue key could have been a treasure he acquired long ago—or it could simply be something he was working on. Either way, he's not getting it back."

Venk nodded. "Good luck with that, then." He raised his voice, bringing Devon into the conversation again. "Send the young mage ta the Breezeway when you've finished with him. I got some work for him ta do, if he's interested."

Devon grinned widely. "I would, sir—I mean I am. I'd be pleased to help you in any way I can."

"Wonderful! We'll all talk soon and celebrate your arrival. Now can we please get on with it?!"

Venk smashed one calloused hand against the hidden crate. "Right, then. Let's go, you lot!" Venk turned and clasped hands with the tall wizard. "I'll be seein' ya soon enough, my friend." The dwarf climbed onto the wagon, plopping himself next to Kiernan.

Panas the Hawk rode up beside the cart, stopping his horse Spiro before the two in front. "Nice working with you, Devon my dear." He extended one long hand, now studded with flashy rings.

Devon took it without hesitation, returning the light elf's strong grip. "I can't say it was *all* a pleasure -- but I will surely miss the company."

Panas winked one golden eye and with a wave to Cornelius, rode on.

Nemesio led Dagmar's brown horse to where Devon stood. He smiled down at the mage. "Don't forget," he said, tapping the side of his head.

Devon nodded. "I will not. As soon as I reach the Breezeway, I will find you."

"Be sure to do that, mage. We will hone that ability of yours. And this time I will be ready for you."

Nemesio turned to Cornelius. The two Malhurians clasped arms. Then the southern elf swung himself onto Dagmar's horse Wren, and followed Panas toward the city gates.

Talesin walked, as Iromanthe was now hooked to the cart. Devon could not imagine him riding on the back of Panas' horse. The ice elf drifted past, barely stirring the dust with his steps. He did not stop to say goodbye, nor did Devon expect him to. Talesin did not strike him as the type to dwell on long farewells.

He was surprised, then, when the ice elf turned around. While continuing to walk backwards, he raised one hand to his head in an odd sort of salute.

Devon quickly returned the gesture. Talesin Darken turned with a nod and continued walking.

"Goodbye, Devon Bane."

Devon looked up into Dagmar's gray eyes. The gash in her head had healed well, but her balance was still off by a bit. Cornelius had advised her against riding for a few more days. Devon directly blamed himself for this, no matter how many times the wild elf absolved him of all guilt.

Devon smiled sheepishly up at her. "Goodbye," he said.

She disappeared behind Venk as Kiernan Nightwing filled the space.

The light elf looked around the dwarf and reached for Cornelius's hand. "I will miss having you as our contact in Preliona, Neil."

Cornelius smirked at him slyly. "You'll be able to visit me by the light of day, Your Highness. Just give Althea some time."

Kiernan nodded. "Give my regards to my sister. I am sure you will speak to her before I do."

Cornelius winced.

The prince laughed knowingly and turned his emerald eyes to Devon. The mage seemed to have grown up in these last few days, if that was possible. His jaw line seemed more set and squared, and he held himself straighter. His eyes had aged. The innocence in them had dimmed, and the mage looked the better for it. Kiernan nodded his approval. "We will meet soon, Devon Bane."

The young mage nodded in return. "Count on it, Your Highness."

"Oh, for Kelina's sake!" The muffled voice of the imp drifted out to them again. *"It's not like we're never going to see him again!"*

Kiernan Nightwing sat back hard against the seat of the wagon as Venk slapped the reins. Four horses jerked forward, pulling the heavy cart behind them.

Cornelius Pav patted Devon on the shoulder and turned for the tower.

Devon did not follow right away. He watched as these exiles, with whom he had shared his first true adventure, rode out of the city that was now off-limits to them. He would count the days until he could see them again.

He sighed and wiped a bit of wetness from is eyes. He shook off the childish response like an old skin and drew himself up straight. He was about to turn and follow Cornelius into the tower when Venk Darkwater spun about in his seat and addressed the White Watch.

The dwarf held the reins in one hand and the back of his seat in the other. "Tell yer new Watch Chief I'll be looking forward ta seein' her when next I'm here. I'm sure she'll want ta have me over fer tea." The dwarf howled with laughter, slapping his knee, and nearly rolled off the cart as he drove out of Preliona.

Devon covered his mouth to keep from laughing. He turned toward the White Watch and offered them an apologetic shrug. But the four soldiers had already turned to go. Their job was done. They did not want to stay a moment longer than they absolutely had to. Acknowledging the dwarf's comments with a collective shake of their heads, they slipped from the alley as silently as they had arrived.

Devon watched them go. He turned again to watch Venk's cart as it disappeared around the bend.

A sudden thought occurred to him.

They were not so different, the White Watch and the *Duak-Thenal*. Both were proud and skilled groups of fighters. Both protected the innocent and helped the needy. They simply followed different sets of rules. Devon did not think the two groups had seen the last of each other. There would be battles to come, much larger and bloodier than the events of this last week. New alliances would be made.

Devon Bane blinked and shook his head. He rubbed his eyes, wondering where these thoughts had come from.

He looked up at the spires of the wizard's snakelike tower. He pushed his way through the wrought iron gate and carefully stepped along the white stones toward the tower entrance.

Cornelius's apprentice entered his new home.

47~Epilogue

LaRante rode northwest, hard and fast on what was now his third horse. He would reach the Institute by nightfall, he was sure.

It was a shame, really. His hasty exit from Preliona had left him no time to ascertain the fate of *Duak-Thenal*. The Prince of the Light Elves was dead, or at least badly maimed. His doggedly loyal crew had no doubt rushed to avenge him. With any luck, Odin Darweshi would have taken at least some of them out along with himself.

That Odin was dead, LaRante was certain. The blundering merchant had fallen for every trap set by the red mage. He would certainly have destroyed the bridge, thinking to erase the evidence of his crimes. A few days ago, that might have worked. But the events of those last few hours made the bridge a moot point.

Odin's killing Alistair had surprised the mage, he had to admit, but the action helped him immensely. Odin had sealed his own fate. LaRante had been spared the messy job of killing the merchant himself. Odin Darweshi had outlived his usefulness. He would be missed by few apart from his own mother.

LaRante's mission in Preliona was finished. *Duak-Thenal* was disbanded, his primary obstacle removed. Althea would recover. She had survived worse. But Alistair was gone, and she would be too occupied filling his place to think of LaRante.

Cornelius still presented a problem, of course, but LaRante was certain his old friend did not suspect him any more than Althea did. He had played the part of the bumbling fool too well. His former partners felt sorry for him. He was still free to act against them. With *Duak-Thenal* out of the way, he could work on putting the next phase of his plan in motion.

And for that next phase to succeed, he needed to continue to play the fool. Kalliroestria especially must never suspect him. She had the power to destroy everything he had worked for. He would have to be most careful with her. But for now, he had her under his finger. She was predictably loyal and trusting when it came to her mentor. So far, LaRante had had no trouble eliciting all the help he needed from her.

That Devon Bane was still alive bothered LaRante more than he liked to admit. His best student could turn out to be his worst nightmare if he discovered his own inherent abilities.

The late Jinin Aurek had twice failed to kill Devon Bane. LaRante would now be forced to finish the job himself. Shame the thief had not lived to complete his mission, for LaRante had been looking forward to putting that evil little man on his payroll. But Jinin was dead. Thanks to that annoying fairy pest, LaRante was robbed of his own prize thief.

Not to mention the key.

He did not have it, but even that did not bother LaRante now. Of the three artifacts he sought, the blue key was the least powerful. The other two were within his grasp—and those he would be sure to hold onto. Cornelius and the princess would destroy the key, never knowing the extent of its powers.

LaRante reached his destination just as the sun dipped below the horizon. The giant red fortress loomed over the trees surrounding the school. The four corner towers overlooked the land like sentinels watching for thieves. The sight of those towers never failed to inspire the mage. Princess Kalliroestria could keep her flimsy pink school of granite and windows. LaRante preferred the heavy, cozy brick fortress of his own home.

He pressed his panting horse to its absolute limit, crashing through the gates and bringing servants running to meet him. The red-robed mage brought the animal to a screeching halt and leapt nimbly from the back of it.

He tossed the reins to the nearest man without giving him a second glance or a word of thanks.

LaRante dropped his head back and removed his red cowl. He breathed in the crisp night air and wiped away all thoughts of the princess and her elven friends. There was nothing he could do about them now. Their time would come, and when it did, he would make sure the battle came on his terms.

He turned and sprang up the stairs of the DeCresler Institute of Magic, in his excitement taking them two at a time. He slammed the door behind him and immediately began barking orders at several students who happened to be in his way.

Lorcan DeCresler was home.

Made in the USA
Middletown, DE
06 June 2022